Praise for Chadwick Ginther

FOR *THUNDER ROAD*

"*Thunder Road* is a fast-paced, thoughtful novel, and news that it's the first in a trilogy is welcome indeed."

—*Quill & Quire*

"Without a trace of antagonistic empires, vast armies, or the schemes of eldritch sorcery . . . Ginther write[s] fantasy that resonates the deepest when it strikes close to home."

—*Locus Magazine*

FOR *TOMBSTONE BLUES*

"The pitfalls facing the middle volumes of trilogies are many. They've got to deliver the same pleasures as the opening volume without feeling like a retread, and they have to point the way forward without seeming like filler that's just marking time until we get to the main attraction. I'm pleased to report that *Tombstone Blues*, Chadwick Ginther's follow-up to the Aurora-nominated *Thunder Road*, manages to avoid those traps."

—*Canadian Science Fiction Review*

FOR ... *FAR GONE*

". . . with action as well as fantastic cha . . . . . . a triumph!"

—Julie E. Czerneda, author of the Clan Chronicles series

"A master fantasy/noir storyteller . . . a deliciously destructive prairie romp."

—*The Winnipeg Free Press*

CHADWICK GINTHER

Graveyard
Mind

ChiZine Publications

FIRST EDITION

Distributed in Canada by
Fitzhenry & Whiteside Limited
195 Allstate Parkway
Markham, Ontario L3R 4T8
Phone: (905) 477-9700
e-mail: bookinfo@fitzhenry.ca

Distributed in the U.S. by
Consortium Book Sales & Distribution
34 Thirteenth Avenue, NE, Suite 101
Minneapolis, MN 55413
Phone: (612) 746-2600
e-mail: sales.orders@cbsd.com

Library and Archives Canada Cataloguing in Publication

Ginther, Chadwick, 1975-, author
      Graveyard mind / Chadwick Ginther.

Issued in print and electronic formats.
ISBN 978-1-77148-463-3 (softcover).--ISBN 978-1-77148-464-0 (EPUB)

      I. Title.

PS8613.I59G73 2018   C813'.6   C2018-900791-5
                                                     C2018-900792-3

CHIZINE PUBLICATIONS
Peterborough, Canada
www.chizinepub.com
info@chizinepub.com

Edited by Samantha Beiko
Proofread by Leigh Teetzel

Canada Council   Conseil des Arts
for the Arts   du Canada

We acknowledge the support of the Canada Council for the Arts which last year invested $20.1 million in writing and publishing throughout Canada.

ONTARIO ARTS COUNCIL
CONSEIL DES ARTS DE L'ONTARIO
an Ontario government agency
un organisme du gouvernement de l'Ontario

Published with the generous assistance of the Ontario Arts Council.

MANITOBA ARTS COUNCIL
CONSEIL DES ARTS DU MANITOBA

The author acknowledges the generous support of the Manitoba Arts Council

Printed in Canada

For Michael Van Rooy
Friend, mentor, and sorely missed

Chapter One

Grave digging takes time. Grave *robbing* goes quicker than you'd think. By now, I could do this in my sleep: get to the top of the coffin and clear enough room to open the viewing hatch. No point in eating the whole box of cereal when you want the toy at its centre.

Straddling the corpse of death cult scumbag, Karl Daher, wasn't high on my list of Wednesday night plans. Yet here I was.

I slipped a small candy ball from my pocket and popped it into my mouth. I bit the candy, snapping it in half. A taste of mint and a rush of air, like I was trying to breathe with my head out a car window, and Karl's stolen last breath returned to his body. His eyes snapped open and the moist earth smell of the grave was eclipsed by Karl voiding his bowels.

"What the fuck?" he screamed.

I pressed the spade against his chest, and put my weight on it. I kept its edge nice and sharp. Karl's head snapped back against the coffin's velvet cushion as he shrank from the pressure.

"Shut up, Karl." I grabbed a handful of dirt, sprinkling it over his Salvation Army suit. "Or I cover you again."

"Nooooo."

Who would've thought such a short word could last so long? Sure, he broke it up with the occasional sob and whine. I glanced around. Noise like that, no way *he'd* miss it. And the last person—living or dead—I wanted to bump into while on the job, was *him*. I didn't want to think his name. Speak of the devil, and all that.

Stupid bastard would get us *both* killed. I didn't have long to piss around.

I pulled a one-litre plastic water bottle from my pack and set it beside him calmly. Such a simple thing, and it startled him back to a semblance of coherence.

"What is that?" he asked.

"Water," I said, smiling.

He licked his cracked lips. "For me?"

I nodded. "You must be parched. When I close up your coffin, I don't want you to die of thirst."

His shoulder twitched, trying to make his hand grab the bottle. Obviously, Karl hadn't been listening too carefully. I elaborated. "I want you to live long enough that the hunger makes you consider eating your fingers, hoping I'll come back for you. Eventually."

His face, already corpse-grey, went white as the moon. Good. He heard. And he believed.

"Would you want that?" I asked.

"No."

Again with the wailing. Whoever—whatever—his master was, they must be pretty hard up.

"You keep shrieking and I'll talk to your corpse." That quieted him. "I'm going to ask you some questions, Karl, and I'd better like your answers." I leaned forward again; his stink wafted over me. "I'll know if you're lying."

He squinted his eyes tightly shut and choked down his sobs. "Please don't leave me here."

Sometimes it paid to be the heavy.

"Who do you work for, Karl?" I asked. I kept using his name. I'd found it created an intimacy that added to intimidation.

What else might I know? Wife. Mistress. Kids. Dog. Anything, and everything.

His eyes were still wide, haunted. I worried I may've pushed him a bit too hard. But then, thinking about what he and his fellows had likely been doing since their arrival, I wasn't too concerned. I'd watched the memorial service earlier, wondering who might show up. Not a popular guy, my mark—hardly surprising for a self-righteous lowlife. He'd served his purpose; I had photos of the interested parties from the funeral. Unfortunately, no one remotely in charge had shown up, and the "mourners" turned out to be dead ends. I still had no idea who was moving in on my turf.

That's why I'd planted Karl. To make sure he'd talk.

"Church of the Risen Redeemer."

I groaned. "You're shitting me."

Everyone working Graveside knew the Redeemers were a sham and a front. A ruse used by any number of cults to suck in ignorant low-level fodder. People who desperately wanted to believe in *something* and with the right leader, could be made to do anything.

"I don't like that answer, Karl."

"Oh, Jesus, no."

If he'd been brave enough to move, he might've tried to cross himself.

"Jesus has no part in what you do." I smiled. My teeth were a row of tombstones. I'd practised this face years ago, when Grannie had shown me what I was. "Who do you serve?"

"I'm dead. I'm dead. He'll kill me."

"Karl, I'll kill you, too. But I'll also stop caring when you leave the city. You won't get any fairer than that. Get gone, stay gone, and to me you'll be gone."

It was a simple technique. Show them the darkness. Offer a sliver of light. Most'll go towards it. Most'll take the easy way.

I still had nightmares about the ones who hadn't.

I wondered which cult topped this branch of the Redeemers. It didn't matter. Whether they claimed to worship God, Hades, Hel, Mictlantecuhtli, or Tuoni and Tuonetan, what Graveside folks followed weren't deities in the way Sunside thought of them. Those Who Dwell Beyond the Threshold used their worshippers' souls to hold entropic forces of the Kingdom at bay—consuming the faithful instead of answering prayers. You bought reprieve from them with your sacrifices, but they'd get you eventually. Necromancers of the Compact—like me—tried to keep them from getting everybody.

Tendrils of fog drifted over the rough edges of Karl's grave. I looked up, wrinkling my nose. Something stank like a dead body in high summer. And it wasn't my patsy.

Oh, shit.

"Say nothing," I hissed at Karl.

The poor bastard looked ready to pull the lid closed on his coffin and call it a night.

Mist wrapped around the open grave, swirling until it coalesced in the shape of a man. He wasn't much to look at. You could see him on any street and not remark on anything other than his pallor. His bald head had a sloping point to it. The clothes he wore—no doubt stolen from his last victim—accentuated his paunch. Despite his shabby appearance, and being shorter than me, Christophe knew how to loom. All vampires did.

"Ah, little Winnie," he cooed.

"My name is Winter." It was hard to keep the edge from my voice, but I managed.

"I am your elder." He smiled his shark-toothed grin. "Surely you will forgive me for using the diminutive."

It pissed me off, but it wasn't worth starting a rumble over. Leastways one I wasn't sure I could win. The necromancer who'd first raised a vampire needed a kick with a steel-toed boot. And I knew right where to put that boot.

"Sure," I said, straining for a light tone. "I can forgive it, this once." This once. He used it *every damn time* I saw him.

"Excellent," Christophe said. His grin fell away and his Hades-dark eyes, small and shrivelled, like rotten blueberries, ran up and down my body. It was hard deciding what was scarier. His smile, or his frown. "I warned you about digging for prizes in my boneyard."

He had. If Frank hadn't been with me, I might've died that night.

So I lied. "I thought I was in McCoy's territory."

"Do not speak of *Mister Bones* to me," he snapped.

I pointed at Karl and tried to keep my tone light when I said, "He's alive, Chris. One of mine."

I could use the diminutive also. I shouldn't be *trying* to piss him off.

The vampire's smile returned and he laughed. There was no blood or flesh caught between his jagged teeth. He hadn't fed tonight.

Not a good sign.

Christophe wiped away a fake tear. Vampires could mimic human bodily functions. Vampires needed to do none of it. They didn't breathe. Didn't tire. They could sit perfectly motionless for hours—days if they need to—waiting for prey. They'd learned the trick of appearing human. Breathing, blinking. The little twitches and shifts in body posture we all do when we're "at rest." They had to, or they'd be pretty easy to spot—and kill. Try sitting across the table from one not playing human. The slight sensation of wrongness growing and growing until you knew you were going to be eaten.

"A necromancer claiming the living as one of 'her own.' If only I had someone to share this jest with." His gaze drifted to Karl and I knew that was it; no more information from this patsy.

Christophe knelt next to the open grave, reached into the coffin, and jerked Karl out by the hair. The vampire's mouth distended slightly, like a snake swallowing a meal, and his gums pushed out past the edges of his mouth. He didn't subdue Karl with his gaze. I tugged my cloak in front of me, to shield me from the inevitable, and looked away as Karl screamed. Keeping the peace was worth more than keeping him alive.

His cry collapsed into a wet gurgle as Christophe bit down. Karl kicked earth into the grave, peppering the hood of my cloak. When his scrambling ended, the night was still but for Christophe's ecstatic moans as he lapped the slowing trickle of his victim's lifeblood.

Karl's body tumbled atop his coffin unceremoniously. The vampire sat with his legs dangling over the edge of the grave. He leaned back on one arm and ran his tongue over his teeth. He missed most of the blood painting his face.

I put my hands on my hips, inching one hand toward an obsidian knife in a leather sheath hidden by my jacket. It should kill Christophe deader than any wooden stake. If—and that was a big if—I could tag him with it.

"I wasn't done with him."

He smiled, feigning innocence. "You should have worked faster. Or scared him less. His blubbering cries brought me here, not your swaying steps. How did you manage to sneak in, my dear?"

"Trade secret," I said.

"I could pull it from your mind."

"Perhaps you could." I forced my back straight. Vampires had powers to sway and control the living. They were among the few risen dead that could do so. A necromancer had power over the dead—including the undead. I didn't, however, want to risk a contest of wills between us.

"You don't need such subterfuge. I could be persuaded to give you free rein of my little domain here."

"Your price is still too high," I said, and meant it. To do as he asked, to let him taste my blood, could give him absolute power over me. Something, once freely given, could never be revoked.

"If not the warmth of your blood, then, your body?"

"No," I spat. "You can't even *have* sex."

He wrinkled his nose in distaste. "Everything is sex with you breathers."

"It keeps us going."

"Yes, I suppose it does. If it wasn't for you beasts rutting, I'd have run out of food long ago." His eyes glinted wolf-yellow as they caught the moonlight. "It wouldn't be the first night you spent with a dead monster's arms wrapped tightly around you, would it?"

Shit. Did he know or was he guessing? Sweat beaded at my brow. His smile said it all.

"Frank's worth ten of you."

"I knew it!" Christophe hooted joyfully, springing to his feet, almost capering. A happy vampire was no less unsettling than an angry one. "And what has he done to earn this . . . value?"

"He saved my life."

"And meanwhile, *I* have spared it. On numerous occasions, I might add." His finger wiped the sweat from my brow. He smelled the bead before a long, black tongue licked it from his digit. "A pale promise of your taste," he said with a sigh. "Someday."

"Not any day soon."

He spread his arms wide and bowed. "I assure you, I have time to kill. You may question his corpse if you wish. I will allow you that much. Tidy up before you leave."

The bastard knew that'd be no help at all. Karl's spirit would need to settle for a full turn of the moon before it could be convinced to come to my call. *If* it could be convinced at all. Taking a bit of his body to compel Karl would be taken as another challenge to Christophe's territory.

Christophe snapped his arms back up theatrically and a cloud of bats and rats tumbled from where he'd been standing to flap and scurry away, squeaking into the night.

I looked at Karl. "Sorry, pal. Not how I saw tonight going."

A sibilant voice whispered, *"I wonder how quick your tongue would be if you'd lost someone you cared about?"*

Summer. My neverborn twin. I heard her loud and clear. No one else could. *Lucky them.*

"If such a person existed."

She shouldn't have been stirring. The new moon was past. It should've been weeks before I'd hear her again. But I was in the 'yard, and she was always anxious around the dead. The looming thirteenth anniversary of my kidnapping wouldn't help.

Neverborn, and Summer still managed to piss me off. I supposed I should be grateful—her and my chimeric nature were my gateway to the world of the dead. *What a gift.*

I grabbed a small flask from my back pocket. I unscrewed the lid and took a long swallow. The whispers stopped. Summer had a child's palate. I took another slug to bolster myself.

It was awkward stuffing Karl's corpse back into the coffin but I managed without getting too much literal blood or waste on my hands.

Figuratively, I was swimming in it.

Chapter Two

After I'd covered Karl, I hit the road. I wasn't worried about him rising from his grave without me. It took more than a fatal bite to create a vampire. Besides, Christophe wasn't the sharing type. To the best of my knowledge, he'd never dropped a spawn.

And goddamn him, anyway.

I'd been hoping to get a lot more out of Karl than I had. I didn't have a hot clue who was recruiting Redeemers this time, or what they were up to. Other than nothing good. At least it was Karl in the ground rather than myself. I shuddered. I was never going in the ground again. Not if I could help it.

I checked over my shoulder, and not to change lanes. Christophe wouldn't appear in my mirrors. I didn't expect the vampire to be tailing me. If he was, my Grave Sight was the only way I'd be able to spot him.

Even then, picking Christophe out of the gloaming wouldn't be easy. Winnipeg was reputed to be among the most haunted cities in Canada. The believers didn't know the fucking half of it. Sure it wasn't as glamorous as other great cities of the dead—Edinburgh, Paris, Rome, Cairo. Necromancers loved the old, the ancient. Cities upon ruins. Death shrouding death.

Ever since the Compact was signed in Rome, necromancers chose a city—sometimes the city chose them—and they were tasked with watching over its dead, dying, and when necessary, doing its killing. Winnipeg was *my* city, and someone new was sniffing around.

Haunted hotels. Haunted churches. Haunted houses. My home might be one of the spookiest cities in the world—per capita, at least. We measure a lot of things per capita, here. It helps us believe we can actually make those top ten lists. We're a leader in violent crimes and homicides, too.

There was a lot more to work with over the pond, but it was also harder to remain anonymous. I'll take the extra effort over bumping into a cavalcade of black-cloaked goons every time I need to visit the 'yard.

Only two ways to get a city without involving the Compact: "inherit" it from your mentor, or take it from someone else— and hold it long enough that Rome acknowledges your claim. The downside to the down-low approach: without regular demonstrations of power, an up-and-coming cult could easily think they'd found a no-hassle powerbase.

I'd have to disabuse them of that notion. This was *my* city.

My Grave Sight lit up as I drove towards the city core, each murder in the city's history standing out, twinkling like a bloody Christmas tree light. Every other—more natural—death, blended into the grey-on-grey blur. The spirits were out in force tonight. Newlydead gang bangers and prostitutes; a few regulars, too. A cannibal victim walking with an awkward gait, showed every line where his body had been dismembered. A grandmother who'd been hit by a bus conversed with a skateboarder who'd been too cool to wear a helmet. A young man whose heart gave out at a German restaurant after an evening of too much *schnitzel* stared longingly through the window, wishing for one more taste of what'd killed him.

You remember the repeaters. The spirits that, for whatever reason, don't move on to the Kingdom.

Even as I zipped by, I knew the skateboard kid would try to rudely proposition me, and when I came to the next light, there would be a soldier standing at attention on the intersection where he'd walked into traffic to die.

Not content watching me from the sidewalk, a ghost jumped out at my car, splattering over the windshield like a burst water balloon. In my rearview mirror, he reconstituted his spectral body and flipped me off. After one had climbed into my car at a red light, I learned to keep an eye out for the dead as well as the living while driving, and to put more than one lock on my doors. I've received plenty of tickets from the cops. I kept my cell phone beside me on the bench seat in case I get pulled over. Driving and texting is more believable than "a dead man tried to claw his way through my windshield."

At least it wasn't raining. When it rained, all those deaths puddled and flowed, and the streets and sidewalks were red with blood. With a new cult in town, I might not need to wait for a change in the weather for the city to get a scarlet makeover.

A honk warned me I'd drifted into somebody else's lane. I was on Portage Avenue; eight lanes east and west cutting through half of the city. Winter sanding and ploughing had erased the dividing lines, and the city hadn't got around to repainting. I joined my fellow late-night motorists in driving by instinct; it was hard to complain about someone being in your lane, when you were all in the *same* lane, trying not to die. Although if people were more cautious, I'd be even poorer.

Grave robbing and monster killing didn't pay the way it used to in the Crusades. I figured being poor was a better option than living as a pawn or slave mage to a magical fetish sugar daddy— or mama.

Necromancers aren't usually high on the list of desirable employees, anyway. We have a bad—and not *entirely* undeserved—

reputation. Consorting with dark powers, and all that. Besides sounding unsavoury, truth is, it's not safe to be around us. Necromancy is more than talking to ghosts and getting hit on by vampires. There's also the "death aura." The fancier-minded among our circles refer to this as thanatomancy.

Frank calls it the "stink of death."

Not every necromancer masters that gift. Grannie Annie passed before she taught me to use it properly. But, if you can't do it, you fake it 'til you can. I may not be able to kill a healthy person with a snap of my fingers, but if you're sick, and I'm feeling generous, I can draw out that illness, put it in an object, and give your ailment to someone else—someone who's pissed me off. I can choose to dilute or concentrate that illness. Or, I give your sickness right back to you—when it suits me.

All it takes is a little nudge to metastasize cancer you don't know about. Not much use in a fight, granted. If I have any warning, your fighting days are over long before I'm in your reach. In a pinch, a little blood clot does wonders. Even the most minor heart attack or stroke will take the fight out of you in a hurry. The concentration required to pull that trick off in a fight makes it a dangerous choice.

Even so, it would be easier to be able to cock a finger at someone and say *die* and have it happen. Probably for the best I can't, or there wouldn't be a single living person left to make my coffee.

Parking my car was a pain in the ass. My 1977 Chevrolet Bel Air is a brute: eighteen feet long with a curb weight of 1600 kilos. It looked like an old cop car because it had been. Handy to be inside the next best thing to a tank when you have to mow over a pack of newly risen zombies or scatter the bones of a skeletal horde. Not easy to squeeze into an apartment parking lot. My place didn't have any parking, so I rented a spot nearby.

After I locked the car, I walked the two blocks home. It was early October, but Winnipeg had been having a streak of unseasonable warmth. That wouldn't last. Never did. And despite being a giant old seventies beater, my ride was pretty reliable. Living in a city where it hits minus thirty, *pretty* reliable doesn't always cut it—hence the need for a place to plug the big bugger in.

My apartment was in an old three-storey brick building near the river. People were dying to get a lease in there. I snorted, thinking of Grannie. Every time we'd be out on a job: "Here we are in the graveyard. *Dead* centre of town. People just *dying* to get in." She'd cackle and slap her knee like the joke weren't already older than death.

My building had those rickety-seeming wooden balconies and stairways on its alley side. I decided to head straight up the stairs to my place rather than round the front of the building. I had a nosy neighbour, and I'd rather not track grave dust right to my door. Though I had no sensation I was being watched, I pulled my cloak's hood over my head, let the Veil envelop me, and climbed. A necromancer couldn't be seen—not by the living—not unless she wished it. The stairs creaked with each step and cast prison bar shadows on the landing as I rounded the banister up and up.

There was nobody waiting for me at home. It's pretty hard to build a life with someone when you've one foot literally in a grave. Aside from that, the only person I trusted enough to fall asleep beside was a dead one.

I didn't keep my outside door locked. At least not in a way that required a key. The protective wards were holdovers from when Grannie was top cloak in town. They'd keep anyone living from trying that door. If an intruder thought too long about breaking in, they'd piss themselves. The less embarrassing, more lethal defences were saved for those who dared cross the threshold. Those wards would do worse to anything dead than run a grue up what remained of their spines.

So imagine my surprise when I saw my door ajar and light from my kitchen slashed onto the landing. The wards weren't broken, or dismissed, I could see that much. After Christophe's little spiel, I didn't want to take any chances. I drew the obsidian knife.

Dangerous to think of it as mine, even if it'd attuned its power to me. If someone took it from me by force, that bond would be meaningless. The knife was hand-chipped obsidian and said to have been carved by Tahl, a snake-boned thing from Beyond, and touched by their power. I couldn't confirm that, but ever since I'd stolen it, the knife had worked like a charm every time I'd needed to make something very, *very* dead.

I slid into the apartment, keeping the knife out of sight. My fridge door was open, and peeking from below it I could see a heavy work boot. It was a man—a big one, too. My boot squeaked on the tile. So much for surprise.

The man behind the fridge door straightened and held a beer in each hand. I smiled as I took in the jigsaw puzzle of scarred flesh he called a face.

"Goddamn it, Frank," I said, throwing back my hood. I carefully tucked the knife away. Frank didn't know its power, and I didn't want him to know I had the means to end his existence. "I could've killed you."

He took a couple heavy steps towards me. "If only," he said.

Chapter Three

Frank was a composite man. A couple years ago, a death cult in Afghanistan had used KIA Canadian soldiers for their experiments. Frank was their first success.

And their last failure.

I gave my head a shake. Composite men were dangerous because they're living *and* dead, and most wards didn't mean shit to them. Which explained how he'd entered, but *this* composite man usually phoned first.

Frank wasn't his real name—wasn't *any* of his real names. It had been an awful joke on my part to name him for Shelley's *Frankenstein*. But, regardless which soldier had donated his funny bone, that name was all he'd answer to. He held both beers, caps' edges against my counter, and snapped a hand down sharply. The caps bounced off the microwave and onto the floor, though he carefully stooped, picked them up, and deposited them into the bin soon after.

"I do have a bottle opener," I said dryly.

"Couldn't find the fucking thing."

"It's where it always is," I said, pointing at the magnetic strip on the backsplash where I kept knives and kitchen utensils.

"Forgot."

He just liked showing off. I didn't call him on it, and instead followed him from the kitchen to the living room where he plunked himself on the big vinyl sofa. I sat in the recliner opposite him.

I gave him the once over. His permanently furrowed brow, scars, and stitches made him look perpetually pissed off. At the moment, his unhappiness seemed to run deeper.

"You need to spend the night, Frank?" I asked.

I didn't say, "You look like shit." He knew. His clouded, mismatched eyes looked damned sad tonight. His hand tightened over the beer bottle. I worried for a moment it would shatter in his giant mitt. He exhaled slowly; forced a smile.

"*Nah*, I'm good," he said, not meeting my eyes. "Thanks, though."

"Anytime."

Frank regarded the floor with the intensity of a man worried he'd fall through. "You don't need—"

"Happy to," I said.

And I was. I also knew it was time to change the subject. If we kept talking about *feelings*, Frank would need to stay over.

Instead, I asked, "How're the Bombers doing?"

He brightened immediately. Frank loved football. His shoulders lost their hunch. Frank took a long pull from his beer and sighed, shaking his head.

"That goddamned team is killing me."

The only thing local football fans—Frank included—enjoyed more than cheering for the home team was griping about them. He attended the odd game, when the weather was cold enough he could wear a balaclava to hide his face. He always sat in the seats at the top of the visitor stands, where the November winds could scare a polar bear. Most games, he listened on his tiny pawnshop transistor radio. Unfortunately, the unseasonal warmth had left Frank stuck in the tiny bachelor apartment I'd secured for him.

Between paying his rent and mine, I was usually tapped out. It wasn't like Frank could get a job waiting tables.

We bantered about the woes of the CFL, and the Bombers, in particular. We'd had this conversation before; terrible refs, clueless head coach, *more* clueless management. Frank enjoyed it. I'd never been a sports person, and missed all the big games while I was out digging up corpses. I tried to pay attention for Frank. I was his only friend, what else could I do?

Finally, he said, "You were out. Business?"

I nodded.

"How'd it go?"

I didn't want Frank to worry, but I couldn't hide my grimace. "Bad. There's a cult moving into town. I had one of their patsies."

"The guy you had me roll?" Frank asked.

"Yup."

"Shit. Death cult accountant, that guy." Frank took in my appearance before noting, "You buried him alive."

"He either had it coming, or he would have had it coming soon enough," I said, knowing Frank would agree with me.

"No doubt." Frank took another sip of his beer. "You get anything out of him?"

I shook my head.

"So we're shitting in the dark?"

"He *claimed* he's with the Redeemers. I'll keep an ear to the ground. If too many people are going into it or climbing out of it, we'll know for sure if they have any real power."

"What'd you do with the twerp?" Frank drew a line across his throat.

"Didn't have to. I dig him up, he starts screaming, and Christophe shows up."

Frank grimaced. "And you let that bloodsucker walk away?"

"Didn't have a choice."

"I don't trust him," Frank rumbled.

"You shouldn't," I said. "He's more dangerous than any idiot cultist."

"You included?"

I swatted his arm. "Be nice."

"No promises," Frank said. "Wasn't made for nice work. Company shows up. Then what?"

"He *chastised* me for digging up 'prizes' in his boneyard. Then he tore the poor bugger's throat out in front of me. Threatened he'd get a taste of me, too." It still grated, Christophe's arrogance.

"Motherfucker," Frank said, slamming his bottle on the coffee table and jumping to his feet. The beer foamed over the neck. He looked embarrassed then, mopped up with his sleeve, and wiped the wet bottle on his coat.

"Don't," I said, gesturing for him to sit. "Please. He's not worth it, and you'll never find him unless he wants you to. And you'll regret it."

Frank acquiesced, muttering, "We gotta do something about him someday."

"We?" I echoed.

"Yeah. You and me. You can't mess with that fucker without backup."

"How do you fight someone who turns into a vermin swarm?" I asked.

"Bring a couple fucking shotguns loaded with silver buckshot," Frank suggested.

"Wouldn't kill him."

Frank wasn't deterred. "Might distract him enough for us to ram a shovel up his ass and through his withered fucking heart."

I had to admit, there was a simple charm to Frank's plan. While it would never work, I did appreciate that he wasn't afraid of Christophe. Even if he should be.

"I'll keep that in mind."

Frank drained the beer; burped. "I may not be on the army payroll anymore, but I still know where to find the good shit."

I smiled, imagining Christophe's surprise when we showed up in the graveyard with a rocket launcher. Knowing my luck it would do diddly. Blowing up Christophe real good would have to wait. The vampire had proven useful in the past. As had his chief competitor for supremacy of Winnipeg's Graveside, Mister Bones. Playing them against each other kept them off my back. Mostly. Until I was certain who would come out on top in our three-way power struggle, I wanted to keep things jake. And Bones paid better when I was looking for work.

"Well," Frank said, "guess I'd better be hitting that old dusty trail."

The sun would be up soon, and it would take more than a hoodie for Frank to hide his face in the daylight.

"Be careful," I said.

He snorted, as if expecting the warning. "Hey, who in their right mind would try to roll me? I'm bigger than Jesus and obviously don't have two coppers to rub together."

That may have been true. I still worried he'd be chased by angry villagers.

"Humour me," I said. "Whoever's in town, I bet they'd love to get their hands on you."

Frank cracked his knuckles. It was the sound of a jackhammer getting warmed up.

"Those fuckers try and take me back, I'll make Afghanistan look like goddamned Ottawa. Say when you need me, I'm there."

I smiled. "Until we know what they're here for, we're in a holding pattern."

"We don't know they aren't here for you," Frank said. "Why don't *you* humour *me*, and be careful for a change?"

I had to admit, his scenario *was* the more likely. He also wasn't done.

"Either way, somebody needs to teach these fuckers to stay out of our city."

"Our city?" It came out with a little more force than necessary. I couldn't help it. Grannie had driven territorial instincts deep into my bones.

Frank couldn't blush, but he sure looked ready to. Embarrassing him immediately made me feel like a shitheel.

"Your city," he corrected himself. "Which reminds me, Mister Bones wants to see you."

I wrinkled my nose. "He would."

"You going?"

I shrugged. "You don't say no to McCoy."

Frank grumbled but nodded. "You should."

"Not an option this time, Frank," I said. "There's a new cult in town."

"You put down the last one without talking to that parasite."

"And maybe if I'd sucked up my pride sooner, a bunch of those cult victims would be walking around and breathing instead of just walking around. Christophe's acting up. McCoy might know why."

Besides, I had a package for him. I wasn't late. Yet. But if I delivered early, he'd just shave the excess time off the next job he offered me.

"Promise me you won't pick a fight unless I'm there to back you up."

"I won't," I said, struggling for sincerity.

Frank clearly wasn't having it. "Promise me."

I guess I needed to lie to him better. I didn't usually make a habit of the practice. He wouldn't leave until I did as he asked, though.

"I promise."

It cost me nothing, and I damn sure wouldn't stage a frontal assault without Frank. He pulled his hood over his head, dropped his gaze to his shoes and closed the outside door behind him. The wards were still intact. I locked the door anyway. Anyone or anything that seriously wanted in would have a nastier surprise waiting for them than a cheap deadbolt.

Evidently, Frank had been here—waiting—for a while. He'd finished all my beer. By way of apology, he'd left a dirty, worn twenty on the counter under an empty with a half peeled off label. Or he'd left it as a hint to buy more beer. While I may still get carded from time to time, it was certainly easier for me to make the liquor run than a six and a half foot tall, grumpy patchwork corpse. I put the empties atop a teetering stack by the door.

Heading deeper into the apartment, my hardwood floors creaked amiably beneath my steps. It was a big place, this. After Grannie's death, I forged sublet documents and made it mine. It was big enough I'd never needed to buy a house—not that I'd ever be able to secure a mortgage. The apartment had two sitting rooms, if I ever entertained. More importantly, it had a fireplace. It's useful having a place to burn evidence.

Most of my furniture had been my mentor's, and what wasn't, I'd gotten second- to third-hand—or salvaged from dumpsters of unknown vintage. I'd had intentions of getting newer furniture, but my criminal acts don't contribute much to my meagre wealth, and being a necromancer doesn't look good on a resume.

Famous corpses have power. The Catholic Church had their saints and reliquaries. Want to be a better shooter? Dig up Annie Oakley. Need to get laid? Jim Morrison. Nobody famous rests in their own coffins for long. The good corpses in Winnipeg had been claimed long ago, by Grannie or her predecessor, and the famous had moved to other cities, and out of my purview, before their deaths. "Winnipeg Famous" doesn't cut it in Graveside circles.

Sure, new people are buried damn near every day. But what they're buried with isn't worth much to me. It's lifting antiques from old corpses that pays the bills. If I use a more recent grave, there's a better chance the theft is noticed. People who'd still recognize the heirloom *are* still walking around, after all. Not a huge risk, but one I'd rather not take. And there are only so many folks that'll pay for Dead Man's Clothes.

My parents stared back at me with accusing eyes from beneath the photo frame glass atop the fireplace mantle. They weren't accusing at the time the photo was taken, true. Their smiles were more of a dagger than their displeasure would ever be. I hadn't spoken to them since Grannie Annie had noticed my gift and "adopted" me. She wasn't my real grandmother, and you'd call it kidnapping, not adoption, but she had saved my life—and my sanity.

Such as it was.

Who I was now, and what I'd done in between past and present, yawned wide as a dragon's mouth. If I let myself walk too far down that path I might never come back out again. What I did now *was* important.

Or so I told myself.

I had to smile at that picture. My mother, tall and long-limbed—the quintessential tomboy when the photo was taken— was wearing tight, flared jeans and an even tighter "Red River Ex" t-shirt. Dad was an inch shorter than her, and sported a severe expression on his broad face; he wore a dapper suit, and more jewellery than Mom.

Somehow those two had made me.

Until Grannie had *remade* me. She'd said she'd kept them safe. Warded them. Made them dead to the Kingdom and Graveside folks. So long as I never contacted them, they'd live. She'd asked, "And isn't it better if they don't know?"

She'd been very persuasive.

I kept the photo nestled in between ugly plush dolls with human teeth; Grannie had made them to trap my childhood nightmares—most of which involved the man who'd kidnapped me. And the woman who, in turn, took me from him. The dolls' limbs were wings or tails, and too many or too few. I was afraid to throw them away, but the photo of my parents made them bearable. Especially knowing they were alive, and my kidnapper was dead.

There were no pictures of my sister. As far as I knew, my parents had no idea she'd ever existed, let alone *still* did.

I stopped in my dressing room and got a joint out of my stash in case bathing wasn't relaxing enough, and headed for the shower. A rock propped open the bathroom door and kept the apartment block's slight lean from swinging it shut. Soaking in the claw-foot tub would be more relaxing, but I was bagged— filthy with sweat, blood, and dirt—and wanted to hit the sack. I'd need to get up early to sniff around. Cultists rarely kept banking hours; if I wanted to find anything interesting without them knowing, I'd have to rise sometime before the sun went down. This time of year, that meant I wouldn't have as much time as I'd like.

While the water ran, I stripped. I gave a cursory glance in the mirror. It wasn't vanity. I wanted to make sure Christophe hadn't given me a tiny wound—small enough I wouldn't feel it—and taken my blood. I'd had caution against leaving any part of me lying around beaten into me. Such a prize could easily be used against me if it fell into the wrong hands—or mouth. And Christophe was both.

It was a shame, given what I do, I could never wear white. I'd look killer in white.

Inspection and introspection finished, old scars stood out, white and vivid against smooth skin, but no new bites, scratches or blemishes, at least. I hadn't intended for Karl to die. There were certainly other 'yards where he could have been interred. It hadn't been my choice to plant him in Christophe's. The mortician only did as she'd been directed.

I tested the water again. Hot enough. Once under the spray, it ran muddy and pink for a long time as the last grit of Karl's grave rinsed from my hair, taking sweat and blood with it. I scrubbed as hard as I could stand. The way that Christophe had gone to town, I'd be picking pieces of Karl from my hair all night.

Chapter Four

Aringing noise went off somewhere outside my bedroom. I burrowed my head into my pillow, and then underneath it.

Another late night filled with mouthy vampires, unpaid debts, and cult conspiracies did not lend itself to me dragging my sorry butt out from under the covers before noon for any reason. The noise would go away.

There it was again. Morning cobwebs had cleared enough I recognized it: my doorbell, loud enough to wake the dead.

Ring.

Go away.

Ring.

Go. The. Fuck. Away.

Individual rings turned into the incessant buzzing of flies on the future corpse of whoever was leaning on the doorbell. The noise continued steadily for another minute before the sound was replaced by the angry pounding of someone who *really* wanted to die.

I was too sleepy to name everyone I'd pissed off recently. I hurled the covers aside, hissing at the influx of cool air. Shaded from the muted light seeping through my bedroom curtains, my obsidian dagger waited on my nightstand. Padding towards my bedroom door, I fastened the weapon's thong sheath around my waist. I grabbed my housecoat and hurried to quiet the pounding—with force, if necessary.

I didn't call out to let them know I was up. I didn't check the peephole, either. Set knew I've made more than my fair share of enemies. Most shouldn't be met eye to eye.

"Winter!" a woman's voice boomed through the door.

I recognized her immediately, and not from the distaste she happened to instil in my name.

I still confirmed the speaker's identity with my Grave Sight, probing through the cracks and into the hall. Tammy Wilmot was alive—not a given for unwelcome guests in my line of work. I gazed deeper. My vision was splashed in red—a lot of bloody deeds had happened here—broken up by the tendrils of death stuck fast to my door, warding against intruders.

The life beyond that door pulsed, heartbeat and breathing calling out to the wards, a life close to being snuffed out. Inches of wood were the only proof between Tammy and death. Our mutual disagreements aside, my dagger and wards were overkill for dealing with her. Probably.

She dated Alyssa Rogers, my neighbour across the hall and best friend. Lyssa and I were close. Tammy and I were not. They'd met because of me and my rented parking spot. I introduced them and initially, at least, Tammy had been fond of me. That feeling hadn't lingered.

As I flipped the deadbolt and fumbled with the latch, the knocking continued unabated. I hesitated before muting the wards. Lyssa would be put out if Tammy shoved past me and ended up a smouldering, soulless husk. Besides, I was fresh out of canning jars to keep a stolen soul, anyway.

"All right already," I hollered. "I hear you!"

There was one more knock for good measure. *Bitch.* I opened the door and Tammy burst in.

Tammy was taller than me, and normally she loomed, as if she was trying to be intimidating. Today, her eyes were red-rimmed and she looked wrung out, as if she hadn't slept. Not a good look to go with two-toned blonde hair, and a body that looked shapeless inside her navy Transit uniform.

I wondered what could make her cry, and that curiosity corked my intended retort. Anger, I expected from her. Not tears. "What's wrong?"

She didn't answer.

"Shit. Lyssa okay?"

She ignored that, too. Her stare bored into me. "Why didn't you come over last night? We heard you come in."

I'm never particularly quiet, so I wasn't surprised they'd heard me. Why were they expecting me to swing by? Lyssa and I hadn't made any plans.

"Should I have?"

Tammy scowled. "You didn't see the note?"

Now it was my turn for a crinkled brow. "No. What note?"

"The one I taped to your door," Tammy accused. "That one."

She pointed to the table by the entrance, piled high with unopened mail and not-yet recycled flyers. There was indeed a note, right on top of the mail Frank picked up for me.

"I came in through the back last night," I said. "I had company. He must have taken it down and left it there. Sorry, this is the first I've seen of it."

Tammy kept her face deliberately neutral. Her voice was tinged with sorrow when she said, "Alyssa's mom passed away yesterday."

People say "passed away" or "gone." Bullshit euphemisms to avoid saying "dead," right? Well. If they knew where the dead had really gone, the word would be no comfort. Snarking with Tammy was second nature to me, but that statement stole the fight out of me. My shoulders slumped. I hadn't realized how tense I'd been.

"I'm sorry. I had no idea."

I could read her face and I imagined her train of thought: *Typical fucking Winter, you've got your head up your own ass and dug deep into the "my shit's the most important" pile, again.*

For propriety's sake, I offered, "Can I get you a coffee? I'll have to put some on—"

Tammy waved away the offer. Instead, she asked, "Can you spend some time with her?"

I knew something about loss, and my heart ached for Lyssa. I wanted to comfort her, but the timing couldn't have been worse.

"Can't you—"

"I took yesterday off. I can't stay home today, too. My boss already hates me. I have no seniority." She paused, floundering. "I . . . I just don't trust her to be alone right now. I've never seen her like this."

That stopped my protests. "I'll get dressed."

She looked suspicious. "I'm leaving now."

"I'll head right over. Promise."

I half expected an accusation about what my promises were worth. Instead, Tammy gave a curt nod, spun on her heel, and stomped downstairs. I closed my door, let out a surrendering breath, and gathered myself to head across the hall.

I could use some tea, coffee, or whiskey (or all three, mixed together in one of those drink dispensing hats with the straws) to prepare for this. I've been around death for as long as I can remember. Death is easy. Grief is harder. There's a reason I don't have many friends—besides Grannie not allowing me any. She'd wormed such notions out of me. Grief. Empathy. Decency. Qualities with no place in the necromancer's world—except to be exploited in others for personal gain or power.

In the end, I didn't bother getting dressed but I left my dagger behind. I grabbed my keys and shut and locked my door, taking a moment to reset my wards. Daylight didn't mean Christophe or Bones wouldn't come knocking. When the wards were active again, I crossed the hall and knocked.

Please don't be crying.

I didn't deal well with tears. Grannie Annie beat the tears out of me when I was growing up. Between losing my folks, losing my innocence, and losing my mind, I'd cried a lot back then. She made me get over it.

Death wasn't such a big deal to a necromancer. I've seen fates worse than death. I've seen a man's skin flensed from his body, waist to toes, teased inch by inch from his bones to make pants, and a gold coin placed in the empty scrotum, "for luck." I've seen a spirit torn from its body and wrung out, everything good tortured away, until all that was left was blackened tar, used for barter in the Kingdom to fuel the darkest rituals. I've seen a brain in a jar, still thinking, still knowing, still praying—begging—for a death that would never come. Ever seen people hollowed out and filled with insects and turned into walking disease vectors? I've seen a flayed man strangled with his own skin. Oh, and *Human Centipede*? Yeah, that's a thing. And all the more reason to stay the hell out of Toronto.

Someone passing peacefully in their sleep usually has a hard time winning my sympathy. Despite what I've seen, I'm not a monster. At least, I try not to be. Lyssa's my friend. I could empathize. I'd lost my parents, too. Lyssa didn't need my tears. She needed her own. And I needed to be there when they came, so she wasn't alone. I could do that.

I couldn't remember Lyssa mentioning her mother since I'd met her. Her sister, Haley, yes. Her brother, Matt, yes. Her dad, Ron, yes. But when it came to her mother, nothing.

Lyssa's door would be locked, it always was. We'd both grown up small town girls, with warnings about "the big city." A habit her years living here hadn't ground down. I didn't knock again. I flipped through my keys to find Lyssa's, and turned the deadbolt.

The first thing I noticed when I went in—the first thing I always noticed—was the beautiful painting of a nude woman on the wall. I had a suspicion Lyssa painted it, but she'd never elaborated when I'd asked about its origins, or who the model might've been.

Her apartment mirrored mine in layout, if not décor. I was jealous of the hanging garden in the south window of her sunroom. She grew enough spinach, tomatoes, and herbs to have fresh salads year round. I have what Grannie Annie called "The Black Thumb." My fridge was more often full of mouldering takeout than fresh vegetables.

Lyssa's voice warbled from the living room, "Hon, you forget something?"

"It's Winter."

She didn't answer. I went deeper into the apartment, heading for the sound of her voice.

Lyssa, still in her pyjamas, looking somehow smaller than normal, was sitting on her couch staring at a glass coffee table strewn with flyers and note paper and an iPad. Occasionally, I thought Lyssa looked sick-skinny. She ate well—better than I did, at any rate—if not a lot. I did check her out with my Grave Sight from time to time, to be certain. Horrible invasion of privacy, but if I can suck cancer out of a friend, and stick it in a bad guy . . . let's say I'll sleep better at night.

Behind the couch, hanging on the wall as if they were in a gallery, were three old wood-frame windows, with the glass panes still intact. I'd helped her rescue them from a dumpster and hang them up. They were all resting cock-eyed. Tammy had offered many times to straighten them out, but Lyssa preferred them crooked.

Her voice was a tired whisper. "I don't need a babysitter."

"How about a friend?"

She gave me a rueful smile. "Tammy bullied you to come over."

"Let *her* bully *me*? I would've been here sooner, but I just heard."

I stopped myself before I said, "Sorry about your mom." I'd said the words to Tammy, I wouldn't say them to Lyssa. She didn't need to hear *sorry*. She'd be hearing it enough over the next few days, weeks, and many months it would take for the loss to trickle to every corner of her life.

I plopped myself beside her and pulled her against me. Her façade broke, and she sobbed. I glanced around for something I could do to help her. The dishes, tidying. Anything but cooking. That help she didn't need.

"Have you eaten today?" I asked.

She shook her head.

"Yesterday?"

Another shake.

"I'll order something."

"I don't know why I'm crying," she said. "Mom and I haven't spoken in years."

"She was your mom," I said. Lyssa flinched. Death may be nothing new to me, but Lyssa would need more time to get used to the idea. "You'll always regret what you haven't done. What you didn't say—"

Lyssa turned away from me. My words brought back the last thing I said to my parents. And how I'd never made up for that childish outburst. Not sure what else to do, I kept her close, patted her back, and muttered soothing words in her ear. We rocked against each other until Lyssa had cried herself out. For now, at least. There would be more tears.

There always were.

We lived in Winnipeg's take on Little Italy—Corydon Village— although you'd never guess it from the sushi restaurants. There was a greasy burger place nearby, and after we both dressed, I took Lyssa for a walk to pick up her lunch and my breakfast.

Tammy's warning had lingered in my mind, and I'd promised not to leave Lyssa alone. Takeout procured, we got down to the business side of death. Lyssa kept listing funeral homes and I kept telling her no, but not why.

"You sure know a lot about this," she said between bites of her chili burger.

"I went through this a few years ago when my Grannie died," was the truest explanation I could offer.

Grannie Annie may not have been nice, but she was the only family I'd had. Instead of spoiling me, she made me fight monsters. She kept me out of a strait jacket and a drug-induced coma when Summer showed up. It wasn't *all* bad.

Only most of it.

"Orchids?" Lyssa asked.

Will animate your mom as a zombie and turn her into cheap labour until she rots into unusability.

"No," I said, keeping the thought to myself. "I've heard bad things."

"Passages?"

Necrophiliac. "Their funeral director hit on me at Grannie's funeral."

Lyssa pulled a disgusted face. "Yuck. Werenick?"

Christophe's Renfield. "Wasn't he under investigation a while back? I'm not sure they proved anything. . . ."

I knew them all. Pastors, priests, funeral directors, and morticians. Over a dozen funeral homes operated in Winnipeg, most were players in the occult. Funeral directors were too useful as pawns and the homes themselves were Costco for necromancers. I'd have to lead Lyssa towards the least dangerous of the dangerous options.

"What about this guy?" I said, tapping an ad on her iPad screen.

She wrinkled her brow, muttered, "Wojciechowski?"

My first thought was: wow, she almost pronounced his name correctly. The second was, *Cokehead and thief.*

Unfortunately, that still made Woj the best option on the table. I'd met him on a previous job and he was, if not stable, mostly on the side of the angels. I could trust him. We still did a little business, he and I. Her mom wouldn't miss any of the jewellery she got buried with. The other options didn't bear considering.

Lyssa feigned reading the ad, gave her head a shake and set her coffee cup on the table with a sigh.

I didn't want to oversell Woj, despite being the only option tolerable to me. I shrugged and said, "It's your choice. This guy seems as good as the next."

"Ringing endorsement," Lyssa said, but she didn't protest further.

I took that as acceptance. "Okay, I'll call and make an appointment. Where do you want the service?"

Lyssa considered, shuffling pages in her notebook. She wasn't a church person, so I wasn't expecting her to say what she said.

"Well, her boyfriend is a Pastor at the Church of the Risen Redeemer. So, there, I guess."

I tried to hide my alarm with a groan. Judging from Lyssa's expression, I hadn't been successful, and I covered by saying, "It's not an attractive building."

"I thought you were going to say they're a cult."

"They're not?"

"Not a chance," she said, more defensively than I would have expected. "Mom wouldn't do *anything* unchristian. You wouldn't believe how long Dad had to fight to get her to sign those divorce papers."

I wanted to warn her, but I couldn't. She'd never believe the truth.

"Mom's church friends are pressuring me to have the service

with them. Dad wants a pastor to preside. Matt said he'd do the eulogy."

I nodded, only half listening. Something was up with the Redeemers, and after Karl's deaths—both fake and genuine—I wanted to get in there and see what. I felt shitty for considering her pain to be my in. A chance to snoop and explore. I wouldn't even have to lie.

I couldn't do it. Couldn't use her. Not like this.

"Have the funeral wherever you think is best," I said. "But it is a hideous building."

It wouldn't help to tell Lyssa a funeral was for the living, not the dead. The dead rarely gave a shit. They had other concerns.

"It's as good as anywhere else. And all of her friends go there."

I gave up. Fate had spoken. "Okay, babe."

"You'll be there."

It wasn't a question.

"Of course I will."

"You won't flake?"

I put on a hurt tone. "When have I ever flaked?"

Lyssa's red-rimmed eyes narrowed. "You were going to cover those shifts at the gallery for me and disappeared for a month."

"Something came up." A month in the hospital after a run in with *Mort Horreur.*

"You flaked. Who disappears for a month on a whim?"

Me. If you call hunting bones in an ossuary beneath the Paris sewers to pay off a debt to a sociopathic walking skeleton a whim. And it hadn't been the only time I'd disappointed her, either. I'd had good reasons on those other occasions, too—not that I could share them with Lyssa.

"Fine, I flaked. It's a habit. But it won't happen this time."

"Promise me. You'll be there to sit with me and Tammy. I need you there, Winter."

I took Lyssa's hand in mine, and kissed the tattoo of linked stars she had on her ring finger. "Hell or high water. Nothing would stop me."

She leaned her head on mine and gave me a peck on the forehead.

"Who's this pastor boyfriend?" I asked, not expecting the name to mean anything to me. It was just small talk.

"Mark. Marcus. Marcel. Something like that. I forget."

If she'd said a last name, I'd stopped listening. Marcus. I had every reason to hate that name. It belonged to the man responsible for my life going Graveside. Marcus. The man who lured me away from home. The man from whom Grannie stole me away in turn.

"You're next," he'd said after every victim he murdered in front of me. He made me believe him, too. Even if each time he reneged and killed someone else, I knew I wasn't being spared. He was a cat playing with a mouse. But in the end, I hadn't been next. He was.

It couldn't be the same Marcus. Grannie had made him very, *very* dead. That whole fate worse than death thing?

I've yet to see anyone deader. I've yet to see anything worse.

And that's saying something.

Chapter Five

Wojciechowski's Funeral Home was farther into the city's south end than I preferred to roam. An unassuming building somewhere between a house and repurposed mini mall. Its too-small parking lot bordered on a residential neighbourhood—lots of spots to steal along the elm-lined boulevards.

Not a necessity today. I pulled into the lot, empty but for one car. My Bel Air rocked to a stop when I slammed it into park.

Lyssa had been more interested in smoking than talking during the drive. I left her to it. I hoped I'd be able to change her mind about having the service at the Redeemers' church. I was fine with scouting the cult under the illusion of acting on the grieving daughter's behalf, but I'd wear Osiris's golden cock as a belt buckle before I'd let Lyssa walk through those doors.

At least she'd said yes to Woj. He and I worked well together, even if I made him . . . twitchy. There was an underground economy for items like Dead Men's Clothes, stolen last breaths, celebrity toe-tags. Another reason for necromancers, hospitals, and the funeral industry to be locked in a death grip. When you accessorize as much as we do, you feel the need to change up, but trust is a harder thing to come by than necrotech. Also, there's the added hazard of your business partners getting arrested.

Or eaten.

Sometimes Woj needed me. He wasn't the first funeral director to have a "client" go missing—and now he tied their shoelaces together so they couldn't chase him far or fast. Our transactions were strictly under the table, but if I could bring a little aboveboard business his way, it would be my pleasure— even if I wasn't happy about today's circumstances.

I left Lyssa outside the funeral home to finish her cigarette while I went inside. I needed to prompt Woj about what to expect. Since I'd made the call, I'm sure he had an inkling this might be a little bit more than his standard day at the cemetery. Weird that if all went well, that's exactly what he'd be getting— instead of *my* standard day at the cemetery.

I walked past the coat rack without hanging up my jacket. I'd stuffed a few party favours in my pockets when I'd gotten dressed, and I didn't want to let them out of my sight.

Woj left his office as the front door closed behind me. His face screwed into a worried frown.

"Hey, Woj," I said.

His eyes were bloodshot, and he looked as if he'd just woken up. He could still use a shave, if you asked me, but Woj pulled off that casually handsome, five o'clock shadow look. On him the scruff looked intentional. He paced the floor, fidgeting with a ring on his pinky finger, but didn't approach me any closer.

"Relax," I said. "You'll spook your new client."

He was hesitant when he asked, "What do you have for me?"

I smiled, trying to set him at ease. It didn't work. "Don't worry. I'll try and make this one easy on you."

His eyes narrowed. "So this *is* a job."

"It's money in your pocket," I said.

He pressed me, almost manic, "Yeah, but are we *working*?"

I closed the distance between us and put a hand on his shoulder, hoping to calm him. He flinched, but didn't bolt.

Progress. "I'm trying to help a friend and keep her out of trouble. There may be a job for me. You should be in the clear."

"I'm always with you, Winter. Always. You can trust me." He spoke as if he worried Grannie Annie might still be listening. Which, I must admit, wouldn't have surprised me one bit.

"I know, Woj. I know."

He still wouldn't meet my eye. I didn't have time for his paranoia. Not if I wanted the shop talk done before Lyssa finished her smoke.

"I am *not* here to kill you."

He looked up after that, as if waiting for me to say more.

"I am not here to harm you in *any* way. I swear."

Whether he ever believed me or not, I was never sure, but he always accepted the oath when I gave it. I wished I didn't have to give it *every* time.

Some tension left his face. "How's your novel coming along?" Woj asked me, rye and coffee fighting for mastery of his breath.

I smirked—I couldn't help it—before I offered my stock answer. "Still struggling with it."

He knew I didn't share his dream. But he still asked. Kinda sweet.

He'd learned I was a necromancer the hard way. A mark I'd been tailing had been the instructor at a writing workshop Woj had been attending. Woj had been particularly intrigued with my story of a modern grave robber.

Woj wanted to be a crime writer, and what little of his writing I'd read, was good. He thought being a funeral director would give him a niche, a platform, he'd called it. It hadn't. At least, not yet. Meeting me had given him a different appreciation of death. I think he'd given up hope of being a bestseller.

The guy I'd been tailing hadn't been a *guy* at all. Turned out he was a revenant. The types of walking dead in the world are too numerous to count. The name revenant comes from the

French *revenir*—to come back. In this case, it had been a Norse individual, not a French one—his variety, *apatrgangr*—the again walker—was more commonly known as a draugr. Not the first time I'd had to put up with viking bullshit in Winnipeg, and it wouldn't be the last.

I never did learn why the revenant came back. Most leave the Kingdom to punish someone from the land of the living. The why didn't matter. He wouldn't be back a third time. Woj's drinking problem started that night.

Mostly, he keeps it together. Today wasn't a "together" day.

Which . . . was probably my fault. He still had nightmares. Which explained his continued self-medication. Not that I'm one to point fingers. And it had to kill him that he couldn't use his best material without outing himself as someone in the know.

He let out a low, relieved whistle. "Okay, what's the deal? Where's this friend?"

"She's outside having a smoke, trying to compose herself." He nodded, understanding, and I continued, "Her mom died."

"And? Possession? Did a ghoul steal the body?" he dropped his voice to a whisper. *"Necrothanatoheliosis?"* I shook my head. He seemed genuinely puzzled. "You wouldn't come to me with just a funeral, much as I appreciate the work."

There was no point in trying to hide it from him; Lyssa would drop the truth soon enough. Better Woj heard it from me, and was prepared, so he didn't go mental when he heard who we were dealing with.

"The deceased was with the Church of the Risen Redeemer. Her boyfriend is the pastor now, and he's insisting the service take place in their church."

Woj paced the floor. *"Shitshitshit."* A moan. "I don't know, Winter. The last time you had to deal with those guys—"

"This won't be like last time."

"Promise me."

"I'll add it to the list." I sure was handing them out pretty freely these days. Giving Woj my word—even sarcastically—mollified him.

"I hate those Redeemer creeps," he said.

"You and me both. While I'm here, I've got another request, since I'm bringing you legitimate business . . . I've got a needy client and I thought a new suit might help."

Woj pinched the bridge of his nose; now he seemed put-upon rather than concerned. "Let me guess: you need it soon?"

"Today would be best."

Woj murmured, "It's for Mister Bones, isn't it?"

I didn't like that Woj knew about McCoy at all, let alone that I did business with him. To the best of my knowledge the two had never crossed paths. I know I'd never brought up who I bought those suits for. But this was a small city, and word tended to get around the wrong circles. Quickly. So I asked him how he knew Bones.

"He's sent guys around before. Dead-eyed bastards." Woj shuddered.

Knowing McCoy's flunkies, I didn't blame him.

"He still insists on only wearing Dead Man's Clothes?"

I shrugged. "The only thing he'll wear."

Woj nodded. "I've got a closed casket Armani I might be able to hook you up with. He decided a pistol made better medicine than chemo."

"I appreciate it."

The door chimed. Lyssa must have powered through that smoke. I'd expected her to have a second right after the first. She usually did when she was stressed.

"Go," I hissed. "Clean yourself up. If Lyssa sees you like this she'll bolt to David Edelman at Passages."

"That sick freak?" He grimaced before straightening his back and assuming a more formal posture. "I have Visine in my office."

"Breath, too," I said. "For most of us, it's not quite rye o'clock."

He scurried off. Lyssa came in and hung up her coat. I caught the sharp whiff of fresh smoke lingering on her clothes. The chill air made the scent contrast all the more striking. I resisted giving her a quick once-over with my Grave Sight, scanning for cancer again. She'd notice the change in my eyes.

Lyssa's brow wrinkled in confusion. "Where's he going?"

"He had to take a call."

It sounded lame, but Lyssa accepted it with no more than a put-upon grunt. I settled her into a wingback chair and dropped into a seat next to her while we waited for Woj to rejoin us.

We weren't off to the best start, which was my fault as much as his. I should have known better. Once you start talking shop, it's hard to let it go. Most of the people I can discuss this with are dead. Or want me dead. Or both.

Lyssa grabbed a tissue from a box on the sideboard and dabbed at her eyes. I gave her a quick squeeze. Woj emerged from his office a minute later and you'd never have known he'd been half-cut and shitting bricks ten minutes ago. He'd straightened his tie and ran a comb through his hair. Eye drops and mouthwash had done him good, too. If he ever sold his book, he'd have a bankable headshot.

He introduced himself to Lyssa, avoiding making the standard offering of "I'm sorry for your loss," instead saying he would help in any way he could, an offer she accepted with a muttered "thank you." Woj beckoned us to follow him to a sitting room and we did.

"Please forgive me for not being able to meet you at the door. A client from last week is struggling with letting go." He gave us a fragile, perfect smile. Only a hint of an upturned mouth. He projected sympathy, but not so much it would put you off for thinking him fake, or a money-hungry ghoul, happy to be profiting on your misery. Seeing *real* ghouls couldn't have hurt. His empathy was also why Grannie and I scared him so.

Lyssa mumbled something I didn't catch. It may have been, "Let's get on with it."

Woj sat across from us, placing binders on the low table separating us, and we got to business. Obituary. Eulogy. Priest or pastor? Neither? Flowers. Music. Slideshow. He showed us his on-site chapel, despite Lyssa leaning towards using the Redeemer Church, in case we "changed our minds."

Good job, Woj.

Planning a funeral is a curious flurry of activity—you never believe you can manage it all—and interminable guilt and sadness of loss. Unless you're glad they're dead, but even then guilt has a way of surprising you, like a spider bite when you reach into a coat pocket. Invariably it is also one of the worst possible times in your life. Much to do in little time when all you want is to stop everything, curl up, and weep. Planning is a welcome distraction. A focus other than grief.

Just because I didn't miss Grannie immediately, didn't mean I wasn't sorry after her passing settled in. I'd always thought she and I would take one another out of this world, somehow.

I hadn't missed my parents when Grannie first took me away. I'd been running away from them, then. And after Grannie had opened me to the Graveside world, I'd been too scared to make the time, to reconnect, afraid of what she might do. To them. To me. Afraid of what my parents might say about my absence. What I'd become. That didn't mean I haven't felt their lack in the intervening years.

It was an ache all the sharper still, despite the passage of time.

Knowing for a fact what awaits the dead in the Kingdom is no comfort, so I never bother sharing. The truth would make people think I'm cracked; the same reason I don't tell them my dead sister still talks to me.

"Come to bury me once and for all?" Summer asked.

I tried not to react. She was my connection to the Kingdom,

to my power itself. Without her, I wouldn't last long working Graveside. Without her, I wouldn't *belong* Graveside. Ignoring her wasn't the problem. Getting her to shut up was, not that I could tell her.

"You can't bury all your problems."

I could, actually. Burying things is easy. It's keeping them from coming back that's the issue. And if burying didn't work, there's always cremation. Woj offered that service, too.

"When you scatter something to the wind, the wind can blow it back in your face."

I didn't have an answer for that, and without any liquor to drown her out, the best way to quiet Summer was to let her win.

Arrangements at the funeral home didn't take as long as I'd expected. Woj was efficient. He needed to drink to cope— who was I to judge? I drank Summer back into oblivion every chance I got.

No meltdowns occurred, but Lyssa was still emotionally spent, and physically tired enough that coffee and cigarettes couldn't keep her from leaning on me on the way home. I was happy to take that weight.

We walked the few blocks back to our building after I parked, staring down the sunset through scattered, stubborn leaves, and the air was crisp with the not-too-distant promise of snow.

Lyssa's phone chirped. I stopped for a second while she dug it out of her purse. With a raised eyebrow, she ignored the call.

"Who was it?" I asked, as she put the phone away.

"*Ugh*, that pastor from the Church of the Risen Redeemer. Again."

His insistence worried me. "Is he pressuring you?"

"No," she said. A sigh, then, "Yes. I don't know when I'm going to get everything done. Tammy's helping. A lot. But . . ."

"Why don't I deal with the church for you?"

Even if the Redeemers weren't tied up in Karl's shit, I had no intention of letting them do the service for Lyssa's mom. I wasn't going to put Lyssa through a death cult initiation.

Their scam worked well in Canada. We're too goddamned polite.

It would be rude to dissent during the service, even if it sounded a little . . . *sketchy*. That's how the Redeemers get you—how all the cults get you. They trick their way in, and blacken your soul by degrees, until you look back and can't imagine being good, or noble. Hell, that's how Grannie got me on board. Going to their church to discuss the funeral gave me an excuse to keep an eye on them and see that new pastor interested in Lyssa's family. I could be abrasive enough they'd reconsider their demands to host the service. She'd be pissed at first, but she'd forgive me. She'd forgiven worse.

"I don't know."

I gave her hand a squeeze. "Let me help. I can do this. How hard can it be?"

Lyssa rubbed her temples. "Well, I do need to meet with the lawyer about the will and I still haven't got the obituary done."

"You could let that slide."

She shook her head. "Dad'll expect one. The words should come from someone in the family."

"So get him to write them."

"They're already doing the eulogy."

She looked fragile, then. "Don't take on too much."

She groaned. "And I work tomorrow. I can probably skive off working the register during the day, but I need to be there for the evening. Fuck, I'm not up to hosting an opening."

"Make Njord do it, it's his gallery. Has his name right on the window in big letters."

Lyssa rolled her eyes at me. "He's great at the meet and greet, and glad-handing, but when it comes to ensuring everything goes smoothly on the night . . ." She shook her head. "Hopeless."

I smiled. She'd complained about this to me several times over drinks.

"If you need time off, I'll take your shift."

Her brow perked up, considering my offer. "You're sure? God, Winter, you've already helped me so much today."

I knew why I offered. I knew I was overcompensating. I wanted to help, but there was nothing I could do to make things better. And worse, I'd use Lyssa's loss to investigate the Redeemers' latest move.

"Friends are the family you choose, my dear." I meant it, too. Which made Lyssa and Frank all the more important.

Lyssa hadn't said yes yet. I pressed on. "Give me a list of what I need to check, you probably had it written out days ago."

Lyssa nodded and I smiled. She was a list maker. They were scattered all over her apartment. Unfortunately, she still didn't look convinced.

I ticked off reasons on my fingers. "Njord knows me, and I've worked retail and waitressed before. It can't be much different than either. We bullshitted about the galleries and museums I'd visited the last opening you invited me to." Baghdad, Delhi, Saskatoon, St. John's, Minneapolis, Dubuque. I'd picked up art and history while investigating various supernatural relics or running my errands for Grannie, and more recently doing freelancing for Bones. Gallery Sig, where Lyssa worked, mostly exhibited local painters, and did custom framing on the side. "We totally hit it off."

Lyssa had a far off look on her face, as if she was trying to remember me telling her about those trips. I tried to remember what I'd told her—I know it wasn't everything.

"He *does* like you."

Didn't I know it. Lyssa invited me to every opening the gallery hosted, but it had been a while since I'd attended. Njord flirted shamelessly with me and a few other of Lyssa's friends. Never pushed his luck, though, and if I was into older guys . . . well, a girl could do a lot worse.

Lyssa still didn't seem convinced. She did say, "I guess I'll ask Njord if it's okay with him."

I waved her off. "Let me call him, I'll set everything up. You try to rest. You have enough on your plate. Besides, I could use the money."

Blowing off shift after shift to run errands for Grannie, long hospital stays to recuperate when a job went sideways, or sleeping in after a too-late night of monster fighting all made it hard to keep a regular job.

"You *do* go through jobs like toilet paper."

I chuckled, glad for a hint of humour. Lyssa looked guilty immediately—at making a joke. It was weird enough laughing around her.

She agreed, after another block of haranguing, to let me help. And a good thing, too, because that last part—needing the money—was especially true. Christophe and McCoy and I bought each other off with favours and threats. Neither of which paid the rent.

We rounded the corner and I got a bad feeling. A long, black car parked in our building's loading zone.

Bones's car.

Lyssa said, "What?"

Double crap. I must have said the first one out loud.

"Nothing important," I said. "I forgot to call someone."

We walked past the car and the windows rolled down. Four men, all with maggot-white skin standing out, incandescent, from their black suits, black hats, and black sunglasses. Anyone else would take their stares for an appreciation of our bodies. We weren't dressed to impress, and I knew these guys better than that. Nothing they'd want to do with us remotely connected to sliding under the sheets.

I stared a hard challenge at McCoy's goons. They lowered their shades and stared right back. Subtle, guys.

When we reached the door to our block, Lyssa glanced over her shoulder at the car and shuddered. "They look like Mafia killers."

I didn't tell Lyssa how close she was.

Chapter Six

I slipped my hand inside my jacket; my knuckles brushed across my concealed necrotech. I usually carried a good all-purpose spread. Today's assortment: a tube of silver leaf flakes that looked like it belonged in a craft store; perfect for keeping a vampire from getting all misty about seeing me. A fountain pen that drew blood like a syringe; good for when I needed to make a signature count. An empty Tic Tac container to trap a riled-up spirit. I kept a sharpened skeleton key on my regular keyring. It was made from a small screwdriver, and if I used it to open you up, it'd make flesh-eating bacteria look like a lazy day at the beach. And of course, resting comfortably in the small of my back, this necromancer's never-leave-home-without-it best friend: Tahl's dagger.

The goons smiled as if they sensed nothing I was packing would work worth a damn on them. McCoy didn't trust human servants. His thugs were recycled souls in new flesh—vat-grown meat stuffed with the evilest spirits he could find. They grew darker and meaner with each iteration. Their flesh lived—sort of—and its artificial nature helped keep them from being susceptible to a necromancer's power. A good line of defence for someone like McCoy.

I switched to Grave Sight and turned my head aside so Lyssa didn't see the shift in my eyes. Suddenly having the cloudy, cataract eyes of a corpse would be hard to explain.

On a good day, I could take any one or two of McCoy's guys and he knew this—probably why he sent the extra help. Since I was walking with a friend I didn't want exposed to the darker side of my life, to say nothing of being drained from supporting Lyssa in her grief, today wasn't that day.

They made no immediate move to follow us, which meant they might have friends inside the building. I had to get Lyssa home and into her apartment before they came for me. Lyssa was already muddled with the Redeemers, I didn't want her caught up with McCoy, too. That dusty old killer made the Redeemers look innocent and he could give Christophe a run for his money in the Deranged and Evil category on *Jeopardy*.

I palmed my keyring and fumbled in my purse, as if I couldn't find them. Lyssa dug out her keys and while her back was turned, I stretched my Grave Sight to its limit, probing the building. The only signs of life were inside apartments, and more importantly, there were no signs of *unlife*. I nodded, relieved to be wrong about the reinforcements.

"What?" Lyssa asked.

"Nothing," I said, forcing a smile. "Long day."

Lyssa responded with a brittle lie of her own. "You're telling me."

I could've kicked myself. "I'm sorry, that was a stupid thing to say."

"Stop walking on eggshells around me, Winter. I'm not going to break."

I still felt awful.

I turned my back to the glass door and followed Lyssa as if I had a target between my shoulders. I glanced down the stairs to the basement where the storage lockers were. Some of Grannie's *serious* necrotech was warded up down there. It might help, but some things, once unleashed, can't be bottled up again. The worst thing I could do was let McCoy suspect I was squatting on Grannie's old hoard. I tried to keep my steps light, and had an ear cocked towards the lobby, hoping to catch the footfalls of anyone following us.

I stopped at the third floor landing. The fire door swung open, and I almost drew Tahl's knife. I shook my head at the dirty look Mrs. Friesen gave me as she shoved past me with her basket of sheets and towels. Unfortunately, the obsidian blade was useless when it came to vanquishing laundry or the disdain of Grannie's old cribbage partner. My downstairs neighbour was also an unwelcome reminder I had a stash of bloody and filthy clothes waiting for their turn in the washer.

Lyssa waited with her apartment door open. She gave me an odd look, but didn't ask what had kept me. I followed her in and closed the door, turning the deadbolt and sliding the chain in place. It wouldn't give us much time if McCoy's goons tried to bust in; any warning would be worth the small effort. To the best of my knowledge, McCoy didn't know my exact address, just the building. Once his boys were inside, it wouldn't take them long to find the place. Not with my wards acting as a beacon.

My stomach rumbled. "I'm going to phone in supper. Thai okay?"

"I'm not hungry," Lyssa said.

She'd curled up on the couch, wrapping herself in an afghan blanket.

"You need to eat something."

She waved the statement away. "I'm still full from lunch."

Another growl of protest from my belly. While Lyssa mightn't feel like eating, she needed to. Pretending to phone in a supper order would give me an excuse to leave the room, and a chance to call Frank.

"How about I order you a soup?"

"Fine," Lyssa said, defeated.

"Where are your menus again?" I asked, knowing damn well where they were.

"Basket by the phone in the kitchen," Lyssa answered.

"Thanks," I said, already heading that way.

I dialled Frank on my cell.

"Yeah?"

I cradled the phone between my ear and shoulder as I rustled loudly through the basket, hoping the noise would mask my conversation with Frank. "McCoy's goons are sniffing around my place."

"I'm on my way."

"They're parked outside, Frank. You can't get here in time to be any use. I'm going to have to bluff them."

"Who'd he send?"

"Huey, Dewey, and Louie," I snapped. "How should I know? His homunculi. Four of them."

Frank's hiss was the sharp sound of a spade biting into earth. "They're not the type to be bluffed."

"That's why I called you, Frank. You're my bluff. Here's the play: I'll leave the line open, you're inside my place."

Silence for a moment, then, "Gotcha."

Good old Frank.

I steadied myself. "We need to sell this, or it could be bad."

"I'll bring the thunder. And if it does go bad, I'll be waiting for you at McCoy's, picking my teeth with his goddamned bony fingers."

"Let's hope it doesn't come to that."

Lyssa called out from the living room, "Did you find it?"

I summoned all the cheeriness I could, which, admittedly, wasn't much, and hollered back, "Yup!"

I tucked my phone into my back pocket and walked to the door. Stealing a quick look through the fish-eye peephole, I could see two goons. They were standing on either side of my door, as if they knew its blind spots. I figured the other two were outside Lyssa's place, since I couldn't see them. Grave Sight confirmed my suspicion. I couldn't rush them. Two I could take. *If* I was lucky and quick.

"*Big if,*" Summer said, rattling my concentration.

What the hell was she doing awake? I didn't have time for her, or to find a drink to quiet her; I crushed her presence down. It worried me that she'd strayed from her usual pattern of acting up only under the new moon. Before Marcus, Summer had been an occasional stray thought I could almost pass off as my own. He woke her up. Made my life hell. He drove me away from my parents as much as I did. Would I have gone with Grannie if Summer hadn't been so insistent?

McCoy's goons would be expecting me to rush them, to pick a fight, since they'd invaded my territory.

I didn't like that they'd know where Lyssa lived once they saw me. Less that they might think *I* was the one who lived there, and could come knocking on her door later. I stayed alive by expecting the worst from everyone and everything. An unhappy way to live beat the alternative. Stranger things have happened than a necromancer putting wards on a neighbour's door to throw witch hunters and angry undead off the scent. While you spend your effort trying to break into the wrong place, I put you under the ground. Not a bad game plan, if you didn't care who else got hurt.

Despite Grannie's best efforts otherwise, I *did* care.

There was no way I'd be able to leave Lyssa's, unlock my door, and get inside before they snatched me. Any fighting would expose Lyssa to my profession. I wasn't about to take the fire escape to my apartment, either. There could be more homunculi. McCoy's ride could have enforcers stacked in the trunk like cordwood.

Any overflow could be waiting for me behind the building. Their numbers had me concerned, but McCoy's goons couldn't think I was afraid. It didn't amount to much of an advantage, but when you're outnumbered, every inch counts.

I stopped at the couch. "Off to grab supper."

I readied my keys. Quietly as I could, I loosed the chain, turned the deadbolt, and burst into the hall. I reached my door, skeleton key in hand. I knew I'd never get the door open and I didn't bother to try.

One of the goons grabbed my arm and spun me around to face him. He shoved me into the door. Energy crackled from my wards. Fortunately they wouldn't hurt me. The homunculus holding me was a knuckle hair's breadth from brushing the door. I tried to shift my shoulders, to make him connect with the wards, but his grip was too strong.

"Where are you going?" the goon said. "Mister Bones wants to talk to you."

Another added, "Mister Bones sent you a note."

Note? What note?

I rolled my eyes at them. My Grave Sight was on, and they knew it. Let them wonder what it told me. Dead eyes also helped me appear unconcerned—McCoy's goons could sense fear and they loved to exploit it.

"Mister Bones has been waiting for you," the guy pinning me said.

He drew out the "waiting," as if he were trying to remind me *nobody* made Mister Bones wait. I could tell he was on his first iteration, a new guy fresh from the vat. The others knew I'd made Bones wait a time or two. They'd told me the same thing. They hadn't liked my answer, then. I knew I shouldn't push my luck, but I couldn't help it. I had to mess with the virgin. It's a fault.

I sing-songed the words I knew were coming next along with him. "Mister Bones doesn't *like* to be kept waiting."

He scowled at my impertinence. "You owe him a package."

I flashed him my brightest smile. "I don't carry something that dangerous on me."

"Dangerous?" he said, sneaking a glance at the guy to his left. The other goons shuffled their feet. McCoy trusted them to hunt and kill for him, they were hardly party to our business.

"Yeah. Dangerous. Christophe has been snooping around. Would you prefer I turn over McCoy's package to him? Because if that vampire knew I had it, he'd have tried to take it."

The goons exchanged more worried looks.

"And I would have let him to avoid the hassle."

The new guy said, "Mister Bones won't like hearing that."

I barked a laugh. "He doesn't like *anything*. McCoy knows the score—"

"Stop using that name."

New guy *really* needed to loosen up.

The floor creaked behind Lyssa's door, her mumbled voice unintelligible. The pauses said she was on the phone.

One of the goons asked, "What's she to you?"

"Same thing she is to you. Nothing."

New guy scowled. "You've got a lot of attitude."

I smiled like my lips were dripping venom. "You came to my place of power to tell me how to act."

"You're not *in* your place of power." He shifted his grip, moving his knuckles away from my door. "Your wards won't save you now."

"This whole building is mine," I said. "You don't know the half of what I have going on."

His mouth quirked in, not concern, but certainly consideration. He said nothing. I debated whether my skeleton key would dissolve McCoy's lab meat. His goons were the main reason I'd had it crafted, but it hadn't been tested. At least not on them. McCoy's homunculi weren't like Frank. He had a semblance of life. He was made from real bodies, had real blood (amongst other fluids) running through his veins. I hadn't identified what McCoy used to juice his puppets. Tahl's knife was still a knife but without a guaranteed lethal strike they'd be on me and that'd be it. I'd be restrained again, and helpless. I didn't do helpless well. I wished Frank was here, and not just listening in. He'd pull the arms and legs off the first one to look at him cross-eyed and use them to beat the rest out the door.

I did my best to keep my face stony. "You didn't come here to fight or you'd be bleeding out. If you're here to talk, quit wasting my time and talk. And you'd damn well better hope I like what McCoy told you to say."

The goon holding me grimaced again. "*Stop* calling the boss that name."

"I'll call *Mister Bones* whatever I want. Won't I, Frank?"

"What's the sitch?"

Frank's voice came from behind me. It was a little tinny; my phone's speaker wasn't enough to carry the menace and presence Frank could command when he wanted to. It *might* fool these jokers. They looked human, but they weren't the smartest stiffs in the 'yard. I had my back to the door, my phone in my back pocket. I hoped they'd think the door muffled Frank.

The impassive faces of the guys across the hall turned worried. The new guy's buddy was filled with outright terror. He must have crossed Frank in one of his misspent lives. I tried not to smirk

"This was a friendly reminder," the frightened goon said, taking a step back. "Mister Bones wants that package."

New guy wasn't having any of their fear. He asked, "Why are you backing off? We've still got the numbers."

I arched an eyebrow. "McCoy didn't warn you about Frank?"

The bewildered look on his face told me Bones hadn't. I smiled. "He's a composite man."

For a guy with no blood in his body, he managed to turn even whiter. He knew *now*.

"*My* composite man."

With a growl even my phone speaker couldn't diminish, Frank added, "Want me to come out and recycle that shit for you?"

I levelled a stare at the guy in front of me. "Do I?"

His lip trembled, but he managed to bluster *almost* convincingly as he took his hands off me. "Your dead pet won't be with you forever."

"He'll last long enough to open that door." New guy didn't have an answer for that. I gave him one. "Keep talking and *this* death will take forever."

"Scram, ya fucks," Frank added.

They did. And as their heavy footfalls stopped echoing up the stairwell, I rested my head on my door. The familiar energy of my wards was a welcome comfort.

"Thanks, Frank," I said, taking out my phone. "I owe you one."

"Ah, who's counting? Stupid dicks need to be taught respect."

A creak sounded behind me. I spun. Lyssa had opened her door.

She asked, "What was that about?"

"Nothing, babe. Just a dick salesperson someone buzzed up. They didn't want to take no for an answer. I ran them off."

"Oh," she said. "Thanks."

"Sorry we disturbed you."

"No problem."

"I'll head over with supper soon and we'll plan more."

"Okay, see you then," Lyssa said, going back inside her apartment and closing the door.

Before I could get supper, I needed to know what the hell was going on with McCoy.

"McCoy wants to see you," Frank had said last night.

"Mister Bones sent you a note," the goons had said.

Frank hadn't mentioned a note.

"Friendly reminder," they'd also said.

Friendly, my ass.

Note, my ass.

I opened my door and rummaged through the unsorted papers on my key table.

Bill. Bill. Flyer. Pre-approved for a new credit card. A courier mailer? I didn't like that. Not one bit. Receiving a letter would excite most people. Not me. Letters can be traps. Grave Sight told me it wasn't enchanted, but it still stood out from the grey. Satisfied, I tore open the mailer and saw a piece of folded vellum. Only this wasn't calf skin. *Nice, McCoy.* There wasn't enough left of the spirit to identify its owner. It was an echo bound to the page, tasked with ensuring only I read the missive. An old, ugly trick.

The letter was crumpled slightly from being inside the mailer and sealed by wax with a Jolly Roger sigil. On the other side: my name, written in elegant script. I guess McCoy knew how to find me after all. McCoy's invitation could mean anything from *I have another job for you*, to *you screwed up the last one and it's time to die*.

I sucked the spirit into my Tic Tac case, to keep him minty fresh in case McCoy left him any other special instructions. Cracking the seal, I read the letter.

> *My dearest Winter,*
>
> *Forgive the imposition and churlishness of sending this letter when scant days remain for completion of your contract, but we both know how you would respond to the more personal touch.*
>
> *Know that I am not unwilling to get personal when I am denied what is mine. Should I continue to be stymied I will be forced to deny you that which is yours. As I know you have spent your advance, I am certain we can find accommodation soon.*
>
> > *Regards,*
> > *Mister Bones*

I had no idea how the bastard could write so well given the state of his hands. Bones had been getting antsy, and unpredictable, as his body failed.

I also didn't want to appear spooked by his goons' visit and rush off, tail between my legs. I had a day or so to let him cool his bones. McCoy needed what I had for him and if the bastard would join the last century let alone *this* one and get a telephone, I'd be happy to tell him so myself. Since McCoy preferred making people come to him, he'd have to wait for the damn privilege of his delivery.

Shit.

I still hadn't called for Lyssa's supper. I grabbed my purse and phoned the Thai place on the run.

Chapter Seven

A buzzing din rose from the gallery patrons. I couldn't make out any individual conversations. The exhibit was at the front of the gallery, and it was *happening*. A crush of people milled from painting to painting. I held down the wine and cheese table while Njord worked the register—and the crowd.

Lyssa's friends, Allie, Gina, Nancy, and Jim had been hanging around the table while their dates (whose names I'd already forgotten) lingered behind them, uninterested. Nancy was outside at the moment, having a cigarette. They'd been disappointed not to see Lyssa tonight, and not just because they had to settle for me.

They'd begun their "professional" lives, while I flitted from dead-end job to dead-end job. Often—tonight aside—I had no job at all. In those rare times when I managed a big score, I must have appeared a criminal to their civilian eyes.

Which . . . I suppose I was.

Allie Olsen was a valkyrie of a lawyer. Six-foot-three, broad shouldered, blonde. All she was missing were the braids. She was dressed as if she'd come straight from her downtown office. She asked me, "Are you going to the funeral?"

I nodded and poured her another glass of red. Her third. Judging from the flush on her face, she'd stayed for the wine, not the art.

"I love your rings," Gina Reyes, a high school science teacher, said. She had a plump and honest face that dimpled when she smiled, which was often. She usually dressed for comfort. Tonight she looked smart in dark-washed jeans and a camisole top covered by a blazer and a scarf.

"What are they? Ivory?" Jim Ko asked, touching my knuckle-dusters.

"Antler," I lied, pulling my hand back, and adjusting the carved rings. There was no good way to tell him they were made from the stolen bones of saints, and the engravings were protective sigils.

"You always wear the *most interesting* jewellery," Allie said.

I pretended her snark had been a compliment. "Thanks."

Gina and Jim had the good grace to be uncomfortable. "Has Lyssa set a date for the service?"

"Still a few details to work out," I said. "I'm sure you'll hear soon."

"You've been a real help to Lyssa," Allie said. "Nice you had the *time* to pitch in."

I shrugged. "I'm happy to help her out, any way I can."

"I hope it wasn't too much bother taking time off." Allie smiled. She knew I wasn't working right now. I let it slide. Allie and I didn't get along—she always made me feel as if I was on trial—but she was good to Lyssa. "You *are* going, right?"

I reminded myself it would be bad form to stab her.

"That's the plan," I said.

A terse nod was her only answer.

Nancy Toews, freshly shrouded in cigarette smoke, returned to the gathering. I slid another glass of Merlot her way, and she took it. She leaned in and dropped her voice to a conspiratorial whisper and gave me a whiff of mint gum not doing enough to freshen her breath. "I wasn't going to say anything, but there's a weirdo hanging around outside. Might be a drug dealer."

I faked concern. Nancy was a nurse at the roughest hospital in Winnipeg. She dealt with dealers and gangbangers every shift, and as a consequence, now she saw them everywhere. Street corner dealers weren't common in this neighbourhood, but she could be correct. Gallery Sig was still close enough to the city core that trouble could wander in. I usually worried more about what went on in the basements of the Stepfordesque gated communities in the suburbs.

Nancy had probably seen Frank. He'd been sticking tight to me since Bones had sent his crew to my place. I hoped he was staying out of sight. The new dark was a good time for *things* to slip through from the Kingdom. I was confident Frank could pass muster as an ordinary thug at a cursory glance during the night. Anyone who took a good look at his scars . . .

It *must* have been Frank Nancy had seen. If not, I imagined he'd take care of the problem lickety-split.

Lyssa's friends hung around the table awkwardly for a few more minutes, eating cheese and fruit while I slipped into serving other guests, thankful for a reason to ignore them. When their wine glasses were empty, they set them on the table and left with a little wave, off to find a less crowded watering hole—and better company.

After I'd cleared the empty glasses from the table, and binned the paper plates with their wadded napkins and empty grape stems, I looked up at Njord Sigurdson, owner of Gallery Sig.

"Thanks for helping out tonight, Winter."

Njord was a handsome man in his early fifties, with iron-grey hair and a ready smile, always immaculately dressed. I appreciated him breaking away from the schmoozefest to say thanks. Good people remembered the little things.

"My pleasure." I added more glasses to the table and filled them alternately with Merlot and Riesling.

It wasn't my pleasure. I had too much on my plate, but I'd promised, and anything I could do to help Lyssa was worth the trouble. The arrival of McCoy's goons at my apartment had upped the ante. When tonight was over, and the funeral was finalized, I could get back to my real business.

"God, I was shocked to hear about Lyssa's mom. She couldn't have been that old. Was she sick?"

"Passed in her sleep is all I know."

Njord was fishing for an age, doing the math in his head. Lyssa was in her mid-twenties. If that's when her mother gave birth, than the recently deceased would be *his* age. I didn't blame him for thinking about his own mortality. It was perfectly natural. Njord took care of himself, and like most people who did, he wanted to live longer, healthier, better. It's as if those in the best health feared death more than the ones the Reapers were actively stalking.

"What do you think of the show?"

Before I could answer, he saw a woman at the register, excused himself with an upraised finger, and hurried to make the sale. I was glad. Now I didn't have to lie to him.

The paintings weren't my taste. They were trying too hard to be sincere. If I'd had the money to blow, I still wouldn't take one home.

Also, the artist, Eliot Aga, happened to be a complete tool.

Word gets around quickly in small circles.

This particular small circle hadn't stopped the artist from complaining to me about every little thing, from the wine we'd chosen, to the "gaudy" framing materials in the back of house. My dark blue dress and gold belt clashed with his colour palette. Somehow, the manner in which I'd arranged the fruit platter managed to distract from his work. He was clever, and didn't cause a scene. He never raised his voice, and he checked over his shoulder for Njord.

Njord didn't notice. He'd never notice. Gallery Sig was his gallery. While he wanted to keep his artists happy, more so, they wanted to keep *him* happy so they'd be allowed to keep exhibiting there. This neighbourhood had disposable income. Njord did well for himself, and for the artists whose work he displayed. The city didn't have enough galleries that artists could afford to piss one off. I imagined the art world was like the supernatural world in that regard.

Eliot was clearly done with his adoring public. He approached my table for a double feature of ogling and insults. While I endured his whispered rants, I wondered how he would've treated Lyssa. At least I'd spared her that. My apparent lack of concern didn't stop him from threatening to have me fired.

It also didn't stop him from looking down my top.

Thin to the point of starvation, with artfully messy hair and glasses he probably didn't need, he would've bugged me *before* he'd opened his mouth.

I filed away every glance that didn't take in my eyes—most of them. I could kill him. Do worse than kill him.

Dare to dream. Of him sliding slowly down a blunted stake.

I was here on Lyssa's behalf. I should keep the murder and soul theft to a minimum. At least while I considered Eliot's unpleasant end, my smile was genuine when I took his next round of abuse. I wondered what illnesses I'd stored inside my aspirin tablets, and whether I could get him to take one in a cube of cheese. Eliot was a dog, but I wasn't sure he'd be fooled in the same way. Maybe if I put the pill down my top.

His smile fell a bit when he noticed Njord had followed him.

"Another sale, Eliot!"

"Wonderful," Eliot murmured.

"Wine?" Njord asked holding a glass of Riesling.

"Oh, yes. I'll take the glass from her. She's *prettier* than you."

Exactly what a girl likes to hear from a cadaverous scarecrow with rotten teeth and coffee breath in competition with fresh wine and sharp cheese. I can usually ignore lame come-ons. From Eliot, it was just . . . *gross*.

Both men laughed. Njord had the good sense to sound embarrassed. I flashed Eliot my best *see you in hell* grin and passed him a fresh glass. His lips twitched as if he'd sipped curdled milk, but he was all smiles when he turned to Njord.

"Lovely evening," he said. "Simply lovely."

They wandered back into the crowd.

I like paintings. I could have been a painter.

I shook my head, surprised Summer had stirred herself. Three times in the same week, and all well before the new moon. I didn't like it. I snatched a glass of white wine and took a gulp. Summer hissed as the wine slid down my throat and settled in my stomach. One of Eliot's potential customers nattered on to me about which piece she should buy now, seeing as how someone had heard her admire her first choice and bought it out from under her. I ignored her and took another gulp, draining the glass.

I usually avoided using wine or beer to quiet my dead sister. It took too long—and both left me with unpleasant hangovers. Hard liquor put her out quick and quiet. As did weed. This didn't seem the crowd to appreciate me slugging from a flask or smoking a joint. Njord was cool, but not that cool. We may use the same dealer, but it's not a side he'd want to present to his clientele.

The front door opened and the barest hint of cool air knifed through the gallery patrons to find me. I breathed it in, an all-too-brief sensation.

You can't quiet me. I can't go to sleep. Not with him here.

Him, who?

There was no answer from Summer.

The customer kept talking, weighing the pros and cons of her new choices, oblivious to the fact I'd been glass-eyed and tuning her out.

"*He's getting closer,*" Summer said.

So who is he? I shot back. *Your boyfriend?*

"*You'll see soon enough.*"

Tapping the table, the customer asked, "Are you listening to me?"

Shit. She'd noticed I wasn't. I beamed a smile back at her. "We sold another one," I said.

Shrilly, she demanded, "What?"

I gestured towards the register with my chin where Njord accepted payment from a stout woman with a purple streak in her grey hair.

"She knew I wanted that one!"

I feigned interest instead of saying *shit or get off the pot*, and hoped she took it as compassion.

Regardless of my opinion of Eliot, his opening was a success. Full house, eight sales out of twenty pieces. I wouldn't get a commission if I made a sale, and I certainly didn't want Eliot to get any more money. On the other hand, convincing the customer to buy something might make her leave me alone.

"I like that one," I blurted, pointing at a piece at random. "There's a weight to it. Looks cheerful, but it's all a front. A disturbing examination of hidden misanthropy. And impotence. I think it's the best of the lot."

Which was a load of crap. I didn't think this lady would call me on my interpretation. Speak with confidence about art and usually the uninitiated, not wanting to appear a fool, would agree with you.

She nodded. "You're right. Subtle. Perfect."

Her elbows rose and she tanked her way through the crowd aiming to leave with something—anything. I blew a strand of hair from my eyes, relieved she'd left.

"*You lied to that woman.*"

True. And I'd do it again, if it would shut her—or Summer—up. It wasn't my fault the woman was gullible.

"You already lie to me."
For all the good it does me.
"You lie to me as much as you lie to yourself."
Then give me a fucking straight answer.

I felt a retort building, a tantrum that would leave me with a Frank-sized migraine. It sucks when you argue with your imaginary "friend." It sucks harder when they win. She'd almost caught me. Stupid wine—I'd had too much, too fast, hoping to quiet Summer, and to deal with Eliot. I wasn't going to get into a conversation with her. It would only encourage her. I grabbed a fresh glass, and inhaled the drink in one go. Summer went quiet.

Njord swung by to congratulate me after he'd rang through the sale. "I'm impressed. She never buys anything, always complains someone beat her to the best of the exhibit."

"Glad to help," I said.

Njord cocked his head to the side, and stroked at his chin. "What did you tell her? I might be able to use it at our next show."

"Something about impotence."

"Ah, that would do it," Njord said. He held a hand over his mouth and whispered, "Her husband left her for someone younger than you."

I grimaced as Njord returned to Eliot's side to inform him of the latest sale. I wished he hadn't told me that. *Not your fault she married a creep.*

A male voice interrupted my thought. "'Disturbing examination of hidden misanthropy and impotence?' Damned if that wasn't the biggest bunch of horseshit I've heard in a while."

I stared at the speaker, who pointed towards my customer. Oddly, I noticed his hands first. He had *hard* hands. Farmer's hands. Mechanic's hands. This man had never moisturized a day in his life. In contrast to his grinning mug, they looked rough and mean.

He was young—my age, give or take a couple years. Wearing

sunglasses, despite the now-fallen evening, and a worn leather jacket over a faded Blues Brothers tee. He stood with his thumbs in his belt, eyeing the table as he hitched up his threadbare jeans. He picked up, and then set down, a wine glass.

"No beer?"

"Afraid not."

His face dropped.

He smoothed his Tom Selleck moustache, which looked natural on him, rather than a hipster affectation, and asked, "What do you recommend?"

Considering the heat in the room and the sweat pooling at the small of my back, I recommended the white. "It's hot in here—"

He gave me a wink. "Certainly is."

I blinked. Was he flirting with me? It had been a while. Catcalls I'm used to. Normally my *piss off or I'll cut you* face scared them away; they assumed I was a bitch and not worth the potential rejection, or they called me a dyke. I stumbled over my words a bit at first, blaming the wine, and decided to ignore the wink, and pretend he'd said nothing.

"I'd recommend the Riesling; it's chilled, at least. It goes well with the Edam and Muenster cheeses. If you're a red man, the Merlot pairs with the Muenster and the Swiss."

He worried at the inside of his cheek with his tongue. "That horseshit, too?"

I shrugged. "It's what the caterer told me. I forgot to confirm how full of shit they were. I've been busy."

He laughed. "Haven't we all."

Weird non-sequitur.

He pulled a king can from inside his jacket and cracked the tab, smiling at the hiss. "Which cheese goes with this?"

"What cheese doesn't?"

He laughed. "I'll skip the glass, if you don't mind?"

"I don't. Njord might. That's not covered in our liquor licence."

The stranger smiled, and finished his beer. "I'll take my chances."

He set the can down and stabbed a healthy serving of cheese with toothpicks, dropping them onto a paper plate. Reconsidering his bounty, he added several more. He pulled up the collar on his jacket, left his beer can behind and walked away with a cocky swagger.

No one in the crowd paid him any mind. Odd, given the clientele he'd shouldered past, and how out of place he was here.

The front door opened again and in that moment, a clear blast of air cut through the crowd and I shivered. A hooded figure waited a moment with the door open before stepping over the threshold.

"Nonononononono. *One was bad, this is worse.*"

I wasn't sure if Summer was talking about Mr. Moustache, but I agreed with her. This *was* worse.

It was Christophe.

He waggled an invitation at Njord, who smiled dumbly.

I yelled, "Njord!"

My warning was too late. Christophe made eye contact. Njord moved in to greet his newest guest like they were kissing cousins. Christophe flashed me a victorious smile.

I winced watching them talk. Eliot also fell under Christophe's sway. The vampire's coal black eyes smouldered at me over Eliot's shoulder as he embraced the artist close and slapped his back.

"*Run. Hide.*"

I had nowhere to run or to hide, thank you for the advice, dear dead sister. I was stuck behind a folding table of wine, fruit, and cheese. I didn't have my cloak and if I did, invoking the Veil and disappearing from view wouldn't help me escape Christophe. Not one bit. I wore some gear, and had more in my purse, but Christophe could kill everyone in the gallery before I'd have a chance to get a swing in with my knuckledusters.

Njord gestured towards me—I'm sure he was telling Christophe about the wine and snacks, but the vampire had a main course in mind, not *hors d'oeuvres*. He hunted for a richer drink than wine.

Christophe didn't head right over to me. Instead, he stayed among the crowd, chatting to each in turn. Shaking hands. Making eye contact. Laughing loudly, generously, at their quips. I wondered if he'd washed off his death stink; no one wrinkled their nose, at any rate. In no time flat, he'd made the entire room into Renfields.

His whammy was a form of hypnosis, only far more effective. If I switched to my Grave Sight, I'd see the phantom chains his words linked around the gallery patrons, and how each touch was a padlock. He owned them all now. Not permanently. Not yet.

I watched those with red wine most closely, but I couldn't watch everyone; the gallery was too crowded. I hadn't seen him drop any blood into their drinks—no Contracts signed. Once a potential Renfield tasted his blood, those locks would snap shut, the chains would turn red, and it would be all over for the poor bugger. They'd be ghouls, serving him until he died—or they did.

Knowing Christophe's appetites, the latter wouldn't take long at all.

I wouldn't let it come to that. Even if it blew my cover. Even if Eliot was a *huge* asshole. Christophe had stepped into my turf and I couldn't let him walk around like he owned it. Or he would, soon enough.

The guy with the moustache hunched behind the crowd, part of Christophe's thralls.

Typical. The first guy to show me genuine interest in ages, and it happened on the same night Christophe wanted to start a pissing contest.

If I surrendered to him, it would be harder to fight him next time he came calling. And he'd keep calling. Wearing me down. And finishing Christophe—no sure bet—would weaken me. Any other rising sharks in the city would smell blood in the water and drag me down while I recovered. The Redeemers and McCoy would fight over the rest, and the Black Plague would look like summer at Grand Beach when they were done.

No, I liked the three-way détente Christophe, McCoy, and I had on the local Graveside. I'd have to be careful. With thirty people under his sway, the vampire could kill me six ways from Sunday. I could be crushed to death by the sheer weight of his thralls. Besides, Lyssa had lost her mom, I didn't want her to have to find a new job, too. I scraped my middle finger over a rough edge on the table, wincing until I broke skin and blood welled up.

Christophe stopped laughing and jerked his head towards me. The crowd froze as they were in a movie that had been paused. He tested the air as if smelling a bouquet. His eyes widened. I smiled and sucked at my self-inflicted cut giving him the finger as I did. He excused himself from the crowd and they waited, silent, in his absence.

He approached so smoothly, it was as if he'd floated over. I kept my finger raised, letting a slow trickle of blood roll down the digit. "Thought this might get your attention."

"Even in this great herd of breathers, *you* always have my attention, Winnie." He smiled his shark-toothed smile as I furrowed my brow at the diminutive. "No need for cheap theatrics. Especially when you have no intention of following through."

"If there's no need, why are you here?"

He waggled a finger playfully at me. "You have been digging where you should not be, my dear." Christophe leaned in close and let his rank cologne of grave dirt, fresh (and stale) blood, and rot waft over me. His playfulness disappeared, quick as a heart attack. He grabbed my wrist, pulling me in close. "Again."

The way he held me, an onlooker might think he was about to kiss my hand. *What a prince.* But he wanted to sneak a taste.

Uncomfortable with our proximity, I didn't want to give away that I had no idea what in the Nine Hells he was talking about. I held up my right hand, showing him my knuckledusters. They'd disrupt his physical form, not kill him. A forced discorporation was painful and would break his spell on the crowd.

He released my hand, but didn't step back. "That grave you were interested in . . . it is now empty."

What the hell?

I didn't bother to hide my surprise. "Wasn't me."

"Do not split hairs with me, *Winter Murray*. Sending your composite man to do your work amounts to the same thing."

"I didn't send Frank." *Much as I might want to.* "And *when* I send Frank to your 'yard, he won't be there to dig."

He arched an eyebrow at my not-so-veiled threat. "If not you, then who? Who else would value that worthless plot?"

"McCoy?" I suggested, reminding myself I had another monster in my life to deal with soon.

"Never," Christophe said. "He wouldn't dare."

"I figure McCoy would dare plenty if he believed he'd get away with it."

Or he'd blame me. It would be just like him to play me and Christophe against one another, then sell me on needing his help.

Christophe sniffed.

"I guess Karl was worth more than either of us expected," I said. "You should have let him live. He could've told us why."

Christophe scowled. I leaned in and touched my head to his. It triggered my Grave Sight without any effort on my part. Spectral chains and ghostly padlocks careened around the room, swirling like a belly dancer's scarves. To my Sight, Christophe was nothing but bones with vermin for flesh. His hateful soul glowed a dour red, and pulsed angrily within his heart's dead muscle.

A trickle of sweat ran down my brow. I didn't dare wipe it

away. "I don't care if you believe me or not. Get out. And buy one of that asshole's paintings while you're here. It'll brighten your tomb."

Christophe didn't buy a painting, but he didn't kill any guests on his way out, either. I dismissed my Grave Sight, and took model glue from my purse to seal my cut. The whole crowd stood still as statues until the door closed behind the vampire. Then, as if Christophe hit "play," they all leapt back into their conversations.

The guy with the moustache was the first to approach my table.

"So," he asked. "You guys always invite vampires to your shindigs?"

Summer screamed. I heard a howling in my ears that wasn't coming from her, and feet running. I tasted the dust of a country road.

Before I could recover enough to say, "What?" he was gone.

Chapter Eight

For the rest of the gallery opening, I wracked my brain trying to guess who the moustached stranger could have been. I had nothing. I knew all the local Graveside players. Maybe he wasn't in *our* world. He could've been joking around. I doubted it.

I couldn't wait for the last patron to leave. I wanted to get Frank and get sober. I was tipsy when I needed to be sharp. In the meantime, I puttered around the gallery and tried to find all the abandoned wine glasses, fell thoughts bubbling up like sewer water in flood season.

I wondered if Christophe had fed on Nancy while she was out for her smoke. I wasn't sure if it had been Frank or Christophe that Nancy had seen. Probably Frank. If it had been Christophe, she wouldn't have come back inside.

It was time to head home. The last customer (who turned out not to be a customer at all) had left, and Njord and Eliot patted each other on the back, celebrating the successful launch. I held the door open for Eliot, happy to see him gone.

Njord passed me a sealed envelope. From its thickness he'd paid in cash. A gesture I appreciated. The Compact's apprenticeship system is shit. Basically slavery. Apprentices toiled doing the grunt work and got nothing while their work is exploited. Meanwhile, the masters lived high on the hog. Gods forgive you if you get a side gig or want your own life apart from being Graveside. Chances are instead of using necrotech, you'd become it. Try to make a little scratch, get sent to Old Scratch.

Across the street, something caught Njord's eye, and following his stare, I noticed Frank waiting. He perched like a gargoyle on the steps of an old apartment block turned condo, oblivious to the old man's ghost standing next to him.

Njord asked, "May I walk you home?"

"I'll be fine."

We stepped outside. I could see him hesitate as he turned the deadbolt for the gallery's front door. "It's no bother."

"I'm meeting someone."

He gave me a peck on the cheek and offered a defiant stare towards Frank. "Be safe."

Good advice. Just not advice I had any intent—or choice—to follow.

After heading north for another block, I turned east, towards home. Frank paced me from across the street. When he wasn't lit by the streetlamps, he disappeared into the darkness. I shook my head. A big thug tailing me would look more suspicious to Njord than if Frank had crossed the street and we'd left together. I hope Njord's nervousness didn't lead him to call the cops, or worse, follow us. Frank didn't like being tailed.

I reached my block without incident and after a quick glance with my Grave Sight, I headed up the exterior stairs to the back door of my apartment. My wards were undisturbed. The door was still unlocked. Good. I could hear traffic from Little Italy's main drag, and the calls of people getting their revel on. After the night I'd had, I wished I could join in; instead, it was time to sober up.

As soon as I entered the kitchen, I shook an aspirin into my palm and bled my minor inebriation into the pill. The fog in my mind cleared as the pill turned black. It was a good way to avoid a hangover, but, unfortunately, usually by the time I was drunk enough to need the trick, I was unable to pull it off successfully.

Good thing I hadn't gotten knackered. I'd forgotten about my Armani peace offering to McCoy, hanging in my hall closet since Woj had couriered it to me. I grabbed the suit and headed to my changing room. I left it on the bed and set the box holding McCoy's artifact beside it.

I slipped out of my dress and into my jeans in a rush and plucked a navy turtleneck from my closet. My door opened and closed, work boots pounded over hardwoods. Frank was here.

He stopped at the door to my change room, and though I was "decent," gave me an embarrassed look, and abruptly turned his back. "How was the art appreciation wank-fest?"

"Great," I said. "Until Christophe showed up."

Frank spun around, ready to burst his seams. I waved him off. "I'm fine."

He growled something I couldn't make out.

"No lasting damage," I said. "Someone else there knew Christophe was a bloodsucker, and I think he knows I'm in the game, too."

"How the fuck would he know?"

"He asked if we always invited vampires to our openings, for one."

Frank's grimace could crack stone and bend steel. He asked, machine gun rapid, "One of Christophe's? A Redeemer? McCoy?"

"I don't know, Frank." I shook my head. "My gut says he's a lone operator. Might be a hermit crab wanting a new home."

Frank let out a grunt. "Let's find out."

"I mean to."

"Who you want to hit first?"

It wasn't a euphemism. He cracked his knuckles, one at a time.

"McCoy sent me an invitation," I said, running my fingers over the box that held his artifact. "I've got Redeemers in town.

Christophe is acting up. And now this free agent is sniffing around. McCoy'll know something."

Frank growled, non-committal, but tossed me my car keys. "Let's roll."

An uncurious consequence of being trained by a woman who ruthlessly exterminated any and all rivals to her power was few people in the magical community wanted to talk to me. My own reputation as Grannie Annie's muscle abroad hadn't made me any friends, either.

Bones and I weren't friends. I'd worked for him before. He wasn't a guy you said "no" to. He was a risen consciousness— little bits and bobs of ghosts and remnants from an ossuary hidden in the catacombs beneath Paris—fused together like a composite man, but without the flesh.

No one knows how a risen consciousness comes together. Or at least, nobody I've ever talked to agrees. What I know for sure: Bones ate over a dozen urban spelunkers before anyone figured out what he was doing. Every now and then he sends me back to France to find a replacement bone. He knows I'll bring home one attuned to him, and trusts me not to mess with it. Contracts are powerful. And we both honour ours.

It's never a fun trip. It's damned dangerous. And since Christophe had put the squeeze on his boneyards, I needed the money. Besides, paid trip to Paris.

Paris had a grand necromantic tradition, one running back at least to its Roman occupation. It was also home to an older, meaner, more powerful necromancer than me. I suspected McCoy and the Steward of Paris didn't see eye to eye, so he clattered around in my town. McCoy turned up shortly after

Grannie's death. And I didn't think *that* was a coincidence, either.

He *claimed* he loved our "quaint little French Quarter"—St. Boniface. I wished he would've settled in Québec, and enjoyed *La belle province* if he missed Paris so much, but maybe he found their French as impenetrable as I did. I didn't ask, and he didn't volunteer. I suspected it may have had something to do with Wolfe and Montcalm, still scrapping all these years after their deaths.

Bones may have been lock-jawed concerning his past when he arrived, but he helped me when Christophe tried to claim the city for himself. I was naïve enough (and at the time, vulnerable enough) to take it. McCoy wormed a lot of free work from me for that help. Now we were strictly contract to contract, job to job. And he paid well.

I wondered if the stranger offered a way out. A way not to side with monsters to keep what's mine. But then, if he worked Graveside, he wasn't innocent.

We're all monsters.

McCoy "lived" in what had once been a wholesale warehouse in the Exchange District. This old neighbourhood was a ghost of a city, the corpse of the promise that could have been, when Winnipeg was referred to as "the Chicago of the North." The district had rebounded lately: trendy restaurants, clubs, and loft condos were cutting into what had been junkie and prostitute central when my parents had first brought me into the city and warned me away from the core.

But there were still bums. There were still stabbings and shootings.

Chadwick Ginther

I had to circle McCoy's block, navigating the one-way streets several times before I could find a parking spot close enough for my liking. Pro hockey's return to the city put parking at a premium downtown. Winnipeggers come in two stripes regarding parking: they'll pay anything not to have to walk, or, will walk twenty minutes not to have to pay at all. Game night had pushed the stereotypical cheap ones to the downtown side streets where parking was free.

I didn't give a shit about hockey, and discovered game nights by being confronted with a flood of arena-bound blue and white jerseys. Frank listened to the game on the radio and tension crept up my spine. McCoy was crafty, and would get more from me than I got out of him. A hazard of dealing with someone who traded in information.

They knew more than you, and they *knew* it.

At least McCoy wasn't able to retrieve what I could get for him, and until he grew a set big enough to go back to Paris by himself, he'd have to play nice, if not entirely fair.

A car pulled out, almost dinging my front end as I slammed on the brakes, tires squealing on the asphalt. Joke would've been on him; my car would've shredded his Cavalier. The car behind me honked at my sudden stop. I nosed into the now-free parking spot. I knew I'd never get the Bel Air straightened out, but the spot would be stolen from behind me if I tried to back in properly.

"You'll never get it straightened out that way," Frank said, peering out the window at the curb.

I gave him a withering stare. "Shut up, Frank." I have little patience for backseat drivers. God, only demons were worse passengers than men.

The honker lingered behind me, leaning on his horn, no doubt hoping I'd give up and leave the spot to him. When it became clear I wouldn't budge, he sped around me, saying goodbye with another honk and a middle finger. As if I gave a damn.

Frank wrote something on his palm.

When he caught me looking, he smiled. "Taking his licence plate."

"What are you going to do?"

Frank barked an ugly laugh. "Nothing serious."

I shook my head. Let him have his fun. It was a rare enough occurrence.

With the hood of my cloak pulled tight around my face, I walked between the steps of the living. Veiled, I slid out of their way. If I struck them, and they noticed the impact, they'd do little more than grunt or swear, and when they turned around, I'd be gone. Forgotten. Invisible. As hidden to them as the homeless who peppered the street, panhandling.

Frank had a different defence. Anyone who saw him coming *pretended* they didn't notice him, scurrying away for the safety of a shop or vehicle.

We'd parked near a familiar warehouse. Across the street was where Marcus had held me until Grannie killed him. This was where I'd seen my first flayed man. His skin had been used to strangle one of Marcus's other prisoners. He kept the skinned face staring at me, hollow sockets fixed. The skin's owner had stared at me, too; pleading. Begging, as if his fate was my fault, and would be until I shared it.

How he'd kept his victims alive during the things he did, I couldn't fathom then, but he did it. As much as I shuddered every time I saw the place, I still checked up on it. I couldn't leave the place be. Footsteps of the dead glowed to my Grave Sight. Nothing fresh, though.

"Miss? Miss?" A woman's voice begged. Nothing living should be able to spot me. "Please help me."

I stopped and turned. A woman lay slumped against a concrete planter. Her spirit stood beside her.

Hades, Hel, and Hunhau. She'd died on the street and no one had noticed. I stepped over beside the body. The pedestrians continued walking, eyes boring straight ahead, doing anything not to make eye contact with downtown's unpleasant reality.

"Help me," she pleaded again.

I held up a hand for Frank to wait for me—he could see me despite the Veil. I knelt beside her, my Grave Sight going over the body. There was a laundry list of things wrong with her. Aside from scrapes and bruises and her obvious malnutrition, a cocktail of diseases, tuberculosis most prominent, had ravaged her.

"I don't want to die," she said.

Her body was scrawny, her clothes filthy. How could someone with so little wish to hang onto it so strongly?

"I have a daughter," she said. "I want to see her again."

I could help her. She was freshly deceased, but not murdered like Karl. In the words of a great movie, her body was only "mostly dead," and a necromancer could still work with that. Grannie Annie wouldn't have bothered. She also wouldn't have left the spirit unmolested. She'd have bound that errant soul before it found the Kingdom, bartered it to another necromancer, or consumed it to delay the disease that'd killed her.

Looking into her shadowed eyes I made my choice. McCoy had waited this long. He could wait a few moments longer.

I drew the sicknesses from her body and held them within mine. I'd never been sick from virus or disease since I'd been awoken to my power. Being a necromancer means one has a naturally (or unnaturally) robust constitution. The diseases *shouldn't* affect me. But they might. That, aside from the general amorality of being a grave robber, kept necromancers from volunteering in hospitals.

Maybe that was how Grannie contracted her cancer. She'd

never been much of a healer, but weaponizing others' sicknesses was the step before healing them. I dropped a handful of aspirin into my palm. To my Sight, the pills turned black as they rested against my skin and the dead woman's diseases leeched into the tablets. I dropped them into an empty bottle and laced the woman's fingers through mine. Few of us chose to help the mostly dead. It pained us. It could kill us.

I steeled myself and tore a heartbeat free and sent the pulse through my body to the woman's spirit and into her still body. I slumped, each breath a ragged gasp. I winced as I put a hand to my chest, and felt my heartbeat normalize. When it did, I noticed, the mostly dead woman was still dead. Saving her was effort I could ill-afford, but I wasn't Grannie, damn it. I gritted my teeth and ripped another heartbeat. Every breath I hissed past my teeth hurt. My ribs ached as if I'd endured CPR. But it worked.

The spirit climbed back into its body, as if getting dressed, and disappeared. The woman's eyes snapped open and she gasped, a loud rasp that startled a nearby clubber into hurrying his steps. She looked around, unable to spot me. She was alive now, to her eyes, I was gone.

Invisible.

A dream.

I tucked a twenty into her jacket pocket and backed away. She stood shakily, and asked a man for change, no recollection of her brief time in queue for the Kingdom. I watched her walk the opposite direction down the street. I wondered if she'd find her daughter. If it were actually safe for my parents to look, I'd want them to find me.

"No," Summer said. "You wouldn't. And they'd hate what you've become."

I wished I had a smart answer. I wiped the sweat from my brow, and motioned to Frank that we were done. I looked back across the street at Marcus's warehouse. I shouldn't have. Spirits stared out the windows. Marcus's victims were tar-black, not translucent. There'd be no peace for them in the Kingdom. Not after what they'd endured. Watching them, I swore they recognized me. That they mouthed, "Next. Next. Next."

I shook my head. Summer repeated their soundless words. I forgot sometimes that she'd been a witness to everything I had. I walked away from the spirits, since I couldn't walk away from my sister.

Frank followed me a few steps closer than he had before.

We stopped at an arched delivery tunnel between McCoy's converted warehouse and the next one over. There wasn't too much tagging on the building, considering its run down appearance. The alcove was too dark to be natural. I couldn't see the street on the other side of the block. McCoy playing around— showing off.

A mortal would walk past that tunnel and shudder. If they were superstitious, they'd ascribe the feeling to the building being haunted. The truth was scarier. My Grave Sight couldn't penetrate the veil. It was an obsidian wall.

Frank held up his hand for me to wait, and walked through that dark curtain bold as brass. I let him go. He was the muscle after all, and he enjoyed his job, and I didn't begrudge him keeping me safe and playing the heavy.

My hackles rose for a second. Under a streetlight, a huge black dog padded across the intersection. It turned and looked at me, eyes flashing in the light. There was something odd about a huge dog roaming free downtown.

I shivered again as Summer stirred. *"I don't like dogs."*

I put my hand on my flask; if she kept talking, Frank would have to take the wheel on the way home. With a tug and a rumbling whine, a man dragged the dog out of the street. I'd been so focused on the animal I hadn't noticed its owner. Seeing its leash now didn't help my uneasy feeling. I wondered if the man had the dog for protection, or if he was running a protection scam.

Frank stepped out of the alcove, and he looked disappointed. "Someone got here before us."

"What?"

He gestured back to the veil. "McCoy's goons. Looks like they went ten rounds with a junkyard dog."

I shot a look across the street. The dog and its owner were gone.

"Okay," I said. "Let's take a look."

The hearse from hell was there, and sprawled around it were McCoy's guys, presumably the same four homunculi who'd accosted me at home. It was hard to confirm identities without faces.

Their suits were shredded, the least of the damage: throats were torn out, arms and legs broken at odd angles, steel bones poking through crafted flesh. The ichor that passed for their blood was everywhere.

"What do you want to do with them?" Frank asked.

"Best to bring them in," I said. "They might still wake hungry."

Frank punched out the car window. Shattering glass echoed through the tunnel.

"I'll put a little sugar in their gas tank. In case there's more of these jokers upstairs and they follow us home."

He popped the lock and opened the door as casually as if he were going to take it for a test drive. Frank lashed out with his foot. His steel-toed boot hit the steering column and snapped it with a sharp crack. Frank wasn't satisfied there, however. He drew a hunting knife that looked tiny in his giant mitt, and gave each tire a deliberate stab.

"McCoy'll be more pissed about the car than his help."

"He should watch where he lets his dogs sniff around, then. We'll tell him we found it like this."

I smiled. "I suppose we did."

I lifted the goons' wallets and pocketed a fat wad of cash from each. Not a proud moment, but they didn't need the money, and McCoy had plenty more where it had come from. No point letting shame stand in the way of a payday. I could help Lyssa out with her mom's funeral costs. At least I could afford to send flowers now.

I gathered their blood, sealing it in a Ziploc with a personal effect—ring, chain, watch—from each body. Maybe I'd be able to use their ichor to bypass their protections. Tidying might also endear me to Bones more than the suit. I wouldn't hold my breath.

"There'll be body bags in the trunk," I said. McCoy travelled prepared for any eventuality. It wasn't as if these guys hadn't killed (or died) a few times already in service to their master.

Frank tore open the trunk. He tossed four body bags on the ground, and we stuffed the goons inside.

With a grunt, I dragged a guy to the door. Frank had one balanced over his shoulder, fireman-carry style, and hauled the other two behind him, one in each hand.

Normally, it would've been Bones's goons answering the door. They'd loom, and threaten, and I'd ignore them. They'd notice Frank and weigh their chances, and open the door, before scurrying into their hidey-holes.

I leaned on the bell, curious as to who would greet us with the regular crowd less living than normal.

A pale blonde woman wearing a tailored black suit with a navy blue dress shirt and matching tie opened the door. She stared eye to eye with Frank and didn't blink. Inge. McCoy's "executive assistant." He didn't use human servants, and she wasn't one of his homunculi. I still hadn't sussed out what she was. With steely eyes she regarded the body bags. Frank nudged the dead goon off his shoulder to fall at her feet.

"Mister Bones has been waiting for you," she said. If she cared about the homunculus, she wouldn't show it. Not in front of me and Frank. I mouthed along with the words I knew were coming next. "Mister Bones doesn't like to be kept waiting."

"I'm here now," I said.

Inge nodded and with no more apparent effort than Frank had shown, she hoisted the homunculus with one hand and carried him away.

Chapter Nine

From outside, McCoy's joint looked sketchy as hell, promising a rat's nest of junk, broken glass, and vermin. Inside was no better. Rats scurried and squeaked, staying well clear of Inge's immaculate heels.

Frank asked Inge, "Your place always a shithole, or did whoever fucked up your goons redecorate?"

Inge smiled and I damn near shivered. "Whoever attacked our interests will be dealt with." She regarded her high heels, and I could feel the willpower it took for her not to bend down to clean the dust from her shoes. "Mister Bones finds few poke their noses beyond our façade. It has its uses, despite its obvious detriments."

She walked us to the elevator, an old open cage affair with a prominent, if dusty, sign reading: *Out of Order*. It was snug in there, between the three of us and the homunculi bodies piled behind me and Frank. As I wondered what the weight restriction on this old elevator might be, Inge closed us in and we headed to the top floor and McCoy's office. Frank whistled an unrecognizable tune as the machinery ground and squealed. Inge hummed along, looking at Frank, openly staring—appreciatively—and I felt . . . what? Jealousy? *Weird*. Frank stopped whistling, and shifted from foot to foot; the way he looked away told me if he still had any fresh blood in him, he'd be blushing.

After years of working for McCoy, I couldn't blame Inge for finding Frank handsome. I'd bring Frank here more often if it would make the Ice Queen act more human.

When we stepped out on the sixth floor, however, the building took on a decidedly different cast. McCoy's office was the entire top floor of the building, and appeared like it belonged in another place, another time. It would be the envy of all the folks buying loft condos around Old Market Square. All original wood, painstakingly stripped and stained. Exposed brick. The hardwoods had seen better days, but were as old as the building and added to its "character." Vintage movie posters for films I was pretty sure had never existed lined the halls. *Never Cross Bones* was the worst title of the lot. It was like stepping into a Prohibition speakeasy. Except all the dancers were dead, and every drink could kill you.

"Leave them in the elevator," Inge said, gesturing at the homunculi. "I will deal with them."

Figures on McCoy's posters moved in the corner of my eye, and the starlets looked more haunted than sexy. I knew if I turned, they'd be still, and back to hawking adventure, excitement. Fantasy.

I didn't bother looking beyond their fictions with my Grave Sight. I'd made that mistake once. I knew what the posters were advertising: Decay. Domination. Death. The first time I'd tried to suss out the queer feeling they gave off, I'd been left with a splitting headache, and a deal with McCoy I'd come to regret.

Beside me, Frank muttered, "This place gives me the heebie-jeebies."

"You will get used to it," Inge called over her shoulder.

Now what the hell did she mean by that?

Inge paused at a gleaming pair of walnut double doors, their hinges shining silver. The handle pulls were cast in the shape of contorted spines, each looking as if it had been ripped from inside the door. I was certain Bones had the doors warded all to hell, and the wrong person touching that door would end up deader than a draugr.

We followed her inside and were greeted by the back of a tall leather chair. McCoy swivelled around to face us. There was a reason he's called Mister Bones by his crew. He was an animate skeleton, which barely scratched his surface.

McCoy's grinning skull gleamed white where the light caught it, as if he'd had it polished. He pushed his chair back, and stood up. He wore a black pinstriped suit that hung hollow on his stick-like body. Even when he wore his suit you could tell there was no meat on Bones's bones. A belt cinched the pants tight around where his ilium and the head of his femurs met, which gave him an even more emaciated look, as if he were wearing a crazy corset and his bones had worn holes in the fabric. For all that, you could tell it had been an expensive suit. Once.

I was glad I'd brought him a new one.

Bones's skeletal hand grasped a silver-handled walking stick. He hadn't needed one before. Or at least, he'd never seemed to. As he walked over to welcome Frank and me, there was the hint of the limp that McCoy tried to hide by playing the walking stick off as a dandy's affectation. I glanced at Frank, who raised an eyebrow. He saw it, too: a potential weakness. McCoy was pretty good at terrifying folks. Fortunately for me, not much rattled Frank.

Unless he wanted to seed false weakness to lure me—or Christophe—into a trap, thinking we could be rid of him.

Until I knew for certain, I'd sit tight, and try to pretend I'd seen nothing. Trick McCoy into believing I'd become rusty. Not that I wanted him probing my corners for weakness, either.

"Winter Murray, lovely to see you," McCoy said, drizzling his French accent over the words like vinaigrette. He stared at Frank for a moment. "And you brought a friend."

"Someone beat up your guys," Frank said matter-of-fact, gesturing back towards the body bags stacked in the elevator.

"I see," McCoy said, clacking his teeth together and turning his hollow gaze over to me. "Terrorizing the help, Miss Murray?"

"At least I'm keeping it to the help, McCoy." I smirked. "For now."

McCoy chuckled. "Inge, recycle them." The Ice Queen nodded. She looked frostier when Bones added, "There's a dear."

In a clipped tone, Inge said, "As you wish, Mister Bones."

McCoy didn't say another word until Inge left the office and the elevator descended. He stepped around Frank and I to close the doors to his office before I could see which floor.

Recycled.

It was more than a euphemism. There was no end to dead gangbangers and ghostly would-be tough guys who wanted one more crack at the flesh. McCoy gave it to them. Somehow. I hadn't figured out how he made his homunculi—yet.

Now that I had a possession, and what passed for their blood, I'd have a hold I could exhort on them.

Maybe.

"There, now that the unpleasantness is out of the way, let's get down to business. Thank you for coming. I assume you received my letter and this is not a happy coincidence?"

"I got your letter," I said, picking at a nail with my thumb. "And your . . . more personal reminder."

McCoy took a crystal decanter from a side bar, and filled a silver goblet with wine. I imagined it would taste excellent. Bones only surrounded himself with the best, goons aside. It would also be an excellent tasting trap.

He offered me the goblet of unknown, and therefore, unsafe vintage. I waved him off. McCoy made no move to offer anything to Frank.

McCoy shook his head and took a drink. Wine dribbled past

his bony jaws and over the red cravat he habitually wore, but most disappeared *somewhere*. "That you would not enjoy a glass of wine with me *hurts*. A physical pain, *chérie*."

"It's a little early in the day for me," I lied.

McCoy barked an ugly laugh. "I am no sidhe and this building is no faerie ring. My food and drink are safe from *geas*."

"Safe from that, but I wouldn't call anything about you safe."

He smiled. "Ever the Careful Cathy."

One could never get through a transaction with Bones without a certain amount of bantering. McCoy loved the ritual of it, made you forget you were talking to a skull and not a face, then gums flapped, and who knew what you might let slip. I played the game as little as I could. I have plenty of secrets I wanted to keep just that: secret. Especially from an information broker.

He sat back in his chair and drilled his fingers into well-worn grooves on his desk and I knew the time for idle chit-chat was over. Bones wanted what he'd commissioned, and I wanted to be rid of it. He gestured at two chairs, but Frank and I remained standing.

I pulled the item from my bag and placed its velvet wrapping on a table in between my chair and McCoy's desk. With as much flourish as I could muster, I unrolled the velvet to reveal the femur inside. It was brown with age and clad with grave dirt from its long-ago time under the ground. McCoy, tilted back in his leather chair, raising the hollows of his skull to the ceiling and took a deep, satisfied breath, as if he was sampling the bone's age, and power, swallowing the catacomb must.

"You are a wonder, my dear." He dragged a sharpened phalange over the bone, scraping more dirt free like his finger was a coke spoon, and took another good whiff. "You've outdone yourself."

It'd been a hard one to find. They moved the bones from time to time and rebuilt the retaining walls to keep the bones from spilling out of their catacombs and into the walking chambers underneath Paris. Locating one that suited McCoy was a more difficult matter than plucking the first bone in reach from the ossuary.

I did my best to keep my voice flat. "It pleases me that you're pleased."

"Pleased is a strong word," McCoy said, setting the bone down. "Considering how long it took you to deliver."

Frank took a step forward, ready to loom. I waved him off.

"As you may have heard, I've been busy."

"Ah yes, with *the vampire*."

"Not just him," I said, leaving the tease dangling to feel out McCoy, hoping he'd offer something. Anything.

To my surprise, he did. "Your mystery cult."

"There's more."

McCoy cocked his head to the side. In the light, one of his eye sockets seemed to deform, like he was arching an eyebrow he'd gone without for centuries.

"It might be nothing," I said, remembering the Tom Selleck wannabe from the gallery. "Might be *the* something that took out your guys."

"Describe them," McCoy demanded, and while I bristled at his tone, I did, down to the last moustache hair.

Finger bones clacked over teeth. "Another necromancer? It has been a while since you had any competition, my dear."

"I've got no competition. And don't remind me of that asshole Barry."

"Forgive me, I misspoke. It has been years since you've had to fight for the city." He gave me the once over with his hollow sockets. "And your exceptional skills aside, you are not your *grand-mère*, non?"

I grimaced. For good or ill, he was right.

"If it is another necromancer, may I count on you to back me?"

"Of course," McCoy said. I sensed a "but" or a "however"

coming in Bones's silence. "As much as I count on you to fend off our vampire friend, Christophe, without proper payment or reciprocity."

So not at all, then. I knew the score. If there was another necromancer moving in, and McCoy took my side, even though that same necromancer had likely offed McCoy's goons, I'd be expected to take his side against Christophe. Something I wasn't ready to do yet.

Still, I tried to turn over the revenge card, to see if McCoy would double down on it. "If this stranger *is* another necromancer, he's already acted against you. Cut me some slack."

"*Proof*, Winter. You have none. And I don't believe for a second you are concerned about my associates' . . . lives." He gestured at Frank. "For all I know, your thug did the damage to earn you a bargaining chit. As for the cutting of slack, I do so many times a day. I enjoy our working relationship, I would like it to continue."

There was an implied "working for me" in McCoy's statement I didn't like.

"And so, I will give this potential usurper the same answer I have given you."

"Unless he throws in with you against Christophe."

McCoy nodded. "A risk one takes in straddling a line drawn in the sand, my dear. How would your companion put it? Shit or get off the pot?"

Frank growled. Nonplussed, McCoy swivelled to face him, bone grating on bone, and let out a hollow hoot. "We are on the same side until we turn on one another, Winter. The same as ever."

Less than I'd hoped for, and about as much as I'd expected. I turned to Frank, motioning for him to hand over our other package. I tossed it on the table between McCoy and me.

"What's this?" he asked, excited as a child with a new toy.

I shrugged. "Thought you'd like it."

McCoy slit the string tying the package using his finger for a knife, then meticulously sliced at the paper's taped edges. Drawing the carefully folded jacket to his face, McCoy's teeth *click-clacked* together in excitement as he pressed fabric to bone.

"Ooh, a cancer suit, how *lovely*."

He held the jacket against his meatless frame. The man it had belonged to had lost a lot of weight before he'd ended his own life. I guess his family hadn't wanted to guess at a new suit size. McCoy would be swimming in it, which was how he liked it.

"To what do I owe the pleasure?"

"I need a reason?"

"*You* do, Winter. Not that I won't treasure it. I assume you hoped a gift would sweeten my disposition."

I grunted, non-committal.

"It will take more than Dead Man's Clothes for that, as you well know." Frank grumbled something unintelligible and McCoy swivelled his skull over to address my muscle. "Does she sweeten you, monster?"

Frank scowled. "Fuck you, toothpick."

"Boys, boys," I said. While I wanted to know who would win in a straight fight between him and McCoy, today wasn't a great day for the main event. And besides, McCoy would cheat.

"It's just a suit," I said.

McCoy grinned broadly. "In that case, I may have information for you."

"I'm all ears."

He tented his fingertips and clacked them together atonally. "Some breather has been asking about you."

I tried to keep my eyebrows from shooting up. "Is that so?"

McCoy flashed his dead man's grin. "Would I lie to you, *chérie*?"

If there was money in it.

Instead, I said, "You haven't yet, which is why we're still friendly."

Bones twisted his skull; almost imperceptibly his hollow eye sockets lined up with mine. "I do not know their name. It was someone Graveside."

I kept my expression blank. He hadn't given away the gender of the snoop. Had to be the moustache. I'd have to track him down sooner rather than later.

"Who?" I asked.

"What is it worth?" McCoy said.

"Not much, since you clearly don't know."

McCoy let out a disappointed *tut*, and held his hand over an empty ribcage, his fingers pressing the suit fabric into the hollow, and tearing through. "You wound me."

Frank snorted, a sound I took to mean *not yet, but fucking soon*.

"Whoever they were, they not only asked about you, they asked about your family."

"Fuck you, Bones."

That wasn't possible. Grannie'd seen to that. They were safe. Everything I did, everything I'd done, was worth it if they were safe. If they never knew.

A skeletal fingernail clicked off his jaw. *Tap. Tap. Tap.* "I don't need to tell you there is powerful magic in familial bones. Their bodies could be a powerful focus to be used against you."

"Try it."

He tilted his head, smiling his rictus smile.

"Try it," I repeated. "And I'll use *your* bones as a focus. I'll burn you down to the *fucking marrow*. I will consume the ossuary you crawled out of, until not even Hades could reconstitute you. I will end you."

McCoy tipped his hat in contrition. "Promises, promises, *mademoiselle*."

"Just watch me."

McCoy hissed, put-upon, like a steam kettle whistling. "Threats bore me."

He held up a skeletal finger before making an exaggerated show of pressing a button. An intercom buzzed. Inge's voice sounded crackly and tinny over the speaker. "Yes, Mister Bones?"

"My guests are asking about our previous visitor. If you'd be so kind as to bring your portfolio."

"At once," Inge said.

The doors opened, and Inge strode in, heels ringing off the hardwoods. She handed a black leather portfolio to McCoy. He opened the case, and after flipping through a few pages, he turned it to face me. The page displayed a pencil portrait of a woman so well rendered it could've been a black and white photograph.

"Many gifts, Inge possesses," McCoy said, turning his gaze on Frank. "Many gifts."

I ignored McCoy, instead focusing my attention on the portrait. I recognized her.

She'd been at Karl's funeral.

"I would offer your payment for our contract, but you've already helped yourself to enough of my money tonight."

I grimaced. "What I took from them didn't cover my fee."

"Then you should not have been greedy."

He had me there.

"Our business is done. Unless you have something else to offer me? No?" He gestured at Inge, and waved towards the doors. "See them out."

Chapter Ten

Inge took Frank's arm like it was prom night and left me trailing in their wake, wishing I could use my Grave Sight in McCoy's domain without going blind or crazier. I considered forcing her to give him up, but Frank was a big boy, and besides which, I didn't know what Inge *was*. Until I did, making a move she might take as an invitation to scrap wasn't prudent. Especially if McCoy saw it as a betrayal of our peace.

There was no whistling, or humming, as we rode the elevator. Inge's hand never left Frank's arm. Instead of being pleased at the Ice Queen's attention when we stepped out of the building, he looked unbearably sad. I shook my head as she closed the door behind us. On a sunny day, all Frank saw was rain.

"Winter," he said, his big lip trembling, and from the way his hands were clenching, if he'd been holding a pool ball, it would've been powder by now. I didn't like what might happen if he was alone. What he might do to himself. Or to others.

I wrapped my hands around one of Frank's giant mitts. "You're staying with me tonight."

I crawled into bed next to Frank, my body still warm from the shower. As always, he was corpse-cold. My bed was too small for him—let alone both of us. Grannie Annie had died in her old king-size, and I'd burned it after I'd burned her—some remnant of her might've lingered inside.

I'd never bothered replacing my little twin. Bringing home dates wasn't a luxury a necromancer could afford—even if she did get lonely—and I didn't trust going blind to someone else's place. Besides, people loved to screw around in hotels. Grannie Annie had always told me to use sex to form bonds with allies. "You're young," she'd said. "Beautiful. Better you win those allies now."

I hadn't put much stock in her advice then. Less now. I had no intention of playing the succubus or lamia. Grannie had never forced me to screw anyone I didn't want to, but she did get the frowny *I'm disappointed in you, Winter* look when I passed up an opportunity.

Frank wasn't such an opportunity, but we did have a bond.

He turned on his side as I spooned against him, running my fingers over the many rough scars stitching his body together. The Y-shaped incision in Frank's torso stood out from the patchwork of mottled flesh and sutures making up his body. He shuddered slightly and I pulled a blanket over us.

Despite what Christophe and others may insinuate, Frank and I have never had sex. They want to believe I keep the big guy around for other nasty business, let them. It makes them underestimate what we really have. Even if *I* wanted to, Frank would never agree. Every time he comes to lie in my bed, he's near suicide. He *would* kill himself, if only he could find a way to die. Sometimes I wondered if I was doing him any favors. He wanted an end, and I was a selfish shit for denying him. Because I needed him. And I'd miss him when he was gone.

Frank's creators had run around wearing their black hats proudly. They'd used Frank in the most horrible ways imaginable—and I can imagine plenty horrible. For the year I'd spent tracking them he'd caused slow death to the cult's victims. Maybe they were trying to break the soul they'd bound to their composite man. Luckily for me, when it came to souls, they'd chosen poorly.

I owed Frank my life several times over. The least I could do was help him to enjoy his own. That he needed help shamed him. I rested my hand on his chest and he growled as if he hated himself. My touch usually settled him and helped him forget his self-loathing. It was worth it if it gave him reason to continue.

"Lies," Summer hissed. *"You do this because you need him. He is a tool to you, nothing more. You use everyone. Even me."*

Bullshit. And she knew it.

I wanted her to leave me alone. Not take up permanent residence. Or be correct. I couldn't slug back a drink because Frank would think I needed the liquor to be with him. Arguing only encouraged Summer. I thought of the time I spent with Mom and Dad, which didn't cheer me up, and sent Summer wailing away into the depths of my mind. It had been a while since they'd leapt into my thoughts unbidden. McCoy's mentioning our dead family must've put them to mind. I'd have to remember that trick.

For now, Frank needed me more than Summer did. I shut down his pain receptors. Every stitch in his patchwork body ached fresh, as if done that moment—without anaesthesia. How he didn't spend his life screaming I didn't know.

He exhaled, the sound a person made when they stood and stretched after a long time at a desk. A moment without pain, when it's all you've lived with, was a blessing. But I wasn't done. The paths to happiness in Frank's brain were pretty atrophied. He didn't have much chance to use it outside of our nights together, but everything was there and everything worked. When I triggered his pleasure centres, Frank's sigh turned into a moan.

I worried one night he'd take a header into the Red River and let the catfish eat him. That wouldn't be enough to end him, and he'd only spend a drowned eternity in greater pain and misery. It had been over a month since he'd last broken down and spent the night. There were tears beading in Frank's eyes. I touched his cheek, and a tear brushed my hand.

I raised his temperature. Sped his heartbeat. Released endorphins. I couldn't do much to cheer him up, but I could make him feel human again.

It was hard not realizing his strong arms could kill me any time in the night. The combined necromancy of Frank's creators hadn't been enough to save them once I'd cut him loose. I felt safe with him beside me, and Frank was safe from himself. It was an approximation of life, but it was the only one he had, and I wanted him to keep living it.

"Thanks," he murmured. Frank tried to get up to leave.

I dug my fingernails into his shoulder. "You're staying."

"But—"

"No 'buts,' goddamn it." I turned to face Frank and twinned my leg in between his. We each had a butt cheek hanging over the edge of my tiny bed. I didn't care. "You're staying."

"I wish I'd met you when I was alive," Frank said.

That was new.

"When I was . . . one man," he added.

"Naw," I chided him. "I'm hard on men."

"You should have someone," Frank said, sounding determined. "Someone who doesn't make you sick to look at."

"You don't make me sick," I tried to joke. "I've seen bodies far worse than yours."

Frank was having none of it. "Yeah. Dead ones."

There was no answer to that. I wasn't happy Frank was lost in melancholy again and I used my touch to calm him, putting him into torpor. I could look past Frank's scars, and all he'd done—even if he couldn't make the same leap.

"Good night, Frank," I said, pecking his cheek with a light kiss. I let myself drift to the metronome of his slow, steady, faithful heart; four beats per minute.

Frank wasn't in bed when I woke. He must've slipped out before dawn and headed back to his place. I hoped he was okay.

Glass clattered and clinked in the kitchen. I grabbed Tahl's knife and called out, "Frank? Is that you?"

It had better be.

"Yeah," he hollered back. "Making coffee."

I took my hand off the knife and let out a breath I hadn't known I'd been holding. I was glad he'd stuck around.

I fuelled up on coffee, preparing to check out the Redeemers and see what their new pastor was made of, and most importantly, get that funeral arranged for Lyssa—hopefully somewhere not cult-infested.

I had no intentions of going into cult HQ there as myself, however. They'd been sniffing around. Asking McCoy about me. Word gets around, my reputation is not a good one. Whoever is banking this iteration of the church probably has a "kill on sight" order out on me.

We'll see.

I checked my wall of shame, with pictures and addresses for the few lost souls that had made an appearance at poor Karl's funeral, clustered among other, older photos. One of them should work if I wanted to make a brief infiltration. I grabbed my Polaroid camera; I'd need a new image. My picture of Corinne hadn't captured the Flicker necessary to assume her appearance and complete a disguise.

It wasn't the safest tactic. Grannie had told me horror stories about a man who'd never come back from the act. Forgot his name. He lost his soul and become a hungry shade, jumping from body to body, burning them out. I shuddered, reminding myself I had to scope out the Redeemers. Turning over the photo of my target, one Corinne Mayberry, I tried to mentally place her address in the maze of suburbs.

I'd come to appreciate all the "junk" Grannie Annie had kept tucked away. Years on from her death, I kept finding uses for old trinkets she'd kept, despite my insistence it was junk and should be thrown away. Grannie was like a dragon in temperament— and power. I wouldn't be surprised if she had many more "hoards" hidden all over the city.

And that worried me. Especially the idea someone else would find them and use them against me. A stranger sniffing around my business lately was less comforting.

Outside the door, Frank shuffled back and forth while I changed into outfit after outfit, trying to find the right mix of stealth, utility, and not scaring the Sunsiders.

Through the door, Frank said, "I don't like this plan," as if he'd been tuned in to my worries.

"You don't like anything," I shot back.

His creaking steps stopped. "You're going alone. *Again.*"

"I can't walk around with you in the daylight."

I felt like a shitheel as soon the words left my mouth.

"No shit," he said, but I heard the hurt through his bluster. I was a terrible friend.

Before I undid last night's good work, I changed the subject and asked, "How do I look?"

He came in, shielding his eyes with his hand, in case I'd played a cruel joke on him. I didn't know why he bothered. He'd seen me naked plenty, but he always played the Boy Scout. He raised the hand slowly, his perpetual grimace intensifying.

"I still don't like it."

"You've told me that already."

Frank's lips twisted into something between a smirk and a snarl. "What now?"

"I steal her shadow and see what her cult knows."

I hated the suburbs. There was no life in them. Giant cookie cutter houses on postage stamp yards in a rush to get the hell out of the scary downtown core. I'd have preferred to stay away, but I doubted Frank would've been on point after the way Inge had rattled him. He'd have killed Corinne, not captured her.

My mark lived in an over-under condo complex in south St. Vital within a group of buildings swallowing the block. I left my old sedan at a park-and-ride—it'd stand out in this neighbourhood of Honda Civics and SUVs as much as Frank would've among its residents—and hoofed it to Corinne's under the Veil. It might be possible to clothe Frank in shadows, too, but I didn't want to get his hopes up. I hadn't met anyone whose shadow would hold Frank. I wished I'd had Frank grab Corinne in the night and bring her to me in chains. After I had her shadow I could keep her in the dark, figuratively and literally, to ensure my disguise lasted a little longer. There was one storage locker downstairs I wasn't using, but I didn't want to shit where I ate.

An elderly man out for a walk with his dog slowed as he walked past me, and the dog barked. Dogs have a good sense concerning the Kingdom and, wrapped in my cloak, I must've been too close for the dog's liking. When you hear them barking for no reason? Cough up a treat. The man gave the dog's lead a tug and hustled away.

It was hard to find anything in these condo complexes, but I saw a late model Cavalier—the same car that'd almost hit me near McCoy's place last night. She *had* been talking to McCoy.

Breaking into Corinne's house was simple. With my skeleton key, no lock could stop me. The key's teeth reformed as I touched it to the door knob, and it slid in as if it had been made to open this door. She worked nights; she'd probably be asleep. I turned the key slowly, though I doubted she'd hear the opening lock's soft thunk.

Corinne had her back to me in the kitchen, washing dishes and listening to music by the speaker of her phone. *Easy-peasy.*

I had a brief desire to make her time hard, since the Redeemers were doing nothing to make my life easy. Plant her at a crossroad. Promise to come back when I was done. Maybe. Grannie's way.

"You buried someone alive not long ago," Summer accused.

"Shut up," I hissed back. Corinne was *right there*, and this wasn't the time to get distracted by whiny siblings.

I eased the door shut. While she wouldn't be able to see or hear *me*, she might still hear *that*.

I grabbed her. One invisible hand on her wrist, the other over her mouth. Her eyes went wide as I gave her a magical chokehold, squeezing her windpipe closed with thanatomancy. Tricky work. Too much and I'd kill her. Too little and she'd wake before I was done at the CRR.

It had to be terrifying for her. An unknown force with ultimate power over her. The violation that came when it happened within your own home. Safe as houses, that's a saying. Houses aren't safe.

Grannie took me from mine. I knew how Corinne felt because I'd been her. If she was luckier than me, she'd rethink her life. Become a better person.

She tried to scratch. To bite. Heels drummed against linoleum. But not for long. A few seconds after her eyes fluttered, I eased my hold on her.

I was sweating by the time I was done. Once I'd secured her, I took my hood off.

There was a large pantry down the hall from the kitchen that would make a handy place to stash Corinne after I'd stolen her Flicker. I just had to cage her shadow and get changed.

While I was in her bedroom I took a few valuables. Nothing major, enough to make it look like a home invasion: whatever cash I could find, bits of jewellery, an iPad. There was no laptop, only an old desktop. I didn't want anyone to connect this to the CRR's activities—or mine—so I couldn't leave behind any "This Home Invasion Brought To You By Your Friendly Neighbourhood Necromancer" calling cards.

I settled on a skirt and blouse combo. Unfortunately, I also saw her wearing nylons. I grimaced, slid them on, and buttoned my blouse. I hated nylons as much as I hated skirts and heels. Hard to run, hard to fight, and if today went poorly, I might have to do both.

Looking at myself in these awful clothes, I packed my jeans, a t-shirt, and a light jacket, and tossed them in a large purse. I'd need to dress the part while I infiltrated, but I wanted out of Corinne as soon as possible.

My Polaroid camera didn't have a zoom. What I got was what I got, and not necessarily what I needed. I watched where my shadow was cast most strongly. Hopefully I'd get a good impression of Corinne's. I waited again.

I pulled out the snapshot and gave it a shake, waiting impatiently for it to develop. I grimaced when I saw it hadn't turned out. No Flicker. I took another picture. Still nothing. Tried again. As the blob turned into a recognizable image, I saw her shadow caught against the refrigerator.

I murmured, "Gotcha."

Finally. It was difficult to find film for the beast, but digital wouldn't work and traditional film had a less than a fifty-fifty chance I'd capture what I needed.

I called the trapped shadow from the image and let it coalesce around me. It had an oily, obsequious feel, like the soul of the woman it belonged to. A yes-woman. I wondered how many horrible things she'd done because she *believed* she was righteous.

My reflection in her vanity mirror showed me the woman's shape. A bit shorter. A bit softer. I blew a lock of blonde hair away from my face. I knew it was a phantom image. I still hated the clothes seeing them on Corinne's body, but at least they looked like they belonged. It was done. I had her shape. Her car. And once I locked her up, she'd be out of the way. It was time to head in.

Wearing someone else's shadow was a dangerous trick. I didn't like it. While I was dressed in Corinne, I wouldn't have a shadow, either. It would be trapped in the Polaroid photograph until I either destroyed the picture to release it, or someone else noticed I was wearing a shadow, not casting one. And the jig would be up. My infiltration was risky and could lead to me being spotted, but I had a purse full of options to escape.

An ounce of prevention . . . I wanted to check the place out, make sure there was no danger to Lyssa and her family. Going in as a cultist would give me a chance to sniff around and hopefully keep Lyssa from getting tangled in with the Redeemers.

I grabbed her car keys and headed away. I'd have to come back for my Bel Air. In any case, it was time to leave the land of minivans and soccer moms, and get to the *real* work.

Chapter Eleven

The building housing Winnipeg's Church of the Risen Redeemer has been many things in its tenure. I vaguely recalled my parents talking about driving in from MacGregor to pick up their Christmas shopping when it'd been a Consumers Distributing.

The Church was a breeding ground for the worst sorts of people and a recruitment site for bad necromancers worldwide. Good, bad. It doesn't always seem like there's much difference between the two. Some of us want to keep the dead resting, and others are into resource extraction. Dig, baby, dig.

Grannie's advice had kept me from trying my damnedest to blast the creeps from my city and leave a smoking crater in their parking lot. She'd told me to axe the ringleaders and wait and see who came to fill their cloaks. At least the Redeemers were an evil I knew, and who they associated with provided useful tidbits of information. They were a necromantic lightning rod.

Usually their followers were misguided idiots, but sometimes a gifted and dark son of a bitch took the reins. Under previous management, the Redeemers had been responsible for missing children and homeless people—all used in their rituals and masses—and had damn near trapped Woj and I in the Kingdom. The Redeemers made Woj nervous. I couldn't blame him. A past figurehead had tried to turn him into a meat puppet and use his funeral home as their own personal murder evidence erasure factory. Not something easy to forget. The Redeemers were still awfully close to his chapel, and cults were always eager to expand their territory.

I half expected Summer to say, *"No different than what you use him for,"* but my dead sister was silent on the matter.

I went inside.

The front of the church hadn't been renovated much since it had been a store. There was still a counter, waist-high, with postal boxes behind it. No numbers on the boxes, though. There were old, worn stacking chairs lining the window side opposite the desk. The last time I'd been here, the way to the public chapel was through a door to the left. The "private" chapel was below the street level. That could've changed. After my last visit they'd needed to redecorate.

I waited, demure in my calf-length skirt and my blouse cinched one button higher than I would have liked. Lots of people were milling around for a day they weren't holding a service.

It didn't take long at all for a helpful cultist to swoop in to save me from having to ask a question. Cults hate questions, but love giving answers. He was big enough to be a threat—given the way he carried himself, I doubted he was. Sandy blond hair and small, bright eyes. This guy struck me as a follower, through and through.

With an oozing smile, and a none-to-surreptitious look up and down my body, he said, "Not used to seeing you around during the day. Is there anything I can help you with, Corinne . . ."

He trailed off, no doubt hoping I'd volunteer my phone number, and my PIN numbers, and my soul.

I decided to disappoint him by offering a wan smile.

"Yes, I need to speak with Pastor Mark."

His eyes flickered. Wariness, perhaps. It looked like I'd have to volunteer something to my knight in creepy armour after all.

"I have a funeral to arrange."

False sympathy bubbled onto his face. "I'm sorry for your loss. Have a seat, please. Let Andy handle everything."

I smiled away my shudder as he mentioned himself in the third person. Andy went behind the counter, flipping pages on what I assumed to be a register.

"We want the service taken care of as soon as possible."

Another obsequious smile. The way he threw them around, he must think it worked like Lemon Gin. "Of course." He rummaged around the desk. "Oh, are you coming to Sunday night's mass?"

Interesting. There had to be something going down. Astronomically and supernaturally speaking, the date was insignificant. Near the anniversary of my kidnapping, but a couple days early, so I doubted it was tied to me personally. I needed to be there. I just had to get an invite. I faked a pout. "Pastor Mark didn't extend me an invite."

My disappointment brightened his face. Of course it did. Now he had a chance to be a white knight.

"I could ask for you." His offer was filled with quid-pro-quo promise.

I pretended to be oblivious and made myself as fawning as possible. "I wouldn't want to get you in trouble."

"Oh, no trouble at all," he said to Corinne's chest. "The more the merrier."

"Thank you."

"I'll let you into Pastor Mark's office," he said. "I'll go and try to find him. He's definitely in."

Yeah, "in." In the basement, eating babies.

He patted my hand. "He'll let you join in."

His palm felt warm and sweaty. Fevered. If I wasn't in disguise, I'd have used my Grave Sight to check him. Regardless, I wanted a bath in hand sanitizer.

Andy gestured past a door reading NO ADMITTANCE and down a hallway, and obviously wanted me to go first. No doubt so he could check out the view from behind.

"Here," Andy said.

I smiled and took out my phone as he closed the door, so I could pretend to play some stupid game when Pastor Mark came around. In the meantime, I would see what his office told me about him, and his cult.

Pastor Mark's office had an "inviting" cinderblock interior sparsely decorated with cheap bookcases and dime-a-dozen landscape paintings. An old dark-stained desk was the only nod to taste I'd seen yet in the entire place.

The wait stretched long enough; I worried the jig was up, and I'd need to make a run for it. There was no exit from the office other than the door Andy'd closed behind me. I eased it open a crack to give a warning before Pastor Mark showed his face.

There didn't seem to be any grimoires on the shelves. Instead they were filled with magazine holders bursting with copies of the church newsletter, books on grieving and relationship counselling I wouldn't read even if I could pan mystical gold from the bullshit river. A book on artifacts from Tutankhamen's tomb perked my interest, but it was only a trade book—glossy photos with nothing about Egypt's Graveside. Same deal with a book of Roman death masks. Popular history, not *real* history. I stopped my browsing when I heard footsteps and voices coming from the hallway.

"I heard Corinne is in the hospital," one voice said. "Someone robbed her or something."

Shit. How'd she wake up already?

A second voice answered, "I thought I saw her here."

"Report could be a mistake."

"Yeah, probably."

A chortled laugh. "Corinne *never* does anything interesting."

Their talk was a momentary comfort, but also meant I didn't have much time. If I bailed now, I might not get another shot to meet Pastor Mark.

There was one other book of note in the office. The lone item marring the desk's polished surface. The Redeemer Bible. Gold letters embossed the book's fake black leather cover, reading: Bible. Nothing Holy in this book. Below the title, also in gold, a glyph like the symbol for infinity, only turned on its head, and broken so that lines stretched out along a horizontal axis instead of completing the figure eight.

I looked over my shoulder at the ajar door.

I've leafed through the Redeemer Bible a time or two before, after busting one cult or another. They claim it's a "new translation" but whoever'd founded the Church must not have been good at Latin, Greek, or Hebrew, because the book's been translated as far away from Christianity as possible.

The words have been twisted, spun into darkness. It seems innocent enough at first. The changes small. It's still familiar. If you've the right inclinations, as you read deeper, it gets darker, and stranger. Just like going swimming in a cold lake, or settling into a hot bath, inching in keeps you from the shock that'll make you bail on the entire enterprise. Some copies change with every reading. The more devout you start, the more quickly you'll be bound to the Redeemers' brand of darkness.

It's no one deed that makes you a death cultist. Camping trips, hunting trips. Just don't ask what's on the grill. Being in a cult is looking up and not being able to remember seeing the sun and wondering how you've ever lived without a bound and screaming virgin on your altar.

Baby steps into Hell.

Several pages were flagged with a rainbow of Post-it notes. I wondered which passages Pastor Mark decided deserved special treatment. Might learn something about the man from how he decided to colour code.

I picked up the Bible. A peek wouldn't hurt. I wasn't worried what it would do to me—I've seen and done darker. Baby steps, I said. Nothing Pastor Mark had noted would shock me. And I highly doubted he knew anything dark enough to make a difference in my already muddied conscience.

Behind me, I heard the doorknob turn, and I dropped the Bible back on the desk and flopped back in my seat, holding my phone at the ready.

The man who entered had a smiling, broad, beatific face. One practically beaming innocence and righteousness. This had to be Pastor Mark. I hated him immediately. Pastor Mark was a broad-shouldered man with a face just shy of handsome. He dressed casually, but it gave off the impression he'd attempted to dress as fine as he could. A red and black plaid collared short sleeved shirt and grey slacks. Business casual. *What's your business, Mark?*

He slid past me and sat on his desk. His smile turned sour.

Looking into his eyes, I didn't know him. Eyes are the window to the soul, the saying goes. I had a saying about that too: Bullshit. Eyes are an organ, and that won't change if you've got a demon or half the Kingdom riding shotgun in your brain. Or a dead twin.

What's beyond control, or alteration, at least for long, are the things which are irrevocably you; posture, gait, mannerisms, they'll tell a person who you are, and I knew I'd met this Pastor Mark before. I just couldn't place him.

Since he didn't seem in a hurry to introduce himself, I'd get the lies rolling. I didn't want to discuss Lyssa with this one. He plucked the Bible from the desk and placed it in a drawer. A lock turned. I wondered what else he had in there. I'd have to sneak back in with my skeleton key, and have a look.

"What brings you in, Corinne?"

"There's a mass . . ."

His mouth twitched in annoyance, quickly covered with a plastic benevolence. "Oh yes, well, Andy has been talking too freely."

I lowered my head, faking contrition. "I don't want to get him in trouble."

"No trouble. The evening was meant for the deacons, so we're all on the same page with the direction our little church is heading, but there was nothing expressly forbidding guests." He leaned forward. "Especially, lovely, talented guests."

Ugh. My gag reflex fought to kick in rather strongly. I forced a smile instead.

"I hear you suffered a loss recently," he said.

I blinked.

"You *were* inquiring about dates to have a service held here?"

"Yes. Right. Forgive me. I'm a little distracted. Andy's suggestion sounded . . . like what I needed after all this sadness."

"I wasn't aware you had any kin in Winnipeg."

Shit. The Redeemers would seek out lonely people hunting for meaning. I hadn't dug deep enough into Miss Corinne Mayberry. My surprise must've shown. Too much going on, in both sides of my life, had made me sloppy.

Double shit.

Marcus smiled, a cat toying with a mouse that didn't know it was dead yet. "I like to stay abreast of my congregations, Miss Mayberry."

"A sign of a great leader," I offered.

Another smile. "I am no leader, I merely follow His way. As do we all."

"Of course," I said. "I apologize for misspeaking."

He waved away my apology, every bit the glorious ruler wearing man-of-the-people clothing. "You are forgiven. One does not learn unless one is corrected."

I didn't do contrition well. Hopefully he couldn't tell how much I wanted to kick him in the balls.

"My friend suffered a loss recently," I said. "I'm helping her with the funeral arrangements."

"How generous," Mark said with an inclined head. "My condolences."

"Thank you," I said.

"They must be taking it hard, to have sent someone in their stead."

I decided to answer as little as I could, while still being as truthful as possible. Unlike most of Mark's "flock," the pastor appeared astute. Crafty. I didn't want him to know anything that could lead him back to Lyssa.

"Yes. They are."

He leaned forward. I forced myself steady as he cupped my hands in his. "Is your friend Alyssa Rogers?"

I tried to hide my sudden fear by plastering on a smile. "You're well-informed."

A crocodile's smile crept over Mark's face. "I do care about my flock. I consider Alyssa's family to be *our* family."

"How . . . generous."

"Despite her life choices, I look forward to meeting Alyssa." Mark nodded. "She's been difficult to get a hold of."

I forced myself to ignore the flare of hate, and continued on, as if oblivious. At least I hoped I did. It wasn't time to agitate the guy. He'd happily bury you alive given the chance and a trumped up excuse. Not time yet, at least.

"Grief," I said, "affects us all differently. I try to do something productive. Others shut down, or bury themselves in work."

"God's own truth."

"Won't you be busy?"

"We will have the service Sunday afternoon. The deacons and I will join you for the memorial later in the evening. I will have time to prepare for both."

I didn't like the sound of that.

He stood and walked around the desk, offering a hand to help me from my chair. One might call it chivalrous. I doubted his intent was in any way noble. "Forgive me if I don't see you out. Things to attend to."

Things, indeed.

"Certainly," I said. "I understand."

He knew. I didn't know *what* he knew, but there was no way I could let Lyssa come back here now. I hoped she'd be okay with the fact I didn't pull through on this one and nail her venue of choice.

When I stood without taking his hand, he brushed it through my hair, tucking away a strand fallen over my face. It felt like he was pissing on me.

As I left the pastor's office, my disguise faded; a prickly sensation, gooseflesh peppered my skin, my temples pounded as I fought to keep Corinne's shadow wrapped around me. Had Mark noticed its absence, or had his touch dismissed it? There was no way I could hold it. The release was inevitable. I held my hands over my mouth, as if I were trying to hold down my lunch. It wasn't far from the truth. It had been a long time since I'd had a shadow forcibly dismissed, and it wasn't pleasant.

I burst into a unisex washroom and locked the door behind me. I was vaguely surprised the washroom had a lock. While they liked their privacy to worship as they pleased, one thing cultists were not particularly inclined towards amongst their faithful, was any other notion of real privacy.

Corinne's image sloughed off me like paint running in the rain. I cleaned myself up, best I could, and steadied myself. Winter Murray's face looked odd wearing Corinne Mayberry's clothes. As Frank had said, they didn't suit me. Fortunately, I had my other clothes in my purse. Unfortunately, I doubted I had time to get changed. I looked for a camera, didn't see one, but that didn't mean there wasn't one. Super creepy place like this, I expected one over the toilet.

I was close to the exit. I could do this. I didn't want to get caught with my pants down while I got changed. I slipped my necromancer cloak on, but left the hood down, and threw on a jacket over the cloak hoping it didn't look obvious. At least then if I had to disappear, I had the option.

I sent Frank a quick text, just in case.

There was a knock at the door. "You okay in there?"

I tucked my phone back in my purse. No time to change. I quietly threw the latch, and jerked the door open. Andy had been pounding on it, and he tumbled inside.

"Thank God," I said. "She's in the stall. I . . . I don't know what she did."

He picked himself up and ran to the stall while I hauled ass out of there. I could see daylight. I was almost free. I doubted Andy had a good enough look to see I was a stranger dressed in Corinne's clothing.

I collided with something hard as rock. A man. Someone I'd not expected to meet again. Someone surprisingly mobile. Surprisingly alive. Or rather, surprisingly undead.

Karl Daher.

Goddamn it.

Chapter Twelve

Y ou. It's *you*."

"Bye, Karl."

His face twisted when I said his name. Karl Daher. My John Doe Trojan horse. I'd seen Christophe rip out his throat and dump him in an open grave. I'd seen him buried twice, and the second time, I'd done the burying myself. And yet, here he was. He wasn't a rotting shambler. There was only one explanation: Karl Daher was a goddamned vampire.

I should've been shitting bricks, but I couldn't show fear. Karl sniffed. His eyes narrowed, trying to mimic Christophe's shark toothed easy menace. He wasn't there yet, but he'd been practising. He was breathing too loud, and he waited too long between blinks, but he'd pass as human. Through the door and a few blocks up Pembina Highway I could make out the lumbering white shape of a Transit bus.

He thrust out his hand as if to grab me. I took and shook it vigorously, smiling all the while. I didn't want a fight. Not here. Not now. Later? Yes. Elsewhere? Hell yes. I treat Christophe with kid gloves, but I could take a baby vampire. In the meantime, I was all about leaving the Redeemer stronghold alive, and revealing myself as a necromancer would be bad for me, and worse for Lyssa.

His hand tightened over my wrist. Karl raised an arm to my throat. He was dead flesh. I could shut him down. Make his body remember what it was: a corpse. I met his eyes as his flesh touched mine, kicked in my Grave Sight. Spider webs of blood pumping through him told me he'd fed. Recently. I also saw the ichor of McCoy's vat-men. Karl must've been Corinne's muscle when she'd visited. If I stared long enough, I'd see his skin rot off him, leaving only bones and hunger. And vermin. Karl didn't have as many rats and bugs in him as his sire. He was young yet.

Vampires were mighty opponents, but Karl's will was nothing like Christophe's and his attempts at malevolence meant nothing when I'd seen him pissing and shitting. I made his body remember me. Set his dead heart a flutter with the terror he'd felt when I'd woken him in his coffin. Fortunately, he had nothing in his bowels to empty, this time. His hand released my wrist. I put him into torpor. Didn't even have to put my lips on the filthy bugger this time.

As Karl stood stock still, I gathered my skirt to run. This would be the last time I wore one, even if cultists fear women in pants more than magic or Satan. I stopped short. Karl's hand clutched my purse strap. And in the purse, Corinne's car keys.

Voices sounded from behind a door. One belonged to Pastor Mark. There was no time to root through the bag for the keys. I left both behind and took off.

I hoped I hadn't tipped my hand, running off, but something gave me the distinct impression that if Karl kept me from getting through those doors, something bad would've happened.

I glanced over my shoulder. Without me touching Karl to maintain my domination, his paralysis would be undone. He was mobile. But he *wasn't* chasing me.

Karl didn't follow me into the sun. If he didn't know the truth of vampires and daylight yet, I wasn't about to share.

Stories say the sun and vampires are anathema. If you listened to those stories, they'd also tell you if Karl had followed me, he'd have turned into a shrieking bonfire. Wrong. Vampires can walk in the sun, but daylight bleeds away their powers—the root of "the sun means death for vampires" bit. If one was recognized away from the old velvet-lined homestead, they'd be goners.

I hauled ass across the parking lot and hopped on the bus, pawing for coins, glad to be out of there. My heart pounded from the run, and the near-disaster at the Church.

"Winter?"

The voice had come from the driver. *Shit.* Tammy's bus.

I never paid attention to her routes, because I rarely paid attention to her unless I had to. I hadn't realized I was still staring, surprised. The door closed behind me and the bus lurched forward and sped towards its next stop.

"Surprised you're bussing," Tammy said.

"Me, too." I hadn't checked the number on the bus. "Where's this bus headed?"

"U of M. Your car die?"

"Something like that," I said, standing awkwardly by the driver's seat.

A grunt. Either non-surprise or, less likely, sympathy.

"How'd it go?"

"What?"

She gestured back toward the Church with her chin. "Booking the chapel. Lyssa said you'd do it."

"Oh. Yeah. That."

Tammy stopped the bus suddenly, knocking me off balance. A few backpack-laden students filed on, shoving past me to get to the open seats near the back of the bus.

"Is the chapel a go?"

"It's not great," I said.

"Did you f—" A breath, catching and swallowing the profanity. She usually didn't bother when she talked to me. Good thing she was on the clock, and not able to chew me out as usual. "Did you even go in?"

"Yes, I went in. The pastor is super pushy, and sketchy as hell."

Her brow furrowed. "Sketchy, how?"

Tammy would've known the pressure Pastor Mark had been putting on Lyssa, I hoped she'd be more willing to buy my story if I slid some truth into it. I couldn't tell her the Redeemers had a vampiric deacon or that Pastor Mark fronted a cult.

"Just a feeling. Lyssa won't be comfortable there. You neither."

Tammy gave a knowing grunt. I didn't need to elaborate—our opinions on organized religion were one of the few points where her and I didn't argue. "It's what her mom wanted."

I couldn't be blunt with Lyssa. I didn't care with Tammy. Any empathy she had for Lyssa's mom was tied up in Lyssa. She'd never met the woman. She could help me steer Lyssa clear of the Redeemers.

"Her mom won't care where we have the damned service. She's *dead*."

The passengers were staring. Bit harsher than I'd intended. I hadn't been expecting this conversation. And I didn't want it. Seeing Karl had set me on edge.

"Jesus, Winter," Tammy said, scowling. "That's cold. Even for you."

She had no idea how cold I could be. I decided not to give her the full exposure.

I sighed. "I'll sort it out with Lyssa."

My desire to get off Tammy's bus, cross the street and get on a Northbound route that would take me back to my car was tempered by the fact I couldn't remember what route would do the trick. To say nothing about how waiting in the open until another bus showed might let the Redeemers catch up to me. I headed to the back of the bus, getting balance practice as Tammy slowed for another stop. It took a serious glare for a kid to lift his backpack and skateboard off the seat next to him, a look I usually saved for guys like Karl—people I'm either about to dig out of a grave, or put back in one.

The kid shifted with a perturbed grunt. I took my seat. Every inch was a border skirmish trying to keep the prick from banging his legs into me. I was so surprised to see Tammy I hadn't asked for a transfer. I wasn't used to riding the bus. Tammy might still give me one if I asked, but then I'd have to ask. And Karl's vampiric turn needed to be dealt with. Soon.

I debated calling Woj to pick me up and drive me home. He'd do it. I wasn't far from his place, but I figured I'd save my demands for a more important favour. From the University of Manitoba I'd be able to bus almost anywhere in the city. It'd been a couple years since I'd been on campus for a Zombie Walk gone wrong, but I figured it hadn't changed much.

After the clown with the backpack left the bus, I sprawled over both seats and stewed, wondering what my next move should be as two teens seated across from me argued the relative merits of the werewolves in the *Underworld* and *Van Helsing* movies and who would *really* win in a vampire-werewolf fight. They didn't want to meet either. Not that any self-respecting monster would turn this lot into spawn.

Spawn. I'd never thought I'd see the day Christophe made one. And he'd thrown in with the CRR. I'd expected *that* even less. If Christophe *had* made Karl, why in the hell had he shown up at the gallery with the ignorant and indignant act? Regardless, our three-way Cold War with McCoy was heating up.

I debated making an offer to McCoy I knew he wouldn't refuse. Of course, it would be all the harder to get rid of McCoy when he thought I was on his side. Because it would be harder for me to act openly against him. Once McCoy grabbed his share of Christophe's pie it might become impossible for me to get rid of him. Insinuating the time was ripe for such an alliance would be problematic. It was still a possibility.

There had to be plausible reasons "why" Christophe had spawned, but I was still uncertain on the "how." How had Christophe pulled off the making right under my nose? Had he gone back for Karl and dug him up after I'd buried him? More importantly: *why* do it? Didn't seem like Christophe. And it had been pretty obvious there'd been no life left in Karl—and I'd double-checked before I'd closed his coffin.

Normally, I tried not to second guess myself; if you did it too often after a fight, you'd start doing it during. More wisdom from Grannie. I couldn't shake the belief I should've killed Karl right then and there while he was limited by daylight. That would've resulted in a definite worst-case scenario: the Redeemers might suspect the truth, regardless of whose shadow I'd worn at the time, but there was no need to confirm it.

I came back to Christophe spawning. Why the hell would he have made Karl a vampire? He hated sharing. Hated death cults. But more than anything, he despised necromancers. Christophe had never revealed the source of those feelings to me. I doubted it was a surprising story. I had no illusion that for all his faux charm, and play at nicety, I was an exception. Just as I doubted Christophe had been made immortal for his looks.

There was nothing new in Christophe trying to keep me out of his 'yard; he'd been doing his damnedest since I'd moved up, and he'd moved in. His threats and visits into my mundane life were getting awkward.

What I did in Christophe's boneyard had no impact on him. Which made it more unlikely he'd have wanted a baby vampire following him around. I'd have to find where Karl rested. I doubted he hung his hat in Christophe's 'yard. Even if Christophe had done a personality one-eighty and spawned, Karl could be bloody anywhere.

Maybe Christophe had made a helper because he'd wanted to double his chances at getting his fangs in my blood.

What Christophe wanted as tribute was something I could never give him. In the supernatural world—as in the mundane—blood is life. I've known necromancers who were paranoid to the point of burning down a building where they'd slipped and cut themselves. Not during a ritual, but preparing dinner.

Overreaction? Depends on the point of view. That same necromancer had spent twenty years as the slave to his own creations for a similar slip. Ignorance is bliss.

I still shuddered at what he'd been forced to do. I knew because Marcus O'Reilly had been the first necromancer I'd ever met, and he'd told me. In exquisite and unrelenting detail. When Grannie had found us he'd had every intention of revisiting every horror he'd experienced upon an innocent.

I was thirteen. Marcus had been looking for his own apprentice. That's why he'd taken me. To help him push Grannie Annie out of Winnipeg. To gain power from Those Who Dwell Beyond the Threshold. Despite his tough talk, he never touched me. These days the Beyonders were happy to receive *any* supplication.

The bus stopped at the U of M, and I exited from the rear doors, so I wouldn't have to walk past Tammy.

I had dug up Karl on Tuesday. It had been a simple matter to corral him after the last service. A church holding service twice a week? Clearly in league with evil.

The Redeemers wouldn't have another mass, service, or bingo night—whatever they called what they did—until Sunday. I had time to kill. I shook my head. The only funeral they'd be hosting would be their own.

Knowing the Redeemers had a vampire in their court, and Christophe was Karl's maker, they had me outgunned. McCoy's "exclusive alliance" offer was looking mighty fine. Still, I knew wasn't seeing everything. I needed something more. I needed someone who'd lasted longer against tougher contenders.

I needed Grannie Annie. Pity she was dead. She'd killed every challenger. Until she'd met cancer—the one she couldn't beat.

Her being dead wasn't going to stop me from getting my answers. I doubted she'd stopped paying attention to "her" town in her afterlife. She might've caught something I'd missed. I also doubted death had softened her. Apprentice or not, enforcer or not, she might take me replacing her personally.

Chapter Thirteen

It was around thirty klicks and thirty minutes to get from my house to St. Andrew's Anglican Church—St. Andrew's-on-the-Red, it was often called here—situated past the Perimeter Highway, and near the Red River. This time of night, and the way I drive, I figured I'd shave off a few minutes.

Normally, I enjoyed driving at night. Especially when I could get out in the country where you could still see the stars, and where my Grave Sight wasn't always blazing. There was death out here, too, make no mistake, it just wasn't as concentrated.

Tonight, I was anxious. It'd felt like an eternity waiting for night to fall so I could make my jaunt. Frank hadn't been at my apartment—or his—and hadn't answered my texts. Unlike him. Especially with how worried he'd been about McCoy and Christophe. I'd have to investigate when I got home.

I couldn't shake thoughts of Frank entirely. I had to laugh at the reversal of the norm. Now the big lug had *me* worried. Worried he'd tried something stupid. He knew enough of my enemies and might try something on his own. He *was* overprotective. He had a temper—and a hate—where anything Graveside was concerned, one he could barely keep a lid on.

Maybe Inge had asked for a date.

That made my concern about Frank's depressive state worse,

given how her earlier flirtations had affected him. Combined with his nature, it might lead Frank to try and go out in a blaze of glory. That *would* be stupid, and if the asshole did it and lived, I'd kill him myself.

It had been a long time since I'd talked to my old mentor, and longer since I'd wanted to. I hated the necessity. I doubted Grannie would like it, either. She'd rub my face in the fact I needed her. This visit would cost me—not only pride but time and materials I could ill-afford to spare when I was beset on all sides. But I saw no alternative other than to keep stumbling around blind.

If all went well, Grannie could tell me a few things. One: Where was Frank? Two: If Christophe hadn't made Karl, who the hell had? Three: What were the Redeemers up to? Finally, who was Mr. Moustache?

The phrase "salt of the earth" gets thrown around a lot. Grannie was more "salt the earth so nothing will grow." When she'd rescued me a dozen years ago, she'd made an example of Marcus that would've done the Inquisition proud. He'd begged for death before she was done with him, and she kept him begging long after.

I'd wanted to watch. Wanted to see him punished. And Grannie had made me see every bit. I watched as all he was came apart, body and soul. When I'd tried to look away, before the end, I'd found I couldn't. I had asked for his punishment, and while I hadn't known what it would entail, Grannie made me see it through. She made me help. We'd revisited everything Marcus had done to others back on him. She showed me everything had unforeseen consequences, for him, for me. Shown me what I was capable of doing. It was the first lesson she ever taught me.

Who knows why the old hag took a shine to me. Or if she did at all. Seeing a terrified thirteen year old girl circled by corpses might've reminded her of her own mortality. Whatever her reasons, she saw the same potential in me my kidnapper had. She saw death living within me. She saw Summer.

I'd believed Grannie was going to kill me, too, after she'd finished Marcus. I'd witnessed so much. Cops still worried me then. Instead, she took me home. Word spread that I was weird—damaged. The kids at school tried making my life hell, but I hadn't given a shit what they'd thought of me. I'd seen hell. I'd been to the gates of the Kingdom and peered in.

Summer talked to me a lot more after that. Whispering advice, encouraging bad deeds. I'd acted out, both at home and at school. Drugs. Booze. Fights. You name it. Nearly expelled more than once. They'd gone easy on me after my abduction. I knew it. And I used their goodness to my advantage. Maybe *that* had been Grannie's real first lesson.

No one had believed an old woman had saved me. Not my rapidly dwindling circle of friends. Not my parents. Not the cops. Not my shrink. They'd all figured I was in shock and inventing stories to explain my survival. A woman had *found* me, they'd suggested instead, as I wandered the train tracks, barefoot and numb, shrouding myself in the dead necromancer's cloak—mine now.

My parents hadn't believed. But they had hope. Hope they could have their little girl back. Their hope had lasted three months until one night, before my fourteenth birthday, Grannie Annie stepped into my room out of a shadow.

"You're real," I'd said, my voice already barely a whisper, and muffled further by the blanket shrouding my lips.

She barked a laugh. "Of course I'm real."

Between flashes of my abductor and what had happened to him and fear for what might yet happen to me, I asked, "It all happened, didn't it?"

She nodded. "All of it."

I remembered the hope that'd sprung in me then, a mad hope. My parents' hope may have returned to them, but it had been absent in me. Not until that moment when my saviour told me magic was real. I'd needed some magic then.

"I'm not crazy?"

With a crooked smile, she'd said, "No more than you ever were."

When she held out her hand, I took it. We stepped into the shadows and I've never looked back.

At least that's what I tell myself. I still half-dialled my parents' number; so long as I never completed the call, they'd be safe. And I'd be safe from them learning what their daughter had become. I still drive past old favourites from when we'd come to the city as a family. When I'd had a family.

Winnipeg is a small city, only seven hundred thousand people, a place where you run into somebody you used to sleep with every time you leave your apartment. After Grannie took me in, I never saw my parents again. I wondered how long they'd looked for me. If they still looked. Was it selfish to cut them out my life? Maybe. And it's not like Grannie had given me much choice. Their little girl did die, all those years ago. Whoever Winter Murray had been, she certainly wouldn't have been rolling to a stop at a gateway to the land of the dead.

St. Andrew's-on-the-Red is an old church, surrounded by a low, mortared stone wall. Grave markers crowded close against the church, as if the restless dead were looking for absolution. Coming upon it, you'd be forgiven for thinking you'd stumbled into a British parish from an Agatha Christie novel. It had a simple structure; stone walls, small pointed windows, and a steep roof, all of which seemed incongruous with the power lines and aluminum chimney that had been tacked on. From beyond the gates, the church's entrance waited in a three-storey rectangular stone bell tower topped by a wooden steeple, its faded paint glowing in the moonlight.

It's the oldest church in Western Canada still offering services, and among the most haunted. There's a good reason for the stories. They're so common, school children tell them. Run around St. Andrew's at midnight—the number of times varies from teller to teller, three being most common. When you stop running, you disappear. Where you go, no one knows, as the phenomenon has only been witnessed or experienced by someone's third cousin's sister-in-law's aunt. Occasionally, someone with an unknown connection to the dead will give the story a try.

I don't laugh at the stories because I know they're true. It was my first ritual jaunt into the Kingdom, when Grannie had helped me inherit the necromantic power Summer's presence promised.

Run widdershins—counterclockwise—around the church, there'd be a red flash and I'd be gone, standing in the sepia-toned land of the dead. The Kingdom.

The dashboard lights were bright enough for me to check the time on my watch. Eleven-thirty. Plenty of time. I killed the engine and got out of my car. I hated that I couldn't bring my obsidian knife with me. It was concentrated death, and would attract the wrong attention. Couldn't bring anything with me, an unfortunate, but important part of crossing over. Any item, clothing, weapon, jewellery crafted in the living world was a beacon to forces one didn't want to attract.

I wasn't wearing any jewellery; I rarely did, unless it was necrotech. My breath misted in the air as I set my Dead Man's Clothes on my car's hood. I'd sure as hell better do this quick. The days may've been warm and sunny for October, but the nights were clear and cold. It was already below zero by the way the grass crunched under my feet, promising a hard frost.

I stripped, shivering as I folded my clothes quickly and tucked them into a plastic bag. The wind slapped my body, peppering my skin with goose-flesh. When one enters the Kingdom it's best not to wear your own clothes. Doesn't matter if you've just showered and laundered your outfit, you'll still reek of life and draw interested and malicious dead towards you.

There are ways around their attention besides Dead Man's Clothes. Sprinkling yourself in grave dirt or cremation ash works for a while, too. The messy method is best taken with a secondary dose of Dead Man's Clothes.

McCoy chose to wear Dead Man's Clothes. For him it was an affectation, an ostentatious display of wealth. Dead Man's Clothes were my only option tonight. Unless I wanted to cross over into the Kingdom and run around starkers. Having Summer rolling around in my head made it a little easier on me, but I still couldn't wear my own wardrobe.

One: they won't survive the trip. The Kingdom is an almost palpable entropic wind and it'll shred and erode things not touched by death faster. Two: there was no guarantee I'd be the only living person there. That moustached guy was unaccounted for, and cute smile and nice ass aside, I'd rather he not see any more than I chose to offer him. At least until I could be certain of his character. It had been a long time since I'd had a date, but I wasn't ready to give the whole show away for free. Three: I couldn't afford to replace my clothes every time I crossed over.

The longer the Dead Man's Clothes have been in the ground, the longer they'll last and the less attention you'll attract in the Kingdom. Both good things. I've learned to stomach a lot of disgusting things. It was always a balancing act between longevity and smell. I can handle powerful odours; laundering would destroy the clothes' unnatural properties. Digging up corpses and stealing their clothes was one more awful item on the list of what I tend to call Tuesday.

More advice from my mother I'd brought from one life to the next—dress in layers. I'd be burning the clothes candle at both ends, my sweat eroding the inner layer's efficacy and the Kingdom shredding the outer. I had the pile of clothes, each item individually sealed in Ziplocs and vacuum-sealed to maintain lack of freshness.

I sprinkled Woj-supplied crematory ash over my head and rubbed it into my skin. Summer stirred as my hand broached the urn. Woj hadn't told me who I was wearing, and it was better not to know. Whoever they'd been, they'd form a barrier protecting my first layer of clothes from getting tainted by life sweat too early.

This time around, I'd opted to add a wife-beater and boxers for extra defence.

"Stop it," Summer whined.

I ignored my sister, and covered my underclothes with snug pants and an over shirt. Baggy suit pants and dress shirt over top. Suit jacket. Formal dress coat. The overall effect made me look wide and shapeless, but I hadn't chosen the clothes to go clubbing. Summer became more agitated with each item I put on. Dearly departed sister hated going to the Kingdom. I don't know why. It should have been her home.

"I don't want to go," she said. *"Don't make me go back."*

"Tough."

"You'll leave me there."

She hated being in my head as much as I hated having her along for the ride. Ditching Summer in the Kingdom was a possibility I'd investigate *if she didn't shut the hell up.*

I wasn't sure if it was because she worried she'd get trapped there forever, or that I'd find a way to leave her. Whenever I prepared to cross over, she reacted like a child being told their dog was going to live on the farm.

There was a bush behind the diocese sign. I stashed my clothes there, keeping an eye out for thrill seekers and vandals. It was a couple weeks until Halloween, and the church's reputation attracted its share of hooligans and shit disturbers. There had been one night when over one hundred headstones had been defiled by punk kids trying to have a good time. The law may not have caught them, but Grannie had. Let's say they'll never do it again and leave it there.

I gave three quick exhales and ran. I rounded the church once. Its motion light bathed the entrance in a soft glow. I kept my pace deliberate. Steady. I didn't want to sweat. That would cut the benefits of my Clothes too soon.

The light was still on when I finished my second lap. Tires crunched to a halt while I was behind the church. Cops? Or someone else? Someone was going to get an eyeful. I'd become an urban legend.

I stopped at the church entrance. The harshness of silver moonlight and halogen glow against black night fuzzed and took on a grainy old-time photograph quality. Red light blinded me.

My world disappeared.

Chapter Fourteen

As my eyes refocused, I stood on the same spot, and a world away. In the Kingdom, St. Andrew's church looked decidedly different. It had gone to ruin. Paint peeled from its steeple, the windows were shattered and gone; bricks had fallen away from the walls, leaving gaping holes. The mortared stone wall surrounding the church was rubble. Only the grave markers were untouched by the entropic effect.

Whoever'd pulled up as I'd left didn't seem to be following me to the Kingdom, but a handful of local burials roamed. The long-interred were clad in the skins of their birth, burial shrouds rotted away. More recent trips Graveside wore suits or church dresses. For now, at least. In death, every soul eventually stood naked for its judgment.

There was no sun, no moon in the Kingdom, and yet there was light enough to see, mostly by the glow of lost lives. Wind whipped past me, but there was no sensation of a breeze touching my skin. It wasn't cold here. It wasn't warm, either. It just . . . was.

This gate wasn't the most convenient place for me to cross over into the Kingdom, but it was one of the safest. And since it was outside of Winnipeg, and therefore outside my purview, by Compact custom I couldn't ward it against other users. Considering the next closest unguarded portal to this realm was thousands of klicks away, I couldn't complain. St. Andrew's was unguarded because only a chimaera with a dead twin rattling around inside them could access the Kingdom from its portal.

My car stood out against the decrepitude the entropic forces of the Kingdom laid over the world. The Bel Air had carried enough corpses, run down enough zombies, hosted enough revenants, it'd become an extension of my power here. If I wanted to, I could drive its shade back into the city and save myself the effort.

The Kingdom still worked its decay on the Bel Air. If I stayed too long, my car's windows would shatter, and brown paint would go to rust (more so), and the rubber would rot off its rims until it died in the real world, too. If that happened, with my luck, its shade would still run the roads, smashing into whatever I ended up driving next.

Yes, ghost cars are a thing.

I patted the hood as I walked past it. The car would draw more attention to me than I wanted.

I was thirteen again in the distorted reflection from the car window. A reminder of my first trip into the Kingdom. Skin seared and smoked away in the touchless wind, as if I were paper—tinder for a campfire. Teeth rotted and fell out, black hair turned lank and grey. I saw Summer there, a second reflection, one untouched by the Kingdom, lurking behind my distorted face. I shook my head and put my will into that image. I wasn't thirteen anymore, and this wasn't my first time in the Kingdom. When I looked again, my reflection was as it should be, matching Summer's closely, if not exactly.

Before her death, Grannie and I had been on good terms. How our relationship might have changed since then, her being dead and me being a necromancer, I couldn't say. I'd avoided her, if not the Kingdom, after her death. Need aside, I wasn't in a rush to see her again. I ran through all the ways asking her for help could backfire. She could try and possess me. She could rat me out to a Hunter and I'd get dragged off as a gift to Those Who Dwell Beyond. Shit, she might've been taken Beyond. Nobody came back from that. What nagged at me the most, was the lingering belief she'd be *disappointed* in me for needing the help.

I hadn't precisely followed her funerary instructions. I wasn't naïve enough to hope she hadn't noticed, or that she wouldn't hold a grudge. Grannie was *all* about the grudges.

I couldn't see any better way. She'd always been straight with me, whether she was threatening to kill me, or burying me alive. With all the snakes circling me, I could use some straight talk, even if it came at the end of a sharp blade and a wicked curse.

Whether I walked or ran here, my body would feel the same exhaustion when I came out. Only the distance travelled mattered, not the speed or effort one expended. The car would've saved me from that problem, while creating worse ones. And since effort didn't help, it was important to stay relaxed. I could sweat here, which brought on greater threats than exhaustion. I walked.

When you walked in the Kingdom, you stepped between the seconds and minutes. Eternity had a way of playing with one's perception. I could cross the ocean to Rome tonight if I'd wanted and be back by morning. The downside was any energy expended here would be visited on my body when I returned to my world. While I could go anywhere, I wanted to have enough stamina left to dress myself when I returned. My round trip to the city centre would be tiring enough.

Many people had died in Winnipeg since the city's founding, and a bunch were ambling tonight, talking to themselves, mostly. I tried not to listen. If I showed too much interest, they'd take me for a newlydead and fun to fuck with. Worse: they'd realize I was alive. *More* fun to fuck with. If that happened, I'd never make it home. I could control the dead, yes. But throwing my powers around would only draw them faster. If it came to a fight, I didn't doubt I'd make a good accounting of myself, but in the Kingdom, it was a numbers game, and the numbers did not favour me.

Odds aside, necromancers are the only living folks with a chance of coming back from the Kingdom. We've surrounded ourselves with the dead, and as an added bonus, I have the whole dead-twin-chimaera gift going for me. Walking around with that tiny bit of dead tissue helps to blend.

A living person with no such connection to the Kingdom, who adopted the right forms, and arrived naked would still be quickly sniffed out. Accidental arrivals died faster. All it took was them asking the first spirit they saw, "Where in the hell am I?" Sending unsuspecting mundanes into the Kingdom and betting on their survival time was a popular necromancer sport.

Looking toward the city from St. Andrew's, its usual dull orange glowed red to my Grave Sight, and the light dripped up into the overcast sky. Home sweet home—Murder City, Manitoba. I've seen the blood shadow cast by Paris and London—old cities with death down to their bones. The pallor hanging over them, and more ancient cities, was one of the only reasons I was glad to live in North America. At times, I still wanted to go west and set up in a younger city. Except I'd met the folks running Calgary and Vancouver's Graveside, and I hated those guys.

Running was futile anyway. I knew that. It was all relative. Nothing and nobody could avoid death for long and any growing city was only playing catch up. For all the layers of death in a city, you tended to see only the newest, or splashiest, deaths. A new death stood out from the gloaming to a necromancer like a four-alarm fire, but didn't last long. One hundred thirty years gone and the Ripper's work still blazed in Whitechapel.

If I wanted, I could dig deeper for an older death, a forgotten death. I've never gone beyond a dozen years. It was dangerous talking to spirits older than you. Grannie Annie claimed to have dug out deaths going back to the first European settlers, but that was her. Tougher than boot leather, mean enough I was surprised death had wanted her.

Souls will drift off on their own. Necromancers can pull them back if they're still in the Kingdom. Often it was easier to find the spirit you wanted than to drag them from the Kingdom. Especially if you were dealing with an obstinate, old, and worse, powerful, spirit. Grannie Annie was all three and more.

She'd taught me all I knew about bonedancing and the world of the dead, and the worlds Beyond, but I was certain she'd held back more than a few secrets. I had a feeling, should I ever summon her, she might not leave.

The gathered spirits knelt back into their graves or wandered off into the fields. A dedicated few hung around, watching me.

The spirits walking the Kingdom weren't ghosts. More like shadows. Ghosts were stuck in the world of the living, too tied to their lost lives to make the jump to the Kingdom. Shades lingered here for a time after death, the more impact a life had cast on the world, the stronger its shadow. Most disappeared after their bodies rotted away. With the preservatives being used by the funeral industry, the Kingdom was getting crowded.

Many spirits were snatched before their time by Those Who Dwell Beyond. Humans had given them many names. Gods. Demons. Devils. Monsters. Old gods who'd lost not only their followers but their names. They took the dead—any dead—and consumed them to keep the Kingdom from working its oblivion on them. If you weren't dead, they were good at making you so. And whether you were slave or pharaoh, mundane or necromancer, it was bad news to cross them.

When I hit the Perimeter Highway, I listened for hoofbeats, or a boat slicing through the rivers. Two warnings our local Hunters were out. The Horseman and the Ferryman, looking to drag the shades that wandered the Kingdom home to their masters and mistresses Beyond. "Horseman" calls up images of Washington Irving and Tim Burton, flaming pumpkins and panicked rides for running water. That wouldn't save you here. Even if you could walk on it. The second your toes touched the surface, the Ferryman would be there. Waiting.

I heard the Horseman's hooves sometimes in the night, when I remembered what Grannie had done to the man who'd kidnapped me. And how she'd made me help her. I rubbed at my brow and a clutch of shamblers stopped. I was sweating. Not good. I took a calming breath, and the shades stepped closer. I acted dead until they moved on. The shades weren't moving on. *C'mon, I'm one more wandering spirit, a wayfaring stranger, hiding from the collectors, and avoiding the crossroads.* They'd believe because I wanted them to. I'd be safe here if I kept my wits about me.

"*They're gonna get you,*" Summer sing-songed.

"Shut up," I snapped.

The shades stared in my direction. They loped forward.

"*Get you and keep you and you'll be dead like* meeeeeeeeee."

The shades stopped, cocking their heads, dogs searching for a strange sound.

"Not going to happen. And if it does, *you'll* be stuck here, too."

The shades wandered closer.

"*I don't want to stay here.*"

The shades stopped.

"You won't," I said. "Because I won't."

The shades' heads snapped up and they bolted toward us.

"Summer, if you don't want to stay here, you should keep talking."

"*Why? You never listen.*"

I could feel her pout. I wanted to reach into my brain and slap my sister silly. "This time I will."

"*Promises, promises.*"

"*Summer.* Please."

Summer's thoughts had to be different than mine. Something about *her* rang out to the Kingdom as dead, just as I still stank of life, despite my preparations. She rambled on about how shitty her sister had been to her in life, and how she'd been forgotten in death, and her parents had acted like she'd never existed, until I was damn near ready to slit my wrists and join her.

"*They've stopped,*" Summer said. "*And you* weren't *listening to me at all. You said you would and you* didn't. *You* lied."

IwillIwillIwill.

I tried to hold the lie in my brain and make it true enough for my sister to believe, but quiet enough the shades wouldn't notice. They hung around, looming, a few steps out of arms' reach. Dead eyes staring. Fingers clenching into fists. Unclenching. After what felt like an eternity, they turned and wandered off.

"*Last time I help you. Liar.*"

Summer's accusing voice grew quiet and distant. I couldn't mouth back at her. It would only draw the shades to me. The longer I dawdled, the faster the Kingdom's entropy would smoke away my suit. Smoke, but no fire. Yet.

The skyline—calling the buildings skyscrapers might be a tad generous—poked out from behind the trees, crowned with a halo of flames. Buildings were forever falling in the Kingdom, collapsing up and down, but until they were gone from the real world, and the citizens' imaginations, they'd remain. Old City Hall, the St. Boniface Cathedral, buildings that *might* have been, and lived on only in the imaginations of an inspired or disturbed few, who mourned what might've been, created the confusing jumbled present, past, and future and never-was that was the Kingdom.

All this river land had been woods or farmland once, no elm-lined boulevards, no war-time homes with their steep-peeked roofs, no stone foundation three-storey mouse traps. Old footpaths still wound through the Kingdom visible through cracked and pothole-riddled asphalt. Dead trees, bare limbs bowing with menace, grew through decrepit houses that were the finest in their neighbourhood back in the living world. Spectral harts followed me; shells of skin stripped of antlers and bones and meat by long dead hunters.

A train rumbled to the south.

I made my way past where street car lines, torn up to make way for buses in the '60s, still cut through the roads, and the Kingdom's wild air carried the sound of distant trolley bells. I knew where I'd find Grannie. Sitting on the front step of her old home, where she'd died, now my home, where I hoped to keep living.

I was almost there. The Red River was behind me. Perfectly still. A pillar rose around a depression. An obelisk. One of many. This one, however, had hieroglyphs inscribed upon it. Among them was the broken infinity symbol of Those Who Dwell Beyond the Threshold, surrounded by wards. No doubt that even dead, Grannie wanted to stay out of their business, and keep them out of hers. I hesitated before stepping over the obelisk's shadow. Grannie had placed these obelisks throughout the Kingdom before I'd come around. I had no idea how she'd done this. They had no corollary back in Sunside Winnipeg. I suspected they were why Grannie had been able to butcher all comers to her territory during the time when the city had been hers. Her mojo was better.

Now I had to hope mine was better than hers. Nothing to do but lock my jaw, dive in, and hope for the best. If Grannie had wanted me dead, she'd had ample opportunity.

I stepped past the obelisk. There was a brief sensation of the wind dying—not stopping—that felt uncannily like I was hopping worlds again. After a momentary shiver, the feeling was gone, and I was plainly still within the Kingdom. I headed deeper in, looking for Grannie.

I found her, as expected, on my apartment's front steps. Her white hair stood out moon-bright against the Kingdom's darkness, and made the craggy, deep furrows in her weathered face seem all the deeper. The clothes she wore had never been in her earthly wardrobe, let alone the outfit in which I'd sent her to the crematorium. Even after her own death, Grannie stole from the dead. She didn't rise. Didn't smile.

"Hello, Apprentice," Grannie Annie said without looking up. "Glad you grew the stones to visit. Here to send me Beyond?"

I ignored her barb, and decided to sweeten the pot by giving her the opening for one of her old favourite jokes. "How's life?"

"Taking forever." Her smile was a phantom, translucent, and I could see through it. She asked, "You dead yet?"

"Been dead my whole life," I said. "And I'm not your apprentice anymore, Grannie."

She raised an eyebrow; her mirthless smile cracked wider. "No?"

"No."

Grannie cackled, and I didn't like it. I knew what usually followed that laugh. A beating at best, being buried alive the worst I'd experienced. Grannie had always said she'd gone soft on me.

"Throwing down will only call Hunters."

She pointed at an obelisk. "Nothing we do here will draw them out."

I didn't want to antagonize her. I needed her. But Grannie also had no truck with weakness, rolling over would guarantee an attack as surely as mouthing off. I had to hope she appreciated strength over deference. I tilted my head to the side, hands on my hips. "Pretty cocky for a dead woman."

She stood and cracked her gnarled knuckles. "If you think you're the master now, let's see what you've learned."

Chapter Fifteen

The cancer that'd killed Grannie ate away her shade's form, until I faced a pulsating, throbbing tumour. Grannie rolled off the apartment steps, howling toward me like a tornado. She threw her entire being at me. I raised my arms to shield my face. My crematory ash washed away in a hateful rain. Her angry wind flayed layers of Dead Man's Clothes from my body as she pushed me toward her obelisk.

Inside the spirit's mass, hard, sharp nails scrabbled over my body, as if Grannie had hundreds of hands. A single scratch would be enough for Grannie's spirit to infect me, to make me what she'd been in her last days, a parasite, filling my victims with the same poison killing me. I was here physically, my form wasn't mutable. Hers was. I had weight. She didn't.

I bit my lip, trying to keep my mouth locked shut, in case Grannie snuck in. My ass clenched tight. Summer cried out in fear.

Grannie must've heard her, too. Her onslaught slowed. Stopped. For once, I was happy for Summer's distraction. I dug in my feet. There was no time to worry about a feint. I pushed back, digging my fingers into her roiling being and started shredding as if I were tearing canvas. She was dead, a shade, and I was a bonedancer. She'd dance to *my* tune.

Grannie had bottled her cancer long enough, before it had been let out to ravage her, that it shaped her even here. I couldn't cure her body back in the real world, and I couldn't cure her spirit here, either. The entire Kingdom was sickness and decay, just like her. There was nowhere to bleed her cancer away into, even if I'd cared to bother.

Instead, I carved her spirit with knife-handed swings. I forced my will on Grannie, opening a gap into the monster she'd become, to reveal the monster she'd always been. The Kingdom's wind tore her tumourous shell the same way it took my Dead Man's Clothes.

She hurled me across the street and into a tree. Its boughs shook, raining leaves, as I bounced off and rolled to a stop on the boulevard. The tree wasn't real, only a reflection, but it was real enough to *hurt*. I didn't have time to hurt. Grannie was back on me in a blink.

Grannie said, "You were good, kid, but you were never me. Never will be."

"I'll take that as a compliment."

"Compliments won't keep Those Who Dwell Beyond at bay."

Shreds of her tumourous self remained behind on the apartment stairs, like boils or sores. Hints of what still lurked within her. She didn't cry out, but from the look on her face, having her shell wracked pained her. If I didn't stop cutting at her spirit, Grannie would smoke away, too, the way she should've when I'd had Woj light her up. All she'd built here in the Kingdom could be mine, too, the way I'd taken what she'd owned in life. Having a space, protected from Hunters, overlaid on my home in the real world . . . with effort I might be able to build a portal directly from my bed to the Kingdom. The only thing I wouldn't get from ending Grannie here: the answers I sought.

Grannie raised her hands in surrender. "I give. I give."

I narrowed my eyes. She hadn't pushed as hard as she could've.

She'd wracked my spirit during my training to prepare me for this life. It wasn't like her to give up without a fight. For all her bluster, there *hadn't* been a fight. Ferocity . . . yes, but the moment I thought I'd had the upper hand, Grannie had called it. Either being dead had changed her or I'd never realized what a bullying coward she'd been.

We circled each other on the boulevard. I didn't want her obelisk at my back, but neither did I want her to get too close to it—where she might be able to access its power and throw it against me.

"Never known you to be a quitter," I said.

"It's been a while since anyone's pushed me," Grannie said. "I'm rusty."

"Didn't feel rusty."

Grannie laughed as if appreciating a compliment. "I see you've been keeping in shape, too."

"Haven't found a shell-shocked kid to dig up graves for me yet."

"Don't sass me, Winnie," she said gesturing manically with her index finger. "I was eighty goddamned years old when I found you, and there'd been a shovel in these hands for most of that time."

"No sass, Grannie, just truth." I shook my head. I hadn't found anyone I could train as an apprentice. No one I trusted, anyway. It was a fine line we walked between the grey and the black. Necromancers didn't have much luck on the white side of the moral line. Anyone who *wanted* my power set, damn sure shouldn't have access to it. Hell, destructive as I'd been when Grannie took me, I'm still surprised she didn't do me the way she'd taken out my kidnapper all those years ago.

"How's your family?"

"Don't have any, Grannie. They've been gone for years."

She cocked her head, as if uncertain what I'd said, and asked, "Worried they're here?"

"No." Truth was, as much as I missed them, I never wanted to see them. Not here. It wouldn't be them. What I'd see wouldn't be what I missed about them. Mom's smile. Dad's rare laugh. Home cooking. Summer days on the farm. Weekend trips to the city. They'd only be two more shades. Necromancer currency.

Grannie smiled. "At least one is still talking to you, even if she's sulking at the moment."

Summer retreated deeper into my mind.

Grannie gave an admonishing *tut-tut*, and said, "Don't be shy."

My eyes widened. I tried to hide it, but it was hard to hide *anything* from Grannie. Always had been.

She smirked. "Oh yes, Winter. Your sister and I are old friends. Older friends than you and me."

I ran through the implications as Grannie's smirk softened. I knew Grannie knew *of* Summer. Didn't know they'd chatted.

She gestured toward the apartment we'd once shared, and walked toward the steps. Infuriatingly slowly. I followed her. "Finding your sister led me to you. She worried about you before you knew she was real. When you wouldn't listen to her. *That* hasn't changed, eh?"

"It hasn't," Summer said.

I rolled my eyes. No one else heard her. Grannie may as well have been talking to an urn.

"Pity, dear," Grannie said. "You two should learn to play nice together. You'll need each other before the end."

So Grannie *could* hear Summer. My sister and I spoke at the same time. As I asked, "What do you mean?" Summer said, *"Too late. I'm already dead."*

"One at a time," Grannie said, with the smiling beatific patience of an actual grandmother.

Her attempting "kind" was unsettling. So was imagining her hunting me through my dead twin. And if she could do it, anyone with Grannie's gifts could.

"If Summer led you to me—"

"Yes," Grannie said, climbing the first step of our apartment to even our respective heights, and turning to face me. "It's how Marcus found you. He was hungrier than I at the time."

"Good thing he bit off more than he could chew."

"Oh, he did at that," Grannie said, a twinkle in her eye, a dead star still glowing despite the time and space between us. "Enough of him. No hell is deep enough for that fucker."

I nodded.

"He's not why you're here."

"I need help, Grannie."

"You still come to me for advice. For help." She shook her head. "You will *always* be my apprentice."

"That time is done."

"Did you heed my death's wish?"

I knew she'd ask. "Of course."

She levelled an accusing stare. "My spirit still feels the crematorium's heat, not the moist press of earth. Don't deny it. Trying to speed my way Beyond, I'll bet. Good thing I prepared for that." She wiped at the ash on my brow. Her touch was dry ice cold. When she brushed me, ash caught in the wind and drifted away. "Are those *my* ashes you wear?"

I snorted. She'd have known if they were. "Are you sure that's the oven you feel, and not approaching hellfire?"

Now, her smile did hold genuine mirth. "*Bah.* No hell could hold me."

"Those you consigned to the underworld might wish otherwise. I'm sure they're lined up for the chance to meet you again."

Grannie closed her eyes, her face taking on a dreamy cast, as if she were reminiscing on dark deeds. "That would be foolish."

She sat down and patted the steps next to her. I joined her. It was strange to sit here, and to not hear sirens whine, or traffic drone, or the shrill cries of crows. As if it heard me, a crow cawed.

Right now, in the real world, the crows should be sleeping. Maybe, because they were carrion birds, the Kingdom was where their dreams went to fly.

They were smart, crows. As they stared at me and Grannie from the trees, they shifted and hopped along the branches, snatching at pieces of mist like they were roadkill. I hoped they wouldn't notice me.

Grannie nudged me in the ribs. Her elbows were bony as ever, and a rent opened in my overcoat, trailing smoke. It widened like slow-burning paper with every moment.

"Here to bird watch, or to get answers?"

"Answers, Grannie."

"I'm not surprised you're here. Bad times are coming, Winnie," she said. Much as I hated the diminutive now—Christophe's fault—hearing her call me familiarly again felt good. Reminded me that our time together wasn't all forced burials and hard labour.

"I figured."

I wish she'd elaborated on what she'd seen. But that wasn't Grannie's way. Her true greeting wasn't the fight. *This* was. She'd make me claw and dig for every scrap. Blurting out everything wouldn't do me any good. Grannie would want to talk. And if I rushed her, she'd dig in her heels instead of helping. She's dead, and I'm a necromancer, but she still had the upper hand—and she knew it. Forcing her to do something was harder than controlling a cat. You could try, but you'd best not hold your breath while you were doing so.

"You've always had a good eye for trouble."

"I've got two, and I use them. If you'd done the same, we wouldn't be here."

I bit back a retort. She was right. Some connection I hadn't seen had allowed events to get out of hand.

"Why don't you tell me what *you've* seen," Grannie said, and it was more demand than question, "and we'll go from there."

"Christophe's being a dick again. McCoy is stretching his bones. New player is in town."

As Grannie considered my words, I fought the urge to check my watch; a downward glance where one should be, would tip her to my impatience. Anything I forced out of her would be coloured by her anger, and she'd try and fool me. Despite what I'd meant to her once—which wasn't a sentiment I was willing to bet my life on—she'd always been tricksy. And I doubted death had changed her character.

"You still haven't bound that uppity vampire yet?" she asked. "Or better yet, made him into ash."

"Not yet," I said. No need to let Grannie know I was afraid to try. Friendly as she appeared now, the Kingdom wasn't the place to show a hint of weakness. Not to anyone. Hell, if I turned the corner and saw my parents, I'd have to play hardass. Not saying I'd do it well, but I *would* try.

"Bah, you're still afraid of him. Shit or get off the pot."

"He's old, Grannie. Powerful."

"Christophe is not alone in possessing power," Grannie reminded me.

"I know what I can do."

"Do you now?" She laughed. "Grannie still knows a few tricks she hasn't taught you. Come back here when that leech is bound to your will, and I'll show them to you."

"I'll do that." I would do *no such thing*. "It's not just Chris. He's spawned."

"Only a free vampire can spawn," Grannie said. "Only good the first sire ever did, was place that limit."

A small thing. It told me something else: Christophe's master, whoever they might have been, wasn't in the picture. Small things can lead to big favours. This knowledge was something. It might lead to bringing Christophe down. "Limit or no, I've still got numbers against me. And the longer I take, the worse it'll be."

"A vampire controls its spawn, but the first vampire was made by necromancers. They brewed a formula to change the drinker from corpse to creature and bind the bloodsuckers to their will."

"You think someone's controlling Christophe?"

"Doubtful, given how you wail about the fucker." Grannie shrugged. "Someone could have slipped it to your Karl before his death."

I was pretty sure I hadn't mentioned Karl Daher to Grannie yet. I was glad she'd let something slip around me for a change. It was pretty clear to me she *had* been paying attention to Winnipeg since her death, and in particular, what our old pals, the Redeemers, were doing. Any other information she might have held better odds of being useful.

I tried not to let my relief show. I needed to get her talking. And not about our good old days. "Why didn't you mention this vampire formula before?"

"You think you're ready to craft and control your own vampire? You hadn't the will then, and you don't now. Not if you're still running from Christophe."

"I stopped Karl."

"A baby. He's nothing."

"Not yet," I said. "But he will be."

"Oh, really?" Grannie asked. "And how is Frank?"

"Frank?" I wanted to know where he was, but I was also afraid of how she'd react when she learned I'd disobeyed her long ago.

She'd sent me over to Afghanistan to deal with Frank's creators. I'd hidden the fact I hadn't destroyed him, too. Told her the job'd been done. He hadn't been named yet. She'd taught me it was always good to have an ace-in-the-hole. I was hers. Frank was mine. Friends were decidedly hard to come by for necromancers.

"Don't horseshit me, little lady. I always knew you kept that composite man for yourself in case I ever turned on you. Proud of you."

"Surprised you feel that way."

She gave my hand a friendly pat. "You played it well, and disobeyed an order while following a teaching. Truth is, by the time I learned what you'd done, it was too late for me to do anything. Grannie was checking out."

The sky burned and shimmered against the mercury currents of the Kingdom's version of the Red. I wondered if she'd watched us from her old room, where I now slept. Probably. She traced a symbol in the dusty step. It looked like a peace sign. Grannie didn't believe in "rest in peace," let alone any hippie notions.

"Frank's missing, Grannie. I need him back."

A shade crow flew off as Grannie said, "You put too much trust in that construct. It's a weapon, not a person."

"Not *a* person. Several."

"Stubborn girl. Always doing things your way."

"It's worked out so far."

"Has it? The *right* way would be better than *your* way."

"Don't talk to me about right and wrong ways," I snapped. "Who's alive and who's dead?"

Grannie's eyes shot from me to the street, head canted as if listening for something, or someone. The crows were gone. She grabbed my jaw. Death had done nothing to diminish her grip. "Best not to be noising that around. Arrogance doesn't suit you."

Grannie felt it suited her fine. I'd pushed her too far. If she knew where Frank was, she wouldn't say now. Not without me forcing it out of her, and there was no guarantee I could.

"I didn't come here to discuss boys, Grannie. Bad things are happening in *my* city. Remember?"

"Your city?" Grannie arced an eyebrow and I worried we were going to dance this dance again. My overcoat was gone and my suit jacked frayed and smoked.

"Mine now."

"Good," she said, nodding. "You don't believe it, can't make it true."

It took a while, but she pried out the rest of my story. Getting a line on a new cult poaching from the Redeemers, trying to break Karl Daher; his murder by Christophe and subsequent rebirth. McCoy's goons and the mysterious stranger. Pastor Mark. I didn't mention Lyssa or Woj. Grannie didn't know I had friends above ground. I wanted to keep them that way, so she wasn't going to hear it from me.

"Seems to me you're tackling this in the wrong way."

"What, you want me to burn down the Redeemer church? You'd always said it was as good a place to keep an eye on the other side."

"True, but times change. You need to change with them, or change against them. If you don't, they'll run you down from a side alley you didn't see while you're looking both ways to cross the street."

"They're actually a threat now?"

"*Times change*, I said. That could be one of them."

That didn't bode well. "Well, I wouldn't mind an excuse to run those buggers out of town."

"You might've missed your chance."

"You think?"

"That's all I can do here." Grannie said. "Think."

She took my hand in hers, flipping it to view my palm. It took a lot for me to trust her with a touch. My gloves were long gone, smoked away into the wind.

Grannie scratched a line through the remnants of my crematory ash, tracing my life line and asked, "Want to know what made me trust you?"

I smiled. Years dead and she could still read me like a book. "Sometimes I wonder, I'll admit."

"Change," she stated flatly. "Years, months—days—earlier and you would've been under my knife. I would've cut out your dead twin and ate her to cross over as you do. Freely. No bloody gates, no bloody bargains."

"What stopped you?"

"I learned I was dying. Some prick had gone and killed me and I hadn't even noticed. Put a slow cancer in me. Got me thinking about what I'd leave behind. This city's far too dangerous to leave to any newcomers. Then that prick took you from your family. Manna from heaven you were."

"Why didn't you see a doctor?" I asked. "You lived for years after you took me in. If you'd known all that time, they might've been able to do something for you."

"Nah," Grannie said. "I knew what the fucker'd done to me. Cancer kept coming back. I used it, passing hurts between folk until it used me up." She laughed. "No sense in regrets. I had a helluva run."

"That's it? You were dying so you wanted an apprentice?"

"Not just anyone," Grannie said. "No need to be defensive, Winnie. There was a balance in you that I liked. Still do."

"Things change," I said, testing her. Death was the ultimate truth. It came for everyone. The dead couldn't lie. They could hide, misdirect, obfuscate—not lie. If anyone knew why, they'd never explained it to me. That was why we summoned the dead for answers. They were more reliable than the living.

She shook her head. "Not that."

That was a relief. I'd hoped Grannie hadn't had anything to do with the cult moving in.

"So," Grannie said, "now that I've passed your test, what do you want to know?"

"What've you seen?"

"Nothing concrete. Whoever's moving in is being careful. Subtle. I don't know that those Redeemer folks are the answer this time."

"I could've sworn—"

Grannie waved me silent. "Not saying someone ain't using them. I doubt that's the whole answer. Most who recruit from that church are easy to spot, amateurs drawn to death for the first time. This is different. Something outside the Compact. Or back from Beyond."

I wished she'd given me a third option. The Compact. Written during the glory of Rome to stop Those Who Dwell Beyond the Threshold. The first time necromancers found themselves comrades, not solo operators. A secret society formed, because there's always a secret society, and secrets were shared. The limits were tested, pushed and refined, all to keep Those Who Dwell Beyond the Threshold at bay. When they ate shades, they took our power from us. Necromancers don't share power.

"You're sure?"

"You would've noticed, you'd paid more attention to your studies."

"Something ancient, something evil?"

"Ancient yes. Evil . . ." She raised her hand and waggled it, non-committal. "Them forces don't have the same morality as we do. Try and think of Beyonders in human terms and you've already lost."

"I'll keep that in mind."

"You better. I'd hate to see you here for real-real."

"Someday. Not today."

Grannie patted my thigh like I was a child. A hole started smoking in my pants. "Not tomorrow, neither."

"I'll do all I can."

"You watch Frank, you hear me? And deal with those fuckers Christophe and McCoy. They've no place bossing you or sassing you. They're dead, you're a necromancer. Let them know who's boss in your city. It *is* your city, ain't it?"

"It is," I said. I wish I felt as sure as Grannie did.

"I'll try to learn more," Grannie said, "but I'll need time."

I grimaced. "Sooner would be better."

She smiled. "I imagine it would."

"Got anything else for me?"

"There might be something." She hesitated before elaborating. "You still maintaining my wards?"

I nodded.

"Try locker six."

I didn't remember ever accessing that locker. As far as I knew, it *wasn't* warded. Before I could question her further, she sniffed the air and scowled.

"Leave. Horseman's out tonight. And you won't want to meet him. Leastways, not here."

I rose. "But . . ."

Grannie stood, her body changed to how it'd appeared at my arrival and slapped my ass. "*Git*, I said. Now."

"I'll be back."

"From now on, *only* come under the new moon," she said, as I sprinted down the steps and away. "Only then, it'll be harder for him to hunt you."

"Who?"

A murder of crows broke like a wave against the trees and the apartment block, scattering into the air as I ducked. When I looked up, they were all in the trees, and Grannie sat as if nothing had happened. Over the din of crow calls, metal rang off asphalt. The crows weren't under her control, or their own, they were forerunners for a Hunter.

Metal crashed against asphalt like the *rat-a-tat-tat* of Tommy gun fire. I knew that sound. The closer it grew, the more I had to fight the urge to shudder. I couldn't show weakness. Not now. Not in front of her—or the Hunter. Grannie had called the Horseman in on me. Bitch had wormed at my trust, bled me dry of ash and Dead Man's Clothes, all the while summoning the worst Hunter in the Kingdom.

"Gods damn you, Grannie."

"If I hadn't they'd know I sheltered you, and I'd be next, and of no help to you. Now, run, girl. Run!"

The Hunter necromancers call the Horseman, was man fused to beast. They might've been separate beings, once. Now, twisted and remade by the forces Beyond. And he was after me. Worse: he'd found me.

Judging from the human torso jutting out of where the horse's head should be, if the man had been separate, the Horseman would've stood over eight feet tall. A giant. The horse body was no slouch, either. It may as well have belonged to a rhino. The shades he'd devoured already tonight glowed blood red inside its black flanks, light pulsing as if with every heartbeat. If the Horseman had a heart, he'd never shown it.

Metal rasped as the Horseman drew a curved sword from the scabbard belted at his waist. The blade drank the light. Gloom ate the glow of the dead souls, and swallowed the light from the river. Tar dripped from the horse's shoes as he approached, melting holes into the street.

He advanced as if he had all the time in the world. Who's to say he didn't?

I ran. Distance is malleable here. Time is not. The city blurred behind me. I jumped and vaulted over cars, buildings, anything in my way. I could hear galloping behind me. The din told how close he was. Too close. No good would come of confirmation.

Run or die.

Chapter Sixteen

Hoofbeats pounded. I ran. My clothes fluttered away, drifting on the ghost winds like cigarette ash caught in a gale. My overcoat was gone. Suit gone. Pants and shirt smouldered and flaked. Muscle shirt and boxers, too. My skin prickled like I was running an ice cube over it. Soon the Horseman would be chasing me in my altogether.

The Horseman was fast. Strong. I covered blocks at a step, pushing my body as I hard as I could, pushing the Kingdom for every inch, and yet every breath I took brought him closer. Every step I took, the Horseman loomed larger. Behind the pounding hooves, and growing closer, I heard a hound baying. How many Hunters had Grannie called?

I was screwed.

Summer's wails of, *"Nonononononononononono,"* were impossible to ignore. The more she'd talked on the way in, the better off I'd been. Now, with a Hunter on our trail, I'd pay cash money to shut her up. But I couldn't blame her. If I wasn't using all my air for running, I'd be screaming, too.

I tried not to look over my shoulder. Fear and instinct made that likewise impossible. I crossed the obelisks' threshold, and Grannie's domain, heedless of whether she'd spun another trap there. When the Beyond beckoned, mortal traps were nothing.

With all my noise, there should be shades aplenty. I caught one peering out a window of a collapsing building. Every spirit has its own sort of energy, as unique in death as they were in life. To bind one, control one, or burn one for fuel, you had to harmonize with them. Something that sounds simple, but was more complex than sharing a pleasing melody. Without Grave Sight and practice, it would be damn near impossible. I stared ahead as I ran, focusing on another peeping spirit. I felt a sync between me and the spirit and mentally jerked it from its hidey-hole and left it on the road behind me for the Horseman.

One wasn't enough. I hauled out more. Hurling spirits into the Horseman's path as fast as I could, hoping he'd be satiated before I exhausted my strength. Hoping I could buy enough time to get home. I bolted another block in the gap between seconds, and turned a corner jumping forward again.

A crash resonated through the dead air, shaking the bones of the Kingdom. The Horseman didn't need to stick to the roads and streets. Had I driven my car right to Grannie's front door, there would be no outrunning him. A glance over my shoulder; he barrelled right through an apartment block, blowing it apart like a matchstick model.

Whatever shades had been inside were either gone, or dragged into his body to fuel his chase. I didn't know where I would be in Sunside Winnipeg anymore. Something told me those buildings weren't long for the world, not with their spirits obliterated in the Kingdom. The Horseman had me in his sight, and he'd ride over children, ride through every hell there was to run me down.

The Horseman snorted. Steam rose from his nostrils. Hellfire crackled, reflected behind the dark, hard stones of his eyes. His hooves gouged the asphalt, sparks lighting from every step.

Would Tahl's knife have had any effect on the Horseman had I brought it? I had no idea, but if the Horseman wanted to drag me Beyond, I wouldn't sell my life easily.

I didn't want to sell my life *at all*.

The hound's barks and growls were closer now, and I thought—I hoped—the Horseman's hooves had slowed. Maybe I didn't need the Ferryman to do the distracting job. Had Grannie conjured whatever dogged the Horseman? I couldn't count on that. Her "locker six" was probably another goddamned trap in case a miracle helped me escape *this* one.

Maybe the hound trailing the Horseman *was* my miracle. I hadn't earned one, but I wasn't about to turn my nose up when one presented itself, either.

There was no sunrise in the Kingdom—twilight always reigned here—but I could make out the steeple of St. Andrew's-on-the-Red all the same. Its crowded graveyard empty, shades in their graves and cowering from the Horseman's horn.

I kept running when I reached the church. I was on the threshold of home, not home yet. The hound's cries sounded weaker, not closer. I didn't dare check what had happened to it. The Horseman's breath burned hot on my back. This time, I ran clockwise round the old church. The Horseman followed. He seemed slower, somehow. Maybe closer to the gate his powers were lessened. Maybe he was fat from the souls I'd fed him. I couldn't take the time to ask. I stopped after my third lap. My body faded.

I was barely there, but the Horseman ran a cheese grater over my mind and spirit as he passed through me. I heard the cries. Shades the Horseman had already devoured, begged me to join them, as if pain shared was pain lessened.

My bare feet touched frosted grass and I stumbled, falling to my knees. It had been a long time since I'd overtaxed myself in the Kingdom. Exhaustion hit first: the desire to fall into a weeklong slumber. I managed a few steps. Pain came next. Muscles stretched beyond human limitation blazed. I crumbled to the cold cement. My breath rose in clouds as my heaving lungs and pounding heart tried to leap from my body.

I'd crawled as far as the sidewalk when the light over the church's doorway flickered on.

"Well, well, well," I heard from beyond the light's radius. "Look who came back."

I forced my head up. There were six of them: five men, one woman. Two I immediately recognized from infiltrating the Redeemer church. Skeezy Andy, and Corinne Mayberry.

This was bad.

I was still far from my shoes and my keys. Andy grabbed my hair, and dragged me back to the church door. He hauled me to my feet; my head lolled on my shoulders as he gave Corinne a good look at me. She was pissed. I was inclined to give her that.

I thought she was going to fight slap-scratch. She surprised me with a balled fist.

The punch was almost welcome. With pain came a dash of adrenaline. Useful for a spent body. Might let me meet death on my own feet.

The big one shouldered Corinne out of the way and gave me a tap—hard enough to let me know he meant business. The punch knocked the wind from me. Not that I had much wind left.

I shot him a look he didn't like. He threw me a punch to the face, and like an idiot, I caught it. That one must have been to let me know they *really* meant business.

My head rang. I slumped in Andy's arms, while the pain radiated through my thick (and evidently, not thick enough) skull.

They dropped me, and I fell, too exhausted to stand, let alone run. But I tried. I flopped onto my back. Stars twinkled in a clear sky, the moon gave me enough light to see who was going to kill me. I tried to push myself to my feet. I needed to get up. To fight. To run. I needed to *stand*.

I couldn't.

The big guy waited for me to catch my breath and gave me a boot to the ribs. My chest heaved, and I sucked air.

"Pastor Mark wants her back at the Church—"

"I'll bet he does," one interjected.

I guess Karl had talked to Pastor Mark.

"Shut up. She attacked Corinne and Karl."

That quieted the protester.

"Get her in the car, Danny."

"Don't use my name," Danny—the protester—whined. "I don't want her to know my name."

"It won't matter what she knows after mass," he said and slapped Danny's head. "Do it."

Danny sputtered.

"You wanna be a deacon?" The big guy snarled, pulling a knife. "Or you wanna be dead?"

"No way, Rod. You're not making me do this. Fuck you. Ben. Aaron. C'mon. Kidnapping? Murder? We didn't sign on for this."

Both stood, still as alligators before a strike, watching the blade.

"Suit yourself," the fourth, Rod, said, grabbing Danny. Metal flashed in the moonlight. Blood streaming black in the dark was bright red as it spattered my body, steaming in the cold air. Danny fell on me clutching at his throat. His life sprayed between his fingers, coating me. I couldn't raise the energy to care about anything besides not being next. I met his eyes as they went dim and licked his blood from my lips.

Rod shook the blood from his knife and smiled at me. "We were gonna kill the little shit on Sunday, anyway. Now we have someone better."

Danny's soul left his body. I could see it as clear as his blood on Rod's hands. He stared, impassive, back and forth between the church and the Kingdom, and his killer, his friend. I wondered which he'd choose, not that either could do me any good. I tried to stand. Still nothing. My tiny taste of Danny's blood was enough to call him back. I could pull one of Grannie's old tricks and burn his spirit to fight. I hated the idea, but when it came to freedom, or being a plaything for the Redeemers, that Line That Must Not Be Crossed wasn't a barrier. It wasn't even a line.

There were no candles. No circles. No cajoling. Danny's spirit was bright in my Grave Sight, and the taste of his blood made it easier to harmonize with him. I imagined chains anchoring him to Earth, holding fast against the Kingdom's pull. I couldn't tell if the spirit was shocked I could hold him, or from processing his death. I didn't have time to care.

I may have been hesitant to work my mojo on the spirits in the Kingdom; here, on Earth, was another matter. When a necromancer called, spirits came. Although in my current state, a newlydead like Danny might prove a challenge. I concentrated on the taste of his blood, and pulled, drawing him through his old meat, and I wore him like Dead Man's Clothes.

His youth flooded my limbs as I drank Danny's spirit into my body. I bided my time. Danny's body still pinned me to the ground as his spirit gave me the strength to run. Rod would have his knife on me before I could get up.

"Ditch him," Rod said, pointing from the corpse to the river with his hunting knife.

Ben and Aaron grunted as they pulled Danny off me and dragged him away into the darkness. Rod loomed; blood dripped from his knife, spattering on frosted grass. He had no idea what I'd done—what I could do—or what I *would* do.

"When we get you to the church," he said, licking his knife clean, "you're gonna take a long time to die."

I lashed out with a kick, and his plums squished under my foot. He screamed and his knife bit into his tongue and slashed his lip. Danny had been a star kicker for his high school's football team.

Rod squeaked and spluttered as he dropped to the ground, managing the words "Fucking bitch" through a mouthful of blood.

I ran for the bush. I would've dearly loved to grab my shoes along with the keys, but there wasn't time for both. I sprinted into the darkness, cold and gravel stinging my feet. I used Danny hard. My body had nothing left; whatever Danny's spirit could muster would have to be enough.

Boots crunched on frosted grass behind me, punctuated by Rod's moans and muttered curses. I felt for the round ended trunk key as I ran. I beat them to my car. Not by enough. Danny's spirit wanted to move on. I couldn't hold him much longer.

I'd have to burn him. It was an ugly thing to do. Grannie had done it all the time. This wasn't how I usually acted. I'd wanted to be different from her. But we are what we're made into, and it was too late for me to change course.

They grabbed me, trying to drag me from the trunk. I drew deeper from Danny. His spirit screamed alongside Summer. He smoked away as I shoved Ben and Aaron back and grabbed Tahl's knife.

Danny begged for release. If I released his spirit now, he might still see the Kingdom, assuming the Horseman wasn't waiting. *He'd* have a chance, *I* wouldn't. I'd be too spent to fight.

Ben and Aaron circled me from either side of the car. Andy and Corinne were on their way, no sign of Rod. Yet. This monkey in the middle game was getting ugly.

Aaron rushed me. I figured he would. He'd been the more aggressive of the two. I feinted running towards Ben and turned back and slid the obsidian knife into Aaron's belly. The dark volcanic glass was invisible in my hand. He hadn't seen me arm myself.

No blood fountained out. Tahl wouldn't waste a drop. Aaron screamed as the skin surrounding the wound dragged itself inside him. Bones crunched and meat slurped. Aaron screamed long after his throat should've been able to make a whisper. His body imploded, disappearing into a red mist; it settled over the blade, seeping into the stone.

Ben stood mouth gaping. He bent over and emptied his stomach. The sharp scent of bile bit at my nostrils.

He held up a hand as he wretched, begging, "Oh, Jesus, no, please no."

Corinne and Andy, brazen before, wanted no part of *this*. They ran.

I slid the knife into Ben's back.

Another scream filled the night. I wondered if Rod would have the sense to book it. Count his losses and run. An engine turned over, revving well into the red, doors slammed, and gravel sprayed as the car peeled out. Nothing living lit up my Grave Sight. I was alone.

I sunk to my knees waiting for the night to be still again. Two shades peeked their heads out from their graves. Danny's paltry spirit wasn't enough to keep me going. I held tight, but his loaned strength turned to smoke and drifted through my fingers. Maybe I wasn't as different from Grannie as I'd hoped. Danny's spirit left my body and exhaustion invaded the edges of my vision. I blacked out.

Chapter Seventeen

I woke to something that smelled like Brady Landfill in August wafting into my face. I opened my eyes, squinting against the sunlight reflecting off frosted trees and grass. A big, black dog had cozied up to me. It panted heavily and licked my face as I tried to raise my head.

Summer buried herself as deeply in my mind as I could remember. Not even the refrigerator buzz of her murmurs was audible.

The cold from the half-frozen earth had seeped fully into my body. I ached all over. A sickness tried to root in my lungs. I'd passed out before I'd been able to get dressed. A shredded camisole and shamrock boxers weren't enough to keep the chill at bay.

Somebody'd draped a blanket over me. I didn't remember getting it from my trunk. I had to get to my car, grab an aspirin and bleed my nascent illness into a pill before it took hold. I didn't have time to get sick. I also didn't have the energy to stand.

The mutt, of indeterminate parentage, pinned me to the ground with a huge paw, and burrowed its head under the blanket and lapped at the blood on my chest.

"No," I said, feebly trying to push it aside.

It growled, and Summer, plumbed from the depths, screamed. I winced. It cocked its head, as if it had heard her. I shoved. The dog stayed put. No chance moving the beast, it weighed more than I did, and if Summer feared the dog, it was no ordinary mutt.

"Bad dog," I grumbled.

"Bear!" a deep voice, vaguely familiar, called. The dog made no move away from me. A shrill whistle followed. "Heel."

The dog's ears perked up and it stood. It turned around, stole another quick tongueful of Danny's blood from my body, and bounded away.

Pushing myself into a half-sitting position made my head spin. Approximating modesty, I held the blanket high to hide my patting behind me for Tahl's knife, a rock, a sharp stick, anything. I saw the owner of the voice, then. My age, give or take, six-one, and whip-lean. His face was in shadow, but there was a hardness in his stance, the way he walked. He was no stranger to death.

My arm was lead as I raised it to shield my eyes to hide my Grave Sight. An invisible leash stretched from him to the dog. I recognized the man and wished I hadn't. Mr. Moustache. Wrapping myself in the blanket, I folded my legs under me and placed an arm across my breasts. I didn't do it because of the cold, or shame, but because covering myself would be expected. Maybe he hadn't recognized me yet.

"You okay?" he asked.

I coughed. "Been better."

His breath misted in the crisp morning air and the slight breeze carried it west and away from us. He snapped a gum bubble with a loud pop.

"That your car?" he asked, pointing to the Bel Air, brown paint too faded to shine in the sun.

"Yeah."

He gave me an appreciative nod in return. "You're a long way from the art gallery."

Shit. I didn't want to open up to him. Lie or get committed. He seemed the sort to sense a lie, but I'd also learned to speak the truth without saying much at all.

"Was out here paying respects. Those guys jumped me."

"That your blood, then?"

"No," I said. He knew the truth already. I *hated* pretending to be a victim. Hated *being* one more, mind you, so I decided to bide my time, catch my breath, and get ready to fight—or run—as necessary. "One of them got cold feet and they killed him. I ran off."

"That explains the body we found."

"You a cop?"

"Of a sort. Why, wanna file a report?"

"A sort?"

He smiled a shit eating grin and tossed a bag at me. My clothes.

"I'm surprised you took the time to fold these when they jumped you. What *really* happened?"

I scanned the ground for Tahl's knife. All I needed was to scratch him, or his monster dog.

"Looking for this?" He pulled the obsidian knife from behind his back. "A lost obsidian knife of Tahl. Serious bit of business. For an art gallery employee."

I grimaced. Mr. Moustache definitely worked Graveside.

I couldn't keep the surprise from my voice. "How—?"

"You're not the only bonedancer around. Not even the first one Grannie took a shine to. That is what you were doing out here, eh? Visiting the old hag?"

I didn't like his tone but "fuck you" wasn't the smartest answer, given he was waving my own magic knife at me. I stayed silent.

A closer look at the man and his dog told me it was a shuck. One of a variety of hounds lurking the crossroads. Winnipeg is known for its thrifty bargain hunters, but just as there are hunters and *Hunters*, there are bargains, and *Bargains*. Shucks meant a

Bargain with power. Harbingers of death and doom. Shucks had many names, according to whatever legend you chose to believe. Black Dogs. Grims. Hellhounds. Yeth Hounds. Cu Sith. Barghest. Moddey Dhoo. Common denominator: they couldn't wait to drag you into hell. Regardless of what you called them, shucks were bad news. Depending on the value you (or someone else) put on your soul, they—and their leash holders—were Beyond's bounty hunters and collection agencies.

If Mr. Moustache had a shuck leashed, it gave me an idea what he was about. Who was he hunting? And who held *his* leash?

His shuck could've been distracting the Horseman on my escape from the Kingdom. That would rankle. I didn't want to be in this jackass's debt. I levered myself to my feet using the trunk of my car and slid into my skirt. To his credit, he looked aside while I dressed. The dog did not.

"You still doing the old hag's business?" he asked. "Or are you working for one of your dead buddies?"

"Buddies?"

"Yeah. Are you in bed with the bloodsucker or the bag o' bones?"

He knew Christophe and he knew McCoy. And I didn't know enough about him to tell him my arrangements with either.

"It's pretty hard to trust someone who shows up in my city with a hellhound on a leash, while a bunch of shit is going down."

"Sweetheart, two things—"

"The first damn well better be an apology for calling me 'sweetheart.'"

He ignored me, and ticked off a finger. "First: you don't need to trust me. I need to trust you. Second: you're not in your city. You crossed the Perimeter. You're in my domain."

He *would* bring up the Compact. Necromancers pick a city, bounty hunters roam the crossroads. By rights, he could take me under if he needed to. I'm sure I've made a few enemies who'd love to pay my way Beyond, and more sure I couldn't stop him if he tried. Not at the moment.

I grimaced as I pulled my shirt over my head. I slipped my feet into my shoes, and crossed my arms over my chest. I hated his "sweetheart." I hated his affected Han Solo swagger. But if I wasn't his target, he might be able to help me.

"What do I have to do to make an arrogant prick trust me these days?"

He waved Tahl's knife idly. "I'll be keeping this for starters. Then, how about your name?"

Names have power in magical circles. Not as much as blood, but knowing a foe's name can allow all sorts of mischief.

If he'd wanted me dead, he and his dog both'd had plenty of opportunity. "Winter."

"William," he answered. "Friends get to call me Will."

"I'd say it's a pleasure to meet you, Billy, but my mom always told me not to lie."

He laughed away my insult. "I bet Mom's *real* proud."

I cast shade at him and he raised his hands in surrender as if I'd pulled a gun. "What the hell would you know about it?"

"Winter Murray," he said. "Kidnapped years ago, returned to her family not long after. Tumultuous months followed, leading to another disappearance. One still unsolved—not that anyone Sunside is looking."

My mouth must have been gaping open. Billy the Bastard flashed me a little smirk. "You've got a reputation."

"How lovely for me," I said sourly. I'd thought I'd stayed mostly under the radar outside my domain. Whatever else they are, necromancers are people, and people always talk. "I haven't heard shit about you."

"William Cairns." He held out his hand. I didn't take it. He glanced at the shuck. "This is Cerberus."

Didn't ring a bell. Cerberus. Cairns. Billy had shitty taste in names.

"Seriously? You work Graveside and go with 'Cairns' for a handle?"

"Says the ice queen who goes by Winter."

I'd suggest he take my name up with my parents if it bugged him. He probably knew they were dead and I didn't want to point him in their direction if not. Despite his protest, I *still* believed his name was an affectation.

"You're well informed for someone who doesn't live here."

"I move around. I assure you I know what I'm doing." He knelt and ruffled the hellhound's fur. "Don't I, Bear?"

The dog kicked at the grass, its tail wagging wildly. It made a quick yip. The sound turned my bowels to water. I'd always been a cat person. Dogs made me nervous. Supernatural killing-machine dogs made me a little more than nervous.

"What's your angle?" I asked.

"I hear you've got issues with the Church of the Risen Redeemer. Me, too."

"They're a boil on this city's ass."

"They've got a new priest. I want him. He's worth a lot to me if I bring him in alive."

"Pity," I said. "He's going to be very dead. Very soon."

He waved the blade. "You think you can take me?"

"*Think* has nothing to do with it. Try not to scratch yourself, the knife's attuned to me."

He hadn't won the knife from me, not the way I'd taken it away from its previous owner, he'd only found it on the ground. If he stabbed me without actually beating me, Tahl would take him, not me. At least, in theory. His eyes flickered and clouded. Grave Sight. His jaw set, and for a moment I thought he meant to kill me to win his own attunement. He hurled the knife into the ground; its leather wrapped hilt quivered slightly as it came to rest. The grass died in a widening brown circle.

Billy turned to walk away. I took a step to follow him. Bear's friendly mutt façade dropped as he looked over his shoulder and snarled. His throaty warning dragged from the depths of hell through sewer pipes and over rusty nails, promising a slow, dirty, horrible end.

"I'm taking the dead one. See what his corpse tells me."

"He won't come," I yelled.

Billy stopped. He turned to face me. "I have my ways."

"I burned his spirit," I explained. "If anything's left of him, the Horseman's snagged it by now. There won't be any answers."

If Billy had any feelings on the Horseman, he didn't share them. If Billy had any necromancy training in addition to whatever gifts his owner had offered him, he'd know that. He grimaced, but recovered his smile quickly enough. "Then I'll keep the little shit on ice, just in case."

There was no point arguing. Hell, even with Frank at my side, I wasn't sure I'd want to go toe to toe and head to head with a necromancer-trained bounty hunter who'd been able to bind a shuck to serve him.

They'd crossed over into the Kingdom. We weren't at a crossroad and I wasn't sure how Bear took Billy along. I couldn't stop them, and I couldn't catch them, so I stayed put, and hoped the Horseman wasn't full, and the Ferryman had room on his boat.

I got in the car and started the engine. It would take a long bath for me to feel human again. Danny's burnt spirit lingered in my nostrils like I'd been sitting around a campfire. Now that I was out of the fresh air, Danny's stink was all I could smell. I hadn't killed with the obsidian knife in a long time. The fact they'd been Redeemers that'd deserved death did little to comfort me. Not everyone who deserves death deserves *that* death. Two new screams I'd be hearing until the end of days.

Chapter Eighteen

The morning sun cut into my left eye as it rose. I shifted the sun visor to block the light, and drove white-knuckled, windows open and music blaring, hoping to keep my eyes open long enough to get home. By the time I hit Winnipeg proper, morning rush hour had me trapped. Traffic was enough to make me want to drop the entire city into the Beyond, and dust off my hands as a job well done.

Billy the Bastard's arrival couldn't be more ill-timed. If his shuck had been doing the howling during my run from the Horseman I'd owe him a life-debt. Much as I'd hate to admit it, and surprised as I'd been he hadn't claimed it. The absolute *last* person I wanted in my city while I dealt with the Redeemers was a leash holder after a contract. He'd get in my way, and he'd value his quarry over demands.

My suspicion Billy was more than he'd revealed aside, I didn't know who he worked for. I didn't know *anything* other than what he'd told me. I don't like what I know, and I don't trust what I'm told. That's how I stay alive.

It took me five minutes to fit my car into its parking space. Distracted, exhausted, and terrified did not make a great combination. After I'd parked I pulled my hood over my head, and made myself invisible to the living. Hades knew I looked conspicuous this morning. I didn't need Lyssa asking about my shiner. She had enough worries.

I dreamed of a shower, a bath, a nap, and a drink. And not necessarily in that order. My wards hadn't been disturbed. Last night had me spooked. I waited for the opening door to come to rest and the creaking hinges to die. I strained my hearing, searching for movement. I pushed my awareness farther inside with my Grave Sight.

Nothing living.

Nothing dead.

At least, nothing dead and *moving*.

"Frank?" He was a son of a bitch to keep track of when he didn't want to be found.

I entered my apartment, and walked through the kitchen and into the smaller living room to the liquor hutch. I grabbed a bottle without looking at the label and poured a liberal splash into a crystal tumbler. I took a quick swallow; its heat trickled down my throat, rum settling into my belly.

I walked back to the kitchen, grabbed a couple ice cubes from the freezer, and plopped them into my glass. A dollop of rum fell onto my hand and I licked it clean without thinking. The liquor thinned Danny's dried blood. It still gave me a taste of the dead Redeemer stooge. Salt and iron. Danny was a meat eater. Crossroads. Blackened bones.

And quick as a cobra, the vision ended. There might be more clues trapped within Danny's life I could use—even if he wasn't for talking anymore.

Stepping out of my bloody clothes, I took a good long look in my floor-length mirror with my Grave Sight. Nothing immediately apparent. I looked deeper. No spots where new life left my body. Summer was there, staring back at me from the mirror, like a double exposure. I raised my hand as if to wave, but she glared, arms crossed over her chest. My heart pumped; blood flowed.

I double checked for anything more serious than a cold: any nicks or scratches I might've missed at St. Andrew's. I'd been covered in blood—stood to reason some could've been mine. And Billy and his shuck could do anything to me if they'd collected any before I'd woken.

Satisfied Billy hadn't dug his claws into me (yet), I unlocked my medicine chest. I took out an aspirin from an unmarked jar, and bled the cold from my body and into the pill. Refreshed, I tucked it away in my "for minor irritations" drawer. Its efficacy would last about as long as the sickness would take to run its course before it had to be discarded. I'd have to do inventory soon, and get rid of the duds.

In the bathroom's light, Danny's blood, once bright red and full of life, was dull, dead, and brown. I felt another pang of remorse for the kid, which surprised me. He wasn't as bad as the other Redeemers he'd rolled with, but "not as bad" was damning with faint praise.

My apartment's bathroom had a claw-foot tub, and it was huge. Huge and old. And big enough for two, although I rarely entertained. The tub, more than anything, was why I'd kept the apartment after Grannie died. There were plenty of bad memories stored away in this place. Soaking my tired bones after digging a grave or three was not one of them. I had time before it was ready for me to slide in. I took another sip of rum and left it on an old wooden chair beside the tub.

Normally, it would be a while before Summer's voice crested the waves of my consciousness and became more insistent, but this month hadn't been normal. Still, I kept a few J's rolled for mornings like this. I opened the baggie, grabbed my roach clip, and headed back to the tub.

When the water reached an acceptable level, I dropped my robe and dangled one foot over the steaming water, hissing as my toes slid in. I braced myself with my hands on the edges of the tub for balance and eased my other leg into the near-scalding water.

The heat stung at first, before its warmth spread to the rest of my body. I slid into the tub. Condensation dripped down my tumbler. I held the glass over my forehead and let the cool drops splash over my forehead. I snatched an ice cube from the glass with my tongue and enjoyed the coolness in my mouth.

Picking up the joint with my clip, I lit it with a match and inhaled deeply. I held the smoke in my lungs for a long moment, enjoying its weight, exhaling with a moan. Advil and Tylenol couldn't compare when it came to dealing with the everyday aches and pains of a necromancer's life. I finished the joint and let the hot water do its job. Sore muscles and exhaustion leeched away. My eyelids fluttered; I slid deeper. It mightn't be a bad idea keeping Billy around. I could use him.

I rolled over in bed and my ribs twisted. I gasped, and crying *"ow"* only made my jaw hurt. If anything, my hurts were worse. I hit the brew button on the coffee maker by my bedside. The scent of percolating coffee was enough to help me keep my eyes open. Only fools would want to walk all the way to the kitchen to get theirs. A stretch and a yawn and another reminder of my sore ribs and jaw. I sloshed coffee into the skull-shaped mug Frank had given me as a gag birthday gift, and reluctantly eased out of the covers, wincing as I grabbed my dressing gown and tied it closed. I padded from my bedroom taking my first sip of coffee, hissing when my lips brushed the hot cup.

I didn't know what I'd have to do today and wanted to be ready for anything. Multi-pocket cargo pants, good for storing necrotech. Sports bra and athletic socks in case I had to run.

Long sleeve shirt. Anarchy vest. I'd gather necrotech to fill its pockets soon enough. I wasn't fully awake yet.

My stomach gurgled. Yesterday had been an exhausting day, and an almost deadly night. I doubted there'd be anything worth eating; I never kept much food in the apartment. I could scrounge a muffin or granola bar. If push came to shove, I could graze on cereal—the milk in the fridge had gone south a couple days ago.

I was wrong about the muffin and granola bar. My cereal had gone so stale I'd be better off chewing plaster. Maybe I could borrow something from Lyssa. I winced. The last thing she needed was the attack of the nuisance neighbour. On second reckoning, a return to normal form might be a relief for her. A chance to help, rather than be helped.

Sniffing the leftover Thai in the fridge, and eyeing spoiled milk that was my only option with which to wash it down, I decided to head across the hall.

I hoped Lyssa wasn't sleeping. I didn't want to wake her. The Thai *should* be eaten today or be tossed—along with the milk, and the cereal. I'd slept until noon, which for me wasn't sleeping in at all, especially given last night. Not as long as Frank might've hoped for, and not as late as I'd needed.

I gave a light knock and was about to turn around and choke down my breakfast of champions, when Lyssa's door creaked open.

"Morning, sleepyhead," she said, then, "Oh God! Winter, what happened?"

Shit. I hadn't thought this through. Hadn't checked out the damage in the mirror to see how Rod's handiwork looked in the harsh light of day.

When I didn't immediately answer her, Lyssa pressed her inquiry with, "Are you okay?"

"Fine," I mumbled.

"Do you need me to—?"

"No. It's sorted." Damn me for giving my friend one more worry when she was already being run through the ringer. Lyssa's look told me she didn't think it was sorted.

"Cyclist hit me. Knocked me down."

"Were they on the sidewalk?"

"Nah, I'd had a few, was on the street. I took some Tylenol, if I don't feel better in a day or so, I'll go to the hospital."

Mercifully, Lyssa gave up on her grilling. She looked better than she had yesterday. That was worth the interrogation.

She gave my hair a tousle and I forced myself not to flinch as she brushed a goose egg. "Why're you here before you're decent?"

"I'm never decent," I said as my stomach gurgled. I hoped she hadn't heard. "Nothing in the cupboard but stale Frosted Flakes and only week-old Thai in the fridge."

"I have bagels, and Tammy's aunt gave us some homemade raspberry jam."

My stomach gurgled again, louder. Mom had been a master jam maker. The offer of fresh preserves was like coming home.

Lyssa motioned for me to follow her into the apartment. "C'mon in. Before your stomach eats the rest of you."

And there went my appetite—I've seen that happen. Not pretty.

I padded into the kitchen behind Lyssa. I glimpsed Tammy watching *Law & Order*. She didn't turn around to greet me.

Lyssa dropped a bagel into the toaster without asking further about my injuries, and poured me a tall glass of milk. It was 1%—considerably less robust than what I had grown up with, but I wasn't in a position to complain. When the bagel popped up, and the jam had been spread, Tammy walked into the kitchen, as I took a giant bite.

She gave me an appraising look, then asked brightly, "Someone else sick of your bullshit?"

"Give it a rest," Lyssa said, glaring.

"Good morning to you, too," I muttered.

"This came for you." She tossed a legal sized envelope on my lap. "Guy had your name, and our address."

I hadn't been expecting anything. And in any case, nothing I had delivered to my apartment arrived via courier.

More hotly than I'd intended, I asked, "Who delivered it? UPS? Purolator?"

"Private courier," Tammy answered between sips of orange juice. "Young guy, cocky. Keeps flirting after you let him know it's going nowhere."

"Moustache," I said. It wasn't a question.

"Yeah? Know him?"

"Unfortunately."

"Aren't you going to open it?"

There was nothing I wanted more than to open it. But there was no way I would until I checked it with my Grave Sight. There was also no way I'd flash my Grave Sight at the breakfast table. Rotting fruit and moldy bagels weren't appetizing, and it did something to you, to let that little bit of the Kingdom into your eyes. I also didn't want to give Lyssa nightmares. If I'd known who'd dropped it off, I wouldn't have let it lie on my lap. I grinned tightly, trying not to let them see how anxious I was. Every single trap and nasty trick I knew a necromancer could pack into a 10 x 12 envelope flickered through my mind. Poison. Bound spirit. Black Plague. Soul jar. Hungry origami bear.

Not helping.

"I've been expecting it," I said, trying to sound sweet. "But it's not important."

"Whatever," Tammy said after a moment, and left the kitchen.

"I wish you two would get along better," Lyssa said softly as she sat next to me at the table. She poured milk into her tea and added, "It's stressful."

"You're right. I'll try harder."

I even meant two-thirds of it. The rest was an accusing stare at Tammy. Lyssa must've sensed that missing third; she barked out an involuntary chuckle before her tea slid down the wrong pipe and her laugh turned to choking.

We hung out long enough for me to finish breakfast and reassure Lyssa all was going as planned for her mom's funeral. I said my goodbyes. Hopefully I'd also cut off any suspicion I was dying to open Billy the Bastard's little note.

I looked at the package with my Grave Sight before I brought it over the threshold into my apartment in case it was loaded with a necrotic bomb. I wouldn't put it past Billy to use the package as a Trojan to blow up my wards—or worse turn them against me. Nothing volatile showed up, but I could see the trail Billy had left when he delivered the package; faded now, yet clear enough to tell me he'd sniffed around my door for a while, and not wanting to try himself against my protections, Billy tried Lyssa.

That was good and bad.

Good, because Billy was at least a little bit afraid to try himself against me. He must have weighed what he could and couldn't see in my apartment's wards, and decided it wasn't worth the risk. If he'd wanted in, and believed he could do it, I'd have woken to him at my bedside, sipping my coffee. Or I'd have woken up dead.

Which brought me to the bad. He'd involved Lyssa and Tammy. I did my best to keep Lyssa out of Graveside. I'd always been torn between warding her place, and worrying the act of protecting her would only bring more trouble on her head. I'd leaned on her being just another neighbour. If I stayed under the radar, so would the people I cared about. With McCoy's goons and Billy the Bastard knocking, and Christophe walking into Gallery Sig . . . that strategy needed work. Pity I couldn't set a ward over her door. Grannie'd only taught me to maintain hers, not build my own.

At least he hadn't brought the shuck in with him. I wasn't sure if that was because it *couldn't* get past my outermost wards, or because Billy chose to leave it behind. I held my hand against my door, probed with my Grave Sight to see if anyone other than me and Frank had been inside lately.

Nothing. I headed in and called Frank. His voicemail gave no name, just a grunted, "What?"

"You better pick up or I *will* find a way to kill you—scratch that, I'll keep you alive." He didn't pick up. "A rogue knows where I live, Frank. Bastard left a package with Lyssa. I'm going to open it. Call me when you get this. And head over. *Now*. I don't want to hear any waiting for dark bullshit, either."

I couldn't put a command whammy on Frank through the phone, but my angry voice ought to do the job. Our friendship had made me go easy on the composite man. I didn't consider Frank a leashed weapon, but if he couldn't hold up his end of our relationship, I might have to revisit our boundaries.

I plopped myself on the couch and opened Billy's note.

We need to talk. Mister Bones will be our mediator. Today. One o'clock.

One. I looked at the clock. Quarter to.

Shit.

That barely gave me enough time to run to my car and get downtown, let alone find parking, get dressed, or arm myself for a face-off with a rival necromancer and McCoy. *Well, Billy, I'm worth the wait.*

At least I'd already decided on the right clothes. What to bring, was a whole other matter.

Tahl's dagger was a given. I was pretty sure that in a pinch, it would sever McCoy's consciousness from his borrowed bones. I hoped.

I didn't have much gear useful against a shuck. They were the underworld's fire-given paw, not beasts of flesh and bone—the obsidian dagger wouldn't kill it, but it would do Billy. Which left me wondering whether I wanted his beastie off the leash. Bear wasn't alive, for all Billy pretended otherwise. The shuck might be Billy's best friend, but he was no dog. I settled for wrapping a scrap of chain mail from a righteous knight around my forearm and hiding it with a long-sleeved shirt. It should keep the shuck from tearing out my throat while I found a way to fend off the beast. My cross nails might do the trick. If nothing else, they'd keep it stuck.

I took my baggies of goo from McCoy's vat-men. I hadn't had time to experiment with it. Didn't have time now, either. In a best case scenario, I'd be outnumbered. Worst case scenario, I'd be *badly* outnumbered. And I wanted to even my odds.

While the ichor acted as the vat-men's blood, it *wasn't* blood. There was no telling if I could use it to compel McCoy's goons. No telling unless I tried—and I didn't like taking an untested weapon into this fight. But it was my best option with the limited time I had.

I dipped a finger into the ichor bag and got a flash of something— different than with Danny. It might be enough. I willed the ichor to follow my digit; like a magnet dragging iron filings, it did. A glance at the other—still sealed—bags and how the ichor within them tried to follow suit told me something interesting.

This should make dealing with the thugs easier. I lacquered my fingernails with the green fluid and waited for it to dry. I was already late.

I didn't run for anyone (*from* yes, and only as required) and used my walk to the car deciding how I wanted to play my meeting with Billy and McCoy. Traffic was clogged, despite rush hour being hours away. Only after the witching hour were you able to get around the city without being stuck behind someone with no concept of driving the recommended speed limit.

Not that I was hurrying.

On my way, I had to detour around a mob of fire trucks, still surrounding a smouldering fire that had taken an apartment block with it. The Horseman had destroyed that block in the Kingdom. Bad news.

I found a side street several blocks away from McCoy's building. Young professionals clogged the sidewalks, heading to and from offices and Exchange District restaurants. I walked past a shawarma place, and if not for the still-punishing line, I'd have stopped for a solid lunch.

I figured I'd kept Billy the Bastard waiting long enough.

There was no sign of Billy outside McCoy's building; he must already be inside. I doubted they'd gone for beers and billiards. McCoy never left his building.

I tried Frank again. Still nothing. I tried him twice more, and again, no answer.

This wasn't like the big lug, and I wasn't happy. With him—or his silence.

Something must have happened to him. And I had three

suspects. I was supposed to be meeting one at the lair of the second. With my luck, Christophe would crash the party, give me the hat trick, and save everyone effort and time.

The main floor of McCoy's building was deserted as always, but my Grave Sight said I wasn't alone. His goons may have been hidden by the shadows, but not to me. There were three: one behind me, one to either side. They advanced like a whisper, their message loud and clear. They weren't happy to see me, despite my invitation. They should've known better. I've learned never to overestimate the intelligence of recycled souls playing toady to a skeleton in a suit.

The overhead lights switched on—I'd never seen them work on this floor—hitting me like a slap. In the brightness of the flare against my Grave Sight, it was as if I'd had a *Shining* experience, and been tumbled ass over teakettle by a bloody wave. Inge loomed over me, to my Sight, glistening like ice in the sun. It was hard to keep my eyes on her, and as that might become a staring-slash-territorial pissing contest, I didn't want to look away. I blinked my way back to regular vision, and Inge still loomed, wearing a fine tailored suit, her heels making her seem a foot taller than me.

I slid my hand behind my back, reaching for Tahl's knife. She growled an almost leonine roar. "Don't try it."

So she knew about the knife—and what it could do. And her tone implied it wasn't enough to finish her. I kept a false smile plastered to my face, and held my hands out wide.

McCoy's goons closed like hyenas, laughing. The ones on my sides grabbed my arms. Struggling hurt my ribs, so I saved my energy in case my plan failed, and I had to fight. Without Frank backing me, I'd need to talk my way out situation.

"Call them off," I said.

"They answer to Mister Bones," Inge said without pity. "Not me."

The third guy circled around me and stood in front and left of Inge. I stared the guy down. "Never come into my domain again. I give Bones that courtesy. I expect it of you."

McCoy's vat-meat muscle all looked the same, but there are subtleties in how they carried themselves, like when you've known identical twins long enough to tell them apart. I was pretty sure this was the chucklehead who'd given me grief about referring to "Mister Bones" as McCoy. The new guy. He wanted to prove himself.

He cocked his fist, ready for another go. If I didn't push back, at least a little, when—if—McCoy turned up again, his entourage would remember, and Mister Bones would know it. And why push back a little, when you can push back *a lot*.

I dug my nails into the goons' flesh. I keep my nails sharp, if not long, and lacquered hard. It was nothing to break their skin. The ichor on my nails mingled with what ran through their meat.

A necromancer can do all sorts of interesting tricks when they've got your blood. Homunculi had something pumping in their veins. And I had it. Their recycled nature wouldn't help them now. I jerked their spirits from their meat. The moment they gave up the ghost, their bodies released their grips as if my arms were on fire. They fell.

I stomped over to the goon who'd decided to start some shit, Tahl's dagger out.

"Hold out your hand," I said to the goon.

He looked to Inge. She shrugged. "I warned you not to do anything rash," Inge said as much to the vat-men as to me.

And just like that his plastic cookie-cutter face looked worried. I smiled at the goon and repeated, *"Hold. Out. Your. Hand."*

He did. Eyes closed. Face turned away, struggling not to obey. Expecting the exquisite, painful, and eternal end the dagger promised.

I slashed it across his palm. Ichor welled, for a moment, and then his flesh followed, slowly melting from his bones, and evaporating. I worried since he didn't have real blood, Tahl wouldn't want him. He had a soul somewhere in his false meat, and the god was more than willing to choke down an unpalatable feast to get at it. It just took him longer to clean his plate. I waited until Tahl consumed the homunculus entirely. Now I knew the knife *did* work on McCoy's goons. I filed that away for a rainy day. The way my life went, the forecast was always gloomy.

McCoy could call back his other two errand boys, but he'd have a damned hard time putting this one back together. He could bill me.

"*He will,*" Summer said.

Inge let out a bored sigh, somehow louder than the goon's last dying shriek. "Satisfied?"

Barely.

"You're late."

Not that she was wrong, I asked, "So?"

"Mister Bones is gone."

"Sick of old Mister creepy? Decided to take over the candy shop for yourself?"

Inge scowled. Her grimace somewhere between hurt and rage. She ground out, "It wasn't me."

Now *that* was interesting. I even believed her. I shrugged. "Wasn't me."

Ice Queen Inge snorted, an oddly incongruous sound, and shot back with, "Bullshit, chimaera."

In the years I've been dealing with McCoy, and by default, his Number One, I've never heard her utter a single profanity. Somehow, that made me believe her more. Believe, not trust. It was hard to trust when she had me surrounded.

"It was probably your vampire."

"One: Christophe's not *mine*." Inge cocked an eyebrow, and I cut off her inevitable follow up accusation. "Two: I'm sure as hell not *his*. If he and I were working together, McCoy would've gone missing the day he arrived."

She sniffed, as if she refused to acknowledge I could be a threat to her employer, while at the same time wanting to blame me for his disappearance.

"Look at Billy Cairns and his canine friend. He's the one who asked me to meet him here," I said. "Your boss could be the bounty he's after."

"They're not responsible."

"How can you be certain? I can only imagine how many revenants and wraiths McCoy has pissed off in the Underworld."

"I'm certain, Miss Murray. And Beyond knows better than to put a price on any bone in my employer's body, let alone his head. I've seen to that."

Interesting. "Noted."

Inge motioned for two more homunculi to go outside on cleanup detail. She led me to the elevator and upstairs. Getting to the sixth floor in an old elevator can feel like an eternity when you're riding with a pissed off whatever she was. There was no small talk. No chit chat. Just a frosted silence. A quiet followed in her wake as she led me down the postered corridor to McCoy's office.

When she opened the door, McCoy's big leather chair swung around. I was ready to be put out when I saw his grinning skull. But it wasn't McCoy sitting at the boss's desk.

It was Billy.

He chewed a big wad of gum, his shuck busy gnawing on McCoy's desk. Billy blew a bubble, snapped it, and looked at me like I'd tried to sell him band fundraiser cookies.

"You're late."

Chapter Nineteen

He was happy to see me. I could tell by the way his cocky steps boomed against the hardwood as he sidled around McCoy's desk. Instead of greeting me, he kissed the Ice Queen on her lips.

When they were done, he asked, "Jealous?"

"Why the hell would I be jealous?"

My voice must've been hot, because Bear growled. Summer fled and dug into her hidey-hole like a tick. She hated being in McCoy's office at the best of times. Scared he might steal her. Scared I'd let him. Billy and his shuck being around didn't help. She wouldn't get any reassurance from me.

Billy's kiss hadn't warmed Inge. There was no raised leg. No passionate embrace. The Ice Queen did brush Billy's shoulder with her hand, which for her was probably the same as fucking.

He spread his arms wide and plastered on a smile for Inge. "She was checking me out."

Inge levelled an icy stare at me, her pupils tiny skulls. I barked a laugh before saying, "Don't flatter yourself."

"At the gallery," he said. "You were interested."

Interested. I snorted. "Until you turned out to be an invader in my territory, and have been a real douchebag ever since."

Inge's scowl augured deeper. My protests wouldn't sway her. Truth or not. If she chose to believe Billy's delusions, I didn't like my odds in any "truce" she negotiated between me and her lover.

"Just what the hell were you doing at St. Andrew's?"

"My business. Sniffing out tracks. Getting the lay of the land."

"Horseshit."

Billy laughed. "You've got a tough rep—you roll with a fucking composite man, for Set's sake. I couldn't appear soft. Had to cover my bases."

"Now you appear desperate. And a liar to boot. You're a bounty hunter for the underworld. Sniffing in *my* business. Don't pretend to be anything other than a mercenary. What'll it cost to get your help—and what'll it cost to make you leave when we're done?"

He grinned. "So, we've both established what the other is, now we're negotiating price."

"Enough," Inge said, slamming her hand on the desk. "We do not have time for your *flirting*, William." When I smiled at Billy being caught, Inge shot me a withering glare. "*Or* your obstinacy, Miss Murray. Not when my employer is missing."

She was right. And he wasn't the only one who'd gone missing. I checked my phone. Still no word from Frank. I asked, "When did McCoy disappear? More importantly: where's Frank?"

"I do not know what happened to your companion," Inge said. "But *Mister Bones* went missing last night."

"Wasn't me," I repeated. Inge stared, trying to suss out a lie. "I was in the Kingdom."

She cocked her head, then turned to Billy.

"It's true," he said. "She'd stayed in her apartment until she left for the portal, and she'd gone through the ringer when she came out of the Kingdom. I doubt she'd have been in any shape— even if she'd wanted to. Unless she was beat up from stashing him there, but I don't see how."

I didn't like that he'd staked out my place. "I don't need you backing me up."

Billy smiled. "Not what you asked for earlier."

I flipped him the bird.

Inge scowled. "We assumed the vampire Christophe had come for Mister Bones at your behest. He wasn't in his boneyard when I tried to question him."

Hades on hot toast—she'd gone after Christophe alone and expected results? What was her deal? I doubted McCoy's protections were down, even with him out of the office. I couldn't trust my Grave Sight to help me. *Someday, Ice Queen, I'll see you out in the world.*

She continued, "Given new information, I'm inclined to believe you're not actively working against us. In Mister Bones's absence, I will act as negotiator between you and William for sharing this territory until such time as Mister Bones returns to his rightful place."

His rightful place was the boneyard. Forever.

"If he returns," I muttered.

Fortunately, Billy was louder than me, and caught the stink-eye when he said, "Not ready to step into the boss's chair permanently?"

Any warm feelings Inge might keep buried for Billy were swept away in the cold avalanche of her glare. "If I choose it, it will suit *me* better than it did *you*."

"God's truth, gorgeous."

Inge smiled, vulpine.

I rolled my eyes. "Enough with the foreplay, then."

"Indeed. We settle these matters and Mister Bones will end this city's vampire problem." Inge turned to me. "A problem *you* have refused to address."

"We still don't know Christophe's to blame," I said. "For all we know, your boyfriend did the taking."

Inge sniffed. "I trust William. Mister Bones does. So should you."

"If you expect me to believe that, I've got a crypt on Pluto I can sell you." I shook my head. "I don't trust *you*. I've *never* trusted

McCoy. That's why I'm still alive and he's not tangoing alone with Christophe."

Inge scowled.

"So sure your boss trusts you?"

"Yes," she said, through ground teeth.

Clearly McCoy *didn't* trust her. I tried to hide my smile. I was happy I'd gotten to her. I turned back to Billy, who was enjoying watching me and Inge scrap.

"Who in the hell are you here for?" I asked. "Because I don't believe it's *me*."

"Don't sell yourself short." Billy laughed. "You know the guy I'm after."

"Refresh my memory."

"Mark Thomas. He calls himself Pastor Mark." Billy worried at a fingernail. "Necromancer apprentice who enjoyed his work too much. A real son of a bitch. Broke rules. Slapped down hard. Wanted revenge. That old chestnut."

"You've described every necromancer operating." Aside from the "son" part, he could be talking about *me*. "Get to the damned point. Why are you after this one?"

"Money. Prestige. Fame. Settle a debt. Same reason any hunter takes a job."

He cocked his head playfully, and flashed a smug little smile that made me want to give him to Tahl, answers—and Inge—be damned.

I made a fist that quivered, wanting to be used, and then released it. "What did he do, besides being an old chestnut?"

"He's been helping out my true bounty."

"Who is *that*?"

"You know him better as Marcus O'Reilly."

I sucked air past my clenched teeth.

"Your worst fear," Summer whispered from her hidey-hole.

"Bullshit." I wasn't sure if I was talking to Summer, or Billy. Or both. Not him. Couldn't be.

"*You know it's true,*" she sing-songed.

Not Marcus.

"His spirit escaped from Beyond," Inge said. "And is operating the Church of the Risen Redeemer through Pastor Mark."

I hardly heard her words. "He's dead." Grannie had made him *deader than dead*. The conviction drained from my voice. Dead doesn't mean much in a world full of ghosts and necromancers. "If ever anyone went Beyond, it was him."

Billy waited, patiently, ignoring my conversation with myself. I couldn't let Marcus back into my world.

Inge asked, "What make you so certain?"

I didn't want to share. You'd think a necromancer couldn't have nightmares, given our . . . proclivities. Not true. There were worse folks out there than me. Maybe it was the sun, and righteousness giving them shakes in their beds, but I knew they had terrors. If all Grannie's efforts hadn't burned them away, then nothing could give a bonedancer a good night's sleep. Nothing that didn't come from a bottle.

There might be a way, after all. If Marcus had help. Summer was my gate to the Kingdom. He might be a chimaera, too. I decided to tell them what Grannie did to Marcus.

"There was nothing left. Grannie filleted him, body and soul. She made me help. She fed him to the Beyond. Bit by bit by bit."

Billy grimaced and adjusted himself. He *would* worry about that particular bit. Inge proved harder to read, other than her desire for me to get on with it.

"She sent me all over the world, to every gate she knew—" every gate she'd *shown* me, at least "—to dispose of his . . . remnants. I fed Marcus's bits to Ba'al, Cerberus—the *real* one—Garm. He was a treat for wight sharks and shadow cats. Whatever I could find. Grannie kept Marcus alive through the torture, to make him suffer for challenging her."

"Yeah, she was a piece of work, all right," Billy said. "But so is Marcus. And my employer will do the same to me if I don't bring him back."

Something in his inflection made me believe Billy had known Grannie. And not just from stories or reputation. And worse: I believed that Marcus *was* back. Why hadn't she told me in the Kingdom? Was she afraid? No. Nothing scared that old broad.

"It can't be," I said.

"Because you don't want it to be true," Summer said, her voice a distant whisper in my mind.

"Why?" Billy asked. "Because you're afraid?"

"I wasn't afraid of him when he was alive," I lied.

There shouldn't have been any way to come back from what Grannie'd done to him.

As if he'd been able to read my thoughts on my face, and his voice dripping sarcasm, Billy said, "But here we fucking are."

Grannie had done her job too well. Her extended vengeance must've given Marcus the time he'd needed to escape. I couldn't imagine how he'd managed. There was no way a simple cult leader could've taken out Bones, or scammed a spawn off Christophe. Let alone have a hunter on their trail. If Marcus was alive, if he was back, Inge was right. He was the Redeemers' real boss, not Pastor Mark.

"At least I know where to find him," I said.

Billy smoothed his moustache. "Aces. Let's go."

"Why haven't you done anything?" Inge demanded. "Why didn't you tell Mister Bones?"

I jabbed at Inge, who parried my hand aside as if we were fencing. "I *buy* information from McCoy. And I sell it—when necessary. Neither of us exchange Christmas cards."

"You didn't think this was information he would pay for?"

"It's not so simple. Marcus has a cult backing him up. He has a baby vampire on the payroll, and unless I miss my guess, he's the one who took McCoy. And Frank."

Inge crossed her arms and *harrumphed*. "His name is *Mister Bones*. You are in his home. Alive at his pleasure. Show respect."

She was right. I *hated* saying the name. "No doubt they have Mister Bones."

Her cheek twitched, acknowledging her small victory. "That changes things."

"You think? How were you planning on getting Marcus back in the ground?"

"Got a hellhound on his trail." Billy patted the shuck, who growled affectionately. "The classics never get old."

I shook my head. "Won't work. However Marcus escaped, it won't be easy dragging him back. And if we don't sort *that* out first, there's no guarantee once we get him gone, he'll stay gone."

"Again, ideas?"

Maybe. The storage locker. I wished I'd had a chance to investigate, especially before I opened it with Billy. Unfortunately, coming home beat up, sleeping in, and nearly missing this peach of a meeting had kept me occupied. "Grannie mentioned an old storage locker when I was in the Kingdom. Might be something there."

"Great," Billy said. "Just fucking great. *Might*. Might be walking into a fucking trap."

Inge added, "And your own deaths."

Billy shot a glance at Inge. Her pronouncement worried him. He gave it more weight than a mere warning. What was she?

"I've been putting out fires. I've had no chance to confirm."

"Where's the fucking locker?"

"Back at my place," I said, not wanting to suggest Grannie had several *other* artifact lockers there, too.

"Got any more certain ideas?"

"Nothing's certain."

Billy laughed. "Death and taxes?"

I rolled my eyes. His jokes were as bad as Grannie's. Normally, I'd take my odds alone with the Redeemers any day. Today, no

Frank. Marcus was back from Beyond and back in town with a cult of followers. If I could trust Billy and Inge—which I didn't—I didn't like my odds.

"They've got a vampire on side. We should get one, too," I said.

"*Assuming* Christophe is not responsible," Inge said. "Will he assist us?"

I tapped my teeth with my fingernail. "Assuming *you're* on the level, let's assume Christophe's jake as well. I'll convince him to help us."

Inge's eyes narrowed. "You'd trust him when his spawn works for the Redeemers?"

"I don't believe he meant to change Karl."

"It could hardly be a fucking accident," Billy said.

"There are rituals where one could create a bloodsucker from a corpse without the vampire knowing it."

Inge and Billy both looked startled. Good. I liked being one up on them. Assuming Grannie hadn't lied about that, too.

Billy shook his head. "What I know about vampires for certain is not to fool with them."

Inge glanced at Billy for confirmation. "How could this be done?"

"The bloody things claim they've been around forever, but somewhere, somehow, a necromancer created them in the first place."

They nodded to each other, and Inge said, "Christophe could control his progeny. Winter is correct, we should talk to him."

Billy pulled a face. "Vampire. Can't trust him."

"We're necromancers," I said, talking tougher than I felt. "We'll deal."

We could. While I was uncertain where I stacked with Christophe in the power department, personally, with a necromancer-trained bounty hunter along, and his shuck to boot, I figured he'd cooperate.

I checked my phone, still nothing from Frank. Not good. With Frank unreachable, Billy and Bear were the only allies I had.

I ground my teeth, trying not to let my worry master me, all the same not *quite* believing. I clearly needed to get a better poker face. I didn't think Inge was a mind reader. If she was, she'd have come at me a few times already.

"I know you don't trust me." Billy sounded like Frank when he said, "Sometimes you have to go all in. Shitty hand or no."

Frank had a similar expression, when he wasn't too depressed about his condition: "You play the hand you're dealt."

It wasn't much, but I'd call it a good omen.

"Let's conclude this, shall we?" Inge said. "And get to work."

"I want Marcus back in Beyond. Where he belongs," Billy said. "So I get paid and keep my employer happy."

I was glad the job wasn't personal for him. If it wasn't personal for me, tanking on the Redeemers would be a good way of getting Billy out of town. Nothing from Beyond was the kind of boss you brought up over Thanksgiving dinner. Grannie sure wouldn't care. Hell, it'd be a tidy way to keep Billy from getting his dog shit on her streets. "I want what you want. And I want Frank found. We ally with Christophe, and return Mister Bones's nonexistent ass to his comfy chair. Then I want you to leave my city."

He considered a moment before thrusting out his hand. "Deal."

Inge put her hands over ours, and spoke a binding word in— Swedish? Norwegian? I wasn't sure. "It is done."

We left McCoy's office. Billy didn't wear a cloak. Granted, the full-length cloak look *was* a little old school, but it doesn't much matter if you stand out when you can also disappear. Necromancers used all kinds of concealers to invoke the Veil. Instead of a cloak,

Billy's faded Chicago Bears hoodie kept him unseen by the living. Bear padded beside him.

The shuck needed no cloak. The Veil was as much a part of him as his black fur. The only time a shuck *had* to be visible was at the centre of a crossroad. I was glad I could see him. It confirmed for now, at least, Bear wasn't hunting *me*.

I asked, "You gonna feed Marcus to your shuck?"

Bear wagged his tail eagerly and howled. The sound cascaded up my spine like breaking glass in a slap fight with nails on a chalkboard. A number of pedestrians near us shuddered and looked around.

"Marcus O'Reilly escaped Beyond, and *me* thus far. Not sure how that bastard is pulling it off . . ." Billy flashed a smile. "We'll get him."

"A shuck won't be enough."

Billy shook his head. "Bear's never failed me. Have ya, boy?" He ruffled the dog's thick black fur and it gave a happy groan.

"You're right. We're gonna get him."

Billy pulled a stick of gum from his pocket. He shoved it into his mouth and chewed noisily. I must've been glancing sideways at him. "Nicotine gum," he elaborated. "Trying to quit."

"How's that going?"

"Better before I met you," he admitted.

Chapter Twenty

I pulled into my parking spot, and walked the two blocks to my building. Billy waited out front. He chewed his gum violently before blowing a bubble and snapping it when I approached. I appreciated he hadn't busted his way in. I knew he could enter— he had before. It was a (very) small thing, but felt like a step in the right direction for our new (and temporary) partnership.

"I like it here," he said, smiling his bastard's smile and gesturing at my tree-lined block. "This is a nice city."

"The welcome mat doesn't stay out as long as you'd expect."

"Well I can't go back to Chicago. That place is *nuts*."

"I like Winnipeg the way it is. So you'll be hitting the road."

Summer said, *"Assuming you actually want him gone."*

Bear's ears perked up, as if he'd heard my sister, and she vanished back into my mind. I smiled. *Challenge accepted, both of you. Once Marcus is gone, Billy's gone, too.*

Billy set Bear to roaming the block—invisible. He'd stand out in this neighbourhood. Hard to imagine *any* neighbourhood outside hell where that dog would look at home.

"No killing," Billy said. Bear whined. "Maim. We won't have to wait a month to summon their dead asses for answers."

The dog seemed to smile, satisfied. I bit my lip to hold back a shudder. If the dog was good for nothing else, it kept Summer quiet.

Reluctantly, I led Billy into my building. Mrs. Friesen was checking her mail. She gave me a blatantly obvious thumbs-up when she saw Billy and headed upstairs whistling to herself and gripping the banister.

"Old lady's got good taste," Billy said.

I scowled and he flashed me a thumbs-up.

"Downstairs, smartass."

Grannie's—and my—storage lockers were in the basement. I preferred keeping my gear close, ready to be used at a moment's notice, but in her long tenure as Winnipeg's necromancer of note, Grannie Annie had accumulated many trinkets. Most I didn't know the purpose of, let alone how to control.

And those were all stored here.

I hadn't known locker six was hers. I should've assumed so. Crossing into the Kingdom was my natural gift. Warding was Grannie's. I shouldn't be surprised she'd made one so complex even Grave Sight wouldn't reveal it. If she'd been square with me in the Kingdom, and its contents were useful—then all was well. If she'd lied about that, too . . . at least Billy would die with me.

Small comfort. It'd have to do.

We didn't need to worry about other folks coming to the storage rooms because every time someone's lease had come up Grannie would somehow finagle their locker away before whoever moved in could lay claim. I'd always wondered why no one questioned it, despite the wards and protections layered over the doors. The apartments were large enough space had never been an issue, or if it became one, they bought a house or moved.

The lockers weren't something I'd considered in the wake of Grannie's passing, though she hadn't gone into the long night alone, and a few apartments became available at the same time, Lyssa's being one of them. With no one to steal the lockers away, the residents took back what was rightfully theirs, and I had to be a lot more cautious accessing what was mine.

Occasionally, and under Grannie's watchful eye, I'd helped her move 'tech out of storage, but I never saw where she took them. My only other experience with the lockers was to learn how to refresh and strengthen the wards Grannie had laid. Exercises always done under her watchful eye, and while there were objects I wanted to examine more, or use for myself, considering what I'd gleaned from repeating Grannie's rituals, I never tested her patience with this. Never acted out.

I'd seen what she'd done to Marcus. She'd buried me alive once a month for the first two years of my apprenticeship. I doubted she had a sense of humour regarding insubordination.

I led Billy down the stairs, leery of letting him know the full extent of my stash. At least the shuck wasn't with us. *One* less monster to worry me. Although it meant Summer was getting chatty again. I'd be vulnerable while I accessed the lockers, and I wouldn't put it past Billy to take advantage. It was comforting to believe Billy would back me up, but I'd feel a lot more confident facing Marcus if I had Frank beside me.

The door to the locker room was open, and judging from the light cutting into the hallway someone was in there.

I touched Tahl's knife hilt, and I could hear Billy's coat rustling behind me and the soft *click* of his pistol cocking. I tensed for a second; my shoulder blades twitched—I couldn't show fear. I wanted to believe this wasn't a trap. That Grannie wouldn't betray me.

"Think this is a trap?"

"You tell me," I shot back.

My Grave Sight blazed with the wards' strength. It was like trying to discern details against the glare of the spring sun on snow, and I shook my head, and let the Sight drop. I took a deep breath (I've fought more than one monster that made the surrounding air toxic, gulping air had become habit) and nudged the open door wide, striding in like nothing was wrong.

Lyssa sat on a step stool, in front of her storage locker, flipping through a photo album. She twisted around to face me. Feigning a nonchalant wave, I removed my hand from the knife hilt. There was another click behind me; Billy easing his thumb from the hammer of his pistol.

I'd have preferred not having Billy around. Lyssa knew I wasn't seeing anyone, and I didn't want to try and explain Billy. As good I am at hiding my supernatural side from Lyssa, she'd catch any lie about my love life before it had left my lips.

I gave Billy a "stay put" glare and walked over to Lyssa. He leaned cockily against the door frame, but actually listened. My guess placed the album's vintage somewhere in the eighties. The picture she lingered over had a woman, roughly Lyssa's age now; her mom judging from the familial resemblance.

"Cutie," I said, pointing at a photo—her on her mother's lap, clutching a cat desperate to escape.

"Yeah, those were better times," she answered. I didn't hear truth in her words.

"You look happy."

"Looks aren't everything, right?"

I knew all too well.

"This was right before my folks split up," Lyssa offered without my asking. "Devastating at the time. In hindsight, not surprising."

I nodded. Lyssa turned the page, turned another.

"What are you doing?"

"Going through some old junk."

Lyssa dropped the album in the box atop several others. "Yeah, me, too."

"You're lucky," I said, without thinking. Then compounded it by adding, "I only have two pictures of my folks. And I'm not in either of them."

Lyssa didn't appear to bristle at my dumbassery—Saying she was lucky when her mom had died? What the hell was wrong with me?—I shook my head. "I'm sorry. Stupid thing to say."

She snorted a little laugh. "Sure was. I'm glad you said it. Everyone is handling me with such fucking kid gloves. Especially Tammy. I'm glad to have your stupid mouth, even if you ruined it by apologizing."

Lyssa tidied the box, sliding the album into a too-slender space in the box, making the cardboard bulge and folded over the flaps to close it up.

"Is that your guy there?" She elbowed me. Not hard—but I had to bite my lip to keep from crying out. She'd tagged me right on a fresh bruise.

"I heard you both stomping down the stairs. I'm not deaf. The same guy who left your apartment the other night?"

"Uh . . ."

"No? *Winter.*"

There was no admonishment in her words. Only playfulness.

"Just a friend."

"Well trot him in," Lyssa said.

Billy strutted in before I could call him, all tight pants and big moustache, flashing a *devastating* grin. I mentally reminded myself of what a dick he'd been since I first met him. It was important to keep things in perspective.

He tapped his index finger to his brow and pointed it at Lyssa. "Howdy."

"Howdy, yourself," Lyssa said. "I'm Lyssa, since Winter hasn't introduced us yet."

"William," he said, shooting me a smug look.

"Pleased to meet you, William." She gestured at a box of photo albums. "Why don't you help me carry this to my apartment? You can tell me how you two met."

I could have kissed Lyssa then, if she wouldn't have taken it the wrong way, and if Tammy wouldn't want to kick my ass over it. She'd taken Billy out of my hair, without me having to do anything.

Billy's smile lost its lustre. He quickly recovered and lied, "I'd love to."

Lyssa pulled a second box from the locker that rattled with unknown loose objects and left the larger, and heavier box, for Billy.

"Be careful what you believe," I called after them. "Billy's a notorious liar."

I hoped he'd get the hint and lie.

Lyssa's voice trailed off. "You look more like a Billy than a William. . . ."

Billy's grin slipped, and I allowed myself a petty snort. But just one. I guess I'm a liar, too.

Chapter Twenty-One

I couldn't see any wards on locker six, but I knew they were there.

There were only so many ways to hide a magical working. Nothing Grannie had shown me did the trick, but the lockers I *knew* to be warded did chime. So it was clearly Grannie's ward, and not me.

"*I can see them,*" Summer said.

What?

"*They're warded in the Kingdom, not here.*"

I thought of Grannie's obelisks, what I'd seen there, and how I could extrapolate that to unravelling wards I couldn't even sense, let alone see. But if Summer could see them, it was a "dead" thing. I needed a spirit to work through.

I patted myself for the Tic Tac box with the spirit McCoy had bound in his letter to me and flicked open its lid. Through the transparent remnant I could see the wards. I almost wished I couldn't. They made all of Grannie's other wards—ones I could maintain, but not hope to replicate—look like a child's scribbles.

Nothing for it. I dove at the wards, trying to unravel them. Hidden in the Kingdom as they were, I had no tactile sense of what I was doing. I could only trust my instincts and hope I was doing it right. I had to trust that Grannie wanted to me to actually see the inside of that locker, and that even in the ward's complexity, there was an underlying pattern to the working that was similar to her other wards.

I followed the rote of what Grannie had done with her other wards. I'd maintained them, I knew them, even if this one was an order of magnitude more complex. Attuning a ward was a lot like calling a spirit: a matter of feeling out the warp and weft, and where you fit in.

Moving past this ward was like trying to sift spider's silk aside without damaging the web so that I could pass without waking up a nest of spiders. Retracing the glyphs that Grannie had used to lock the door would neutralize them. When the ward dissolved, I'd either neutralized Grannie's protections, or I'd sprung my last trap. My fingers trembled as I touched the padlock on my storage locker. What if I'd missed something? A single thread wrong and you'd armed a bomb.

I didn't want to know.

I did. Grannie had a mean reputation in magical circles. She'd spared me, when she'd never taken a hindward glance at kindness trampled underfoot, but she'd kept me alive. Raised me in her own way. Given me a sense of self. Purpose. I believed she'd been trying to help when she'd sent me here.

The door was open. And I was waiting. Shivering. Doubting. I stepped in.

The locker was four feet wide, eight feet tall, and ten feet deep. Stepping inside felt like falling into a grave. The fluorescent lights didn't cut deeply into the locker. Stirred-up dust fell like snow. The walls were only two-by-four stud frames. Masks hung from those studs, two on either side.

Death masks. So this was where they'd ended up.

The masks were a reminder of what happened to those who stuck their noses into Grannie's business. Death masks were plaster or wax casts of a person's face after death. Sometimes they were made from clay. The ones Grannie had collected were much more elaborate—and I didn't see any recent enemies here. I'd had time to get used to them, and they no longer gave me the willies. Most Sunsiders have seen a death mask, even if they didn't call them by that name. King Tutankhamun's mask is the most famous example. Usually death masks were made as mementos of the dead. Sometimes—especially if a necromancer is involved—they bind a soul to the material plane, keeping them from ever moving Beyond.

Grannie had always moved her treasures around—from hoard to hoard. Never kept items in the same place twice. Never told me where everything was. I'd assumed she did the moves whenever she sent me away on an out-of-city errand. I'd tried to catch her at it once. My snoop never came back to give a report. I'd ended up in the dirt. The last time Grannie had needed to plant me.

And here I was snooping again.

As I regarded them, the masks' eyes seemed to follow me. I wouldn't be surprised if they *were* watching me. I'd given them names the first time I'd seen them. Before Grannie had told me what they were, or that they'd have something to say. They hadn't appreciated my nicknames, but Grannie hadn't told me their real identities, and they hadn't been inclined to share.

Argentus. A Roman senator.

The Pirate. Youngest, and wildest, mask in this bunch.

The Pharaoh. An Egyptian tomb architect.

And Baba. A Russian witch.

Their chains were each unique to them. Rusted iron, draped in seaweed for the Pirate. A cobbled road for Argentus, scarabs for the Pharaoh, and chicken's feet for Baba.

Lines stretched from them into the Kingdom, where their spirits roamed still. As long as their masks existed, they could never go Beyond. They'd never be taken by a Hunter, but they'd never know peace. Someone had hated them with a passion.

"Hello, lass," the Pirate said. "Long time."

"Yes. Too long," Baba added.

Argentus asked, "How've you been keeping?"

"Well," I said. "Still above ground."

"They weren't talking to you," the Pharaoh said.

Strange feeling a half-hidden part of your own brain blush.

I thought you'd forgotten me, she said sadly.

"Locked away, lass," the Pirate said. "Like you."

The masks' glares boring into me. They *would* greet Summer like a long-lost friend.

How the fuck did she know them?

I used to come here, Summer said.

I blinked. I had no idea she could leave my mind and become a free spirit. I asked, *If you hated being trapped, why didn't you stay gone?*

"Grannie wouldn't let me."

"Aye, that woman always got her way," the Pirate said. "A lesson we all learned, eh lads?"

Agreeing murmurs came from the other masks.

"She knew you were wandering?" I spoke aloud. Summer gave an agreeing murmur. The masks could eavesdrop on my conversation with Summer. Using words not thoughts might force me to consider what I kept from them. "How did *she* know, when *I* didn't?"

"You weren't as careful," Summer said, *"when you didn't believe I was real."*

My knuckles cracked as I clenched my hands into fists. "You *stole* my body."

"You stole my life," Summer accused.

I couldn't believe Grannie sent me here. These masks wouldn't be any damned help. Only a potential danger down the road.

Their dead faces all tensed, but it was Argentus who spoke. "You've seen her?"

Not a good sign, if they were getting into my head, without me placing their masks over my face. Their accusations became louder, echoing off each other and the walls in the locker. I wondered if they, like others Grannie had bested, had hoped she'd found her way Beyond the Kingdom, where she'd bother us no more.

"She said something in this locker might help me."

"I do not think it was us to whom she referred."

"Then *what*?"

Their empty eyes seemed to turn toward the back of the locker, where the wall was black, despite my flashlight's beam.

"There's nothing there," I said.

Baba chuckled. "And is there anything there for mortal eyes to see when you do your business?"

I refocused my Grave Sight, peering deeper. Still nothing. The locker door banged shut behind me and I saw something against the far wall. A ripple in the blackness.

"I don't like it in here anymore," Summer said. *"It feels wrong."*

I didn't comfort her. I chose not to mock her either, since I agreed. The closing door had rattled me more than it should have. I left the locker, wedged the door open. A bead of sweat rolled down the back of my neck. I headed back inside.

The murmurs from the death masks followed as my steps echoed off the locker walls. Closer now, I could see the bare stud walls didn't carry through to the far wall. I also couldn't make out the cinderblock lines I knew *should* be at the far end of the locker. A foot from the wall, my light pointed straight at it, and all I saw was blackness.

Grannie *had* left something here.

But what?

And how could I get it without triggering any trap Grannie might've left for me? It was as if a necromancer cloak hung over that wall, keeping what Grannie wanted hidden, hidden. If it hadn't been for a faint ripple when the door had closed, I'd never have noticed it. Could it be so simple?

"*Don't do it*," Summer said. "*I don't want to see.*"

I ignored her.

Grannie may've been arrogant in her power, but she was also cautious—practically draconic—when it came to guarding her treasures.

"Listen to your sister," Argentus warned.

"We have to," I said, steeling myself.

I tore the black fabric from the wall revealing a fifth death mask. A face I'd never expected to see again, despite what Billy had said. *Marcus*.

Summer screamed, and I wanted to join her.

This was no plaster cast. Marcus O'Reilly's death mask was his flayed and cured face. A pained rictus forever etched into his tanned skin. Grannie had formed her tether from old bones, ancient bones; she'd dug up fossils to make something strong enough to hold Marcus. There was still a shard of spirit in this mask tethering Marcus to Earth. That was how Pastor Mark had helped him escape, and they'd followed the chains back to Winnipeg. Why the fuck had Grannie saved even a scrap of Marcus?

At least it looked like he'd be in pain forever. Until he smiled in greeting. I blinked. Had his face changed or was it a trick of the light? I couldn't believe I had to face this again. When Billy'd said he was after Marcus, it hadn't seemed real. *Couldn't* be real.

My kidnapper. The man's soul was a canker and his life was hadn't done a shred of good for anyone he'd ever touched. Myself included.

I wondered how different my life would've been had he not taken me. Would Summer's voice have grown more and more insistent? Would I have lost control in the same way? Would my parents, sick of my perceived madness, have abandoned me at the Selkirk Mental Health facility? Or would I have outgrown Summer's whispers? Would I have been happy? Would I have become the person I pretended to be when I was with Lyssa?

It's one thing to idly consider a past that can't be changed. A whole 'nother damned thing to dwell on it. Chances are, had he not taken me, Summer's voice would have driven me to madness—a fate shared by many necromancers. And when Grannie crossed my path then, she would not have hesitated to kill me. I'd have been the villain, not a victim. A threat to her city—and to myself—wielding a power I didn't understand.

It could've been *my* death mask hanging on the wall, not his.

I'd never know. I'll think of it until my dying day, and I'll never forgive him for that. Not that I'd been lining up to forgive him before.

His spirit waited.

"I knew you'd come back," his mask said. His laughter filled my head. "You want the truth?"

"The truth has little home in you, Marcus," I said.

I didn't know what to do. I couldn't rebuild Grannie's wards. I couldn't hide him away again. If I tried to just leave, his spirit would try to overwhelm me. Soon Billy would know I had his target and I doubted a bounty hunter would hesitate to use his tombstone bullets with Marcus driving my body.

I'd been Marcus's puppet once. Never again.

"Lass, you shouldn't be doing this." I smiled as the Pirate warned me, though he was probably talking to Summer. "I'm plenty hard enough for you to do what needs doing. In my day I've killed more than my share o' bleeders. A stiff drink and we'll leave on the evening tide. We'll leave a wake o' destruction and wailing widows behind us, we will."

He was sweet to be concerned. But that concern would get in the way of what needed doing. Now I just had to do it.

"*Sooooo* frightened," Marcus's voice mocked me through dead lips.

It was hard not to let his voice get to me. I plucked Marcus's death mask from the hook on the wall and stared into its concave darkness. What would it mean, seeing the world through those eyes?

Easing myself to the floor, I pressed the mask to my face. I expected his presence to hit me like a backhand.

Instead, Marcus seeped in slowly. At first I wasn't sure he was doing *anything*. Oily sweat covered me in a sheen. A rancid scent filled my nostrils. The smell puckered my taste buds. I wanted to gag. Marcus oozed deeper. Sliding down my throat, hitting my stomach like a hunk of lead. He found that old fear like I was the prisoner, not him, and he dug in, widening the gap between who I was, and who I had become, trapping me on the other wrong side of my fears.

"Lovely to see you again, Winter."

"At least one of us is pleased."

"I've been thinking about the time we spent together. Before Mother Anne killed me. Before you escaped me. Oh, how Summer and I talked while you slept the night of the new moon. Do you know what your dear, dead sister asked?"

Mother Anne. I'd never heard her called that. I didn't answer him. I knew what he'd say. Summer remained silent. Marcus's mask forced my mouth to smile.

"She asked me to kill you," Marcus said. "*Harvest* you." He spoke in my voice now. I let him. This wasn't worth fighting over. I knew he'd try to expel me from my body. Tension crept up my neck. Blood pounded in my temples. My mouth dried. He tested me. Pushed at my boundaries. If he trapped me in his mask, would it take the shape of *my* face? Or would he take that from me, too? Marcus's pleasure washed over me, a wave as foul as his spirit. But this tiny violation was nothing. The real battle was yet to be fought.

"Summer begged me, promised me anything."

He ran my fingers through my hair. He was pushing his luck. "Anything," he said again. "No man is made of stone. All I needed to do was crush your will, break your spirit and expel it. She wanted to live, you see. *She* deserved to live."

He'd wanted a willing servant years ago. Maybe Summer had promised him one. I didn't know, and I couldn't fault her wanting to be alive. I *could*, but I doubted she'd answer my complaints right now.

She'd known nothing but the limbo of my subconscious. Outside the days surrounding the new moon she'd been truly dead.

Marcus's laughter shook my body. "So easy," my lips said.

If Marcus kept his precious memories locked in the crypt of his mind, my defeat had effectively kicked in the doors of his will.

Marcus's spirit was a clenched fist as we walked together through his thoughts' dirty labyrinth. He'd try to finish me deeper in his core. Somewhere quiet. Somewhere private. With each shift in time and place I fought. Insignificant, but I still fought. My struggles forced him to consider the truth of what he had done. It tore holes in fabricated memories. These holes in his ego might be my golden thread to escape his maze. To get home.

"You don't have a home," Marcus said. "Or a family. Nobody."

"I did. Before I met you."

"And how is what I've done different than what *you* did to your family when you left with the hag, Mother Anne?"

"I protected them," I said.

I could feel Marcus's syrupy amusement. He forced me to laugh.

"Your *protection* harmed them more than I ever could. Every day they are left with the hope you might call. Or burst through the door. And yet they don't know *why*. At least when I took someone it was final. Final as death. Those left behind could go on with their lives."

"That's horseshit and you damn well know it. You watched those families years afterwards. How well were they going on with their lives?"

"Don't blame me for their weakness." He may as well have said, "meh" for all the emotion he gave his defence.

A passage opened.

Sadly, he said, "There's no coming back from this place. It will consume you."

"I'll take my chances if it means finding a way to end you."

"Easy to say now," Marcus shot back. "You'll change your song, chickadee."

"Try me," I said.

He dragged me deeper.

Chapter Twenty-Two

I steeled myself for the many horrid memories likely to be running through Marcus's mind. Torture. Murder. All the horrific violations I knew a necromancer could wreak.

I *hadn't* expected my own apartment. But it wasn't mine—not yet. By the ramshackle décor and uncertain cleanliness, this memory was before Grannie'd rescued me from Marcus.

Grannie sat in her sunroom, decidedly unladylike with her legs spread wide, enjoying a cigarette, and swirling a glass of whiskey. She slugged her drink, set it down and drew a long drag from her cigarette. I could taste the tobacco in the air. A breeze from an open window in the sunroom blew the smoke down the hall.

If events were going to play themselves out here, I thought, I may as well grab a seat. There were ample cushioned chairs in the sun room, and Grannie took no notice when I claimed one.

A toilet flushed. Marcus walked into the room, still fiddling with his belt. He wore a '70s-style black leather jacket, but the fringes on the sleeves were crow feathers. His navy crew neck shirt and blue jeans were both stained with dirt and dry clay. He'd been digging. Somebody. Somewhere.

My first thought was: "What the fuck is he doing here?" Quickly followed by: "There's *no* way he took the time to wash his hands."

Grannie dropped three ice cubes into a crystal tumbler and filled the glass to the lip. The ice cracked as the liquid hit it. She passed the drink to Marcus.

His face gave away his hesitance.

"You weren't always the man you are now, were you?"

Marcus snorted. "That's being kind, Mother Anne."

Mother Anne.

"A callow youth, impressed by his power, and afraid to use it." Grannie's eyes sparkled. "We changed that, didn't we?"

"Sure did," Marcus agreed. "That's not all that changed. You said if I ever darkened Winnipeg's streets again, it'd be my grave."

Grannie smiled. "I did, didn't I? As you say, times have changed. I need you to do something for me, Marcus."

"Anything," he answered. There was no hesitation. It was how I'd answered Grannie's requests when I'd been her apprentice. "Who needs to die?"

"Oh, not die. Not yet, anyway." She pushed forward a photograph—a close-up of my face. The background wasn't in focus, but something in my smile sparked a memory. I'd been at the zoo with my parents on the day that photo was taken. "On the night preceding the new moon, I need you to take this girl."

I sat in stunned silence while the woman who'd been a second mother to me (okay, wicked stepmother) bantered with the man who would soon be spending a month trying to break my spirit.

Marcus licked his lips, sipped his bourbon and swallowed hard. He grabbed Grannie's cigarette pack. "May I?" he asked.

"Of course," she replied.

"Interesting," was all Marcus said. His silence afterward implied, *why*.

"I have use for such a person."

"I know," Marcus said dryly. "But why *this* one?"

Grannie laughed. "Dear boy, what moment have we ever shared that would make you think I would tell all my secrets to you?"

"Age changes a person."

"Not that much," Grannie said flatly. "You will take her on the night before the new moon. You will keep her for a full moon turn. Frighten her, torment her. But you *may not touch her*. A single out of place hair, and I *will* end you."

"*Hmph.*" Marcus snorted. "You take all the fun out of the job."

Fun. It was *fun* for him. And for all her talk after, she'd *allowed* it to happen. No. She'd *caused* it to happen. Why?

Grannie said nothing.

Marcus grimaced. "This will require more control than I'm used to exerting."

"Yes, it will." Grannie nodded. "Take whatever you need while you are in my domain. I will conceal your work from the Compact. Hades knows we have enough people who won't be missed. Don't forget the price of failure."

"How could I?" He chuckled. "I've lived with the headsman's axe brushing my nape for as long as I've known you, Mother."

"As it should be," she said. "It gave you your edge."

"So it did," Marcus agreed.

I couldn't believe Grannie had been the one to engineer my kidnapping and not Marcus. Okay, I *could* believe it. I just didn't want to. I'd wanted to believe the best of her. But her "rescuing" me from Marcus was a damned lie. She'd set everything up. Every awful thing she'd done to me, or forced me to do to others was acceptable, because she wasn't *him*.

Baby steps into darkness.

We'd been a cult of two. I'd been as gullible as any Redeemer. How had he managed to hold this back? His spirit whimpered in my clenched fist. It dissipated, slipping between my fingers. When Grannie had slain him, when she'd made me take his remains and scatter them, I'd thought the plan had been for him to be destroyed. Forever.

Instead, she'd purposefully created a means for Marcus to come back.

I wailed. I poured my will into holding together. I needed more. I needed everything. I refused to drift into blissful infinity. Though, knowing Grannie, there would be no bliss in the destruction of her "dear boy's" spirit. Any other time, that would have pleased me immensely.

The scene shifted from Grannie's sunroom to the abandoned Exchange District warehouse where Marcus had kept me imprisoned for a month's time. Most of those days were still a blur of terror. After Marcus had used it for his . . . operations, its tenants would not be sleeping soundly, no matter how much they'd paid, or how many guards they'd hired.

I watched every indignity Marcus supplied to both myself and his other prisoners, jaw clenched. A movie montage on fast forward. I'd seen it all before. I didn't have the time to linger, and Marcus would only enjoy the spectacle and draw strength from it.

Judging from the partially vivisected homeless person, I'd reached the fateful night when Grannie Annie had come for him—and for me. The man's screams had long ago turned to frothy gurgles. Even a sadist like Marcus couldn't stay amused indefinitely. He'd taken the man's tongue and placed it in a fluid-filled jar along with other . . . choice bits. The man slumped forward, blood streaming continuously from his ruined, gaping mouth.

I spoke, but the words weren't mine. They were Summer's.

He stopped toying with his other prisoner, slitting the man's throat with a quick slash and sauntered over to where he'd kept me tied up. He flicked the blood from his blade on my face and knelt, as if to lick it off. I shuddered; his eyes, milky as a corpse's, swollen with Grave Sight. I felt that pulse of desire. The throbbing need to take me, to foul me in every way imaginable to me now, and unimaginable to me then.

"You're next," he whispered.

I'd given up—resigned myself to the fact I was his next victim. This time he meant it. This time he'd follow through. Marcus never got his chance. His knuckle brushed my belly and the door exploded. Grannie Annie strode in like hell on a bender.

I'd been too far gone, Summer too ascendant for me to understand Grannie's words at the time.

"Too soon, you fool. That wasn't her. I warned you."

Marcus was paralyzed in fear as he faced his angry mentor. Unlike me, he knew what fate awaited him for crossing her wishes.

"You didn't say she was a chimaera."

No one, necromancer or not, should have witnessed what Grannie did to her dear boy that night. Nor what she would make me do to him later. I'd struggled to see and Summer kept the sight from me; but I do remember my dead twin saying *Good.*

I didn't have the luxury of Summer's protection this time. Grannie dragged his entire nervous system from his body, kept it alive, kept it connected to his meat, so he felt *everything*. I witnessed Marcus's terrible fate with my own eyes, and felt every torture as the necromancer's spirit faded from my sight in the vision. It was satisfying despite knowing it hadn't really been his end. An appetizer for the meanness awaiting me.

His warnings about what I would see in his memories weren't idle threats.

Even trapped in this vision, I felt a tentative connection to my body, back in the storage locker. My mouth grew dry, parched, tongue fat against sunken cheeks. My head pounded. It was as if I'd been exposed in the desert for days. If I didn't get out of here, I might feel myself die. I saw a gap I hadn't rent in his mind. It looked like scar tissue compared to the bloody gashes I'd left in my wake. *Something* had been there. But what?

I dug into that old wound, until I felt a familiar hand. Not Grannie's. Not mine.

Summer's.

Grannie had used Summer to dig something from Marcus's mind. It hit me then what it had to be. And why she'd sent Marcus after me: Marcus *had* been a chimaera, too, and Grannie was hunting for that bit of him that connected him to the Kingdom. And apprentice or not, Pastor Mark was some chump who'd had a rogue bit of Marcus sewn inside him—the reverse principle of what the masks were designed for. Instead of preventing the spirit from moving on, Grannie had made something that couldn't die.

Had she meant to do to me what she did to Marcus from the beginning? Was my survival a fluke? Was I alive only because Marcus got sloppy? She'd never, in all the years, intimated such a thing, even when she was burying me alive. I'd always thought she'd kept me around because she wanted an easy way into the Kingdom. She'd never hinted at anything like this. There were only two reasons she would've sent me here. Allowed me to learn this. She expected me to die, which I didn't quite believe. Or, so I could clean up her mistake. Marcus. A mistake that wanted her deader than dead. *Whenever he was done with me.*

I dragged myself away, through Marcus's hall of memories, back to Grannie's. To the betrayal she'd hidden. I followed the trail of scars to where Marcus's torture had really begun: with Grannie Annie.

Marcus's death mask didn't contain the entirety of his soul. Not yet. This remnant had years to plan and plot, and lay this trap, but he didn't have the power he'd corralled in life. Trapped in this bit of Marcus's consciousness, skin I took pains to moisturize dried and cracked. My limbs turned to sticks. Eyes clouded, and breasts shrivelled. My cataract-clouded reflection in Grannie's table was not good. My hair, grown grey and wild, touched the floor, winding its way through the chair and around furniture legs, binding me.

My face flashed a slack-jawed, senile smile. Marcus's trap attacked me at the roots of my self-image, altering it to bind me within the futility of my opposition. Any other necromancer this thoroughly webbed would no doubt have surrendered by now.

But then, I've always been stubborn as a mule. And twice as prone to kick.

It must have seemed to him that I'd given up. But I was waiting. I appeared to be a husk before I acted. A necromantic rope-a-dope. This was not me. I wasn't alone in trying to change who I was, or who I'd had been with selected memories. I'd be damned if I let Marcus or Grannie do it for me.

I knew who I was.

The bands Marcus had woven into his fantasyland hardened, but hardness isn't strength. Hard is brittle. Prone to shatter. I'd seen enough, and had all I needed to break free. Marcus never should've left that vision of Grannie. He believed her betrayal would break me. He didn't know me.

Grannie turned from her knitting to regard me. I could almost place the pattern of her work, like her wards, and how it wove in and out of the scar cut into Marcus's soul. "You will never escape, Winter Murray." Grannie raked her eyes over me. "Tell me, little Winnie, was this how my body looked when the sickness took it? Was I withered and bent?"

"I cried over your corpse, you fucking bitch."

"More the fool you were, then."

"Who got you? I've wasted years trying to find and punish them."

Grannie laughed. "You don't know? Truly?" Her face was hard as steel plate. "It was you."

My confusion must have shown.

"Your sister, anyway. The first new moon after I took you in. At Marcus's behest, true, but she did it. You'd drugged yourself senseless to be able to ignore her insistent voice that something was very, very wrong." Grannie shook her head. "You had no idea how right she was. Neither did I, I suppose. She suspected I was going to find a way to carve her out of you. Put her in *my* head. She was right. Summer is more gifted than you are, Winter."

"Then you should've made *her* your apprentice."

"Oh, I tried." Grannie smiled over her knitting. "But she was too locked up in you by the time we were done with Marcus. I couldn't oust you and take your body without losing her."

"And losing your new convenient way into the Kingdom."

"A pity you were not the remnant, and her the necromancer. A pity you never learned to work together. Then, you might have somewhere near the power to survive."

This wasn't a shade. Or Marcus's memory. This was *her*. I would've missed it if I hadn't just faced off against her in the Kingdom. And this remnant of Grannie would lead Marcus to her, just as the bit of Marcus sewn up in Pastor Mark had been a beacon to light his way out from Beyond. But this bit of herself she'd hidden away in Marcus's death mask which was meant to be her way out, could be my way out.

This remnant had Grannie's personality—and arrogance—not her raw power, and while it might have her know-how, as a remnant, she couldn't hold a candle to the real deal.

Especially when the real deal was as pissed off as me.

My spirit drifted away. Not pulled screaming and ruined as Marcus's had been. Pushing my luck, but I needed to show Grannie I wasn't afraid of her. Or Marcus. A leisurely exit from the spirit world, the ultimate necromancer flip-off.

Even having left a breadcrumb trail of torn spirit, and Grannie having her own pathways, it took some doing to wind my way back to the death mask.

Goosebumps peppered my sweat-slick flesh as my spirit and body reconnected. I undid the knot binding the mask to my face. It remained stuck fast until I slid my thumb between mask and face and pried it off. A hollow, sucking sound filled the locker as the mask squelched free. Marcus didn't want to release his hold on me. I didn't want to believe him, but Marcus had no need to lie about who Grannie had been. Or what she'd been capable of.

I stared into my abductor's face. This, and his chimeric twin walking around calling itself Pastor Mark, were his only remnants in the physical world. Physically destroying an empowered death mask was difficult, but not impossible.

I'd blamed Marcus for so long. I still did. "Following orders" was no excuse. I still had nightmares from the "orders" I'd followed in my time. He wasn't getting a free pass there. My anger at him hadn't dimmed, only spilled over onto the true fiend. The real thief of my youth.

Grannie Annie.

There were many days and nights during my training to be a necromancer—and after—I'd hated Grannie. Looking back, that emotion was a flickering candle compared to how I felt now. But knowing she'd wanted to use me to cheat her own eventual death, before cancer got her . . .

I'd murder every memory of her I had—if I could allow myself the luxury. If I killed the pathways to those recollections I'd still be able to function, if I did it right. I'd still have my powers—and a lot of unanswerable questions about myself. I'd leave myself open to her enemies—and to her.

For better or worse, she'd earned her place in my brain, and I deserved to have her there.

The revelation in Marcus's memories had hit me like a comet strike. Destroyed everything I'd built up. But the hate was still there. Growing.

No, I couldn't destroy Marcus. Not yet. I'd send him to join Grannie. But first . . .

I bounced Marcus's mask on my palm, then I tucked it into a bag. I doubted I'd have time to come back for it and I couldn't leave it here. Grannie'd never shown me how to reset the wards that'd bound Marcus. I couldn't trust leaving his dead face behind in my home.

Chapter Twenty-Three

"Thanks for leaving me on moving detail," Billy groused as we left my apartment block.

"You thought I'd let you watch me in that room under *any* circumstances? Get real."

He pulled a face. "I should've figured you for the secretive type, given your master."

"Given my *former* master, consider yourself lucky you're still breathing."

"Point," Billy said, pulling his keys from his pants pocket.

"We're taking my car," I said.

"Mine's closer." He pointed at the Mustang, giving the gesture a "right the fuck there" emphasis.

Already suspecting the answer, I asked, "Do you know where we're going?"

Billy grimaced. "I'll find it."

I shook my head. "I'd rather take you there than feed you directions."

Billy spat his gum on the boulevard. "Fine."

I smiled. Small victories. Get the smarmy bastard used to listening to me now, and it'd be easier to force him out later. By capitulating to my demand to drive, he'd lost a bit of power. It was no Constantine Binding, merely a first step. And Billy knew it. He'd acknowledged my control in this domain, and he wasn't happy.

"Shotgun," he said, looking at Bear, as if to salvage a victory.

We drove in blessed silence. There was no chatter. No innuendo. Only Bear panting out the open rear passenger side window, wind rushing past the glass, and tires over rough roads, punctuated by the occasional horn blast informing someone they didn't know how to drive. Pity it didn't last.

"Aren't you going to ask?"

"Ask what?"

"What I told your friend with the nice ass and no bra."

"That you were barking up the wrong tree and her girlfriend could kick your ass?"

Bear chuffed, laughing like some terrifying Muttley. I bit back a smile, but I'd have to watch what I said around him. Nice to see the shuck's loyalty to Billy the Bastard wasn't complete. Billy scowled. He'd aimed for mean, but it came closer to petulant. It was a cute look. Shame it was on him. I couldn't hold my laugh back any longer.

"I told her all about you. Grannie. Mister Bones."

"Bullshit," I said, staring into Billy's poker face. It wasn't as good as he believed. "Doesn't matter *what* you said. You won't be sticking around long enough for the lie to be important."

My stomach growled. The journey into Marcus had tired me, and I hadn't grabbed a meal before I ran out for my meeting. The protein bars I kept stashed in my glove compartment wouldn't do the job. I pulled into the first fast food burger place we saw. Shit food, but calories. I didn't want to face Christophe hungry.

Bastard would likely be hungry enough for the two of us.

I filled Billy in on most of what I'd learned in between bites of burger. At least, what directly related to the job, and not me. We'd made a deal after all, and if I had to rely on his help to put Marcus back where he belonged and survive long enough for the door hit Billy's ass on his way out of town, cooperation was key. It was a strange feeling.

He didn't react to Marcus being a chimaera, or that Pastor Mark wasn't his target, beyond grunting, "Close enough."

He turned from me to load his pistol. The gun looked like a revolver, only made of bones, not metal, and I knew despite its looks, the enchantment binding those bones made them tougher than steel. The cartridges he plunked into the chamber didn't have the soft, greasy sheen of lead. They were stone.

Tombstone bullets. Carved from a murderer's broken tombstone. They kill dead things deader. Billy had an impressive array of necrotech. I didn't ask if he'd made it himself. Curiosity might make him think I cared.

As we approached the 'yard, I said, "Let's hope Christophe is in a good mood."

"Vampires have good moods?" Billy shuddered. "News to me."

"Don't worry, I'll offer you up to him to get my own ass out of the 'yard if he isn't."

Billy smirked. He must've thought I was kidding. "Funny."

"I'm not joking." *That* shut him up.

After, Billy asked, "What's the deal with you and the vamps?"

I shot him side-eye. "There's no deal."

"Most necros I've met don't fuck with them. Unless they have *one* bound for muscle—one they created, not a free roamer."

Billy's assessment was correct.

"You a blood junkie or something?"

I snorted. "Hardly. Christophe is old. I'm not sure how old. Grannie didn't mess with him." She'd lost the right to be anything familiar to me. She may have put up a kindly façade when we were out in public, but it'd never been her. It was a lie, hiding the rotten old monster she was. "She had the power to compel him, she rarely chose to exercise it, is all."

Unless she had to.

"And you?"

"I could, if I had to." I believed it, too. That was the strange thing. For the first time after facing Marcus, and my mentor, two people more dangerous than Christophe, I believed I could take the ancient vampire. I liked that feeling.

"Power untested is no power I'd trust."

"Good thing it's none of your damned business."

Billy shook his head. "I beg to differ. You've made it my damned business. Your vampire is hip deep in the shit with the cultists behind all your—our—problems. We're on the same side."

"For now," I said. "And for the record: Christophe *hates* the cults more than necromancers and trespassers. Right now, you're both. I wouldn't rile him any further with accusations."

"Thought you said you could control him?"

"I did. What makes you think I'd do it for you?"

Billy snorted a laugh. "That likeable, am I?"

"You're an interloper in my territory. Professional courtesy, my ass."

"And you and your hag of an old mistress have a rep as long as my dick for killing any bonedancer who sets foot beyond the Perimeter. I needed to suss you out, and keep you off balance."

"My rep is *a lot* longer than your dick," I tried to say it without chuckling. I almost made it.

"Ah, she laughs," Billy said, smiling.

"You haven't seen anything yet."

"Maybe I'll shut my big mouth, then."

I nodded, serious. "Maybe you should."

Even in daylight, this graveyard would give a person a chill. A gibbous moon shone over the hilly 'yard. Hard-edged shadows cast from memorials stabbed into the deeper darkness of the tree line. Wind rattled the branches, and the stones seemed to stretch on *endlessly*. Strange walking in bold as brass, and not skulking around, shovel in hand.

It wouldn't have mattered if I *had* come to dig. There was no one around. In the distance, I could hear the burr of a tractor's rumbling engine, growing distant.

Despite my best efforts, my hard-soled boots betrayed my movement as a stray, fallen leaf crunched in the still night. The majority of the trees still stubbornly clung to their leaves. They shone silver or golden, reflecting the light of both moon and street lamps penetrating the graveyard. We headed deeper.

A heavy footfall sounded. I put my hand to the hilt of Tahl's knife. Billy drew his revolver.

Another step.

I'd strained both my body and senses hard tonight, and couldn't pinpoint the sounds. A hulking shape slid incongruously from the shadows and into the weak light under a streetlamp.

Billy levelled his pistol at the shape.

I knocked his hand up. The bullet strayed and knocked out the streetlamp. Billy's gun didn't boom, or bang, when he pulled the trigger. It was more a muffled *whump* followed by a keening wail as the ammo cut through the air. The smoke drifting from the barrel smelled more like a wood pyre than the sulphurous reek of gunpowder.

"What the fuck?" he asked.

"It's a friend," I said, smiling. "Evening, Frank."

Frank took several steps forward without speaking. I hoped he didn't think Billy and I were fooling around.

"Never seen a composite man up close," Billy said nervously.

"Frank, this is Billy the Bastard. I imagine he prefers to be called William."

I took my hand from Tahl's knife. When I turned to face Frank I was greeted by his fist. Pain flooded my brain as my nose flattened and blood gushed over my lips and chin. I doubled over cradling my face. I couldn't breathe. I couldn't see. Something big and heavy slammed into my back, knocking me to the ground. Squinting through the pain and tears I looked up.

"Oh God, they got Frank."

"Bullshit," Billy shouted. "He got us."

I didn't bother with my Grave Sight, I could see well enough with my own eyes what the problem was. Clear as the autumn sky above us, anyone could see the self-loathing in his eyes.

The conflict.

The powerlessness.

Frank had begged me to kill him—after he'd finished off his makers. He still did. It was hard to hear his rueful laugh or his animated discussions of football when I looked into his eyes as he approached.

There was nothing of Frank left in those mismatched eyes. Something compelled him. Controlled him. I could've interrupted the link, if I hadn't been too tired to sense it. Now, I couldn't concentrate hard enough to break the control over Frank. Whoever puppeted him must've known that.

They'd crushed all conscience from him. And I knew who to blame. "Marcus."

Frank's smile would've curdled milk. "Hello, Winter. Nice to see you again."

He'd turned Frank into a weapon again. And pointed him at me.

Another shot fired. Frank didn't grunt at the wet thud of bullets impacting his torso. Instead, he closed his hands over Billy's head, and squeezed.

This is how I die. Christophe had been right.

A growl. Something big and heavy shouldered past me. Frank thrust out his arm and Bear closed his slavering jaws over Frank's wrist. A shuck's jaws could break an arm like it was a candy cane. Frank didn't care. He hurled Billy aside, and the hunter bounced off a tombstone. Frank kept his eyes on me while he pried Bear's jaws open wider and wider. I winced as his inexorable progress. With a loud snap, Bear's jaw broke and Frank tossed the beast aside. Bear landed with a thud and his jaws clacked shut. The shuck rose unsteadily to its feet without a whimper, its ruined mouth already healing.

Billy yelled, "Son of a bitch!"

His voice sounded thick, like his jaw had been wrecked. He charged Frank, gun pointed, before I could yell, "Don't!" and he fired.

Tombstone bullets, he'd said. Good against a vampire, if—and that's a big if—you hit it while it's solid. But a composite man isn't one dead body. It's many. And it would take more bullets than Billy had to bring down Frank. We weren't ready for this.

Frank staggered as each stone bullet hit him. Bear clamped his teeth over Frank's knee, but Frank ripped the shuck free, wrenching it by the tail. Grasping its jaws in his other hand, he snapped the beast over his knee and I heard its spine snap. Frank pounded towards Billy, dragging the crippled shuck by its hind legs.

I circled around Billy, not wanting to draw Frank's attention.

Billy dug for bullets in his pocket. He snapped the revolver's chamber open, and pounded a quick loader into it. I've never seen one for a bone gun. With an obviously practiced twist of his wrist, Billy snapped the cylinder closed.

I'd have to be careful, and not because I didn't want Frank to tag me. To my Grave Sight, a cloud or shadow had been draped over Frank and wrapped tight with fossilized bone chains. There were so many chains enveloping Frank, they may as well have been mummy wrappings. A spirit shroud. Bullet holes turned the shroud into a Charlie Brown ghost costume. They weren't stopping Frank. Nothing could stop Frank.

Except me—and Tahl.

I tightened my grip on my obsidian knife. I wouldn't—*couldn't*—kill Frank. But I wasn't going to let him kill me, either. A bullet wailed past my ear.

"*Goddamn it,* Billy!"

"Get in the fucking fight, then!" Billy yelled back. "I'm sick of carrying you."

I had no time to be gentle. If Billy shot me—accidentally or otherwise—it might not kill *me*, but it would kill Summer. And my connection to the Kingdom would die with her. Billy wasn't being careful. I'd have to risk it.

The shroud over Frank moved like a living thing as the bullet holes mended. If I could cut through that shroud with Tahl's knife without hitting Frank, it would flense the possession off him. Same principle as Billy's new tactic: ball-and-chain bombs. The eggshell-thin casings loaded with silver dust shaved from relics were a perfect way to separate a possessing spirit from a body.

I heard a loud grunt and I chanced a look. Billy was on the ground, wincing and clutching at his side. Frank used the shuck as a weapon, swinging the black dog by its legs, beating Billy.

I needed that shroud off Frank, but I didn't like my chances if he killed both Billy and Bear. For once in my life, I'd help the living first. I pulled a cross nail from my pocket and pushed it through the shroud and into the ground, pinning it to the earth. Frank didn't react to the first, when I put a second, his drapery shuddered, and after the third, I had his full attention.

Shit.

I rolled to the side as he spun and slammed Bear to the ground beside me. Backpedaling, I leveled the knife at Frank. He squinted, and I saw the shroud dimple over his eyes, as if it, too, was examining the knife.

Billy wasn't moving, neither was Frank. He stood stock still and I could see the shroud pulling back. It recognized the power in the knife.

Somewhere, despite his mind being held prisoner, Frank did, too. Because he surged forward as if he wanted to impale himself. As if he knew one well placed—or misplaced—strike could end it all.

Billy still had a ball-and-chain bomb resting in his palm like a poison apple. I only had to get past Frank to get my hands on it. I tried to deke Frank to one side. He was focused on the obsidian knife in my right hand. I could throw it, aim wide and if he followed, I'd have a clear line to Billy's prone body, and a weapon that might stop Frank without killing him.

If I was too slow, and Frank grabbed Tahl's knife . . . I didn't want to consider that. Because if Marcus had the knife, he could kill *anything*.

The obsidian knife wasn't balanced for throwing, it didn't need to be. I hurled it wide, waiting for his eyes to follow it. They did, and I bolted. I ducked under a wild swing from Frank, and rolled to a stop next to Billy. He was breathing. That was something. I reached for the ball-and-chain bomb, but Billy's hand tightened over it. He murmured something that might've been, "Bear."

I couldn't use too much force without breaking the bomb. A couple more seconds was all I needed.

Seconds I didn't have.

It's easy to forget how goddamned *fast* Frank is. Built like a rhino, but he moves like a cat. His fist was a blur, and I couldn't see if he had the knife.

Chapter Twenty-Four

Wherever I came to was dark as hell. My whole body ached. From Frank's beating. From lying on cold cement for gods-only-know-how-long on. I smelled ... wet, and musty. Underneath were vague scents of earth. Body odour. Mine, and a man's. And blood.

Lots of blood.

I tried to say Billy's name. No words came. I'd been gagged. A funny taste lingered on my tongue. Blood.

I was in a basement or crawlspace. I'd been tied up while I was out. My hands were bound behind my back. Legs, too. The bindings were hard, and cut into my wrists. Zip ties. I was surprised I hadn't been blindfolded, but the lack made a sick sort of sense. Marcus wanted me to know I couldn't see. He wanted as much fear and doubt as he could, and since my Grave Sight would cut through a blindfold, he hadn't bothered.

I wormed my body around to probe the cell's dimensions. The effort hurt. I ground my teeth on the gag against the pain and did it anyway. Something tiny scurried away from me. Pill bugs, silverfish, or millipedes. From a further corner I heard the soft skittering feet of a mouse, or rat. A muffled squeak; a louder cry.

I kicked out towards the sound. I hit something heavy—and hard—the firmness of muscle, not steel. The mysterious shape had to be Billy. I kicked at him again. As precarious a situation as we found ourselves in, it was satisfying to put the boots to the mouthy bastard. A man's voice moaned. I kicked a third time for good measure.

If it was Billy, he was alive enough to register pain, and not conscious enough to answer it. Unless he was gagged, too.

I ran my tongue over my teeth and tasted old blood. *My* blood. Something else, too. Something sour. Neither boded well. I had no idea how long I'd been out, and I'd broken one of Grannie's cardinal rules: *never* let them get your blood.

Possessions. Spontaneous combustion. The Death of a Thousand Crows. All the terrible things Grannie'd warned me could happen. Everything I'd seen her do. Everything she'd made *me* do. Everything I'd done with no urging but my darker nature. It was all on the table.

Not a pleasant thought. Maybe if I could escape this place—or burn it to the ground—I could exercise damage control. I doubted that. I had no idea how long I'd been out. By now, an information broker like McCoy could've bought a taste. Christophe had always wanted to try my vintage. Our showdown might not be so far off.

Wishful thinking.

Marcus wouldn't sell me. He wanted revenge. He wanted to finish what he'd started thirteen years ago. No matter how much McCoy (assuming he was still animate)—or anyone else—might be willing to shell out for a taste, Marcus wasn't the type to share. He'd taken my blood to take me.

I *would* burn this place to the ground. Scour the Church of the Risen Redeemer from the earth and from the Kingdom until no ashes remained to be blown Beyond. When I was done, everything Grannie had made me do to Marcus would seem like a stag night in Atlantic City.

The skittering sounds increased and booted feet echoed off the cement walls. My skin crawled. Because *things* were crawling all over me. I felt the mass of the bugs pushing at my body, lifting me up and out of the hole.

There was a thud and a groan. Billy—it had to be Billy—was unceremoniously dumped onto the ground. I couldn't see what'd dragged him out. There was a sound, like a melon cracking, and I winced. I judged it to be about a three foot drop. Not pleasant when I was already beat up and unable to control my fall, but survivable.

Another groan from below me as the bugs scattered. I felt a momentary sensation of weightlessness, and I dropped. My landing was softer than Billy's—since I'd landed on him and not the ground.

"The fuck," he murmured. Conscious. That was something.

And not gagged, either. Which pissed me off. If you were only going to gag one of us, Billy was *clearly* the way to go.

"You okay?" he asked.

I grunted an affirmative through my gag.

"Don't worry about me. I'm tougher'n I look."

From the strain in his voice, I hoped Billy was tougher than he sounded. He'd have to be to live this long.

"Beautiful, isn't it?" Marcus's voice said from somewhere.

Wherever they'd dumped us was slightly brighter than where we'd been stashed and I could see niches of deeper darkness— like crypts had been carved from the cement and into the earth.

A stream of vermin; rats, mice, and insects dragged Billy away from me. I rocked myself, trying to get my feet under me. The vermin swarm stopped and rose into a man's shape. A man I knew. Karl Daher.

He stepped forward. The individual bugs and rodents forming his body disappeared into his pallid corpse-like visage, scrambling inside his mouth, ears, and nostrils.

Karl smiled, showing off his new vampiric grill. "Wonderful to see you again, *Winter*." He used the same tone with my name

I had when I'd dug him up in Christophe's 'yard. "*I'm* the one who gets to pull *you* out of the ground now. I am the master."

He hissed and leaned in close, his breath rank against my face. Spittle dripped from his fangs and onto my neck.

From behind Karl, Marcus's voice boomed. "There is only *one* master here, Brother Daher, and it is not *you*."

Karl's eyes flashed red as he withdrew. They glowed dully in the darkness, making it look as if he'd painted his fangs in blood—which was hardly outside the realm of possibilities. Maybe Christophe hadn't spawned after all. Maybe Grannie had shared how to make a vampire with Marcus when he'd been her apprentice.

"Bring them," Marcus commanded.

Karl hesitated a moment, as if weighing his options and whether he could take a great gulp of my blood, and whether it might be enough to give him power over Marcus. His consideration didn't last long. Chains stretched from Karl, into the darkness. Karl was a follower, not a leader, no matter how much he wanted to play at tough. I'd read him right when we'd first met. The glow in his eyes faded.

"Of course," he said, dragging me by the feet toward the soft glow of a candlelit chamber. "Master."

Great. Cultists and their fucking candles. I was in for a fun time. Both Billy and I had been dressed in bloodstained cassocks, thrown on over our clothes. Dead Man's Clothes, judging from the stains, and the corresponding rends in the fabric.

"My dogged pursuer, also," Marcus said. He chuckled at his own joke, and I found a new reserve of hate.

Karl grumbled under his breath, no doubt he'd meant for me to hear, but my ears were sharp—when they weren't ringing from a beating. It might help to know Karl wasn't happy with his lot in the Redeemers as Marcus's underling. I wasn't sure *how*.

Karl stooped to grab a handful of dirt and sprinkled it over us. He clutched Billy by his collar and dragged us through the portal and into the light. Some of the symbols. They were like the ones on Grannie's obelisk, and just as warded against Those Who Dwell Beyond the Threshold.

I tried to look away, but couldn't. The light beyond the gate burned at my Grave Sight. My blood pulsed with razor blades. The candlelit chamber looked like a natural cavern turned ossuary. It reminded me of the Paris catacombs. Using femurs for wainscoting might've been a shade too far. Winnipeg had been built on a floodplain, and I was pretty damned sure there were no such structures under Manitoba's prairie clay gumbo soil.

Marcus wouldn't leave his place of power—not now, not with me prisoner—it would allow him to have an edge. Or it would allow him to *believe* he had an edge when it came to our inevitable final dealing. As likely as not, we were somewhere below the Redeemer church on Pembina Highway. I also knew we weren't. We *couldn't* be. We were there, *and* somewhere else. Somewhere not in the Kingdom, and not Beyond. Marcus wouldn't want to go back there—he'd be doing Billy's job for him.

My Grave Sight showed winding threads, like a spider's web of crossroads, a space hidden in between spaces. Although there was a physical anchor holding it to the church basement, its access point kept shifting along that maze of roads, from nexus to nexus. Skimming. Real enough to find—if you knew the way—near impossible to stumble upon if you didn't. Very clever.

If I wasn't tied up and about to die, I'd have been more impressed. While I'd heard such places were possible, I'd never seen one. Until now. I guess Grannie did love Marcus best, she'd never taught *me* anything like this.

Now the damned candles made sense. There's no shadow without light, and here, the shadows danced on the walls and ceiling; flickering intangible monsters beyond knowing, ready to reach down and take us when the darkness descended.

Marcus still wore Frank's body. A necromancer putting their soul inside a composite body would be terrifying. The control they'd have over their own flesh would be unimaginable. And if Marcus animated a custom crafted body, his power would eliminate the few weaknesses composites were known to have.

Pastor Mark was stripped to the waist and wearing that stupid crow-feathered leather jacket Marcus had sported in our death mask chat; his pastor's "business casual" slacks and Oxfords traded for slightly out-of-style blue jeans and bare feet. Drawn in blood on his chest was the same not-quite-peace sign Grannie had traced on her steps. He wore his master's death mask. A connection to his power, or knowledge. A chain ran from Marcus to mask—and to Mark. It pulsed. A chain can be jerked both ways, and Marcus might need his apprentice to carry out his plan, but right now, the master was sending *something* to his acolyte. Knowledge. Power. I couldn't say. They needed the mask to forge their chimeric connection. And I'd brought it right to them. The mask watched me, smirking.

There was no stone altar, no slab of sacrificial slate, but there was a heavy wooden bench worked every inch in Norse runes. There was a pile of meat on the table that should've been dead, and somehow wasn't. I recognized it—the big thug who'd worked me over outside St. Andrew's. Rod.

Karl dragged me and Billy through the crowd, dropping us right in front of the bench. No doubt to ensure we had a good view of what awaited us. He joined the Marks on the other side of the bench, trying to loom.

They had Frank—good for them. A point for the away team. Marcus wouldn't have him much longer. Not if I could help it. It would be difficult to break his hold on the composite man— especially here, in his place of power—but I'd find a way. I owed

Frank that much and more. And I owed Marcus whatever Frank wanted to pay him, plus my own interest on top.

The rank and file Redeemers entered the chamber, surrounding the table in a semi-circle. A few familiar faces there. Andy. Corinne. People who wanted *me* hurt. I wondered when Marcus would give them an opportunity.

I could see the ties between the cultists and Karl. Thin little chains—necklaces dipped in blood—stretched from the vampire to the entire congregation. Karl had been busy. He'd barely been in the ground. It was hard to believe he'd had the time to make so many Renfields. But there they were. He couldn't turn them fully. Not without killing Christophe first.

The cultists' blood chains weren't strong—*individually*—but they were many. A much stronger tether ran from Marcus to Karl, and it was obvious who held the leash.

Christophe and McCoy hung above the rune table. Christophe, bound in silver, wore garlic bulbs like bandoliers. McCoy had been stripped of his suit and hat; a bare skeleton, his mismatched bones staying together with will and hate. He was short a few pieces, including his most recent addition. Pastor Mark held the femur in his hand. It turned black by inches, and a shadow chain stretched from Marcus's death mask to Bones. Both the vampire and skeleton glared at one another, as if laying fault. When they noticed me, I felt the weight of their blame. I matched their gaze, defiant. If they'd learned to play together, we wouldn't be in this mess.

That's where McCoy came in. Marcus wanted to build his new body around McCoy's bones. That was why he hadn't destroyed the risen consciousness yet. If Marcus ripped what passed for McCoy's soul from the bones he animated, they'd lose their power. They were tied to McCoy's consciousness, made of dozens of souls. Without that force holding them together, they'd not work for the base Marcus needed to build his new, invulnerable body.

This was uncharted territory. It didn't matter if he didn't know how to make it all work. He'd keep turning people into meat and use them for as long as it took. Unless somebody stopped him.

For once, I was glad it fell to me.

Why hadn't they destroyed Christophe? With the elder vampire destroyed, Karl could've filled the Redeemers' ranks with baby vampires. Tougher than ghouls and Renfields, and easily dominated by their sire. Perfect soldiers.

Marcus wanted to be the sire, but he didn't want to be the vampire. He wanted Christophe's power without his natural weaknesses. So he'd engineered Karl's death and turning. He needed Karl to be able to make progeny vampires the Redeemers—and by extension, Marcus—could use, but only if *he*, not Karl, had ultimate control over the bloodsuckers.

Smart move. Karl may've been a yes man in life, but power changes a body, and it wouldn't be long until Karl realized he didn't need anyone's say-so to feed, to fuck, or to kill, and he'd form his own cult. If that happened, and Marcus lost the flock Pastor Mark had shepherded for him, well, even Pastor Mark must have an idea how valuable Marcus would find him when he had nothing to contribute to the cause.

Marcus didn't want to share power. None of us did.

It's one reason necromancers find it easy to pick off an incumbent and steal their territory. We don't make easy friends, and while we may have entrenched power, there was no one to miss us when we were gone, and a long list of people wanting us replaced. It wouldn't matter if the new guy was a bigger dick. There was hope the new party would keep their promises and treat you right while the old guard were proven deceitful fuckers with only pain to bring to the negotiating table.

Tears streamed from Rod's eyes. He screamed with every part of his face, but his mouth was clamped shut as if it'd been stitched together. His entire body lay stock still. I wondered how he'd ended up on the altar. He'd been a pretty enthusiastic follower. One who'd failed to bring me in. Or he'd enjoyed hurting me and Marcus viewed me as *his* to play with. Whatever the answer, I wasn't swimming in remorse for the bastard.

Pastor Mark slid a scalpel over Rod's leg, flensing away skin and meat from the bone. There should've been more blood. Buckets. Instead, only the smallest amount showed on the scalpel blade. I heard a crunch as he disarticulated the bone and a sick squelching as he pulled it free of Rod's body.

The pastor was a skilled necrosurg to keep Rod alive through such a procedure. Almost as skilled as Marcus had been. Vivisection was tricky business. Marcus must've been an encouraging coach. The bones littering the cult's hidey-hole also told me he'd had practice. Together master and apprentice slid Bones's corrupted femur into Rod's leg and reconnected tissue. Green homunculus ichor ran into Rod through an IV, creating a tiny river map of green in his veins.

What are you trying to build yourself, Marcus? Not a composite man. Not a homunculus.

"Not the prettiest, is it?" Marcus said, gesturing at Rod with Frank's arm. "Once it's prepared, I'll be able to make it look however I want."

Pastor Mark touched his fingers to Rod's temples, tilting the head toward me, and his face shifted like putty being molded— into the face Marcus had worn before Grannie had cut it off and made the death mask. He made it turn to me. Made it smile. Mark released Rod. A slick of snot and blood ran from Rod's nose as his face shifted back.

"Doesn't matter what it looks like, it'll be hideous, if *you're* wearing it."

"Charming. You won't be so flippant when I've taken back all that was owed to me. This city. Everything it holds. Everything it hides. *You.* Mother Anne's inheritance should've been mine."

Pastor Mark patted the thug's head as if he were a good dog. "Stay strong, my son. We need you to be strong."

So that was it. Marcus could wear Frank, but not control him completely. Another necromancer could cut through the spirit shroud he'd wrapped Frank in, given time. The composite body alone wouldn't be good enough for him. Not with the enemies he'd made. Me. Billy's boss. Grannie. He left himself vulnerable to another necromancer when he wore dead meat, and he couldn't possess a living body or he'd have already done so.

The shadows lowered Christophe. Pastor Mark carved off a bit of his dead flesh. The meat should've been desiccated and wormy with age. It pulsed red as if it'd been carved from a living person and blood ran from Mark's fist. The meat slithered and slipped. Mark clutched a bat, not flesh. He crushed its wings and it bit his hand and became a rat. Mark didn't cry out, he just poured the squirming meat into Karl.

"When he's consumed you entirely, Christophe, Karl will be a sire, and you will be gone."

He spoke like a kindergarten teacher and I really wanted to hurt him.

Instead of being annoyed, Christophe laughed, jutting his chin at Karl. "You stupid breather. Even if you kill me, *he'll* never be more than a thrall."

I tried not to laugh, too. If I could see them, so could Christophe. Through his apprentice, Marcus forged chains around Karl as he fed him his sire's power. Karl grew more powerful, yes, and he also bound him deeper into service with every bit of it.

"The Kingdom will come to Earth. And we—you—will be exalted above all when it does."

He was lying, of course. They'd be among the first to die if that happened. If not, Marcus wouldn't be troubling himself with such an elaborate new body, he'd just take over Pastor Mark or any of the other clueless believers in his flock. He also wouldn't have bothered with the wards to keep the Beyonders from noticing his hideyhole.

"This woman," Marcus yelled to his assembled cult with all the power of Frank's voice. "She sought my end. She feared our good works. She would betray me to those who tried to destroy me and the filth they sent to hunt me. But like our Lord, I have risen. I have been granted his blessing. The blessing of blood will change me. As I will change you. Soon you will be like me. Like Brother Karl. Like our Lord. Invulnerable. *Immortal*."

A holler rose from the Redeemers. Fists stabbed the air as if Marcus had announced they'd met their fundraising goal, or Eunice had won the Legion meat draw.

"Then, and only then, will our good works become great."

"You're not a servant of any god." I jutted my chin from Karl to Marcus. "He's a walking corpse and you're a puppet. What Elder Thing is up your ass making you talk?"

The crowd made indignant noises. Marcus silenced them. "Like the serpent itself, evil's servant will try to sway you with sugared words."

"Serpent," Billy murmured. "The Thrice Serpent is the one who offered the Contract."

A booted foot kicked Billy into me, knocking us both over. I hadn't expected Marcus to actually be working for one of Those Who Dwell Beyond the Threshold. He was too arrogant. And they'd never want to announce that someone had escaped them. Bad for business, that.

Marcus gestured in Frank's body, and Karl's rough hands turned me to face the Redeemers.

"The Kingdom on Earth?" I said, incredulous. "This is what the Compact was meant to stop!"

"It'll happen eventually." Marcus shrugged. "By ushering it in, I'll be on top."

"Bullshit. You'll be the first against the wall."

"Not the first," Marcus said. He clucked at Karl, who tore my shirt. The fabric of my collar burned my skin as it ripped free. I tried not to wince. I didn't want to give him any more damn satisfaction. "They try to mask their bitterness, their hatred. We see them for what they are. We know all."

"And we will bring her to the Lord," Karl yelled.

He sank his teeth into my neck.

Osiris, Hades, and Hel. The crazy bastard meant to make me a vampire. He couldn't be that stupid.

"Kneel," he whispered harshly.

"Go to Hell, Karl," I spat back.

He flashed a toothy smile.

"You first, bitch."

Karl grabbed my hair and the oh-so-witty response I wanted to unleash died in my mouth as he bit me again. I spat blood onto a candle's flame, snuffing it.

"Don't kill them here," Marcus hissed. "Their deaths will bring Hunters running."

They were afraid of something. Good. It was too much to hope the Hunters could arrive in time to save us, let alone that when they were done with the Marks they wouldn't turn on us next.

Chapter Twenty-Five

The coppery smell of blood filled the trunk. My whole body ached from the beating the rough roads and trunk were giving. It was cold, too. Billy's skin was my only warmth. They'd pulled off our clothes, ready to put us in the ground in our underwear.

I rarely went sadistic with punishments. Okay, that was a lie. I shook my head. I did what I had to do. Always had. My marks got what they had coming to them. No more, no less. I should know better than to cast my deeds in the best light before my last trip to the Kingdom. I may've done terrible things, but at least I hadn't enjoyed it. The energy expended didn't pay off in any concrete power gains in my eyes. Grannie Annie had felt differently, though. When I escaped this mess, Karl and Marcus would be begging to be let go with gangrene of the dick.

The car must've rolled over a pothole. The impact jarred my bruised body. I bit my lip. Billy bounced into me, hitting the top of the trunk.

"Motherfucker," he cursed.

"Can you call Bear?" I asked. "Could he track us?"

"Yeah," Billy said. "But after the number your buddy did on him, he'll be off the table for a while."

"Shit."

"It's just you and me, baby."

I flopped over to face Billy. My hands were bound to the front, his behind.

"William," I hated using his full name, but I did, hoping my seriousness would register. "In all likelihood, we're both going to die screaming. That's pretty damn far from okay. And your face and voice being the last thing I see and hear is in no fucking way a comfort."

"I'm sorry we didn't have time for anything else."

I rolled my eyes. Even that hurt. "Hel wept, you're a jackass."

Billy's ease at pissing me off reminded me I still had a slight chance of escape: kill Billy in the trunk, and capture his spirit. A leash holder's spirit would have a lot more power behind it than a callow youth's. Enough for me to break my bonds, kick open the trunk and survive the tumble to the road. Possibly enough to kill everyone who'd put me there when they circled back.

I doubted Billy's spirit would hold up long enough for me to fight Frank. Especially since they'd taken my necrotech. I had no idea how long I'd been out, or where in the hell they were taking me. I didn't know if they'd sent Frank along.

I'd lost my best weapons, not *all* my weapons. Thanatomancy could kill Billy—not my strong suit on the best of days. It would have to do. Maybe he had a pre-existing condition I could exploit. While it was bad form to murder him after we'd made an alliance, there was only one ally I'd consider following to the grave, and for now Frank wanted to put *me* there. Even if Marcus was behind the wheel.

It would sour matters with Inge if I killed Billy, but I'd never liked her. Better to focus on that, than killing him. Much as I hated to admit it, the jerk had grown on me, and that would make an already unpleasant job more difficult. I'd have to put a pin in the death plans and focus on getting back to home base.

"You're thinking about killing me, aren't you?" he asked.

I clenched my teeth. He'd noticed my power building. Half-trained, not *untrained*. Something I'd best remember.

"Desperation always makes you sloppy, Winter," Summer said.

I ignored her, focusing on Billy. I didn't want him to get ideas. "I've thought about killing you since I first met you. Why should now be any different?"

He rolled over to face me. "You bitch! You totally were. You were gonna snuff me and burn my spirit to escape."

No point denying it.

Billy's groan, hot and resigned as his none-too-fresh breath wafted over me. "I considered it, too."

The car came to an abrupt stop and I rolled into Billy, conking heads. A door opened, the chassis rocked as someone stepped out and slammed the door shut. Boots crunched over gravel and the trunk opened, revealing Karl backlit by the moon. His form blocked what little light there was, making the night seem darker. He hauled me and Billy out and dropped us on a gravel road.

Karl threw me over one shoulder. Billy tried to get to his feet. Karl kicked him in the ribs, sending Billy skidding ten feet over the stones. Casually, Karl walked past, dipped down and dragged the moaning, but otherwise pacified, Billy by the neck.

I didn't know where we were, other than somewhere in the country, presumably *my* country. It was prairie. Probably Manitoba, but if I'd been out long enough, it could've been Saskatchewan or the U.S. Wherever we were, I knew immediately *why*.

They'd taken us to a crossroad.

Manitoba's backways are crisscrossed by a grid of gravel roads that intersect every mile. Mile roads. Crossroads have a long history of mystic underpinnings; in modern folklore as well as old myth. Bluesman Robert Johnson sold his soul to the Devil at a crossroad. Suicides used to be buried at a crossroad with a stake in their heart to keep them from rising as vampires. The list goes on. Dark pacts. Dirty deeds. All done by night where two old roads crossed one another.

Most of what you've heard is true.

They're impossible to miss—the veil is thinner between crossroads, the Kingdom, and Beyond. I wasn't that senseless (yet).

Billy and I were shoved roughly to the ground while Marcus and Karl's bug-eating cultists dug a hole in the centre of the road. I supposed I should be thankful they weren't making us dig our own graves—Grannie's favoured punishment. Having to dig my own fucking grave *really* stuck in my craw. I wondered how many times she'd made Marcus plant himself when *he'd* been her apprentice.

I remembered weeping the first few times, sweat and tears stinging my eyes, cutting troughs through the dirt on my face. Wailing I was too young to die, that I didn't *want* to die. Grannie'd always answered the same way: "Want ain't got nothing to do with it."

She'd light a smoke, one of her hand-rolled Drum cigarettes with no filter, building it slowly and making me alternately glad of the delay, and anticipating more dread. She'd usually add while leaning on her shovel, "That hole ain't gonna fucking dig itself."

And I'd go back to work, choking on sobs and snot, trying to parse a world where a thirteen-year-old girl was forced to dig her own goddamned grave at necromancer-point.

Staring into Grannie's Grave Sight eyes when she told you to dig or die (and she could still make you dig after), I believed her. Every goddamned time she took me out to be buried, I believed I'd die. It didn't matter she'd always dug me out before. Whenever I went under the earth, to my heart, and bones, and marrow, I believed *this is the time I don't come back up.*

I had that old feeling again.

The cultists dug with picks and shovels, tearing up a country road that looked like it hadn't been maintained in a decade. They'd worked fast. The crossroad needed to be an active one. Looks aside, there was a real chance someone could stumble on us. Witnesses might give me and Billy a chance to escape, but far more likely, Karl would get a late night snack.

A grave dug by hand has power. Using a backhoe—or Frank, had he been there—would've been faster, but the sweat, the blisters, the blood, the *effort* of making that hole, and filling it, keeps things in the ground better left buried. Never thought *I'd* be the thing better left buried.

Frank couldn't sweat, and didn't tire. Easier into the ground means easier out. While the chuckleheads at the Church didn't know much, they knew that. Besides, Marcus had other plans for my composite man.

This was never how I saw myself going. I'd *been* buried alive. I'd always figured something new would take me out.

"It will," Summer said.

I wished I had Summer's confidence, this once. I wasn't dead yet, but my future looked bleak.

Karl stared down on me. He might've swam through a river of blood with how death clung to him. A swollen black tongue worried at flesh and sinew caught within his serrated teeth. A shovel full of earth struck me in the face. I spat dirt. The digger looked mortified (or terrified) that he'd hit Karl, too. Specks of dirt stuck to Karl's blood-tacky body.

"Sorry," the digger stammered.

Karl smiled wider, and licked a bit of the earth into his mouth.

"Let's see how you like going in the ground, bitch," Karl said to me.

I didn't see a coffin. They were going to plant me. While I was still alive. But I doubted they wanted me to stay alive for long.

Something wet dribbled on to my face, sliding over my lips and into my mouth. It was salty, sticky.

Blood. Karl's blood. Vampire blood.

He really was that stupid. I opened my mouth as far as my brutalized jaw would allow. Gulping everything he offered me. I felt it in my gut, sour and rancid like turned milk, waiting to make me sick. A thing like Karl. His blood could be useful. Just . . . not right now. If I used it to heal, they'd notice. If I tried to fight, we were outnumbered twenty to one.

Necromancers are always looking for a way to stretch their lives beyond nature. When you piss off as many dead people as I have, there's good reason not to rush into the Kingdom. A taste of vampire blood, and the power it gave might be too much temptation.

There was a sure way to live forever.

Or at least live until a hunter gets lucky, puts a stake in your heart, cuts your head off and stuffs it with garlic, and buries you in hallowed ground.

No thanks. I'd rather keep my apartment than a crypt.

The goon who'd hit me with the shovel of earth received the honour of wrapping me in a linen shroud. Karl shoved me into the open grave. I hit the ground, knocking the air from my lungs. I took another breath through the linen as a shovel of earth slapped my face, choking me. Billy landed beside me with a thud and a moan.

A phone rang. Judging from the ringtone, it was mine, and Lyssa was the caller.

Karl tossed the phone to me. "Go ahead. Take the call."

It had to be a trick. My tiny inner optimist said I could give her a message to give to Woj. My much heftier inner pessimist chimed in saying, "They gave you the phone because who the fuck are you gonna call?"

Hard to argue with that.

Summer cackled, as if she knew I'd break. *"You're going in the ground."*

I focused my will, shoving my sister aside. Things weren't so desperate I needed her company.

She was probably right. Karl hadn't been stupid to leave me my phone. I was bound. Who could I call? Frank? Giving me my phone wasn't stupidity, it was cruelty. One more torture piled on what they'd already inflicted, an *amuse-bouche* of what was left to come. Assuming I did get a call from someone willing to help, how could they? I didn't know where I was. We could be buried anywhere in the world.

Or outside it.

The call ended, going to voicemail before I could get a bare finger on the touchscreen. She called again. I managed to put the phone on speaker.

Lyssa couldn't help me. I answered anyway. This was probably the last time I'd hear her voice, or she'd hear mine.

"Hey, Lyss," I said, my voice sounding thin.

"Did I wake you?"

I ran with it. "Yeah, grabbing a nap at a friend's."

"Your *friend* Billy?"

Her voice rang with happiness for me, and I didn't want to disappoint her. "You caught me. I don't want to wake him." I'm about to be buried somewhere, Lyssa dear. Best case scenario, I was an hour from downtown, maybe two. More. How many square kilometres could be in that radius? Yeah, Lyssa would find me in time. Easy-peasy.

"I wanted to say thanks for setting everything up with the funeral."

I hadn't done anything. I doubted Tammy would've stepped in without mentioning I'd dropped that particular ball. There was a sharp, crisp knock that sounded grim as a funeral bell.

"That's Pastor Mark now. He said he needed to come over, finalize details and I wanted Tammy here with me. Talk soon?"

"Is—" I almost said Woj "—Mr. Wojciechowski there?"

"He is."

"If they disagree . . ." How in every hell could I still help her? ". . . do what he says, okay?"

"Why would they disagree?"

"Humour me."

"You sound all weird. Are you drunk?"

A door opened, across the miles, and the crackle of a bad connection, I heard Marcus's voice.

"Hello, Alyssa. Tammy. Wonderful to meet you both. Shall we begin?"

Karl stretched out his hand, elongated like a shadow following the sun, and snatched my phone. He ended the call, snapping his thumb through the device.

Marcus had Lyssa. And if Woj was there, they'd both be dead. Or worse, turned into bug-eaters like Karl and Corinne. I hoped Woj would fight. That he'd have Lyssa's back. The supernatural terrified Woj, but he was no coward.

He was mostly afraid of me. And without me there to egg him on, Woj would run. If he could. If he wasn't already dead.

"Cover her," Karl said turning away.

Shovel after shovel of earth cascaded over me.

"Karl," I tried to keep my voice steady. The effort made me wince. "See you real, real soon."

If you're buried alive, you're not going to claw, dig or punch yourself out of the ground, whether they put you in a coffin or not. I bit my lip and forced my breaths to be as infrequent and shallow as I could. It would give me a couple minutes. Not enough.

"Dead, dead, dead," Summer mused. *"Finally together."*

"See you on the other side," I said as much to Billy and Karl, as to my sister.

There was no other side. Karl had forced his blood on me. He'd fed on me. If the Redeemers managed to end Christophe before I suffocated, if they hadn't already, I'd be a thrall to Karl, and a servant to Marcus and his clowns. Best case scenario right now: I'd die before Christophe.

I closed my eyes. I wasn't here. I was in bed. The new moon was a week away. There was no reason for me to be hearing my neverborn sister. I walked myself through the steps to banish Summer and control my fear.

Use your Grave Sight. Refocusing my vision, I could see, clear as a digital countdown, how much air I had left. And it wasn't enough.

Don't scream. Save your air for the son of a bitch that put you down here.

I wasn't sure if going in the ground without a box would be better, or worse. This was hardly the first time I've been planted. I never knew when she'd do the burying. Because necromancers can hide from the living if they want, there were times I was buried under the noon sun, while people grieved for a dead loved one not twenty feet from where Grannie had forced me to dig my grave. After two years, Grannie stopped the torture. I think she just got tired of the digging.

It was always the same. You go into the ground. You try not to soil yourself. You do. You gag on the stink. The shame. Then you get beyond it. You deal, or you die. Simple.

I wasn't worried about that happening. Yet. I wouldn't live long enough to care about voiding myself. There was no one waiting to pull me from the ground. No one had a stolen last breath to bring me back after I'd suffocated, as Grannie had done with me, and I'd done with Karl.

Thinking of Karl, my heart sped up; a staccato jackhammer against my ribs. I wished him an end at which Christophe and McCoy would shake their heads and say, "Was that necessary?"

Oh yes.

I covered my nose and mouth as best I could without disturbing the shroud, and squinted my eyes shut. Before long my ears filled with dirt and I couldn't hear the hiss of the shovels sliding into earth or the patter of my burial. The fall chill seeped from the earth into my skin. I welcomed it until I no longer noticed it. The only sensation was the vibration of shovelfuls of earth. And blackness.

Cheap bastards weren't even gonna give me a coffin. *Somehow, some way, I'm coming back for you, Karl.*

Chapter Twenty-Six

Buried. Panic.

No, covered; not yet buried.

They expected me to kick and scream, or at least, they *hoped* for it if they didn't expect to see it, and I gave them a show. Pride doesn't matter when you're being buried alive. Keeping your head does.

They were planting me with Billy. My not-entirely-fake struggles would help mask the fact I wanted us to remain in physical contact. I didn't know how he planned to escape this, but if he could summon Bear, assuming the shuck had survived Frank's attack, I wanted to make sure the black dog dug us both up, and not just his master. Keeping contact with Billy would also, in a pinch, allow me to keep going longer. If I had to steal a breath, or heartbeat from him, despite our pact, I'd be glad of the option. Inge might make me regret doing it later—assuming I lived long enough to see later.

Right now, it wasn't looking promising.

My hand brushed Billy's arm; he jerked it away. The prick. I was trying to help him.

"*No you're not,*" Summer said. "*You're trying to bury him in the dark.* Just. Like. Me."

I couldn't argue with her without swallowing grave dirt or making my splitting headache worse.

I pawed around for Billy's hand again. The weight of earth above us made it hard to move, but I found him. I wrapped my hand around his wrist and dug my fingernails into his skin. I slowed his heartbeat. Stole his breaths. Fed them back to him at a trickle.

His struggles eased.

I wasn't sure what would've been worse: putting me in the box, or leaving me bare in the ground. In fresh-turned earth, we had a different problem. Its weight would suffocate us if we didn't choke first. Karl wanted me turned, so he had to plant me. Three days to return is traditional, not set in stone. It's more to ensure the person you bury does, in fact, die. If you dig them up and they're alive, you have to bury them again.

And who needs *that* hassle?

I opened my eyes and turned on my Grave Sight. There was no light. No moon. No headlamps. They tamped the turned earth, as if they were sinking a fence post.

My shroud kept most of the dirt away, but it wasn't perfect. I could sense with my Grave Sight. Breathing, however, proved more difficult. Weight crushed me, and each breath threatened to be my last. Dirt cascaded into my hollow.

I couldn't *see* Billy. Holding his hand, I had a sense of how he was doing. Not good.

Billy was tough, maybe as tough as he claimed, but this terror was different for him. He clawed out of his shroud. He had dirt in his mouth and no air in his lungs. Not good.

He tried using his death aura on me, trying to take my life to keep his body running when it should be dying. He'd been trained further than he'd led me to believe. His admission in the trunk hadn't been bravado.

"*No. Only what you'd meant to do to him,*" Summer said.

I let the comment pass. I didn't have the energy to waste arguing with my sister. Not if I wanted to stay alive. Especially when she was right. And the more I considered it, the more I needed to keep Billy alive, too. He wasn't a perfect ally, but he was on my side. I couldn't say that about many people—living or dead.

And the Marks had Lyssa. Probably Tammy, too. I'd tried to keep this shit from them. And now they were in it deeper than I was in the ground. Tammy and I might not see eye to eye, but she didn't deserve what would be going on at Redeemer headquarters. Nobody did.

Help was thin on the ground. I've been backed into corners before and fought my way out. I'd had my gear—and Frank—to rely on, or Grannie. Or Woj. Now there was just me. And Summer.

Thanatomancy was not my strength as a necromancer. I'd be lucky to give Billy a cold by touching him and trying to kill him. I could steal breaths, but he didn't have many those left. At least there was still life in the earth. I stretched my death aura as far as I could, trying to push it away from Billy. There were rodents. Worms. Microbes. Small lives. It was something.

I stopped breathing, and swallowed their deaths instead of air, like a whale feeding off krill. And I even sent a few breaths Billy's way.

It wasn't a perfect solution. Planting me in the crossroad meant I didn't have much living earth to use, and there was far less inside the road. Soon, I'd expend what the ground had to give. Scorched earth. Nothing would ever live here again. And Billy would die, and I would die. And when they dug me out, and I was a vampire, many, many more would die.

Billy tensed. His heart sped up. He wanted to gasp, and I forced his mouth shut. It cost more life than I'd have liked, but the sooner he died, the sooner I died. If I let him go, his spirit might be enough to free me, but then what? The option, once discarded, felt so appealing now. Baby steps into darkness. Cross this line, then the next, and before I knew it, I'd be no different than Grannie.

Or Marcus.

Summer could talk to me. Maybe she could talk to Billy, too. Tell him to call his shuck. Assuming Bear was still alive.

Summer?

A naked figure stepped from the darkness, glowing silver with moonlight despite being underground. It was me.

And it wasn't me.

The body was mine. Only a small freckle dotting her left breast was different than mine. It was Summer as she would've been—had she lived to be born.

"*I'm here, Winter.*" She spread her arms wide. "*Welcome to the crossroad, sister.*"

Will you help? Can you make Billy call the shuck?

Summer glowed eerily in the moonlight. Reflected star patterns twinkled over my twin's naked body.

I wondered whether getting Summer to convince Billy to call his shuck was the best idea. She hated Bear. He terrified her. Her fear made sense, as much as I hated to admit it. The dog's purpose was to bring lost spirits home to the Beyond, when it wasn't dragging the living there. I guess I wasn't too keen on relying on Bear's help, either.

"*Why should I? You never care. Never listen. You always lie.*"

I've been a terrible sister, I know.

Summer's silence hung there, agreeing with me.

You won't just be helping me, you'll be helping Billy—

"*You don't care about him.*"

Marcus has Lyssa.

Reality settled in, and I could've wept under my shroud. I knew what he'd do. Not being in the know was little protection. I wasn't sure which fate would be worse: Lyssa's, who wouldn't understand, or Woj, who would. Their terror would be candy to Marcus. It was too much to hope they'd die quickly, or well.

The only thing Marcus's sadism gave me to work with was *time*. Time to find a way out of the ground, and after all these years, to bring the payback. To him, to Grannie. To bury my past.

I exhaled as I took her hand. I couldn't see my breath mist from my mouth. Instead, Summer formed an "o" with her lips and rocked her head back and forth. A cloud drifted lazily from her mouth and she giggled. A curious, sharp pain stabbed my chest. I put my hand over my left breast. My heart had stopped. Summer mimicked my motion. Her eyes grew distant and she made a contented moan.

"Come walk with me, sis," Summer said.

I shook my head and slumped. *I'm dying.*

"Everyone's dying, you're just doing a better job right now."

You want me dead?

"I want us together," Summer put her hand around my shoulders and steadied me, pressing my body against hers.

I'd prefer us to be together and alive, I said.

Her eyes glittered. It made me worry. We were still at the crossroad. Wishes and words had to be carefully formed here. There could be unexpected—and unpleasant—consequences to a stray phrase.

Summer pressed her lips to my forehead. I expected them to be cold. Cold as my name. Cold as death. They weren't. My sister's touch burned. Burned like liniment. She wrapped her spectral arms around me. Her legs twinned with mine.

"Okay," Summer said. *"I'll talk to Billy."*

I blinked and the slight motion allowed a trail of dirt to infiltrate my shroud and slide over my eyes. I hadn't expected that.

"It's enough that you care for someone to weep over them, even if it isn't me."

Summer *should* have no trouble talking to him. I supposed the question was: would he have enough sense to listen? Her words washed over Billy's consciousness. He'd been beaten, bloodied, and buried. He was only alive because I fed him stolen life.

If he couldn't call Bear . . .

"*You will* not *abandon him.*"

Keeping him alive could kill me.

"*Then we'll have something in common. Maybe you'll talk to me without needing something,* then."

Harsh, but fair.

I kept feeding Billy's lifeline. Stretching my thanatomancy, trying to pull in as much life as I could, but I already felt the lack. We'd poisoned so much soil larger living things would run from this crossroad. I'd hoped Marcus would've left some Redeemers watching the spot to welcome newly undead me into the fold. If they'd left anyone behind, they were staying far enough from the grave I couldn't find them. I couldn't chance using Karl's blood, either. If he'd stuck around, he'd notice, and spent as I was, he might be able to stop me. I could do this without him.

Now *would* be the time the Redeemers decided to do something right. I bit back a snort. Because things had been going so fucking well for *me* lately.

I couldn't hear what Summer said to Billy. I got impressions, as if overhearing a whispered conversation in a crowded room. Snippets bubbled to the surface here and there in the silent shallows between my heartbeats, but her words, other than "Bear," "shuck," and "crossroad" were lost to the grave.

Time had no meaning under the earth. After minutes, hours, or days, Billy made the call. Cerberus's name being spoken from Billy's lips sent a ripple through my Grave Sight, like a shimmering mirage on a hot prairie day, and it echoed in my ears like the tolling of a bell.

The shuck would come. It *had* to come. I'd felt the power in Billy's summons. The only thing preventing Bear from coming would be the black dog's final death. Somehow, that wasn't comforting. I'd seen what Frank had done to him. It might've happened already.

Sitting back and waiting to die wasn't my strong suit. It felt like I was stuck in rush hour traffic. I'd take a longer route if it meant *moving*. Stillness was death. Movement was life. For my life, I couldn't think of a move to make.

Karl's blood burned in my belly. I wasn't dead yet—close enough it wanted me to make the change. I wasn't sure what that meant for me. Or for Christophe, who'd have to die for Karl to become a progenitor vampire. I didn't care if Christophe died anymore, other than Karl would go on a feeding orgy and leave me with a much bigger vampire problem. For a complete prick, Christophe practiced his nature with restraint.

It was possible I could tap into Karl's blood and use it. He couldn't possibly be dim enough to ignore that, in the same way Billy's summoning of Bear had resonated to me.

I wondered if Marcus had heard the call. Would Frank be waiting topside to have another—final—round with the shuck? Had Woj escaped? Had he taken Lyssa with him? Too much to hope for. I'd been buried enough times to be a realist. As much as I loved the idea of my funeral director coming to dig me up, our best chance was Bear, or nothing.

"Done," she said. *"And thank you, Winnie."*

When she said it, I didn't hate the name. Then, we *merged*. There was no other way to describe it. Without Summer to hold me I dropped to the ground in the crossroad. My mind was clear as my body convulsed. It was as if I watched myself from a distance.

Headlights barrelled down the dirt road. Distance and clarity disappeared as I snapped back to awareness. Adrenaline flooded my body. My heart exploded back to beating. I pushed myself to my feet. There was enough time for headlights to light me up like a halo. Not time to run. No time to dive out of the way.

"Watch and learn, sister," Summer said.

I tried to put my hands over my head; to clench my eyes shut. Summer wouldn't allow it. Instead, I passed right through a car. Or the car passed right through me.

Tires bit into the gravel. The hearse skidded, caught a rut and slid sideways right through our spirits. Brake lights lit up the road, red as hell.

Underground, as the microbial life dwindled, there was something else in my Grave Sight. Something blazing red. New death. And blood staining the parched earth, and following the call of my thanatomancy, that spent life flowing to me. As my power touched the blood, I had a vision of topside. I heard the muffled *whumps* of gunfire. Cries of pain. Anger. Hate. Fear. The concentration of death was caustic, and at the same time, my heart raced like I'd mainlined Red Bull.

I'd looked at Woj many times with my Grave Sight. I'd never seen him like this: a wild man. A berserker. A warrior. And as soon as I saw that, I saw who'd inspired this change: Inge. She blazed against the Kingdom's black like a full moon on a cloudless sky; silver, cold, and merciless. Death personified. I knew that wasn't right. She wasn't death, merely its instrument. Its chooser. And she'd chosen the Redeemers to die.

The Redeemers died and died as Woj fired. Out of bullets, he hurled his gun at a cowering parishioner and charged drawing a knife. An aura of death filled Woj, with a sense of invincibility as he did Inge's will. It was false. No matter how much he'd wanted to avoid my world, there was no helping him out of Graveside now. If that bitch got Woj killed—even for the price of *my* freedom— she wouldn't be the only one choosing death.

There was a growl and the sound of digging. Bear had found

us. Summer dragged me back underground, cramming my spirit back in my body. I gasped, swallowing dirt.

My thanatomancy might not affect the shuck, or it might. I couldn't say for sure. While I'd heard a fair bit about the black dogs, I'd never tangled with one. Few survived such encounters, and the tales were mostly second-hand, or pure fabrications. I doubted my death aura would be enough to kill him, but I didn't want him to associate me with pain or hurt. He might only dig me out to kill me.

The timing was the tricky part. Shutting down the aura before it touched Bear, while still allowing us to eat enough life not to suffocate.

Bear grew closer, and his strangled whine, and Summer's presence, were gone. That was the sign. If Bear was close enough for her to run off, he was close enough to hurt. I had to hope he was close enough to get me and Billy out of the ground while we still had breath.

I cut the aura. Blind, the weight of the grave was heavier. No sensation, other than dying. My lungs compressed as I drew on the last air I had left.

Billy's grip tightened against my wrist as his air supply was cut off as well. I dug my fingers deeper into him. Pain was the only sensation I could give him to combat the fear.

I didn't know where Bear was. I stopped caring. I didn't know where I was. I swore Summer beckoned me to join her. I was so close to the Kingdom.

I just had to take her hand. Sisters and we'd never been so close.

I reached out.

Chapter Twenty-Seven

My fingers slipped through Summer's and caught Bear's mane. The shuck surged out of the ground, dragging Billy—and me—from the grave.

Topside, Woj was still alive, panting with exhaustion as he leaned on a long black hearse. The idling car was a little the worse for wear, riddled with dents and bullet holes. At least we had wheels. Inge was there, looking frostier than normal in the chill night. Bear licked Billy's face joyfully, his eyes on me and full of blame.

Staggering, breathless, away from the grave, cold air peppered my skin with gooseflesh. I hunched over like an old woman, my shuffling steps and beaten, tired body would do little to dispute that image.

The sky held a peculiar dark and quiet in the country. A solitude someone who lives in a city can never fathom. Where were the street lights' reflected halos? Where was the noise? Out here, any sounds were foreign. Frightening. Light was at the stingy moon's discretion, and pinpoints here and there, like stars, marking the farmyards. After being buried alive, I was glad for any light smiling upon me.

Most of the cultists were dead. One still cowered by a rusted white van. He was going to pay. I was glad they'd left me one.

Bear growled at him every time he inched toward his feet, and he dropped, prostrate, before the shuck.

The cultists' spirits only hung around for moments. I tried to grab as many as I could. Billy, too. A few slipped away from him as I wrapped myself in spirit armour, using them to fuel my exhausted body like I had at St. Andrew's.

There was no time for morals. For recrimination. For cursing that I wasn't so different from Grannie after all. Marcus had Lyssa. He had Frank. Soon he'd have my city. Compact be damned. I ate the spirits, burning them to heal the damage the Redeemers had done to me.

I asked Billy, "You gonna be okay?"

"I'll be fine. Bear'll lend me strength."

He *did* look better already—cuts and bruises fading. One thing in our favour: no thralls had turned after death. Which meant Christophe still "lived." We'd still be outnumbered when we got to the shadow church. If we could turn Frank back to our side, and free the vampire—and McCoy, too—I liked our odds. If we couldn't do all of those, matters were worse.

But first . . .

A hand stopped me before I'd taken two steps—Woj's, judging from the pinky ring.

"Winter . . . are you okay?"

"Fine." I shoved him away and pointed at the living cultist. "Better than he'll be."

I gestured with my hand, puppeteering two corpses to their hands and knees.

Woj jumped back as the corpses rose. "Christ!"

"No," Inge said. "They are merely animate, not *risen*."

I walked the corpses into the grave they'd dug for me and Billy and dismissed their animation. They fell like discarded toys.

"They were alive once," Woj said.

I whirled on him. "So was Marcus."

"Winter, don't do this."

His eyes pleaded as much as his voice. I ignored both. "They made their choice."

Woj didn't approve, but outnumbered, and overpowered, he let it go.

The cultist whimpered, leaking as much snot and tears as blood. Woj looked uncomfortable. We needed him on board, which meant he had to believe that any crazy, evil-looking thing Billy and I did to get to Marcus was for the greater good. It became hard to see that line at times, and I couldn't blame him. Shit. My own line seemed so far behind me lately, I didn't know where it was—and I'd drawn it.

"No sympathy, Woj." I pointed at my face. "He'd have done worse given the option."

"He *has* done worse," Inge said.

I wasn't sure if her approving tone was reserved for the cultists' deeds or my desire for revenge. Knowing what she was, I wasn't surprised she knew, either. She needed to see into a soul to see if it was worthy to die, and worthy of whatever version of Valhalla or Hel Beyond had to offer. I'd never visited either, and I wanted to keep it that way. Hopefully getting her boss back to her whole would keep me off her list of chosen.

Woj dropped his eyes to the side and sloughed off his jacket, handing it to me. I accepted and zipped it up. The coat smelled strongly of wood smoke, with a hint of sweaty male musk. Not unpleasant. Homey, rather. I do spend a lot of time around corpses.

"Karl?" I asked.

Inge shook her head.

"Disappeared the second we rolled up," Woj said.

I walked the rest of dead Redeemers into the grave. They pulled dirt in over themselves. I kicked dirt over their bodies, wishing I could do more.

"Let us leave this place," Inge said.

"Agreed," Woj said.

He didn't sound nervous any more, which surprised me, although there was a hint of exhaustion in his voice. He stared, fascinated, at Inge, and I worried he'd found a new supernatural woman—one he *should* be terrified of, and wasn't. I didn't like sharing. I was still surprised by the pang of jealousy. I'd kept Frank for my own when Grannie had told me to destroy him. I was as pissed that Marcus had taken something—someone—from me, as anything else the bastard had done.

Now I worried Inge was doing the same. Only Woj was a person. If he wanted to waste his life making death for her . . . I could argue his choice's merits, but I had no right to complain. Frank hadn't been given that choice. I'd kept him existing after he'd been made, and strung him along with the hope I could find a way to end him, when it'd been in my hands all along. I was as bad as the cult who'd made him. I'd free him from Marcus's control and I'd let him know I could end him, and if he took that news without killing me, and still wanted me to do it, I'd give him peace.

I wondered if pining after Inge would make Woj drink more, or less.

Billy shot a dirty look at Woj. Typical. It was perfectly fine for him to put moves on me and Inge, and he couldn't stand the idea someone else might want to be with "his" woman.

"Night like this has as much light to see by as the Pope's dick," Billy muttered, scanning the sky.

"It'll get darker," I said. "If we don't find Marcus. And soon."

We needed to find a way back to Marcus's shadow church. So I could burn the fucking place out of existence.

"Simple," Billy said. "You know where his bug-eaters hang their hats."

"Not simple." I shook my head. "We weren't in the Redeemers' basement. Not really. There was something off about where they took us, and how they got us there."

Inge asked, "Off?"

"Here, and not here. I didn't get a good enough look to figure out how Marcus did it. Felt *like* the Kingdom, but we weren't *in* the Kingdom. Even Billy would've sensed it if we'd been taken Beyond."

Billy muttered, "Even Billy," before adding, "Bear can find it, wherever it is. Ain't nobody can hide from a shuck. We'll find them, but I'm not sure we're enough to finish them."

"You're not," I said. Frank had messed us both up solo. "No offense."

He grunted in admission. "Bear'll take me along through the crossroads." He pointed at Woj and nodded towards me and Inge. "He won't survive. Not sure about you two. It ain't pleasant."

"I'd rather not chance it," Inge said. "I have enemies on the other side I'd rather not face again."

Woj ran a hand through his hair. "Me neither."

"We can't take the time to get to either St. Andrew's or my necrotech stash to help even the odds."

"Yeah, we need to be there, like, yesterday," Billy said.

"I opened the vaults," Inge said, gesturing at a coffin secured in the hearse. "Given the circumstances, I imagine Mister Bones will give you all a deal when he tallies the cost."

I snorted. "The cost of his own rescue? He owes us whatever you took plus interest."

With a sniff, Inge said, "I'm not his accountant."

She slid the coffin part way out of the hearse, and opened the viewing port to reveal Mummy wrappings among them. How rich *was* McCoy?

I'd have to make Summer remind me to up my fee the next time he offered me a job.

She laughed. *"If he exists long enough to offer you another job."*

Also inside the coffin: a black spear, with glowing red runes engraved the length of the blade and flowing down its haft. Inge took it before I could. In its stead she passed me a knife made from a sharpened spine.

Woj got a set of aviator goggles with red lenses. Grave Sight goggles—they'd allow him to see once we crossed into the Kingdom. He put them on and shuddered. His knees buckled and I thought he'd collapse. I reached out to steady him but he shook his head. I couldn't see his eyes through the lenses, only skeletal sockets.

Billy received an AK-47 made from bones and a case of tombstone bullets. I'd never seen a fully automatic bone gun. Billy was a good shot, but his weapon worried me. "Accidents happen." "Collateral damage." "Friendly fire." Lots of chances he could make my city his.

We'd be okay if we had to traverse the Kingdom, and we were armed if things went south. We needed to leave the living world for wherever Marcus was hiding. We swaddled ourselves and dressed in silence. The Dead Man's Clothes and mummy wrappings would help keep things off our tail once we crossed over into the Kingdom, and with luck, we'd still be dressed when we faced Marcus.

Inge's gaze lingered on the living cultist. "What will we do with this one? I sense he's fated a death with purpose."

The cultist shrank from her words, murmuring useless prayers under his breath.

"Yeah, I've got a purpose for him," Billy said. "This piece of shit is gonna grease the wheels."

The cultist shook clasped hands toward me, in supplication. "No. Please. No. I'll do anything."

Billy smiled as Bear dragged him towards the crossroad. "All we need you to do is die."

I nodded. "He dies as Bear opens the way—"

"Your sister pushes us all through," Inge finished.

Billy whistled. "We get a free ride."

"Timing is gonna be important," I said.

"We don't have time to walk the shadow ways," Billy said. "Not if we want to stop Marcus."

Woj asked, "What if we drive there?"

"No car could survive. Entropy'll seize it before we get through two jumps."

"Even a hearse? This car has put more bodies in the ground than any of you." He inclined his head towards Inge. "Except for you."

Woj was on to something. I'd never tried to take my car into the Kingdom physically, but I figured any vehicle a necromancer drove would've soaked up enough death it could make the trip. A hearse should work, too.

I nodded. "Worth a try."

"Great," Billy said. "At least the car has room for us *and* our body bags."

"I didn't bring any," Inge said, and I couldn't tell if she was serious or playing at deadpan. "I plan for success."

The cultist jerked his arm away from Billy, and elbowed him in the ribs. His eyes sought a way out. There was none. Inge's fingers closed over the man's shoulder like an eagle's talons and her grip forced him to his knees. Blood seeped through his shirt, painting her nails.

Billy muttered, "I would've had him."

"We are short on time," Inge said, "and you are long on life."

"Get the fuck in," Billy said. He gave the cultist a deserved, and unnecessary, punch in the nose, which drew a reproachful glance from Inge.

The man cowered.

I asked, "What's your name?"

He blinked, as if surprised I'd bothered to ask. "I'm not supposed to say."

"We're a bit beyond 'supposed to,' don't you think?"

He nodded slowly. "Travis. Travis Beach."

"Well Travis, we *are* going to kill you. It's only a matter of how." He whimpered and I worried I was going to lose him. I gave him a good once over with my Grave Sight. *There we are.* He was sick. Terminal. I wondered if he knew. Wondered if that was why Pastor Mark's rhetoric had won him over. In the end *why* didn't matter. Not to me. "This can be over—" I snapped my fingers "— quick."

"Or?" he blubbered.

"We run you down in the hearse and drag your body and spirit through the shadow crossroads, burning you like fuel until we find your boss. If we're done with you then, we'll let you die."

He didn't like either choice. When I was ready to just murder him then and there, he said, "Quick. Oh, Jesus, please, make it quick."

"Deal," I said and spat on my palm, holding it out. Travis did the same. We shook on it. "Now get in the fucking grave."

Billy wasn't satisfied with my promise. I hadn't told him thanatomancy was, generally speaking, not my strong suit. Whether he knew or not, he wanted insurance, and a modicum of revenge. He splayed Travis's arms wide and sank a coffin nail through each palm. Those nails ensured Travis would stay put until he died—and after. Standing on the cultists' bodies already had Travis's head and shoulders above the grave and overlooking the road behind us. I guess Billy wanted insurance in case I couldn't flip the switch in the cultist's brain.

I couldn't fault him. Travis still looked as if he'd been betrayed. He had no idea what awaited him Beyond. Did he expect to arrive in a verdant land full of singing cherubs and be reunited with his childhood dog? I wished I'd be able to see his surprise when he was proven wrong.

"Okay," I said. "Quit torturing him. Let's do this."

We piled into the hearse. The doors slamming sounded an awful lot like a coffin being closed.

Chapter Twenty-Eight

We backed up to take a run at the crossroad. It would be our first gate into the shadow paths that only shucks were supposed to walk.

Help me, sister.

"Why should I?" Summer asked. It was the first time I'd been happy to hear her voice in over a decade. "So you can leave me behind again?"

Never. I meant it. *I didn't know. I didn't understand what you had done. I was too young. Too scared. I'll never ignore you again.*

"Prove it."

How can I make it up to you?

It was a little creepy feeling my dead sister smile within me.

"Give me your body," she said, "and I'll take you where you need to go."

I'll be wanting it back.

"Of course you will." It was hard to tell if Summer was being sarcastic or resentful. "You ask my help, but you still don't trust me."

Think of it as, "trust but verify."

"You are Grannie's creature."

That hurt, but I bit it back. She was right. *When we're through, I get my body back. Marcus is mine.*

I knew I wasn't helping my case, demanding vengeance against Marcus, but it was *my* life he'd attacked. Summer had to see that.

"If that's what you wish. That's what will be done."

Done.

Our Bargain struck, my spirit drifted away. Not pulled screaming and ruined as Marcus's had been when Grannie and I had first taken him apart. It was as if I'd found an escape hatch and the gradual invasion of Summer's consciousness simply . . . displaced me. I'd fought my whole life against my other half. And here I was, acquiescing. Giving over my body to her.

"Then why are you terrified?" Summer laughed.

It was a dangerous trilling sound, and I worried, mad. I could only hope she planned on keeping our bargain.

"No worries, little sister. I keep my promises."

That statement wasn't encouraging. I remembered the promises Summer had made when I ignored her. Now I had a taste of being her; a thin candle in a mind's window. I could see, hear—everything but touch. At least she'd have a damned hard time drinking *me* away. I needed her. She had to be happy or Winter might go to sleep forever.

"Would that be terrible?" Summer asked.

For me!

"If you say so. I know how conflicted you are about our life." She buckled the seatbelt. I supposed it couldn't hurt.

Bullshit I'm conflicted.

"Why, then, do you drug yourself into submission whenever the dead moon rises?"

Because of what you were going to do to us to save your skin.

"Ignorance, sister, doesn't become you."

And you seem to forget who was there.

"Do I now? I saved our life."

If I'd been in control of my body, I'd have gripped the seat. Billy was saying something to Inge. I didn't want to listen.

At what cost? You were going to let Marcus—

"You're a fool. I wouldn't let Marcus do anything. Without me, we wouldn't be speaking now."

That would be a relief.

"*Would it? Do you long for the black? What lure does the Kingdom have for you? Do you want to give it all up to live among the shades?*"

I didn't know how to answer her question. Secretly, I worried the answer was yes. Oh, I had Frank. And Lyssa. No other *real* friends. No lovers for more than a night or two. What *was* keeping me here?

Lyssa was still trapped with Marcus—Tammy, too—and no doubt they weren't enjoying any sense of hospitality. Marcus's cult still had Frank under their thrall.

"*Don't,*" she said.

Don't what?

"*Don't feel guilty.*"

Can't help it. You and I both know what Marcus is capable of.

"*Do you?*" Summer asked aloud, glancing at my reflection in the rearview mirror.

I thought of what Frank could do. And how the woman I'd viewed as a mother, father, grandparent all rolled into one had set me up to be kidnapped. To be tortured and abused. To be killed in order for her walk the earth again in my body.

Yeah, I figure I do.

"*He has no idea what we're capable of.*"

What was still keeping me here? *I'm too stubborn to die. Yet.*

"*Then listen to me. Stop wasting your body. If you die you take me with you, and I've spent enough time in the Kingdom already. Three nights a month is not enough to live.*"

It was among the hardest things I've ever done. Hard as it was, it had to be done right. I stopped where I stood. The words had to be spoken aloud.

I'm sorry, Summer.

"*Was that so hard?*"

Woj stopped the car. I couldn't see Travis in the headlights. Not sure how far we'd backed up, enough to get a head of steam,

I supposed. Woj revved the engine. There was no sense in being quiet; Marcus would know I'd survived.

"*Go,*" Billy demanded.

Woj looked over his shoulder at the hunter, and his eyes were grimmer than I'd ever seen, including when Inge'd whammied him with her mushrooms. "I deal with the dead every day. Every person, good or bad, is something unique gone from our world, and I treat them with respect, regardless who they might've been. I hope you get the ends you've forced on others. All of you."

Ouch.

"*I'm sure he didn't mean you,*" Summer said.

"You better hope your car holds up," Billy said. "Or you'll be meeting your end today."

Woj flashed Billy, and presumably the rest of us, his middle finger, and we shot forward. I closed my eyes, trying to ignore Billy's muttered ramblings of vengeance, and juvenile dick measuring with Woj. I had to find my thanatomancy and time this right.

Too soon, and we'd drive over an already dead Travis and into a mass grave, not the shadow crossroads. Too late, and Travis would splatter all over the hearse. Which, to be fair, *might* still open the way.

"Winter," Woj said.

"*You're talking to Summer.*"

Woj flashed a worried look.

Almost got him.

"*Almost,*" Summer repeated.

Through gritted teeth, Woj muttered, "Sooner would be better."

Travis hit my death aura. I opened my eyes, and the road blazed in my Grave Sight. I could see the fear in Travis's eyes in the split-second before he disappeared below the hood of the car, slid past the grill and out of sight. I held that dying brain, as if it were a toothpick between a thumb and two forefingers, and I snapped it.

Travis died instantly.

It was a bumpy ride. Woj turned on the radio.

Soft, peaceful classical music of an unknown-to-me vintage filled the car. It wouldn't ramp us up for a fight, but if it kept Woj calm, and his head in the game and not a bottle, I'd take it.

I'd never been to this place tucked away between our world, the Kingdom, and Beyond. I had no idea what opening the windows would do. I had no idea if keeping them closed would keep us safe, either.

Summer?

"You are safe," she whispered. Her voice, while quiet, didn't hold the same timidity it had in the past. *"For now."*

Unspoken, and just as clear was: and not for long.

We'd kill that corpse again when it woke up.

Bear alternated between pressing his head against the passenger side window, and the air vent. It might be better for the shuck to have his head outside to follow the scent to the shadow church. It wouldn't be better for us.

In the same way the Kingdom reflected the living world, the shadow ways looked like the country roads where Karl tried to finish me and Billy. I could feel his blood in my gut, and through it, feel him out there. Somewhere. In a night that stretched forever, only the hearse's headlights gave away what lurked on either side of our path.

A good thing. *Stairway to Heaven, Highway to Hell.* There were no stars here. No moon. Only night. And fog. At times, the mist cleared enough we could see images in the afterglow of the headlights. On one side, it looked like still water, reflecting the black sky, yet somehow I knew it to be darker, deeper. On the other, a fire that gave no light, no heat. No comfort. Only pain.

A perfect resting place for Marcus.

"Or you," Summer said.

She was right.

Out beyond our vision, something howled, and the hairs on the back of my neck stood on end. I knew that cry. A shuck. Not Bear. And it wasn't alone. A howling chorus shrieked in answer. I glanced behind us. Eyes, reflected red in our taillights, paced the hearse, bodies hidden. They grew in number with every crossroad we passed.

The shucks moved like living gloom, disappearing in and out of the fog and dark.

Bear growled, softly, almost inaudibly, and the shucks fell away and didn't reappear. Billy patted his partner.

"Good job."

I didn't trust any of them. Without Frank along I had to hope each would keep the others honest. Better behaviour through paranoia.

Travis's spirit clung to the car as we howled through the Kingdom; a spiritual hood ornament.

The cultist's tattered remnant of existence billowed in the wind, our motion distending his spiritual remains. His howling was deafening over the hearse's engine. Travis's final moments were going to be painful. I'd promised him no physical pain. Our bargain hadn't said anything about after.

It was a distinction Grannie would've made, and I didn't like that such word splitting came easily to me. I was no hero, for all that I kept worse things in the ground, and put worse folks than me there, too. It wouldn't be long before a better person than me got screwed over by something I'd done—if it hadn't happened already—and it would be my turn.

It had probably already happened. I've killed enough people one of those dead enemies must've left behind a loved one to come gunning for me. Maybe they'd find their way Graveside, learn enough to take me down. Maybe I'd take a bullet in the back of the head at an ATM. Every necromancer knows: death comes for us all. No matter how much we fight it, or refuse to admit it. Only a matter of time.

I worried something had broken in Woj. His fear didn't seem gone; rather, managed. A side effect from Inge's gift. Knowing how he was with booze, he was probably addicted to berserker mushrooms now. I wondered if he'd get sick of being used, even by my relatively soft hand. Too much contact. Too much familiarity. My mystique was being burned away with every moment we spent together in the car. I both liked, and hated, the realization. Maybe we could become real friends, finally, if he lost his fear.

And if anyone in the car could ensure my body disappeared, it was the man who owned a crematorium.

It was hard to concentrate on good thoughts, especially now, when all I wanted was two kinds of revenge, one hot and flashy for my recent beatings, one cold and slow for Marcus's part in making the necromancer's life *my* life. Marcus waited at road's end, and while Grannie may have given the order, he'd carried it out. He could've said no. He didn't have to be her creature.

"Neither did you," Summer reminded.

I wasn't.

"Sweet you believe so."

I said no to her plenty.

The fog coalesced into a humanoid shape, biting off my retort. The fog man rode on the air in our wake, its fingers misty tendrils clawing for Travis's spirit.

What the hell is that?

Summer asked Billy for me. He shrugged. "Damned if I know."

"You're the one who's been here before."

"Easy to walk the roads with a shuck and not get disturbed. What we're doing . . ."

"—will draw out Hunters," Inge finished.

As if on cue, I heard the piston scream of a horse tortured beyond endurance. Pounding hooves rang out against the road. A sword hissing from its scabbard somehow cut past the hearse's engine.

The Horseman had found us.

Chapter Twenty-Nine

P unch it," Billy yelled.

"What's your—" Woj's retort died on his lips when his eyes flickered to the rearview mirror and saw the Horseman. *"Shitshitshitshit."*

The hearse lurched forward as Woj dropped a gear. The Horseman closed. Fast.

Billy looked over his shoulder. "Does this fucking brute go over fifty?"

Despite being clad all in black, the Horseman somehow stood out from the darkness behind the hearse. As if he were so foul night recoiled from touching his edges.

Bear turned. A low growl building in his throat. He launched himself over the seat, landing in Billy's lap.

"Ow, fuck!" Billy yelled.

The shuck scrambled, pawing at Billy's chest, trying to get into the rear of the hearse. His every bark hit the wall between Summer and I like a hammer on a pane of glass. She'd run soon. Try to escape the shuck and Horseman both. If she did, we'd be stuck. Lost.

And dead.

"You're not gonna tangle with him again, goddamnit."

The shuck didn't seem to listen, still scrambling to escape the car. Billy couldn't hold Bear on his own and I couldn't help. I had to hold on to Summer, keep her in control. Keep her in my body. My spirit wanted her to rabbit as much as my brain didn't; it wanted her gone to rush into the vacuum she'd leave behind, and my body and soul would be together.

Billy had both hands on Bear's collar. The shuck had his rear legs against the back of the seat, straining. He was gonna take Billy with him.

"*Sit,*" Inge demanded, and the shuck stopped. Bear looked over his shoulder at the Ice Queen, whimpered, and his tail drooped between his legs. He looked ready to leap. "Now."

Bear eased his straining, and Billy roughly hauled him back over the seat. "We need you to chase Marcus's scent, not the Horseman."

Bear acquiesced. He let out one last howl I shuddered to hear, and clambered, silent, into the front seat.

"We're still being followed."

The shucks were back. Bad to worse. They came out of the shadows, howling and following on the Horseman's heels.

Bear growled.

"Jump coming," Billy said.

The shucks nipped at the Horseman as if obeying Bear's orders. The Hunter barely slowed, but he *did* slow.

"Try and lose him at the next crossroad."

"Here's hoping," Billy said. "Got a horseshoe up your ass?"

The Horseman scythed his sword in a wide arc, cleaving a shuck in two. But not before the shuck crunched down on the Horseman's foreleg. They collapsed in a heap.

"Good work, Bear," Billy said.

We jumped. When my vision cleared, I could see we'd lost the shucks, not the Horseman. *He* was still right on our tail. His sword slashed at the car, metal shearing through metal. He drew a pistol longer than my forearm and cocked it. It sounded like "doom."

Woj jerked the wheel of the hearse. Its tail end slid and broadsided the Horseman. His horse legs gave way and he tumbled into the fog.

"Yes!" Woj said, pumping his fist.

"Won't do any good," Billy said.

He was right. I could already hear his hooves. If there'd been a jump right then we could've lost him.

Calmly, Inge unbuckled her seatbelt and slithered over the back seat and into the back of the hearse. "Let him catch us," she said.

Billy grabbed her shoulder. "Are you fucking high?"

Inge slapped his hand away. "I do not choose you to die this day, William. I will hold the Horseman. Do what needs to be done. Grim One willing, I will join you when this gnat is made to stop nipping our necks."

I didn't expect we'd see Inge again. We could've used her power in the fight against Marcus and the Redeemers. Inge dying didn't scare me. Far more terrifying was she'd *live*. If she could face the Horseman and walk away, if she could *kill* a Hunter . . . I was going to be a long time digging my way into her good books after all the shit I'd talked to her.

Inge's visage changed from Ice Queen beauty to ancient hag, as if centuries piled on in moments. In showing her age, she gave off no sense of weakness. Despite her hair going grey and her skin wrinkling, her already cruel mouth turned more vicious. A liver spotted hand clutched her spear tightly as she crouched in the back of the hearse. Somewhere I could hear a wolf's howl.

Inge said something under her breath as she crawled into the back of the car. It sounded like a blessing—or a curse.

Inge kicked the rear door off and yelled, "Horseman, I choose you. Death comes."

She leapt into the night and was gone.

We jumped from crossroad to crossroad, following Bear's urging. When the hearse approached a point that would get us closer to Marcus's shadow church, the dog barked, and Summer opened the way. Every jump we made, Travis's spirit was scraped thinner and thinner.

Good riddance. Except the moment we lost Travis, the road would go to work on Woj's hearse. His car had an association with the dead, and would hold up better than most. But it wouldn't last forever. And when it died, we walked.

Time was our biggest enemy in this chase, not Marcus. We'd have to beat this level before we could get to the boss fight Marcus and his allies represented. Winnipeg's red Grave Sight glow flickered closer and further and absent on the horizon as we drove. With our next jump, it blazed brightly.

"This doesn't make any damn sense," Woj said. "We're headed west."

Bear barked in agreement.

"West, east. Doesn't matter here," Billy said. "There's no directions. We're not on a road."

Woj shuddered and placed a hand inside his jacket pocket. No doubt he had a flask tucked away in there. Or more berserker mushrooms. He was getting better at handling the monster side of the job. The weirdness . . . Driving with no direction will get to anybody, and I wasn't about to set him off by being a backseat thanatomancer.

Travis screamed. His spirit shroud was tattered. Each rend in his self seemed to cry *"please"* as each crossroad eroded his existence. Skeletal fingers sunk into the hood of the hearse were Travis' only remains; somehow, without a mouth, still screaming.

We jumped again and we were inside the city. A version, at least.

Where cities in the Kingdom were a hodgepodge of what was, what is, and what might have been, Marcus's shadow version held no recognizable landmarks. I knew my city well— you could drop me anywhere and within a few blocks, I'd be able to tell you were I was, where the nearest graveyard was, and the quickest route home to my place.

Not here.

This was a Winnipeg that could have been, and thankfully never was.

Parts of the city were flooded, and the roads left behind were pockmarked and broken, never repaired from whatever imaginary calamity had breached the Floodway. Our drive slowed to a crawl. Growing blooms of rust decorated the car. Paint flaked away, and over Travis's screaming, spider webs of broken glass appeared on the windows in a slow crackle.

We jumped again.

Travis was gone.

So were we. Well outside the Perimeter.

"God fucking damn it," Billy said.

"We need to get to the next crossroad," Summer said through my lips.

Steam rose from the hearse's engine. A tire blew and the car fishtailed over the gravel road. Woj bit his lip as he fought to control the car. We straightened out, and the car lurched as he hit the gas. Another tire blew. Rims ground on gravel.

"Almost there," Woj said, more hopefully than I felt.

"No way the next jump takes us to the church," Billy said.

Summer nodded in agreement. "Marcus would have anticipated pursuit, and would've made his altar as difficult to find as possible."

"Keep the car on the road," Billy said to Woj. "You were the one who had to fucking drive."

Woj glared at Billy in the rearview mirror, muttering, "Should've left you in the ground."

Bear growled.

"We don't have time for this," Summer said.

I agreed. Our mummy wraps and Dead Man's Clothes would protect us when the car disintegrated, but then we'd have nothing left to diffuse the crossroad jumps. We didn't belong here. I figured if Billy could survive taking the crossroads, I could, too. I wouldn't lose Woj to Marcus.

There has to be something that'll keep us on the road.

"Almost there," Woj grunted past his teeth.

Bear barked and Summer opened the way. The hearse jumped, and we were back in Marcus's twisted Winnipeg.

Sparks shot out on either side of us. No tires left. A crack sounded from the front. Bear ducked and Woj threw his hands over his face as the windshield shattered. Glass stung my face. I didn't feel it. Summer cried out in my stead.

"Oh shit," Billy said, pointing down.

The floor of the hearse eroded, holes growing larger with every foot, every inch, we drove. Behind us, our gear-filled coffin tilted like the *Titanic* sinking, knocked a hole through the roof, and dropped suddenly through the back of the hearse.

"Fuck!" Billy yelled and dove backwards.

He snagged a handle, and grunted with the effort of holding the coffin. I had to give him props. I was strong, but that would've dislocated my shoulder.

"Little . . . help," he said.

Summer leaned over the back seat as the roof tore away. I wished Inge hadn't ditched us. From what I've seen, she could've hauled that coffin, everything in it, and us, too, over her shoulder and not broken a sweat.

Our help wouldn't amount to much. Two people aren't enough to carry a coffin. There's another reason they use six pallbearers;

in case your corpse feels lively, it doesn't hurt to have a numbers advantage.

We tried anyway.

Billy ground his teeth, his ass to the driver's seat, feet braced against our seat and back being flayed by the winds. Summer grabbed a handle, and jerked the coffin to the side, and off the track. Billy eased it down crossways over the hole in the floor of the hearse. A stopgap measure. The hole kept growing.

Metal scoured asphalt, sending sparks to be eaten by the darkness, but there was no sound other than the whipping wind, and galloping hooves. Sounded like Inge had only chosen delay for the Horseman, not death.

"I'm sorry, Billy," Summer said in my voice.

I *wasn't* sorry. I'd never liked Inge before I'd known what she was capable of. Billy's hands clenched and unclenched. In the rearview mirror, Woj's gaze dropped from the road. I wasn't sorry she was dead—and she had to be dead if she'd faced off with the Horseman. I was sorry we couldn't count on her muscle when we stormed Marcus's church.

Bear barked, another jump coming.

"This better be the last goddamned one, buddy," Billy said.

Bear gave an uncertain whine. Time was more pressing now. Not only did they know we were coming, we were being chased there. I didn't like our odds of finishing off the Redeemers, let alone getting the hell out of the crossroads before the Horseman showed up.

And I knew he'd show up.

Billy's gaze darted from Bear to the coffin. "Get ready, Winter."

"Summer," my sister corrected.

We hit the crossroad and Bear opened our way to the next link in the chain. Summer pushed us through. Still in Marcus's twisted shadow Winnipeg. That had to be a good thing. We were near its downtown, and the junction of the city's two major rivers. This had been a train yard once, in the real world, not here. It looked more like the provincial legislature grounds, if, instead of statues, tombstones and open graves littered the dead grass.

A great imposing building, done in the Gothic style—Notre Dame on acid—all angles, and juts. Gargoyles and buttresses that'd never been imagined in the real city cast shadows over the graveyard. No sun, no moon, no stars, and still it cast a shadow. There was a crucified golden idol, where, on Notre-Dame de Paris its rose window would've resided.

"Holy fuck," Woj said.

"Somebody's compensating," Billy said, adjusting himself.

I strained, searching for the sound of the Horseman. He'd tracked us past a few crossroad jumps; I had no doubt he'd be able to find us again. I could only hope the hooves I heard were a mental echo, and not the real Hunter.

The hearse's front axle tore away, taking the rear axle with it. The car ground to a halt, and its final death. Inge's tickle trunk fell through the hole in the back to hit the earth with a resounding boom. Summer flipped open the viewing port, and handed out the necrotech.

Once outside of the car, I could feel the pull of the Kingdom, even here, wherever *here* was. Our Dead Man's Clothes were degrading. More slowly than they would in the Kingdom proper, but the effect was still happening. Tiny wisps of smoke rose from me and Woj. Billy, in contact with his shuck, seemed unaffected. For now. I didn't want to think about facing Marcus with our protections gone.

"We gotta move," Billy said.

"It's time, isn't it?" Summer said to me.

Summer's hand reached, tentative, at first, despite our need for speed. I couldn't blame her. I'd resisted her, and was such a shitty friend to everyone, that she no doubt figured this ride had been her one and only chance to have a body. I could've seized her hand, forced the switch back. I didn't. She needed to know, she was my sister. I'd keep my promise.

When Summer took my hand, she said, *"I love you, Winter."*

Don't say it like we're about to die.

She laughed. *"I'm already dead."*

I laughed, too, and Woj jumped at the sound, as I took over control of my body again. *Summer . . . I love you, too.*

Family. I hadn't considered Summer in those terms; she'd always been my sister in name only. Never family in the way that Mom and Dad had been, and yet, her and I had stuck together longer.

I smiled grimly, looking at Marcus's seat of power. "Who's ready for a walk among the tombstones?"

The rows were endless, stretching past the horizon. No matter how many steps we took, we never drew closer to the Redeemer church. I glanced at the nearest tombstone. It read: *Winter Murray.* They all did. As far as I could see, my name inscribed on simple granite slabs. No "Rest in Peace." No dates. Only my name. I'd faced death as long as I'd been working Graveside, but it was rough seeing this reminder that it would happen, likely soon, and it wouldn't be pleasant.

Billy let out a whistle. "This fucker sure has a hard-on for causing you pain."

"You have no idea," I said.

A cry echoed on the wind, and I recognized Lyssa's voice.

"Goddamned Marcus," I muttered.

"He's doing it to get to you," Woj said. "You can't let him."

"He has Lyssa," I said. *"Don't* tell me what I can and can't do."

"Getting killed isn't going to save her."

Woj was right, damn him. "Let's just get there."

I wondered if Marcus would bother to fill in more details of my death on every tombstone if he won tonight. Marcus was the obsessive type, he'd complete his little memorial. He'd take satisfaction in pissing on those metaphorical plots, too. "Let's get the hell out of here."

Heavy steps fell, sounding like thunder. I knew those steps long before the man dragged my name through clenched teeth and dead lips.

"Hello, Frank."

Chapter Thirty

Frank reclined against one of my many graves, one leg lying straight out, the other bent at the knee. Something in his posture looked . . . wrong. Frank was *never* that relaxed. Tahl's knife dangled idly from his hand, braced on his raised leg.

My knife.

Except it wasn't. Not anymore. I'd been beaten. The knife taken. It wasn't attuned to me anymore. I couldn't believe Marcus gave it to him. Maybe Frank had sensed its power—suspected it could kill him—and held it back.

"Go," I said to Billy and Woj through clenched teeth. "Now."

"You can't take him on your own," Billy said. Bear growled as Frank stood up.

"Watch me." I interposed myself between Frank and Woj. "Find Lyssa and Tammy. Keep them alive. If you can kill Marcus or Karl—great. I'll be along soon."

"Winter," Woj said, "You don't have to do this alone."

"Yes. I do. Go!"

They went, running through a graveyard meant for me. That fact wasn't reassuring. Just because Marcus had made this 'yard for me, didn't mean my friends couldn't die here, too.

"You know I can catch them," Frank growled, his voice sounded strange. Forced. He stalked closer. I did know.

Looking closer—and I didn't want to get *much* closer, remembering the way he'd rung my bell in Christophe's 'yard—his lips were stitched shut. I didn't remember that from earlier. I gave ground before Frank's inexorable advance. There were many reasons why you'd stitch someone like that, none good.

The spirit shroud Frank had worn the last time I'd seen him was gone, but the stitching over his mouth told me it'd likely been bound within him. Maybe I'd damaged it worse than I'd believed, and Marcus had taken it internal so I couldn't weaken his hold on Frank any further. I could dig it out. It'd take time.

Time wasn't in abundance when you were facing an angry composite man.

Frank could crush the life from me with one hand—if he put that hand on me. Over the years I've had to get pretty good at ducking angry undead arms. Frank looked bulky, slow even, but he wasn't a shambling zombie.

I'd seen Frank chase down a speeding car and shoulder block it off the road. He was bigger than me. Stronger. Faster. A scratch from Tahl's knife and I'd die horribly. The faster our fight ended, the faster he'd run down Billy and Woj, and they'd die, too. Now I was the one stuck on the tracks facing the big train.

Except for one lingering doubt. I *knew* Marcus didn't want me to die fast. Frank had kept the knife hoping to die, not to kill me. It was the only answer I wanted to believe, because it meant my friend was in there, fighting Marcus's control.

Too many maybes to bet my life on. Frank had always come through for me in the past. He wasn't pieced together from criminals and cultists. He was made from soldiers. Warriors. Duty and service were carved into his bones. He wouldn't follow Marcus if I gave him any way out. I had to make him see the truth of who he was, and hope the *real* Frank didn't want to kill me for forcing him to live.

Marcus didn't use Frank's natural speed. He stalked me like a slasher in a bad horror movie. Every step measured against the surety *my* body would tire, *his* would not. Even when he wasn't in his own body, Marcus was still arrogant as hell. He waved the knife in front of his face and it ate all the light of the sky.

Frank shifted the knife from hand to hand, he feigned rubbing a thumb over its edge. Marcus wasn't stupid enough to make that mistake. Frank, being ignorant of the blade's power, *might* have. I didn't know if Marcus was trying to give me hope that he might end Frank, or despair that he could.

"A Tahl knife," Marcus said, his voice somehow clear through Frank's stitched lips. "An impressive weapon. Pity I *took* it."

"Admire it while you can," I said. "You'll be seeing it up close soon enough."

"No wound that isn't fatal," Marcus said as if he hadn't been listening to me—or if he had, as if it didn't matter to him what I said. "Your composite man wants an end. So. Very. Badly."

"You're the one who's going to get an end."

"Does he know, Winter?"

"Shut up, Marcus."

"He doesn't?" Marcus laughed, his manic, crazed trill sounded *wrong* on Frank's lips. "He. Does. Now."

Frank's eyes widened, and his gaze darted to his side, where the knife shivered in his hand. His grip loosened. If I was fast enough, I *might* be able to snatch it from his hands. *Might* being the operative word.

I must've unconsciously inched forward, because Frank's mitt closed tight around the hilt. There'd be no getting it away from him now short of sawing his hand off. Frank was in there somewhere, fighting Marcus. He had to be. Because in a straight fight Frank could've had me on the ground and turned my ribs to powder and my face to pulp by now. I could help Frank fight. It would mean getting close. Inside the arc of those haymakers.

I ducked a punch that shattered a tombstone and rock shards pierced my cheek. I rolled away and onto my feet. Another worry. If I bled on Frank's body, Marcus could use my blood against me. Judging from the doofy smile he'd screwed onto Frank's face, Marcus had been counting on that.

I charged forward. *Don't think of where Frank's punches might land, but where I want them to land.* Moving those limbs from their desired path was like lifting Everest.

I scrambled up Frank's body and jammed my thumbs into his mouth, sawing at the stitches with my fingernails.

A couple stitches popped as Frank exhaled, *"Urrr,"* with a mouthful of death breath. I was too slow. Marcus's shroud leaked out as Frank's arms closed around me, pinning me against his chest.

I managed to fill my lungs before Frank's bear hug enveloped me. That cushion of air might help prevent him from immediately crushing my ribcage. It wouldn't last.

"Your friends will die." I hated hearing Marcus talk through my friend's lips. "And it'll be your fault."

Everybody dies. I can bring my friends back.

"You won't, though," Summer said. *"The cost is too great."*

She was right. Another yardstick on the way to becoming worse than Grannie Annie.

"The leash holder and mortician you brought will make good meat," Marcus said. "Better than the pitiful cult my brother managed to raise."

"C'mon, Frank." I scraped another breath. "You're better than this . . . a . . . soldier. You fight . . . kill . . . monsters."

Another breath. Hard won.

"Please . . . Frank. *Fight. Him.*"

I couldn't force Frank to drop me. Couldn't make him drop the knife. His dead heart still, despite the manic energy Marcus had imbued in him. I started it. *Faster.* Beat. *Faster.* I forced his mouth to open. A stitch tore. Beat. *Wider.*

Frank didn't need both arms to hold me. I was pinned against his chest by one arm, while Marcus raised the Tahl's knife behind me. I pushed off against Frank's body with my feet. I may as well have been a kitten he was drowning.

Grey stained the sides of my vision. I was spent. Out of options. Another stitch ripped in Frank's mouth as Marcus made him laugh. No. I had an option.

I lunged at Frank's lips and bit down, hard. I snagged the thread in between my teeth and jerked my head back. The stitches tore free, shredding Frank's lips into a jack-o-lantern smile. Marcus's shroud poured from Frank's mouth as if I'd lit a fire in the composite man's belly. I had an instant to act, and instead of breathing, I forced Frank to carve through the escaping cloud of Marcus's power.

His eyes went wide. Marcus's presence fled, his face appearing over the tombstones as he darted into his church.

Frank's grip was no longer crushing, but not comforting, either. His arms were still wrapped around me. He could still crush me. He didn't.

"I knew you had it in you."

Frank pulled his hands off my body and his face screwed into a frown. I stepped back as he looked at Tahl's knife. "You always had this."

I nodded.

He slapped the flat of the blade against his palm. "You could've ended it for me. Any time."

"Yes."

"You *knew*," he growled.

I backpedalled, hands in front of me. "Frank—"

He slammed his fist against his chest. "This entire goddamned time you knew how to end this."

The distance between us seemingly evaporated in two footsteps. He slashed at me and I darted backward, colliding with a gravestone.

I scrambled, trying to keep a grave stone between us. "I'm sorry. I needed—"

"Need? *Need?*"

I held up my hands. "Don't do Marcus's work for him."

"You could've killed me." I'd never heard such betrayal in Frank's voice. "I *wanted* to die."

Frank said "could've." He *meant* "should've" and he was right. It had been what he wanted.

"You can't always get what you want."

"I can't, but you can?" He looked at the knife, looked at me. "Fuck you, Winter."

"Frank—"

He wasn't going to come after me; he wanted to finish himself. Unless I stopped him. Again. Proved I was as bad a friend as he believed I was. I needed him. I rushed forward as the knife crept closer to his chest. Diving under another slash, I managed to get my hand onto Frank's forearm. I made him twist his arm, keeping the obsidian blade away from him.

And away from me.

"You said you'd try and find a way to end this." Frank shoved me, breaking contact before I could calm him. "For years. You said you'd try."

Frank backhanded me, sending me flying ass over teakettle over another tombstone.

I rubbed my lip with the back of my hand. "Don't do it, Frank."

"You have a chance to keep your promise. Find it fast. Because I know *this*—" he waved the dagger at me "—will do the fucking job."

"I'm sorry, Frank."

"Sorry. *Sorry.* You'll find your sorrys in the dictionary between 'shit' and 'syphilis.'"

"There's other words there, too, Frank." *Think, Winter. Think.* All I thought of was myself. Sneak. Sorrow. Slime. Soul. Special. Soldier. Not good enough. Summer gave me the word. "Survivor."

"I didn't survive," Frank said, gesturing at himself. "None of me did."

I recognized the hangdog note in his voice. I also noticed he no longer had the knife pointed at me.

"I've been selfish. You were too useful."

His face fell into a frown. "Useful."

The anger, the loathing Marcus inculcated in him returned; not mystical infection, rather his disappointment in me. Shattered hope.

I wasn't done, and I hoped he'd hear me out. "That's how it started. You were insurance. Against Grannie Annie. Against the world. Against future fear. I needed you. But that's not all you were. Not anymore. Not then. You were my first friend, Frank. The only person I could share this life with."

Friend. That word had weight behind it. "Friends don't do that to each other, Winter," he said. "And this ain't no kind of life. Rot in hell."

He plunged the knife at his dead chest and I betrayed him again. I forced his hand open, and he dropped the knife, his fist hitting his sternum with a meaty thud. He stooped to grab the knife and I dropped him to his knees.

I hated controlling Frank. Hated it. I used necromantic tricks to ease his pain, to make him feel more human. I'd never told him I'd controlled him. I guess he'd always figured being near me had done it.

This time, when he picked up the knife it wasn't to stab himself, or to stab me, but to return it to its rightful owner. I took it and unlike Marcus, I didn't force Frank to smile, and his face told me what he thought of my actions. I had too much invested in Frank to let Marcus win, and allowing Frank to die counted as a win for Marcus.

When this was over, Frank and I would have another long talk. In the meantime, he was a soldier, and the fight wasn't over.

"This is the big one, Frank." I looked at Marcus's church. "This ass is why I'm Graveside. He took my life from me and made me into someone who'd use you."

"Not good enough."

"He took your choice from you, too."

"I *expect* it from pieces of shit like him. Not you."

That cut, and I nodded, letting it bleed. "He'll do worse. He needs to be stopped, and I need you to do it."

Frank looked at me, at the knife, as if weighing oblivion against enjoying a pilfered beer on my couch and discussing a football game. His hand clenched into a shaking fist. His stare darted over my shoulder.

"When it's done, *we're* done. And then I'm done."

I nodded. "I won't stop you."

"Don't try." Frank growled out the words and I shuddered to hear them.

"Get up," I said. "And fall in."

A gun cocked behind me and it sounded like a bone breaking. A growl quickly followed. "Billy. Bear."

"You made it," Billy said, eyeing Frank warily. "Everything good?"

I smiled at Frank. "I never doubted."

Billy snorted. "I did."

I turned toward Marcus's church. Its shadow stretched over my crop of tombstones. Billy and Bear were there. Woj, too. "I told you to go without me."

Billy stared at Frank. "Just wanted to make sure our six was clear."

Frank's cheek ticked, and I wondered if he was going to snap Billy's neck right there. Instead, he shouldered past Billy. I could see Frank's rage at being used. We weren't good. Not by a long way. But I pointed him at something worse. Using him again.

Business as usual.

Frank turned to us and cracked his knuckles. "Let's go put that fucker in the ground."

Chapter Thirty-One

Marcus's church loomed, cyclopean and gothic by turns of the shimmering red skies. Featureless stone slabs would, when one turned their head just right, reveal in their shadows grotesques of the foulest sort amid bone spires, and windows where the stained glass was stretched human vellum. Knowing Marcus, it *had* to be human.

Unlike most places in the Kingdom, Marcus's place of power showed no entropy. Strong places of death never did. When I'd visited Grannie, my apartment building had looked as new as if it had just been built. More her influence than mine—it's easier to maintain something than to establish it. I wondered if this structure was birthed since Pastor Mark had busted Marcus out of Beyond, or if it was up and running back in Grannie's day.

I couldn't believe I was going into the church by choice. But my friends were Marcus's prisoners. My allies, too. Much as I hated the idea of Christophe and Bones running free, I had little doubt something far less agreeable would move into any power vacuum their destruction left behind. Bones and Christophe I could work with. Usually. And if I pulled this off, each of them owing me a life-debt was not an advantage to be ignored. Might save my ass the next time someone came looking to replace me.

The doors swung open on our approach, because of course they did. Woj crossed himself. I was pretty sure he wasn't Catholic. Whatever gets you through. Marcus may've hoped to keep anyone from finding his redoubt. Now that *I* was here, he didn't want to appear weak, or frightened of our inevitable confrontation.

He didn't need to.

Marcus still held most of the cards. I may have drawn Frank back to my hand with a lucky deal, but Marcus had prisoners, a tamed vampire, and gods-only-knew what else working his side. I hoped he hadn't finished his fancy new body yet.

I asked Frank, "You remember where he's hiding?"

He grunted, "Follow me."

The doors creaked closed behind us. Skeletal hands on one side of the stone clasped a mate on the other. Overlaid with the *thoom* of the stones shutting us in you could hear the *snap, crackle, pop* as bones locked the door in place. The pull of the Kingdom disappeared, and our Dead Man's Clothes stopped their slow smoulder.

Beyond the doors was a great room, filled with skeletal pews bent in backbreaking poses holding up seats made from gallows wood. Vaulted ceilings were held up by columns made of interlocked titanic bones—dinosaurs, or something from Beyond.

It was an imposing entrance, but its depth was an illusion, a *trompe l'oeil*, and once past it, we were in the Redeemer building as it appeared on Pembina Highway. Unobtrusive. Utilitarian. It was a waste of energy and effort for the entire complex to be a false construction. Someday, if I failed, it would be finished, and our bones would shore up Marcus's power. I knew where the stairs were—their reflection should be in the same place here.

Even before we found the stairs, it felt as if we'd tunneled hundreds of feet under the earth. I'd been in enough catacombs to know the sensation, and I didn't like it here any better than I had in the real world. The feeling became worse once we found the stairs stretching forever downward into darkness.

Our steps rang off the stone, echoing, as we made our descent. The path into the church was narrow, lined by stacked bones, dotted by the occasional skull painted with arcane symbols. The remains were stacked to the arch's vault at the top of the tunnel, and they jutted out more at the top, looming like a grisly tree canopy, threatening to topple upon us. The air was moist. Foul. Freshly turned earth hiding a rotting corpse. The stink intensified with every step, until even I wanted to empty my stomach.

Niches cut in the rock held empty burial chambers. I knew Marcus's ambition, and it wouldn't be long until those were filled. I wondered if he'd like his shadow reality to become the only reality. It would suit his opinion of himself, but even if he gorged on the power of an elder vampire and a risen consciousness, I doubted he'd get the power to flip off Those Who Dwell Beyond. But with a custom-made body that couldn't die, one that he could control every part of, he was getting closer.

Frank's steps boomed the loudest, drowning out the rest of us—and hiding Billy's retching. Odd that he broke first. I guess both Woj and I were more used to dealing with bodies after their deaths—Billy was more accustomed to making them dead. I'd have hushed them, but I *wanted* Marcus to hear us coming. To know death could come, even to him.

Deeper we went.

We broached the room where the Redeemers had kept Billy and me before they'd taken us for burial. Karl and the remainder of the Church waited. It was larger here than in the real world—an auditorium rather than a cramped basement. And lit by enough candles to burn Rome to ash. Tammy and Lyssa were on their knees on either side of the vampire, staring blank-eyed as he ran his elongated fingers through their hair.

Stacked bodies beside the altar were in varying states of articulation, staring at me with dead eyes. Behind them was an arch built from the bodies' missing meat and propped up by bones. A portal, but to where, I couldn't see. Its interior shone with a dull, sick green light.

"Far enough," Karl said, tightening his grasp, and jerking their heads up, exposing their throats.

Two cultists laid nasty looking blades against Lyssa and Tammy's skin.

"Let them go, Karl," I said.

He smiled, flashing fang. "No."

Bear growled beside me, whipping his head side to side. Something was wrong. Shucks were often seen as harbingers of disaster—usually the viewer's—but I was inclined to give Bear the benefit of the doubt. He smelled a trap.

"You will submit to the church—"

"Or what?" I snapped. "You'll kill them? They're dead whether we fight or not."

Karl conceded the point with a nod. "True. They can die easy . . . or hard. I'll give you that much choice for them."

I knew Karl was in no position to give any such choice. It all lay with Marcus and Pastor Mark. I suspected if they didn't renege on the vampire's bargain, there would be no easy option open for *me*. All the cultists had tasted Karl, but none had been turned. If Christophe would allow it, Karl could make his own progeny. The fact Karl *couldn't* meant he hadn't finished eating Christophe.

Tammy and Lyssa had been covered in crematory ash, and since I didn't recognize their outfits, what I assumed to be Dead Man's

Clothes. They didn't react to the threats or my seeming disregard for their welfare. They'd been whammied. Good. What I had to do would be harder if they were screaming and crying and laying justified blame. Pastor Mark and his church sure didn't know people, and Marcus, for all his protestations otherwise, sure as hell didn't know me—or what Grannie had made of me.

"Kill them," I said. "I'm a necromancer, you fucking half-wit. I can bring them back."

Karl's eyes widened. I could smell his fear when he realized he had no leverage over me.

Bear clamped his jaws and Pastor Mark blinked into view behind Billy, stabbing him before I could call out a warning.

Billy dropped to a knee and grunted, "What the fuck?"

Bear bit Mark's forearm, and shook, pulling him away from Billy. Mark didn't drop his knife, instead, he punched down at Bear with my antler ring. Bear yelped and let go, but didn't discorporate.

Before I could get there, Mark was already gone.

"He has your cloak," Summer said, and that made the reality sting all the more.

Marcus's voice rang off the cinder block walls. "Take them."

The cultists rushed us.

"Take care of the cultists," I said to Frank. "And Karl."

Pastor Mark gestured me forward with both hands, taunting as he appeared before me, Marcus's death mask smiling. I had to get through the portal. Had to free Bones and Christophe. The room shook and the ceiling rained bones, building a skeletal fence in my path.

"Bring the women," he yelled. "I want to finish them myself."

I screamed out, "No!" as Lyssa disappeared.

Marcus would need someone innocent to seal the deal and wake his new body. And she was. She and Tammy both were— at least in Graveside terms. Those Who Dwell Beyond could care less who or what you slept with. How much weed you smoked, how much you drank, or if you dropped E for special occasions. They didn't even care if you were a thief or a murderer. It took a particular stain for your soul to garner their attention.

"He's mine."

It was a grunt from Frank. I knew he'd keep the others on point. They were as afraid of him as they were of me.

Woj followed in Frank's wake as the composite man bulldozed his way through Marcus's followers, snapping necks and shattering skulls with every punch. Every time they got close to Karl, the room rose against him, firing sharp phalanges, skeletal hands erupting from the floor to trip or out from the walls to snag and delay.

Billy braced his body against Bear, borrowing strength, and laid down suppressing fire with his bone AK-47, firing in short bursts. The bone gun must be more accurate than its real progenitor, as Billy's shots weren't of the "spray and pray" variety. Frank beat a corpse with another corpse. They kept the cultists off me while I tried to get a clear line to Karl.

The moment a cultist died, Marcus's power washed over them. They hit the ground, and they stood again. We *were* fighting a necromancer, but every temporary death bought us time and cost Marcus energy. Frank took to crippling strikes to slow them. Disarming them, literally. If I could get Marcus's hostages out of his church alive, I'd call it a win. While I *really* wanted him dead for all he'd done, the living had to take precedence.

Billy kept his back to the wall's dubious safety, strafing Karl with tombstone bullets. The vampire turned to mist, believing the bullets would pass harmlessly through him. They *did* pass through him, but harmless they were not. Each shot gouged a hole in Karl's mist. He screamed. The cloud exploded into a stream of rats. They fell to the ground and scattered, running under the cultists' steps. Billy shot at them, too. Only a few rats died, turning to dead hunks of Karl meat before smoking away into nothing.

I shifted my focus back to scanning for Mark, and skirted the wall. Hands scrabbled over me. I wasn't master here, but I was strong enough to make them miss.

The others knew what to do. They had their tasks in hand. They could clean up the cultists. As much as it pained me touching any part of Karl, I found the blood he'd forced me to swallow. It gave us a stronger tie than the last time I'd dominated him. That tie also gave him a better chance to fight back.

His blood pulsed molten in my belly, mixing with my own. It had been under the ground long enough for my stomach acid to attack it. It would be weakened. I wouldn't have long for the blood to be carried to my whole body. For the power to infuse my body. I bit my tongue until it bled, filling my mouth. I pinned my mouth shut with my hands as I forced my gorge to rise, making Karl's blood mix with mine. He laughed as I choked it all down.

I tensed as I touched that power. Karl smiled. He'd felt it.

His body reformed, eyes flaring red. "I have you. *So. Easy.*"

I had to laugh. He believed making me taste him would give him power over me. That *I* wouldn't dominate *him* as I'd done in the real church.

The fledgling vampire figured by giving me his blood he could control me. Had he been an ancient, like Christophe, he might've had a chance. Linked as we were, through his dreamy mind's eye, his followers knelt around my grave. Pleasure emanated from Karl, as they debased themselves at his will. I flushed, euphoric with power. It drained my urgency, my need for anything but more blood. Lyssa didn't matter. Tammy didn't matter. Only Karl.

"*Winter!*" Summer cried my name.

Her insistence dragged me back to myself. A reminder the job wasn't done and that I was nobody's thrall. For good or ill, my decisions were mine. Always would be. My dead sister had saved me again.

"How was your time in the ground?" he asked.

"I didn't shit myself," I shot back. "How was yours?"

He grimaced. "Pity you couldn't have stayed there longer."

"For you."

I wasn't a vampire. Yet. But I drew on his strength through the tie he'd bound to me. I burned the smallest fraction of the power Karl had unknowingly given me, and I misted. I rose like steam flowing past, and around, Karl in a gush. I solidified behind him.

"What?" Karl yelled. I'm not sure what bothered him more: me using his power, or that I used it *better*. He spun, lunging at my throat, fangs bared.

"Stop!" I yelled, and he did. I *tsked*. "You should've read my scouting report before you joined the big leagues, Karl. There's a damn good reason I've held this city against all comers."

He gestured at a clutch of cultists, pinned behind the altar. They'd tasted his blood, too. I could control them through Karl if I wanted to. He didn't know that, either. It wasn't necessary, and I had another idea for them.

They rushed me, each wanting to be the one to take me down and win their master's gratitude. Hoping to be made into a vampire for their good work.

Billy fired his AK. Sense couldn't beat its way through Karl's command and the cultists ran on, heedless of the danger. Billy mowed them down. Only one was able to crawl through the hail of tombstone bullets to get to the vampire's side.

I touched his blood tie to Karl and broke his will. A simple thing. A twig snapped between two fingers. He stopped, eyes glazed. Waiting.

"Your servant is mine now, Karl."

"Impossible," the vampire whispered. If his dead body could cry, he would have. Karl couldn't cry. He couldn't slink away. He couldn't do anything but stare down a face greater than him.

"You should have done your research." I smiled. With my

tongue I probed the slight elongation of my canines the vampire blood had caused. "I did." I pointed at Karl's servant—mine now—and made a gift to Tahl.

I released him before the obsidian knife touched his skin. I wanted him to be fully aware of his end. His scream sounded like meat dragged over broken glass. I paced over to Karl while the wet sounds of death filled the church.

"P-p-please, don't kill me," Karl begged.

"Silly rabbit," I teased. There was no mirth left in my voice when I spoke again. "You're already dead."

Karl's body smoked. His meat bleeding into mist. He wanted to escape. Too bad for him.

"Stop."

He did. He didn't want to know *why* he did. Karl was powerless to resist me. The rancid green glow of Marcus's portal bathed Karl's still body. It was so close. So close to Lyssa. So close to Marcus. I drew the spine dagger from my belt. Final death would find any vamp you plunged the dagger into and I wanted to make sure when Karl was gone, his second death permanent.

I wagged my finger. "*Never* give your blood to a necromancer. Not unless you're bigger, badder, and smarter." I slid the spine dagger between Karl's ribs and into his heart. "And besides: we control dead things, moron."

Too bad Karl didn't crumble to dust, like on *Buffy*. He was far too newly made for me to be that lucky. He dropped to his knees, mouth working dumbly and eyes disbelieving. I burned his blood to carve Tahl's knife through his neck and sever Karl's head in one swing.

Karl's death took his power with it. His borrowed vampiric strength left my body in a moment. My teeth rounded. Exhaustion flooded me. Hunger gnawed my stomach where his blood had been. Without Karl's blood, I collapsed atop the newly re-dead undead. His body changed. His head rolled to a stop, staring. Old blood stained his face. His eyes clouded. He leaked from everywhere. And he *stank*. More than normal. Full of shit as he was, he had none left in him.

At least my wounds had healed. The rush from using that much vampire blood still tired me greatly. My heart pounded like a jackhammer. Renfields get used up in a hurry, and they didn't access half the power I had. My fingers tingled and my knees wobbled as I stood. I couldn't let exhaustion get to me. I had to fight through it. I had to save Lyssa and Tammy.

I stared at the portal. Mark would be there. Marcus, too. They had Lyssa and Tammy. Bones and Christophe had to be there as well. I couldn't open the way. I had no key.

One more time, sister.

"It's a Chimaera Door. Like St. Andrew's." Summer examined the portal. "I can get you there. No one else."

I saw it, too. Marcus wanted me on the other side. Everyone else, not so much. Woj wouldn't be able join without dying. *Bear might get Billy in. Maybe Frank could join them.*

Might wasn't much to go on. Neither was maybe. Marcus knew me. Knew I had friends and allies. Knew I'd used them to fight him. And he'd made a scenario where I had to face him alone. Again. And no Grannie would be coming to my rescue this time.

"We're on our own," Summer said.

It was good enough for me. "Let's go."

There was no spectral hand to take this time. It still felt as if I were reaching out for my sister. Our joining came easier this time than before. In the past, I'd never have considered Summer and I as "we." Times change. Summer opened the way, and I dove in, hearing a cry. It was hard to discern who the voice had belonged to over the din. It didn't matter.

I had to stop Marcus.

And then I had a shitload of bodies to bury before dawn.

Chapter Thirty-Two

Marcus waited. The portal had taken us somewhere else, somewhen else. And I remembered it well. In the real world, that portal had taken us to Marcus's altar room. Here in his shadow city, it went to the warehouse where he'd held me. Or a twisted recreation from his memory. It was still decrepit, filthy, and Marcus had a lot more bodies stacked in here than the last time I'd been through.

He had a physical body again—Rod's—though I'd only recognized it from its size. I knew it was him because he'd taken back his crow feather jacket. Pastor Mark was with him, shirtless, and wild-eyed. Lyssa and Tammy lay beaten, but breathing, in front of the altar. An animated body stood guard. It hadn't been embalmed. Rot and bloat had twisted it beyond identification. Maggoty eyes stared impassively. Another needless cruelty perpetrated in a lifetime of needless cruelty.

Lyssa and Tammy had put up a fight. Meaningless, but sometimes a good right hook was all you had to give.

Pallid flesh and gleaming bones stood out from the shadows where Christophe and McCoy were suspended from the ceiling. The vampire had been burned, scarred, and was a lot less substantial with all the rats Karl had eaten out of him. He'd replenish, and so would his vermin. Assuming I won.

Or I cut him down.

From where I stood, Bones was in much worse shape: only a skull and ribcage.

"Hello, Winter," Marcus said, his voice alternating between pleasure and hate, as if my name was equally shit and sugar to him. He gestured at his new body. Until he ritually killed Lyssa or Tammy, that body wouldn't be wholly his. Marcus may've walked around wearing Rod's body, but Rod wasn't there anymore—even if technically, since I couldn't see his spirit hanging around, Rod hadn't died yet, either. "Like what I've done with the place?"

I didn't give him the pleasure of hearing me say his name. Fuck him and his name. I was there to wipe both from my mind and memory. I glanced around, checking for an ambush. The dead goons Pastor Mark had brought through with him were all but a twin to the rune-marked altar, waiting to join the fun. Crucified skeletons hung from the rafters and decorated every load-bearing post, as if Marcus had shored up this hidey-hole with every death he'd ever perpetrated.

"You'd have made a lovely vampire. Pity Karl couldn't turn you. Pretty Winter, cold as ice, cold as death, forever."

"Go fuck yourself. If I wanted advice on my appearance, or was open to comments on it, I'd never listen to you."

Marcus laughed. "And yet you turned out just like me."

"I never wore such a lame-ass jacket."

Marcus must've loved that jacket. He sent zombies after me. They moved pretty good for dead guys, but they *were* fresh meat.

"Maybe I'll pay a visit to your family when I'm done with you."

A risen cultist clawed at me, its head lolling on a broken neck. I spun around stabbing it in the chest with Tahl's dagger. I jerked the dagger free and the corpse shuddered; a stream of gore and viscera dropped as if the corpse shat out its entire chest cavity. It fell and didn't rise for a third go-round.

"If you could've, you would've," I snarled. "You impotent fuck."

Marcus gestured at his maimed follower with a jut of his chin. "But wrong on both counts."

I blinked. There was no way Marcus would try such an obvious lie. Unless it was truth.

Marcus laughed.

"One more reason to kill you," I shot back. "Again."

Marcus turned to his brother. "Deal with her."

Pastor Mark flipped up the hood of my necromancer cloak, invoked the Veil, and disappeared. I opened my eyes to my Grave Sight and screamed. It was too bright. So much death. It was like McCoy's office, only worse. I dropped to my knees, breathing hard, and trying not to vomit from vertigo.

"No Grave Sight here," Marcus teased.

Too much death. I shook my head, looking around. An invisible boot cracked into my jaw, knocking me back on my ass. I still couldn't see him. I *could* hear his mocking laugh.

When Grannie had given me that cloak off Marcus's body, it'd felt like a prize. A trophy. Now I knew it for what it was. Every bit of necrotech Grannie had given me over the years could've been Marcus's hand-me-downs. The thought made me sick. Made me want to destroy my gear as much as I wanted to destroy Marcus.

A fist slammed into my back. I clenched my hand tightly over the dagger's hilt and I slashed behind me. I didn't connect, but I heard Pastor Mark curse. I kept swinging. Kept kicking.

"Goddamn you, Marcus," I cried out. "Afraid of me?"

He ignored me and stole another bone away from McCoy's body. His corruption trick moved faster now. More of Bones's body belonged to Marcus than McCoy, and it was speeding his ritual along. Marcus opened up his own chest and tore out a rib. He didn't even grimace. Blood spurted as he dropped another piece of Rod to the filthy floor and eased McCoy's rib into place.

Pastor Mark laughed. His manic exaltation bounced off the walls and I couldn't place him. I ran for Marcus instead. I needed to keep him from finishing that body. And I tripped.

I tumbled, sprawling into the dirt. Bastard was toying with me. My dagger skittered from my hand and across the floor. I clawed for it. Pastor Mark was faster. He kicked the knife away. I pushed myself up, a kick to the ribs helped me off the ground, but not to my feet. I gasped for breath, crawling towards the obsidian knife. I couldn't let them have it.

With effort, I forced myself upright. I panted, leaning my hand on my thighs, bent over. It would've been easy for someone to slide a knife in my back then.

Where is he?

"*I'll find him,*" Summer said.

Where? Lyssa looked at me as if she were in a dream, and as much as I wanted to comfort her, I couldn't. Not yet. Not here. *Where is he?*

"*Give me your body.*"

Summer had given it back before. I had no other choice. There was no finding Mark here. He was too prepared for me. No way in hell would he let me at his brother. He wouldn't be prepared for Summer. What we had was new. I didn't understand it yet, and I'd lived with her in my head for over a decade.

Do it.

This transition was easier than at the crossroad. The dead were still in my vision, shadows of themselves, compared to how they'd appear in my Grave Sight, but the living . . . they blazed bright. Lyssa, Tammy. All the shadows, all the dead upon whom Marcus had built this place.

Behind the altar, Marcus glowed, too, as he finished whatever ritual he'd hoped would keep the Beyond from finding him. Bones screamed through the process. When the rib had been entirely corrupted, Marcus hadn't bothered to stitch up the gash in his chest, or stop the bleeding. He pulled another rib from Rod's body, replacing it with McCoy's blackened bone as if they had no substance. Pastor Mark's face, where the death mask rested, was a grey shadow.

I didn't want to let on I could see him but the second Summer approached the altar, Marcus would know the jig was up. I had him, and I didn't know what in every hell that existed to do with him. He thought he was hiding. There was no hiding from me.

I wasn't the only one with a dedicated sense of finishing folks off. From outside the church, I could hear the Horseman's hooves. Marcus jerked another rib off McCoy. Black seeped into it.

I'd need to choose quickly or the decision would be made for me. No doubt letting the Horseman take Marcus would be adequate punishment, but I doubted he'd stop there. I imagined we'd make a good accounting of ourselves if we fought him. My imagination was enough to know that wouldn't matter in the end. Thirteen years Graveside and I've never heard of a necromancer destroying a Hunter.

Summer and I slid among his corpses, giving them their rest. I fought my way toward Pastor Mark, serpentine. The tricky part wasn't killing his zombies, it was getting close without letting him know we could see him. Pastor Mark had no idea Summer could see him. *I* couldn't, but my sister could. My arm jerked out, grabbing his hair. Pastor Mark screamed and tried to wrench away. I slashed with Tahl's dagger but he dodged. Pastor Mark's body was slick with sweat, but now that we had him, I wasn't going to let him go.

His hood fell as he whirled around. Summer tore at the death mask but it wouldn't budge.

Where Pastor Mark had first wanted to get away, now he couldn't hold on tightly enough. I followed his chains from Marcus's death mask to the prick himself. He was trying to open another portal to some other redoubt even deeper in the Kingdom—it'd kill Tammy and Lyssa if he succeeded.

Never fails—think you've bearded the dragon in its lair, and it still finds another place to run. But Marcus wasn't going to run. I wouldn't let him do to anyone else what he'd done to me.

Never again.

We wrenched at the mask again. Summer dug my nails into Pastor Mark's face while I heaved on the binding between him and Marcus. We ripped the mask free. *Now* I could see Pastor Mark. From his frenzied wailing, we'd taken his face along with the mask. The chains stretching from the mask to Marcus's new body shattered and he cried out in pain as his nascent portal shattered.

"Nowhere left to run," we said.

It's hard to maintain concentration and the desire not to be seen when you're in blinding pain and begging for help. Pastor Mark had no skin on his face—his eyes were gone, too. Son of a bitch was also getting blood all over *my* cloak.

"You get wound up by the smallest things," Summer said to me.

Some things won't stand.

Summer spun the cloak off Pastor Mark's shoulders and snapped it back in place over our head. We didn't disappear. We *wanted* Marcus to know we were coming for him. Summer rubbed at a wet stain. My fingers came away red. She ran her thumb over the blood, spreading it around my hand, and gave me back my body.

We had Pastor Mark's blood. That meant we could control him. Good. He was tied to Marcus. Better. His screams were already tiresome.

I shut his larynx and cut off his airflow. His cries died, replaced by muffled gasps as he kicked and clawed at the ground, silently begging for air. I gave him none.

"Billy might want him alive."

Summer was right. *Then he'd better hurry.*

Pastor Mark had the pill bottle full of illnesses and the antler rings I'd had on me when Frank had taken me out. There were nasty illnesses in there. Necrotizing fasciitis. Tuberculosis. Mummy Rot. I didn't bother choosing one. I dumped the lot into Pastor Mark's mouth and forced him to swallow. Easy-peasy when he wanted to gasp for air. I didn't want him to die fast, or clean, and Marcus might have a use for him if he was dead.

All it took was a touch to make the diseases bloom. Pastor Mark wept blood, coughed up more. He burned with fever. I gripped the death mask tightly and I fed his disease cocktail to Marcus through their brothers' bond.

The Horseman drew closer. And louder. Hoof beats shook Marcus's entire church; bones rained from the ceiling. I stalked over to Marcus.

"He's coming for you." His brashness gone, I couldn't hide my smile when I said it. "There's no escape for you this time. If I don't kill you, the Horseman will."

Marcus knew it. "What then for you? If the Horseman takes me, your precious leash holder is as good as dead as well. His owner doesn't care for failure."

I shrugged. "What's he to me?"

"Even if they don't kill him," Marcus said, his voice taking on a sing-song tone, "you'll be stuck with him."

"Better him than you."

"Is Winnipeg's Graveside big enough for you both?"

We circled each other. I had Tahl's knife. He had McCoy's rib. The longer I kept him talking, the closer the Horseman got, and the longer it took him to corrupt McCoy. Good for me, bad for Billy. Bad for Billy would end up being bad for me. Lord, he could be a pain in my ass. I'd wanted him on the other side of the Perimeter and gone.

Not much hope left there.

I cut Marcus. Not deep, but he cried out. I could see shards of his spirit drift off, floating through the bone rain towards McCoy. I'd touched damn near every bone in McCoy's body over the years, procuring him replacements, and I could bolster the bastard's fight. I wondered if Marcus had known.

Marcus got in a good stab with McCoy's rib while I helped Bones rebuff his corruption. I cried out, but only when he twisted the rib. He stared, grim-faced. Marcus's corruption was in that bone, an oil slick over already rancid water. I couldn't let him get his taint any deeper in me.

It gave me a chance to get in a stab of my own. I raised my obsidian dagger—it was the only way to be sure.

"All of this," he rasped, "is because of *her*, not me."

Grannie Annie. Mother Anne. Mentor to both of us. If she'd lived any longer, would I have turned out like *him*? Would I have followed them both, dancing all the way into darkness? Or had I already?

Summer had an answer, but I couldn't hear it. Her voice seemed far off.

We *were* the same in most of the ways that mattered. I wanted his death to be as horrible as he'd wanted mine. Grannie hadn't shown him mercy. She hadn't known mercy, no matter that she'd "saved" me. She'd ended my life even as she'd kept me breathing.

Tahl's knife trembled in my hand. Was this really what I wanted, or was I just cleaning up one more of Grannie's messes?

"*Winter, no!*" Summer's scream cut through my doubt, and my sister forced my head down to show me Marcus's hand, and where my blood had sprayed his skin.

"Bastard," I growled.

He'd been using my own weakness against me. Trying to give him a mercy he hadn't earned. Well I had *his* blood, too. I felt for any weakness in his body. His sutures were invisible, but they were fresh, hadn't fully fused together. He was like a newborn's skull, and I pushed his pieces apart. It was like trying to wedge open a stone door. The homunculi ichor in his veins made him resistant to my power. But not immune. He was still wrapped in real meat. And his body hadn't been completed. I pushed harder.

Marcus screamed and McCoy's bone fell out of his hand.

"I may not want to be like Grannie," I said through clenched teeth. "But she's not the only one who wants you dead. *I* don't have to kill you myself. *I* don't have to torture you to make you suffer. Good news, I'll let you live."

A gun fired, loud as thunder over my shoulder. Marcus shrieked as a tombstone bullet dug into him. I had a chance to kill him. I didn't. In the end, Marcus might find satisfaction that I'd been the one to end him. I'd deny him anything, everything, I could. I turned and there was Billy the Bastard, with a big grin slashing his face.

"Nice work," he said. "Need a hand with the cleanup?"

Fuck you. He must've read my expression. Billy smirked.

"I've gotta give him to my boss. Before the Horseman shows."

"He's all yours."

"Please," Marcus begged. "I'll give you anything."

Bear growled, and snapped at Marcus.

"You have nothing we want." He blew on his fingers and limped closer to Marcus with his bone AK leveled at the necromancer. "You're only a payday."

"You have no idea what it's like Beyond." Wails didn't suit Marcus. He could've at least gone down with some fucking dignity. "What the Thrice Serpent can do to you."

Billy wasn't having Marcus's protests. "I know. And *you* bought yourself the fucking ticket. No one *ends up* there. You chose to be there."

The building shook. "Better hurry, Billy."

"Bear! Get over here!" He pressed the bone AK to Marcus's forehead. "In the name of—"

He was too late. He couldn't get his benediction off in time to make the kill and get his pay. The Horseman blew through the portal with a sound like a sonic boom. Billy whirled but was thrown against the wall. To his credit he stood up. We both knew he would lose. I stepped in front of him.

I stared down the Horseman as Marcus and his apprentice wept and whimpered, and it should have made me feel something other than tired, but it didn't.

The souls trapped inside the Horseman's body, fueling him, shrieked, their cries like steam escaping from a kettle. The Horseman taking Marcus Beyond was the best, surest way to guarantee I'd never have to deal with him—or Pastor Mark—again. It would damn Billy. Worse, if I abandoned my pact with Billy to settle with the Horseman, it meant the annoying shit would likely stick around, and become a much bigger thorn in my side.

Part of me welcomed that idea. If I couldn't convince Frank to stick around, I'd need *somebody* on my side.

If we were fresh, it would be worth a go. I had Tahl's knife, mummy wrappings swaddling my body, my necromancer cloak, and most importantly: backup. Billy held his bone AK almost hesitantly. Bear's growl rumbled, echoing off the walls of the shadow church.

The Horseman didn't spare the shuck a downward glance. His eyes remained focused upon me. With his arrival, the Kingdom's pull resumed. Smoke rose from my Dead Man's Clothes, not enough to hide me from his gaze.

"You would try yourselves against me?" His voice was the sound of meat in a grinder.

He spoke. I didn't know he could. Speech meant he could reason. I swallowed a lump so my voice wouldn't break. "If I have to."

"You mean to abjure me?"

"No," I admitted. I glanced back at Billy, and winked. "I mean to destroy you. There's a difference. You have what you came *for*. I suggest you go back where you came *from*. Now."

Inge's voice rang out like a bell as she entered the chamber. She'd managed to cut a way through Marcus's portal. Frank and Woj were on her heels. "For once, Winter Murray, choose the sensible path."

Billy gaped at Inge. "How?"

"The Horseman agreed to set aside our enmity." The Ice Queen's eyes dropped. "I am sorry, William."

"You—"

I cut him off before he started a fight I didn't want to finish.

The time where I let Marcus have any space in my life or mind was long past. I handed over Marcus's death mask, bowed to the Horseman, and stepped aside. It pressed the mask against its armoured horse body. Marcus screamed as what had been his face stretched and wound itself to the Horseman's armour until it was subsumed into the Hunter's body. The bone chains that'd tethered the mask to Marcus reappeared, rattling and clacking. The chains dragged Marcus and Pastor Mark into the Hunter, and they were gone.

Their cries lingered long after the Horseman's hoof beats had faded.

"What the fuck were you thinking?" Billy said, wheeling on Inge the moment the Horseman was gone. "I'm fucked without him."

I asked, "You wanna argue with the Horseman?"

"I am sorry, William," Inge said. She brushed her fingers through his hair. A gesture I almost took for kindness. Couldn't be. Not from her. "There was no other choice."

Billy grimaced. "People who say that are the ones who don't want to make the *hard* choice."

"Had I made any other choice, I would not be here, and neither would you. The Horseman would have overtaken us en route. And either he *still* would've taken Marcus's soul, or Marcus would've succeeded and the city would've been offered up to Those Who Dwell Beyond. The only difference is you'd have no chance to win back your master's favour."

"Fat chance," Billy said. "They're not the forgiving type."

"Perhaps you require a new employer, then?" Inge said, looking up at Bones.

Billy's smile returned. "You offering?"

Inge lifted McCoy from the hooks restraining him, and set him down in Marcus's ossuary. In moments, he stood with a chorus of clicks and clacks. He looked more together, wearing the cast off bones. His movements were stilted, and I worried this fresh introduction of spare parts would make McCoy unpredictable. A problem for later.

"I always have uses for talented operatives. And our mutual friend—" McCoy inclined his head towards me, speaking from his perch above the altar "—often proves unreliable."

"I'll remember you said that the next time someone kidnaps you," I said.

Chapter Thirty-Three

Lyssa's face had a haunted cast as she embraced Tammy. I can't say I blamed her.

I checked them out with my Grave Sight. I needed to make sure Marcus hadn't left any bombs waiting to go off. He was the sort to have a doomsday option kicking around. I know I had contingencies in place for my death; he and I had both learned from the worst in that regard.

There was nothing I could see. Marcus must've been too busy with Bones and Christophe to bother. There was only the lingering taint of Karl's blood in their bodies. Nothing to be concerned about—the bloodsucker was too dead to do anything with the bond, and what was left would fade.

Lyssa and Tammy's bodies were fine. Their minds and spirits . . . that'd take longer to judge. I've seen what they've seen and there's no going back to blissful ignorance. They could go forward, change their worldview to accept things that dwelt in the dark—or break. It was hard being caught in the wake of such evil, and horror. Lyssa and Tammy's trials and been rough. Soul-damaging, but not soul destroying. At least she hadn't participated in the acts herself. They'd recover. With my help, assuming they'd still have me.

Tammy asked, "This is why you flake?"

I nodded, hoping they'd understand. "I never wanted you involved in this."

"There's more out there like him, isn't there?"

"Oh yeah," I said, gesturing at the ruined Shadow Church. "I've faced more powerful, but none worse."

I immediately felt like a shitheel. Taking what might be the most horrible, terrifying experience of Tammy's life, and denigrating it, making it nothing in its commonality. She headed me off before I could apologize.

"Tell me some time," Tammy said.

I blinked. Surprised. Lyssa scowled and said nothing. Sometimes knowing about things is what brings them knocking in the middle of the night. Knowledge is power. Having power makes you dangerous, and being dangerous in my world puts a target on you as sure as weakness. At least so long as Grannie was still out there, I could imagine there was someone worse than me.

I didn't tell Tammy that. Instead, I said, "Sure."

They stood stock still, and I pulled Lyssa into a fierce hug. I buried my head in the crook of her neck, and listened to her heartbeat pound against me.

"I'm sorry this happened to you." I looked at Tammy. "To both of you."

Lyssa didn't answer at first. She pulled away from the hug, and took Tammy's hand. "After you get us home, I don't want to see you again, Winter."

Her rebuke was a heart punch. I forced a smile, barely a twitch at the corners of my lips, to keep from crying. "You won't."

I sent Woj out with Lyssa and Tammy. Woj offered a hand to help them up the stairs. Tammy shook her head, warning him off. They didn't need to see what came next. Frank followed them out.

Without Marcus to act as an anchor, this place wouldn't last long. Fading away to nothing wasn't good enough. Since Marcus had chains of power connecting him to his cultists, we used his cultists for kindling. I didn't want anyone to find and save this place before the Kingdom reclaimed it.

I debated leaving Christophe here to burn away with the Shadow Church. If I did, I'd finally be free of him. His territory would be mine. Maybe without the vampire nipping at my heels I could concentrate on digging McCoy out of Winnipeg's Graveside, and make the city *fully* mine.

But that was the easy way out. The Grannie Annie way. Christophe had been as much a victim in this scenario as any of us. And with him diminished by Marcus's ritual, I didn't fear him. I severed his chains with Tahl's knife. He bowed low, but said nothing.

Marcus's portal had brought us here from the Redeemers' basement once, maybe it could get us home. I hesitated to use it, but I saw no traps with my Grave Sight, and in any case, we were truly out of options. None of us would survive taking the Kingdom to get home. With Summer's help, I activated the portal. It was similar to trying to unlock Grannie's wards. We focused on the feelings, and impressions experienced when we were last there, and connected it to our world, and the Church of the Risen Redeemer.

We walked out of the Shadow Church and into the Redeemer building, and the real Winnipeg. I stretched my Veil over everyone who couldn't hide themselves. The fires had reached the fake church in the real world. Smoke chased us up the stairs as the Church of the Risen Redeemer burned in both worlds. In every world it might've touched, flames rose—scouring away every vestige of Marcus's power with them.

Good.

"We did it," Billy said.

"We did."

The city's Graveside had irrevocably changed—and it was too early to tell if that was a good thing. Billy would bring trouble to my doorstep, but since he'd also bought me a lot of vengeance, I was inclined to let him hang around. It wouldn't hurt for me to have more folks on my side should Bones and Christophe decide to revisit *our* non-aggression pact. Bear padded behind his master, glaring back at me, as if blaming me for their failure to bring in their bounty.

There was no sign of Frank. Billy broke into a car in the parking lot. Inge helped Bones into the passenger seat. Billy and Bear hopped into the backseat; they drove off together without a word.

The vampire inclined his head, the sun beaming off his bald pate as he backed into a shadow. "For your help, I owe you a boon," he said, and was gone.

Woj looked at me, weary. "I'll give you a ride home."

Frank wouldn't answer my texts once we'd left the church. When I went to check on him, Frank had cleared out of his apartment. All he'd left behind was a full ashtray and an empty matchbook for a joint called the Red Circus. A bar run by a ghoul named Camilla. Frank was used to working for someone, for something. Even before he'd become a composite man. Red Circus was of the few places Frank could find employment for his skill set, or, more worryingly, an end to his existence. And I couldn't be sure which he'd chosen.

I'd promised Lyssa she wouldn't see me again. I hadn't promised I wouldn't see her. I sat in the back of Woj's chapel for her mom's funeral service with the hood of my cloak up, invisible to the only friend I had.

The funeral turnout was small.

But then, we *had* murdered most of her church. Besides Lyssa and Tammy, I could see who I assumed was Lyssa's dad, her brother, Matt, and sister, Haley, Njord, his partner, Ron, and Lyssa's friends and their significant others (whose names *still* escaped me). I'm sure they were loving my apparent no-show. One or two other strangers who hadn't been on my Redeemer watch list rounded out the attendees. Billy sat beside me. He'd recovered his Chicago Bears hoodie and was as invisible, and unwelcome, as me.

If I worked at it, Lyssa might forgive me. Tammy no longer hating me would be a good start. She'd need time, and space, and I'd give her as much as I could without letting my world come after her again. I still doubted things would be easy between us once the glow of my saving her from torture, mutilation, death, and soul imprisonment had worn off, but Lyssa was worth fighting for.

The funeral itself went as well as could be expected. There were a couple readings from the Bible—thankfully not the Redeemer version—and that was fine. Religion had been central to the woman's life. "I could arrange for Lyssa to talk to her," I said to Billy when we were the last two by the grave.

He took a long time to answer. "I think she's had enough talking to dead folks. No one else gets to do that. Why should she? Talking to a ghost won't change anything. Won't bring her mom back. Won't make her welcome you back."

No one else gets to do that.

I do.

I talk to Summer, although it took me most of my adult life to start listening to my dead sister again.

I *could* talk to my parents. Somehow their being alive made it harder for me, not easier. I'd missed them—I knew how to deal with that—but I didn't know how to do this. To see them again. To speak to them.

Snow fell as I pulled into the lane. I stared at the wards Grannie had carved in the fence posts and telephone poles. Her "protection." I looked with my Grave Sight, and I saw her watching me from the Kingdom. Half there, half here, as if she too were on a Shadow Road. A lot of crossroads in the county, a lot of places for her spirit to wander over.

I had to be certain.

They were alive. I could see them. My parents. They were both outside, getting the yard ready for the winter. They were both alive.

When she'd taken me under her wing, with the vile things I'd done in Grannie's name, I didn't believe I'd *deserved* parents. I sure hadn't wanted them to know what I'd become, and so I'd believed her. I never came home to check. The thought of seeing someone else on our land, hurt worse than knowing we weren't there. Ninety minutes away, but if I never made the trip, I could pretend.

Grannie had worked hard to beat and cut away my illusions when I'd become her apprentice. That was the one falsehood she'd worked hard to reinforce.

I kept my sunglasses on, hoping it would be enough for them not to recognize me. And to watch them with my Grave Sight to make sure Marcus's taunts hadn't sent me into a trap. Sunglasses, a hoodie under a leather jacket, and a scarf wasn't much disguise, but the idea of coming home wearing someone else's shadow didn't sit well.

They approached my car as I rolled to a stop. I got out to greet them.

Mom asked, "Can we help you?" Dad had a slight frown as he looked me over.

"*They don't recognize us,*" Summer said, and the hitch in her voice made me want to cry.

I know.

As much as I didn't want them to see me, it was also the worst thing that could've happened.

In my Grave Sight, I saw the scars from the cancer that'd tried to kill my dad when I'd been a teen, and the broken bones from the accident, since healed. There was something else, in their minds. It lit my Sight. Dead pathways in their brain. Grannie's "protections" had killed their memories of me.

They saw me, only nothing was there to make the connection between my present self and who I'd been. They weren't *Mom and Dad* in any way that mattered to me, and *Winter* was nothing to them. I wished I could believe it. They were the same as I remembered them, despite thirteen years separating us. The only thing missing was *me*, and I wondered if they were better for it.

Of every torture Grannie had visited on me and the world, *this* was the worst. My breath caught, and it was as if I'd been buried all over again.

Dad asked, "Are you lost?"

A tear rolled past the bottom of my sunglasses. True pain always helped to sell a lie.

"Yes," I said. "I'm trying to find the Smiths' house?" There *had* to be Smiths around here somewhere. "Got turned around on the mile roads."

"They're not far," Mom said. "Head east for two more miles. Then south for one. Can't miss them. There's a bunch of old license plates nailed to the first Hydro pole on their lane."

Now that she said it, I knew the place, and that hurt, too.

I gave them each a hug—Mom returned it warmly, Dad patted my back awkwardly—and I got back in my car and ran away from home again.

I didn't have it in me to tell Mom and Dad I was alive. That I was theirs. I *could* summon the person who had taken me from them. But I wasn't ready for that conversation with Grannie. I guess the one thing she hadn't cheated was death. Better for her if she stayed in the goddamned ground.

Grannie's apparition waved at me as I turned out of the lane and onto the country road. It was too late to change anything that happened between Grannie Annie and I. Too late for Lyssa and her mom, too. I knew Lyssa as well as I knew myself, and her current anger at me aside, someday she'd ask me to raise her mom. And I'll summon Grannie Annie for a talk of our own. For now, she and I have said all we needed to.

Because the next time we met in the Kingdom, it wouldn't be to talk.

Acknowledgements

It's my name on the cover, but there's a lot of people who helped get this book into your hands, dear reader. First, I gratefully acknowledge the Manitoba Arts Council whose financial support helped make *Graveyard Mind* a reality as I was revising my first draft.

Thanks to Sandra Kasturi, Brett Savory, and everyone at ChiZine Publications for making a great looking book. I initially debated whether this manuscript belonged with ChiZine until I accidently pitched it to Sandra at a convention, and her enthused, "I love vestigial twins!" sealed the deal that I'd submit it. I've loved ChiZine books for as long as they've been publishing, so it feels great to join the family officially.

My editor, Samantha Beiko, whipped what I thought was a tight book into even better shape. Sam, I can't say enough good things about working with you. Between the edits and book layout, you went above and beyond. Leigh Teetzel for the proofread. Erik Mohr created a kickass cover. Not going to lie, I've often imagined what my ChiZine cover might look like while admiring Erik's work and he sure didn't disappoint. Don Bassingthwaite, thanks for introducing me to Brett all those years ago at CBA in Toronto and insisting I should read *In and Down* (Brett, that book is still one of the weirdest things I've put in my brain-hole). Also, huge thanks to Michael Rowe for the warm welcome to the ChiZine family.

My first readers: Shen Braun, Laurel Copeland, David Fortier, Mike Friesen, Frank Krivak, and Chris Smith who read earlier versions of this book so you didn't have to. Jill Flanagan, Sandra Wickham, and the crew from Patricia Briggs' workshop at When Words Collide who scoured Chapter One for flaws. Also thanks to Patricia Briggs for the kind words about said chapter, and encouraging me to stop workshopping *Graveyard Mind*, and to start submitting it.

In between drafting this book and selling it, I've had to attend far too many funerals, but I want to thank all of the funeral industry professionals who took care of my family, friends, and neighbours. Winter's views of your profession and mine are vastly different, and if you're reading this, please don't sell me to necromancers after I die (and if you do, at least bargain hard).

Julie Czerneda and Kenneth MacKendrick, thanks for the blurbs. Many folks contributed art, hospitality, or have had my back in the book stack trenches since *Too Far Gone* released, so Carol Antrobus, Steve Benstead, LeeAnne Berkvens, Jean Cichon, Mike Cichon, Sarah Johnson, Shanleigh Klassen, Clare C. Marshall, Kevin, Madison, Jeff Nadwidny, Brad Neufeld, Jocelyne Quane, Robin Righetti, Amanda Sanders, Clark Sheldon, Chris Szego, John Toews, and Tyler Vitt, thanks for everything. Robin Smith, thanks for loaning Winter your old car (I intend for her to mistreat it even worse than you did, but not as much as that moose).

Friends and family. Mom and Dad.

Wendy, always Wendy.